CRACKED COFFINS

BERONIKA KERES

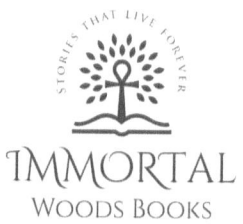

IMMORTAL
WOODS BOOKS

Cover design by www.trifbookdesign.com
Editing by Eliza Dee (www.clioediting.com)

ISBN 978-1-7771514-3-0 (paperback)
ISBN 978-1-7771514-4-7 (hardcover)
ISBN 978-1-7771514-1-6 (ebook)

CONTENT WARNING

Cracked Coffins is the first book in a dark fantasy thriller series that explores the horrors of abusive relationships with a vampiric twist. This series is not a romance with a HEA, but a story of survival.

This series contains heavy subject matter that may be triggering for some readers. Elements include, but are not limited to:

- **Violence:** Graphic Violence, gang violence, assault, kidnapping, stalking.

- **Abuse:** Domestic abuse, child abuse, rape & sexual violence.

- **Other Mature Content:** Alcohol & drug use/abuse, profanity, suicide, prostitution.

Visit www.beronikakeres.com for detailed information and a full list of series triggers.

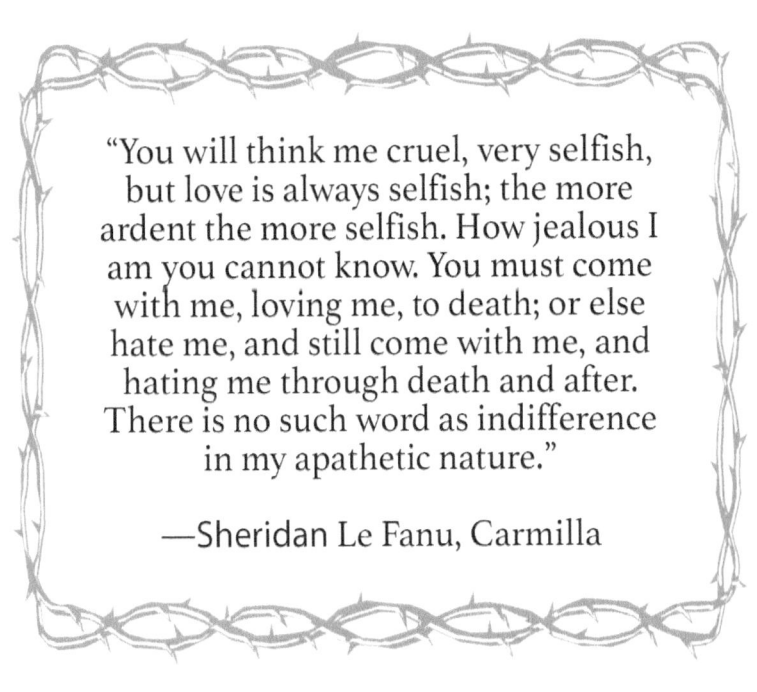

"You will think me cruel, very selfish, but love is always selfish; the more ardent the more selfish. How jealous I am you cannot know. You must come with me, loving me, to death; or else hate me, and still come with me, and hating me through death and after. There is no such word as indifference in my apathetic nature."

—Sheridan Le Fanu, Carmilla

Another year has passed, and though nothing has really changed, everything is different.

For the second year in a row I stare at my history quiz. *Ancient Civilizations Unit Test* is typed across the top of the page, the questions only half filled out. I'll be lucky to pass with a fifty percent mark, which is twenty percent more than the last time I did grade ten. I've attended more classes this time around, but still, the information I have on ancient Rome and Egypt isn't relevant enough to the questions that have me glowering at my paper.

It's unfortunate my teachers stopped mercy-passing me once I finished ninth grade.

My leg bounces as I flip back and forth through the stapled pages. I root through my brain for the answers, but only facts of unknown origins present themselves to me and I can't remember anything Mr. Derek taught us that I didn't already write down. Even if I had studied or attended every class, the feeling of impending doom that runs through me like a cold chill makes it hard to concentrate.

I do my best to focus on the test and distract myself from the fact that I turn seventeen tomorrow, but the reality that I'll likely fail again still doesn't overshadow my birthday.

With a frustrated exhale, I lean forward in my desk. Any information that might have been on its way to me is intercepted by the feeling of my cigarette pack in the pocket of my jeans as it presses into my hip bone.

I inhale sharply and tap the back of my pencil against my test. While I tuck my long sandy-brown hair behind my ear, my gaze shifts to the clock. *Five minutes left.*

Birthdays have always been hard for me. While most kids would celebrate their seventeenth birthday with joy, knowing that they only have one more year before freedom, the reality of it makes me want to smoke until I can't breathe anymore.

All my birthday represents to me is that I have one year left before aging out of the foster care system. I know I won't be dropped onto the street as soon as the clock strikes midnight, but the statistics and the flimsy promise of government help do nothing to aid my anxiety.

My heart thumps with each tick of the second hand, the sound echoing in the silent room. I remember to write my name quick on the test—Marianna Cortez—and leave the pencil on the desk where it was when I sat down.

As soon as the minute hand hits twelve, I stand and weave through desks before dropping my test down in front of Mr. Derek and turning back on my heels. If he says anything, his voice is lost in the sound of the dismissal bell.

Classrooms empty, the hallway of our overcrowded high school filling with the noise of rowdy students and slamming lockers as I step into it. I shove my way toward the closest exit while digging in my pocket for my lighter. The deep and familiar voice of the security guard yelling a warning at someone near the far end of the hall makes me stumble, but I continue until someone grabs a fistful of my hoodie and stops me in my tracks.

I'm pulled out of the rush of students and find myself between a pastel yellow locker and Carston—a senior who has no good reason to be in the tenth-grade hall right now.

"No," I growl as his lips part to speak, trying to shove around him so I can get outside and smoke before break is over.

He holds his hand up, flashing the dark glob of heroin in the corner of a tied and torn sandwich bag.

My heart skips and I gasp, my back pressing against the locker as I take a step away from him. Eyes darting around the crowd for security, I bat at his hand.

"You're going to get us both expelled if they see you with that," I snarl.

Getting myself expelled is one thing, but I'm not going to let anyone else ruin my life for me.

He lowers his hand, but even with it out of sight my arms still itch, and my throat is still dry.

"You look really sexy today. What are you doing after school? Come over. Dad won't care if I got a girl there." A coy smile shapes Carston's lips as his other hand brushes down my bicep.

I jerk away from him, the heel of my fist pounding against his chest. He isn't moved, though, his smile only growing wide and toothy.

"Fuck off. I've been clean for a year. And like I said the last twenty times, I'm not going to screw you for drugs." I adjust my baggy blue hoodie and ball my fists up at my side, though I can't help that my eyes dart back to the heroin in his hand.

"Whatever, Marianna. Sobriety is overrated." He steps closer to say, "It'll be fun."

His words crush the air from my lungs, the sound of his

voice replaced by the voices of a dozen other men as the phrase bounces around in my head.

It'll be fun.

Even with the heroin it was never fun.

I shove down the decade-old memories of my mother's drug-fueled abuse and fight for a breath before squaring my shoulders.

"Fuck off," I reiterate.

"Come on. It's a birthday present. Don't you want to celebrate?"

"My birthday isn't until tomorrow." I give him another shove, my knuckles connecting with his sternum and making him flinch through his grin.

When he takes a step forward and I think he's going to pin me between him and the locker, my hand jumps to his wrist and I find myself twisting his arm and throwing my shoulder into his chest.

I'm not sure what comes over me, not sure why I wrestle him against the locker, kneeing him in the groin and yanking on his arm and wrist until the heroin is out of his hand and in mine. Maybe I just want to take it away from him since he's pissed me off. Maybe it's because I dreamt last night—and every day this week—about how much easier things would be if I didn't have to constantly feel everything.

Or maybe it's because nothing is truly different. Maybe everything is exactly the same—exactly as awful—as it always has been.

I leave Carston behind and groaning in pain as I scramble into the nearest bathroom before locking myself in a stall.

Staring at the substance in my hand, the first thought I have is to rush home and shoot up. My eyes flicker to the toilet in front of me, but even if I wanted to flush the heroin, I can't loosen my grip.

My sobriety thus far has been passive. Isolating myself over the past year from anyone but my three best friends and staying home has kept me out of the direct path of drugs. But now, with it in my possession and without a good enough reason to convince myself to get rid of it . . .

Turning seventeen may be no different than turning sixteen, or any of the years before, but eighteen? At eighteen, everything changes. Everything will be different, and I'm not sure I can handle it.

The bell has long rung by the time I can make myself take a proper breath. I swallow a lump, my head lowering in defeat as I shove the baggie of heroin in the pocket of my jeans. Thinking that security or a teacher might come looking for me soon, I drag my feet to my next class and mumble an apology to my teacher as I slump down in my desk.

My mind circled around the idea of getting high during the entirety of class. I couldn't help but glance at the door every other moment, my heart racing at the idea that someone saw Carston and me with drugs and that a police officer could walk in with a drug dog.

And if it weren't for my three best friends—Camille, Daina, and Jenna—I would have already gone home to dispose of the evidence. By injecting it, most likely.

The buzz of the cafeteria is far from my mind, the smell of greasy food from the lunch line making me nauseous. A group of rowdy boys rushes by our table, and if it weren't for one of them tripping over the leg of my chair, I might not have even noticed.

"Are you psyched for your birthday tomorrow?" Camille asks, her excited green eyes poking out from beneath her golden bangs.

Cheek in the palm of my hand while the other rests on the

lump of heroin in my pocket, I offer a grunt. My response makes them frown before Jenna's head of dirty-blond hair turns toward a slim figure as it moves toward us.

Daina's voice, thick with a Spanish accent, draws my eyes upward as she approaches the table. "Aren't you going to get anything to eat, Marianna?" With a plate of tater tots in each hand, she sets one down in front of Camille before sitting across from me. "Do you have lunch money?"

Even if I did, I would only end up puking my lunch back up. "I'm not hungry," I mumble, staring at the doors across the cafeteria. I know it's only a matter of time before my legs start moving me out of here to go home, and I can't find a single reason to resist the pull.

Daina sighs as she pulls her dark brown hair up in a pony-tail before picking up a tater tot and dipping it in ketchup. "Are you still coming to the mall with us tomorrow after school to pick out your birthday present?"

Jenna looks up from her red flip phone. "You can't say no," she warns before going back to furiously pressing buttons on the keyboard.

"Yeah, sure, I'll go," I agree, not wanting to know what lengths they'd go through to make me have fun on my special day. The last thing I want to do is bus all the way up to the North End Mall with them to look at things we can't afford, but I know my birthday is an excuse for them to do exactly that. With the high crime rate where we live in the west of Lorimer, New York, the closest mall has hardly any stores worth visiting for fun.

I only last another ten minutes in the cafeteria before the idea of sitting in my room with a needle in my arm coaxes me away. Despite the thin thread that still holds me to sobriety, I know I can't sit around school with contraband. Not wanting my friends to think I'm skipping—and to avoid a lecture from

Camille—I feign sick and promise to meet them at the mall tomorrow if I don't make it to class.

My legs are jittery, my teeth chattering as I meander through students to get to the front door. The security guard scrutinizes me with a hard eye as I follow behind another group of students leaving campus for lunch—likely to one of the fast-food destinations a handful of blocks away—and I brace myself for the possibility of being stopped and searched.

Thankfully, I step out through the front door of West James High School and into the cool of day without being harassed. I can't help but wonder what it would be like to attend one of the richer schools in the north of Lorimer, or even one in the stable middle class of the east. From what Camille recounted before her mother and she were forced to downgrade their lives and move from their home in the east, it was like a different world.

Though, I suppose it could be worse. I could be in South Sutton High, where they have full-time police officers and metal detectors. West James High School may be the second most dangerous school in Lorimer, but we are lucky to have an open campus at lunchtime, a lunch program and extra funding since the other high school on the west side merged with us, and only a lockdown every other month instead of every other week.

Things could be worse.

I frown and jam my fists in the pocket of my hoodie.

Things could also be better.

Between my worn sneakers and the spontaneous ache in my knees, the twenty-minute walk home seems twice as long. I keep careful eyes on my surroundings as I smoke a cigarette, my gaze shifting over the roads and old houses that are telltale of the crime in our neighborhood.

The unkept fences and yards, the worn paint of old houses, sagging roofs, and graffiti have all become normal to me now. West Lorimer doesn't have nearly as many of the abandoned and structurally unsound buildings as the south does, but after seeing them so often—and growing up in one with my mother —I'm always in awe on the rare occasions I travel to the north or east side of the city.

Speeding by, a red muscle car revs the engine just as I inhale a long drag of my cigarette. I sputter and cough, my heart slamming against my ribs as my hand jumps to cover the black-and-red tattooed double Rs on the side of my neck. I'm not sure why I've never had the gang tattoo covered, since it's become a bull's-eye after I killed another member in self-defense. Maybe I have a death wish. After all, since I left Venganza Roja last year—or Red Revenge—death is all they have to offer me.

When I see that the man driving is black and not Latino, I exhale a breath of relief but quicken my pace. Between the risk of being seen in the street and the heroin in my pocket, I know I won't be able to stop my paranoid glances until I'm in the safety of my bedroom and near the gun beneath my bed.

My heart settles when I approach my foster home, the off-white bilevel house no more inviting than the rest of the homes in our neighborhood. It's a different foster home than the one I was in last year, but a foster home nonetheless. After I climb the concrete steps and go inside, I kick my shoes off and dart across the living room to the stairs. Reality sinks deeper into me with each step toward my room.

If this year is hardly different than the last, then I'm no different either.

I sigh and close the door of my blue room, the sound of my foster mom's television turning up like she thinks she can make me go away if she can't hear me.

After navigating the mess of dirty clothes, papers, books, and garbage, as well as the few boxes that remain from when I moved in, I clamber onto my black futon and stare at the popcorns on the ceiling. I find myself slipping the baggie of heroin out of my pocket and rubbing my thumb on the lump like it's a worry stone.

My mind flip-flops between wanting to use and knowing I shouldn't. On one hand, I'm already a year clean and I know if I relapse it could open the door to full-time use. It's a terrifying idea. I haven't been a full-time user since my mother was the one injecting me. Even if I didn't want to get high, how would I get rid of it? I know I'm not physically capable of flushing it myself, and if I tell Pam she'll call the police. If I call my social worker, I go to rehab. I suppose I could hide the heroin in the shed . . . but that's only moving the issue.

I feel like I'm flying high on a swing set. It would be much easier—more enjoyable—to let go of the swing and soar through the air than it would be to plant my feet against the ground to stop. But if I let go, how do I land? Will I land gracefully on my feet with a burn in my ankles that I can walk off, or will I hit the ground and have trouble getting back up again?

Could I use again—only this once—and go back to being clean? Or will I make my fear of ending up homeless and a drug addict on the street once I age out a reality?

I think myself into stasis, my thoughts chaotic with uncertainty as I stare at my ceiling. It's like I think my unwillingness to decide can get me out of the situation. But the rest of the afternoon moves on without me, and soon I find myself falling asleep with a lit cigarette in my hand before an ember lands on my finger and wakes me.

After putting my cigarette out on the windowsill and flicking the ashes off my hoodie and onto the floor, I rub my eyes and turn the baggie of heroin over in my fingers. With a deep breath, I stuff it in my pocket and follow the smell of chicken nuggets downstairs to the couch, where my foster siblings are.

My eleven-year-old foster brother grins at me as I flop down beside him and steal a nugget from the silver bowl between them.

"Want some ketchup, Mari?" Samantha asks from the other side of Charlie, her deep brown eyes glittering as she holds up the white bowl for me to dip it in.

I smile and dip my nugget, thanking her before asking, "Has Pam left her bedroom yet?"

He shakes his head of blond hair and wipes crumbs from his lips with the back of his hand. "She said she got called off work today and told me I could cook the whole bag of nuggets this time if I left her alone."

I'm not sure how to respond, so instead I turn my attention back to the cartoon playing on the television and stuff my face with food. When we're done eating, I wash the dishes and clean the clutter off the kitchen table before making a lunch for Samantha to take to kindergarten and scrounging up change so Charlie can buy lunch.

"Do you want to work on your word exercises?" I ask Samantha as I flick the TV off.

"Sí, Mari." She sighs and hops off the couch, her shoulders slumped as she follows me through the kitchen's swinging door and to the table, where Charlie is already working hard on his math homework.

Once I have them in bed, I find myself glowering at my foster mom's door with my hands in fists. The television volume has turned down a few notches since she would have heard me put the kids to bed, but I want to storm in and demand she do everything tomorrow so I can just be seventeen on my birthday and not Mom, but I know I'll wake Charlie and Samantha up when Pam and I start yelling.

Instead, I leave. I shove my gun in the back of my jeans for security. After throwing my sneakers on, I step out into the night with a cigarette dangling from my lips and five dollars from the emergency money that Pam thinks she has hidden from us behind the microwave.

My head spins, a flurry of thoughts and feelings making me feel off-balance as I hasten to the corner store a few blocks away. I take greedy drags of my cigarette, my throat raw and my brain tingling by the time I reach the door of the brightly lit building. I stomp the butt of my cigarette out on the sidewalk and dip inside. After pacing down the aisles, I buy a bottle of root beer and a bag of chips in hopes that the junk food will distract me from my drug cravings.

Not wanting to take too much of a risk by walking around at night, I light another cigarette and head home. Halfway down the block, the hair on my neck lifts and I can't shake the feeling of eyes on me. With a hard swallow, I flick my cigarette into the road so I have a free hand that can go to my Beretta in the back of my pants if need be.

My eyes search the empty roads. Headlights shine from an alley past a few houses ahead. I wait for whoever it is to turn onto the street, but instead the headlights turn off. Still able to hear their engine and the slow crunch of tires, I quickly dart across the road to avoid whoever is trying to hide.

I walk so fast I nearly trip myself, my heart hammering in my chest as I scrutinize every shadow and road for threats. A few minutes later, when the sound of an engine behind me makes me glance over my shoulder, I spot a black car prowling at the end of the street. It moves far slower than the speed limit, and I can't help but think the driver is purposefully trying to keep distance between us.

Adjusting the bag on my arm, I break into a sprint, quickly covering the last block home. I race across the sidewalk and scramble up the steps. But when I grab the doorknob, my hand twists off it.

I gape at the locked door. "What the fuck," I breathe, my

voice coming out high-pitched. "Pam," I accuse, knowing damn well I left the door unlocked behind me.

The sound of an engine makes me look over my shoulder again, and I see the black car turning onto my street. My hand jumps to my gun, my fingers clutched around the grip as I turn to face the road. As if it had never been following me at all, the black car—now close enough to identify as a Mustang—resumes a normal speed and drives past the house.

It takes a few deep breaths to take my hand off my gun, but I know I have bigger problems to focus on now. Turning back to the door, I grit my teeth and bite back a frustrated shriek. Knowing I have no way of getting inside, since she won't unlock the door with any amount of hammering, and that I can't sneak in with the security system, I can't help but give up.

I squeeze my eyes shut and make up my mind. One more high. I don't want to feel anything else tonight.

Any energy I might have had left vanishes after I climb over the six-foot-tall fence to the backyard. I roll my ankle when I land, but I can't find it within myself to care. Soon I'll be too high to feel it, to feel anything.

Emotionally numb and feeling the chill of night to my bones, I drag my feet through the shin-length grass and to the shed at the back of the yard. After pulling the key out of a fake rock, I slide it in the lock and force the heavy wooden door open, the rusty hinges protesting.

Unloading a heavy sigh into the cramped space full of old bikes and lawn care supplies, I turn on one of the tiny flashlights I left behind on the shelf last time I slept in here. After shutting the door behind me, I crawl onto the lounger that takes up the entire floor space and stretch out. With its thick cushions—though dusty—it's almost comfier than my futon.

Trying to keep my heavy heart from beating too fast with some deep breaths, I shine my flashlight on the shelf by my arm and find the tackle box where I last left it, a spoon, needle and shoelace still hidden in the bottom.

I stare at the supplies in my hand and swallow a lump. My hand shakes, and I want to be strong enough to put it all back and stay clean, but I know I'm not. I know I'm not strong enough to deal with tomorrow, to deal with the fact that I'm locked out of the house the night before my birthday, or that tomorrow is the first day of my last year of security. I almost don't want my seventeenth birthday to come at all, or my eighteenth.

Just this once. I promise myself that after this, I'll never get high again. I'll be strong after this. I'll face my upcoming years with more strength than I did the last sixteen, even if I must fake it.

Pulling the heroin from my pocket, I turn it over in my hand and can barely see the dark substance. Putting the end of the flashlight in my mouth, I gather everything I need on my lap and prepare my drugs. With the sticky substance on the spoon, I heat the underside of it with my lighter until it's ready to draw up into the needle. When the needle is full, the air in the shed thick with a vinegary stench, I tie my shoelace around my bicep and rest the flashlight on the shelf before searching my inner elbow for a vein. All of my old track marks are healed and faded. It's almost a shame when I press the tip of the needle against my skin.

"Happy birthday to me," I sing to myself, my heart hammering, veins eager.

I slam the plunger down and quickly pull the shoelace off my arm. Roses bloom under my skin, my mind finally empty. The burn in my chest and legs lifts, and I no longer have to think about breathing.

When I try to reach for the needle in my arm, I can't lift my hand off my stomach.

My legs don't move.

My eyes droop.

Bliss holds me down like a brick pulling me to the bottom of a river. I don't care that I'll be sleeping in a shed, that Pam locked me out, that it's my birthday. All I care about is the peace swirling in my blood.

My mind is finally empty of chaos, just colors and sounds luring me away from consciousness. The wind opens the shed door, the dark of night crawling into the tight space with me and making it hard to breathe. It takes half my vision, the weight of it heavy on my head and eyelids. But through what's remaining of my sight, the outline of a tall figure appears between me and the moonlight.

"*Marianna*," the wind whispers as the darkness drifts over me.

Then, there's nothing.

II

I find myself staring into the bloodied water of a toilet bowl, my head resting on the seat. The large shadow cast over me blocks out the bright light that shines through the black spots of my thin vision.

"Who are you?" a voice asks from the doorway, the sound so quiet I question hearing it until my eyes roll to find Charlie standing in the doorway in his pajamas.

I try to tell him to go back to bed, but only a groan rolls in my chest and my skin flashes with heat as my stomach clenches.

"Go back to bed, Charlie," another voice says, though I'm not sure it's mine.

The sound of my own vomiting covers the following words that send Charlie on his way. I feel my head pull up and hear my own gasp when a hand tightens on a fistful of my hair.

"What—" I hear myself say, my voice so far it sounds like it's coming from another room. The taste of vomit is strong on my tongue, and my vision fails.

"*You're overdosing,*" a man's voice says, the sound comforting.

When something presses hard against my mouth, my protesting whine rolls in the back of my throat and I gag on the sweet and thick liquid that flows over my tongue.

I fight to open my eyes and connect to my body so I can find and question the source of the voice, but it feels like I'm floating in blackness.

The next second comes and I find myself lying in bed, disoriented and groaning as my hands root through the blankets. I touch something that moves and feel coldness sweep against my face as I gasp.

"*It's okay, Marianna, you're safe,*" the sweet voice murmurs.

Morning is suddenly around me. The smell of puke and sweat clings to the early-morning air. I sit, a headache pounding in my temples that chases away the memories of last night. Passing out in the shed is clear to me, but how did I get in my own bed? My sweaty skin makes me recall the feeling of puking last night, but looking around, I see my bed isn't covered in puke and I'm in different clothes than I passed out in.

Then, vaguely and like a fading dream, I remember the comforting tone of a man's voice and Charlie standing in the bathroom doorway while I puked. My heart jolts when I remember how he asked someone who they were and whoever was there told me I was overdosing.

The realization that someone brought me into the locked house while I was OD'ing makes me scramble out of bed and rush downstairs to the kitchen, where I can hear Charlie making Samantha breakfast.

"Who was here last night?" I demand, the swinging door bumping me as I stand disheveled in the doorway.

Charlie hip checks the cutlery drawer shut while looking me over through narrow eyes. "You were . . . you stumbled in the house and went upstairs. You spent half the night puking in the bathroom."

I fold my arms over my chest. "I saw you in the doorway and you asked whoever was with me who he was."

Without taking his eyes off me, Charlie carries the spoons over to the table and plops down beside Samantha, handing her one for her cereal. "I don't know what you're talking about. Only you came in last night. I didn't hear anyone else."

Annoyance adds to the pounding in my head and I glower at him. "Through the locked door, Charlie?"

"What are you talking about, Marianna? There's no way it was locked. I stayed in my bed, but I heard you come in and your puking kept waking me up. Are you sure you didn't hallucinate it all or something?" He takes a bite of his bran cereal, milk running from the corner of his mouth before he wipes it with the sleeve of his pajama shirt.

I gape at him. But knowing that he's not one to lie to me, I sigh and plunk down in my chair. Was I really that messed up? I suppose what Charlie is saying makes sense. If the house had been locked, the alarm would have been blaring if a stranger broke in to help me through an overdose and put me in bed. Who would do something like that anyway? Was I merely so paranoid about that black car that I was only half paying attention when I tried to open the door?

Rubbing my hands over my face and groaning, I say, "Sorry, Charlie. I didn't mean to wake you up." With the blood I saw in the toilet bowl, I must have been puking for quite a while.

He gives me a forgiving smile. "It's okay. Are you still sick?"

I almost tell him that I overdosed, but if I did, why do I feel okay? Surely I should have more than a pounding headache and a shaky stomach if I had. Besides, how would I have gotten myself inside? I'd be dead in the shed right now. Maybe I was so high—so close to overdosing and delirious—that I couldn't tell the difference between my dreams and reality. Or, could have there been something else in my heroin?

"I'm okay," I mumble, offering Charlie an apologetic look. The reality of my actions makes me stare at my lap. I should have known better than to let him see me high like that, especially knowing how he found his own parents overdosed when he was six. "I'm sorry I came inside like that."

"Hey," he says, making me lift my head. "Happy birthday."

Samantha grins from beside him. "*Sí*, happy birthday, Mari."

My smile quivers. "Thanks," I whisper.

Stepping off the bus at the North End Mall, I unwrap the plastic from the new pack of cigarettes Pam gave me for my birthday so I wouldn't steal hers. After discarding it in the bin beside the entrance, I wait for my best friends on a metal bench. Opening the fresh pack, I flip three of the cigarettes over and decide I'll celebrate today by smoking the other seventeen before midnight. Plucking out the first, I place it between my chapped lips and light it, the first inhale that hits my dry throat making my muscles relax.

The cigarettes are more fitting than the unoffered alternative. At least seventeen cigarettes do a better job at representing me and how I feel about today than seventeen candles stuck in bright icing would.

I rake my thin fingers through my hair, strands singeing on the end of my cigarette. Shoppers pass through the door with a low hum.

A chill rolls down my back, something changing in the air. I look around, trying to shake the feeling of being watched. When I don't see my friends and nobody else sticks out, I blame the paranoia on recent events.

Ember hitting the filter, I crush it against a childhood scar from my mother's cigarette before flicking the squashed butt into the bushes and lighting another.

I burn through two more cigarettes while I wait and am about to pull out my fifth cigarette when familiar voices yank me from my tobacco-induced fog.

"Marianna!" my friends squeal while hastening toward me.

My head hammers when I stand, and I almost lose my footing. I jam the cigarette pack into my pocket and brace myself as Daina throws her arms around me.

"Happy birthday!" Daina squeals, her hug more suffocating than the stench I've wrapped myself in.

Jenna and Camille meander up behind her with glimmering eyes and wide smiles. "Happy birthday, Marianna," they take turns saying before we slip inside the mall.

They seem more excited than I, their loud banter carrying above the hum of shoppers as we traverse the packed mall to the food court, but it doesn't quite reach my ears.

In the packed food court, the pizza place we line up at offers a free meal on your birthday if you show them your identification. I use the gift card my social worker gave me since I lost my identification again and can't be trusted to keep my birth certificate safe. It wasn't until years after I was born that the government found out about me and made my mother register my birth. Even then, my mother was always high. She likely had me at home, so there's no real proof March 18th is my birthday.

It doesn't feel like my birthday anyway.

With pizza in hand, we gather around a white-topped metal table after brushing off a stranger's crumbs.

"What do you want for your birthday?" Jenna asks after her first bite of pepperoni pizza.

I think through my mouthful of ham and cheese pizza, mind wandering to the camping and utility store upstairs.

Dropping a small stack of bills on the table in front of me, Camille says, "We pooled together fifty bucks for you, so think."

Through another bite, I smile and say, "Thanks. I want that knife upstairs."

Daina groans and leans back in her chair, flicking her long hair over her shoulders. "Come on, why not something fun like a new outfit?"

"That knife upstairs is fun," I counter before devouring the last of my pizza and half of my root beer.

Once we're all done eating, they begrudgingly follow me upstairs to Outdoor Trek. We pass by a few green tents and a rack of mountain bikes before making it to the cashier. Jenna and Daina take off and plunk down in a display of camping chairs and tents, pretending to sip fake beers while they jabber on about which tent would be best for camping when they're rich.

I find the rainbow chrome knife I've been eyeing for months and jam my finger against the glass. "That one," I say to the cashier.

"Sure, can I see your identification?" he asks with a haughty smile, like he knows damn well I'm not old enough yet.

My lip twitches as I pat my pockets for an identification card we all know I don't possess. "I forgot it at home," I lie.

He rubs the stubble on his chin. "Sorry, I need to verify your age before I can sell it to you. You could always go home and get it."

My hand curls into a fist on the glass. "Dude, I'm eighteen, *I promise.*"

He crosses his arms and straightens, eyes challenging mine.

I'm about to unleash another retort when Camille grabs my arm and drags me away, growling, "Don't, Marianna, you'll get us kicked out."

"I want that knife," I tell her, glaring at the cashier over her shoulder.

She herds me to the back of the store, where Daina and Jenna have climbed onto a couple of display Jet Skis. "It's your birthday, and it's just a knife. Why not pick out some clothes or something? You've already got so many knives. Just get that one next year."

Arms folded, I scowl, hating how rational Camille is. But ever since the four of us got grouped up in seventh-grade art class, she's always been the voice of reason in our tight-knit group.

A man maneuvers between us to reach the shelf of climbing ropes and hooks. When he excuses himself, the smoothness of his honey voice makes my heart skip and I move aside without a second thought.

"Come on," she continues. "Hell, if it's so important maybe we can try to find the same one online."

Fire singes the nerves in my fingertips and scorches my stomach. I know I shouldn't be so upset about a stupid knife. "But it's my birthday." I just want things to go my way for one day.

The man looks up from a package of carabiner hooks. "It's your birthday?"

I shift my weight to my other foot as I look up at him. "Yeah." Likely near six foot four, he stands so close it feels like he's towering over me.

His grin is wide and friendly, a perfect set of white teeth exposed. "Well, happy birthday," he says, tone sweet.

My arms tighten across my chest. "Thanks."

"Is the cashier giving you trouble?" he asks. He sets the package of hooks back on the shelf and slips his hand into the pocket of his black leather jacket.

"I'm a year too young for the knife I want," I tell him, feeling ambitiously hopeful as he fishes out his matching leather wallet.

I hold my ground as he steps closer, only to take a discreet step back after a tiny breath. I can't help but smile at the inadvertent nicotine barrier I've ended up surrounding myself with.

He must be used to worse smells than mine, as he steps back toward me to speak, and I'm not sure whether to be impressed or appalled.

Quietly, he asks, "What knife is it, birthday girl?"

Pulling my birthday money from my pocket, I say, "It's the rainbow chrome folding knife on the top shelf."

He waves my money away, which brings my scowl back, and says, "It'll be a birthday gift."

I cock a brow. "A birthday gift from a stranger?"

His smile twitches like he's trying to hold back a chuckle. "Yes. Strangers do nice things for each other all the time, don't they?"

Not wanting to risk losing out on getting my knife, I say, "Yeah, like coffee trains and whatever. Right."

Grinning, he nods as he brushes between Camille and me. "I'll bring it out to the bench."

As soon as he's out of earshot, Jenna and Daina climb down from the Jet Skis and we move to stand near the bench outside the store together.

"Oh my God, he's so hot," Daina gushes from beside me, Jenna giggling along with flushed cheeks.

Camille fights a smile. "Guys . . ."

"Don't you agree, Marianna?" Daina asks.

He is horribly gorgeous, in a sweet way, though there is just enough severity to his features and the way he carries himself to stop people from taking that sweetness for granted. Yet all I say is, "Yeah, so?"

Daina's grin only grows, her eyes sparkling. "He looks like the type of guy that goes camping and canoeing all summer. We should seduce him into taking us with him. I need a tan, and ever since my mom and auntie had that fight, I doubt I'm allowed to visit her in Mexico anymore. I don't want to get grounded again for trying to have my cousins pick me up."

Jenna giggles. "I'd like to go canoeing. If we run out of space in the canoe, I can sit on his knee and help him hold the oars."

Daina releases a dramatic gasp. "As if. I'll flip the canoe if that happens."

I look up as he approaches. "You guys shut the hell up, he's coming."

He hands the plastic packaging with the knife inside to me. "Happy birthday."

"Thank you . . ." I trail off, realizing I don't know his name.

"It's Den," he says, flashing a gleeful grin again. I can't help but wonder if he's the ridiculously over-happy type. Buying gifts for strangers would be something someone with that personality would do.

"Oh, okay," I start. "Well, thanks for the birthday present, Den."

Smile remaining, his eyes tighten as he mulls me over. "I'm sorry, I keep thinking about how familiar you look."

I fold my arms back over my chest, package gripped in my fist as I become painfully aware of how I must look to him in my cigarette-burned hoodie and worn-out jeans. This fact makes me want him to go away quicker. "We've never met." I'm sure I'd remember him if we had. With a face like his?

"Are you sure?" he presses.

"I've never met you, Den," I repeat, a little more firmly this time. My heart beats so hard that my knees wobble.

He rubs the back of his neck, his messy medium-brown ponytail made of curls and waves sliding over his hand. A chuckle slips through his apologetic smile. "I'm sorry, Marianna—that's what your friends called you, right? I must be thinking of the wrong person."

"It's whatever," I mumble, waiting for him to walk away. I

should have worn something nice for once. After all, it is my birthday and we're in a richer part of town.

"Well, regardless, what kind of plans do you have for your birthday?" He glances between my friends and me. "I'd love to treat you to dinner, Marianna. I know a nice restaurant around here."

Overly friendly, or calculating? Why would he want to ask *me* out?

At the mention of dining in this part of the city, my friends' faces light up.

"A date?" Daina asks him.

Camille smacks her in the arm and hisses, "Shush. Of course it's a date."

His smile is patient. "What do you think?"

Birthday dinner? In the rich north of the city? I've never done anything like that before. "I don't know," I say, upper lip stiff. "Did you buy me the knife so I'd feel like I have to say yes to dinner?"

His smile plummets into a frown. "No, really, it wasn't premeditated. I'd already bought it when I had the idea."

I glower—hating that I feel embarrassed in his presence—and Camille jabs me in the side with her elbow.

His smile sneaks back to his lips. "Five-star restaurant . . . I can pick you up in my car . . ."

"She'll go," Daina answers for me, Jenna unable to hold back her laughter at Daina's brashness.

I sigh, just wanting to have the shitty birthday I've already prepared myself for.

"So how about it? Will you let me take you out to dinner tonight?" he asks.

I clench my jaw, deciding to agree so he'll leave sooner. What would the chances be that he won't show up even if I do? I rearrange my expression to something friendly. "Sure."

Daina squeals happily.

"Great," he says.

"Where are we going?" I ask, my smile having a hard time staying on my lips.

Den gives the name to a fancy five-star restaurant, which only makes my friends more excited, like they're the ones being asked out. He tells me to dress formal, which makes dread fill my limbs.

"What's your address?" he says. "I'll pick you up."

I laugh. "I'm not giving you my address."

His nod is understanding. "Okay, I'll see you at the restaurant."

Den gives me the address of the restaurant and what time to come, which Camille quickly types into her phone.

His dark eyes catch mine, his stare heavy. "Please show up."

"I will."

He grins. "Perfect. I'll see you tonight, then," he says before stuffing his hands in the pockets of his dark blue jeans and walking away.

I watch him until he's out of earshot. "I'm not going."

Daina whines and does some kind of tantrum flail. "*Come on*, Marianna. You have to go."

"He seems nice, though," Jenna adds, Camille agreeing.

I slip my knife into Daina's oversized purse so I don't have to carry it. "No, *I don't* have to go."

The three of us walk again, weaving between shoppers.

"Yes, you do. You can't just stand him up," Daina says, tone matter-of-fact.

"Why not?"

We step back onto the escalator, going down.

"Because he seems like a nice guy, and it'd be mean," she adds.

I cross my arms. "So? I'm mean."

Camille groans, making someone look back up at us for a

moment. "Stop with all the angst, seriously, Marianna." She leans back against the rail. "Why don't you want to go?"

Jenna says, "I think you could have fun."

I twist my fingers together. "I'm not ready to date," I admit. That, and I'm not sure I could even handle being near someone so put together without questioning myself every moment. What does someone as attractive and sweet as him want to do with me? I can only imagine it's the same thing the boys at my school want. I'm not even good enough to be someone's daughter, never mind *girlfriend*.

It'll be a first date that turns into nothing. I've got enough to be upset about, and I don't need to add heartbreak on top of it all.

Daina leans her head back and makes a protesting noise. "Come on. You've never even been on a date before. Live a little."

But technically, I have if you count the men who paid my mother for *special alone time* with me when I was a kid. I'm not ready for dating, because sex is one of the things that usually comes along with it, and I'm definitely not ready for that either.

I give everyone an explanatory look and they fall into a unified silence for a minute.

"It wouldn't be the worst thing to step out of your comfort zone," Camille says.

Jenna smiles. "What if we waited with my mom in the parking lot and you can make a break for it if you need to?"

I pointedly look away from them and scowl.

"Marianna, it's just dinner," Camille says as we step off the escalator. "He seems like a decent guy. He's better than any option you have at school. Maybe an older guy could be better for you, more maturity and all. I doubt he's partying and getting high every night like the guys that have shown interest in you."

We make our way through the flurry of customers to find the exit, dodging salesmen who try to give us soap samples.

"What if he's awful? What if he figures out too late that *I'm awful*? I don't even know how old he is," I counter. Old enough to buy my knife, at least.

We push the heavy glass doors open, stepping into late-afternoon sunlight.

"Then you don't have to call him back," Jenna says. "He doesn't seem that old, anyway. College, maybe."

"And you're not awful," Camille interjects with a scowl. "Just a little . . . abrasive sometimes."

Daina grins. "Yeah, and I'll have my brother steal his boat if he's a jerk."

I don't respond, following in their steps as I squeeze between my friends and the red brick of the mall so we can all fit on the sidewalk.

Camille touches my arm. "Come on, give it a chance. Maybe you'll have fun. Maybe you'll even like him. If anything, you get an expensive meal out of it and a bit of dating experience."

I sigh, stopping at the confectionery window when my shoulder touches glass instead of brick. "Maybe." Or maybe the date will be one more thing that makes my birthday suck.

They stop at my side as I look into the display window. Colorful streamers and flowers are strategically placed around the display case, cakes and other fresh desserts placed for show.

My eyes drop to a cake just big enough for two people. White icing covers the square surface, the edges a bright ocean blue, a sugar dolphin with enough space for a name underneath stuck on top. I cup my hand against the cold glass. Spotting the price tag, I decide what to use my birthday money on. I can't remember the last time I had a birthday cake. Would it be pathetic to ask to have my name iced on it, or should I buy it as it is?

But an employee in her black apron slides into the display,

icing-stained hands snatching my cake up. She hauls it away to whichever customer beat me to it.

"God fucking damn it," I snarl, reaching for the cigarettes in my back pocket. They fall from my jeans and spill from the package and all over the concrete. Now I've got no cake *and* no candle stand-ins.

Jenna and Daina reassure me they're still good as they squat to pick them up for me.

"It's fine," Camille says. "You don't need to make it into a big thing. It can just be dinner, and I'm sure *he'll* buy you a birthday cake, okay?"

I ignore her and stuff my cigarettes back into my pocket, making a beeline for the bus stop as the bus nears it. My friends hasten in my steps.

We step on the bus, dropping change into the slot to get a ticket before finding seats at the back. I pinch my nose, the smell of piss and summer sweat filling it. Thankfully, Camille opens the window.

"We still have a couple hours to convince you," Daina says smugly.

"You'll need it," I grumble.

For the entire bus ride, they spout reasons I should go, saying I need to take more chances and stop hating everyone before I get to know them. I ignore them most of the time.

But once we're alone in my bedroom, they dig deeper, telling me that just because I go on a date doesn't mean he'll want to have sex, how if I end up liking him and seeing him again, I still don't have to, and if he doesn't respect that, then he's not worth it. Daina says that if I end up having sex, it won't necessarily be bad because of past experiences. I counter that I could avoid it all by not going, but she won't have it.

Eventually, I agree, but only begrudgingly.

"You better not sabotage this date," Daina hisses. She flips through bent metal hangers in my tiny closet after I've washed my shield of cigarette smoke off in the shower and applied makeup to the new mark on my inner elbow.

Lying on my futon, I stuff my face into the pillow, wishing the date and heartbreak was over already. I just want to get over hearing that sweet voice telling me he doesn't want to see me again.

I roll over when a hanger and fabric land on me. Blue sequins scratch my bare arms. I hold it up. "This thing? I'm going to look thirteen. Don't I have anything better in there?"

She shakes her head. "At least you'll look pretty. Besides, blue looks nice with your brown eyes. Den won't even care what you're wearing, he'll be too busy trying to impress you."

"Remember," Daina says, "*you're* out of *his* league. Make him work."

Camille rolls her eyes at Daina. "Just try to have fun," she says to me.

I pull the strapless dress up violently, a few sequins ripping off and disappearing into the mess of clothes and papers on my floor. I wonder if the dress will have as hard of a time staying up as it did when I was thirteen. I haven't exactly filled out yet.

When she pulls a makeup bag out of her backpack, I fall back into the bed and shield my face with a pillow.

"Let me do your makeup, you brat!" Camille hollers while sitting beside me, trying to rip the pillow away.

I growl like a dog, and she sighs.

"Why are you being so difficult?"

"I don't like makeup," I say, voice muffled. I only ever use it to hide bruises and relapses. It's too much effort otherwise.

I tighten the pillow when I hear her unzip it.

"Please! Just mascara."

I slowly lower the pillow, eyes turning to slits at the clumpy black wand that's waiting. "Fine," I agree, thinking it might help draw attention away from the bags under my eyes.

She grins, bringing the thing to my eyes. I blink against the wand. She puts it back in her bag, and I pull my lips into my mouth as she tries to attack me with red lipstick. Thankfully, Jenna and Daina agree that mascara is enough, with Daina convinced she knows his type enough to assume he'd prefer me natural.

My foster mother, Pam, pokes her head into my room as Jenna brushes my hair. "What are you all dolled up for?" she asks with her croaky voice, a cigarette hanging from her wrinkled lips.

Camille stands and smiles, smoothing out her peach-colored blouse. "She's got a date."

Pam laughs, heavy steps continuing down the stairs. "Good luck with that."

I grit my teeth, fists on my lap.

Camille rolls her eyes, turning back to me. "I can't believe your social worker lets you live here."

I shrug. "She's a poster mother to them. You should see how much effort she puts into her show. I've never seen the house so clean on those days."

"You should ask for a new foster home," Jenna says. "Can you do that?"

"It doesn't matter," I whisper. "I age out in a year." It was easier than saying I'd already made my way through my fair share of foster homes in the city, and that there wasn't a lot about me that made people ready to take on a "troubled teen with a history of drug abuse, gang violence, and severe behavioral and emotional issues," as my file put it. I haven't seen any point in trying to get that file—that I wasn't supposed to read— to say anything different. It's not like I'll get adopted no matter how hard I try to be a cookie-cutter good girl. Hell, I'm barely fosterable.

In a welcomed attempt to lighten my mood, Camille teases that we should all get jobs and rent a house together in the rich north of Lorimer.

The sound of cartoons disappears from the living room downstairs, shouting starting up about unwashed dishes. I hear Charlie calmly apologize, saying something about how he planned to do them after homework. Pam keeps yelling.

By the time Pam leaves for work, it's time for my date. I ask Charlie to help Samantha with word exercises if he's not too tired after his homework, since we both know Pam will never help her, and the two of us seem to be the only ones who want to help her prepare for first grade. I set her in front of the television and change the channel to Discovery.

Back on the bus, Daina tries to give me dating advice, reminding me to be civil and make little body movements to make him swoon. I intercept the handful of condoms she tries to stuff in my purse—saying they're so I can be safe if I change my mind—and they end up all over the floor.

They get off a few stops later, but not before making me promise to show up and to play nice.

III

Long before fancy sports cars pass by me as I walk down the street and past the valet, I feel out of place. I prepare myself for dirty looks and under-the-breath comments as I approach the entrance and am glad I'm spared when none come.

A man in a suit opens the door for me, and I'm immediately bombarded with classical music and the red-and-gold scheme of the restaurant. The staff are dressed more nicely than I am— in black-and-white outfits—but then again everyone seems to look better than me.

I definitely don't belong here.

I think of backing away and going home, but I make eye contact with the host.

"I'm supposed to meet someone," I say.

He looks me up and down. "I see. Your name?"

"Marianna Cortez." I look around at the tables behind him for Den, but all I see are fancy diners in a smear of suits, dresses, and jewelry. What are the chances that I'll be stood up?

He searches for my name in the leather-bound book at his

stand and is about to speak when Den appears behind him, smiling.

The host recognizes I've been found and waves me past him.

I follow him to the back of the restaurant, the feel of his hand on my lower back turning my throat into a desert. A table for two awaits, and a waitress quickly approaches as he pulls out the gold-silk-upholstered seat for me.

"I see your date has arrived." The waitress dons a warm smile. "What would you like to drink?"

Brave, I say, "Wine."

Her eyes dart between me and Den, her lips parting for her low tone of hesitation. "Uh . . . are you twenty-one?"

When his fingertips brush the hand she has planted on the table, her eyes turn to his and they lock.

"Bring my date and me a bottle of red wine, okay?" I miss what kind he tells her, the foreign words refusing to stick in my mind.

With a wide smile and cheery voice, she says, "Oh, okay, sure thing!" She walks away, almost getting plowed over by a woman who trips over her heeled feet.

I grin, doing my best not to look away when his dark eyes meet mine. "Thanks."

"Of course." He pushes his glass of water toward the middle of the table, passing me a menu before opening his.

"Thanks." I open it with a shaky hand, the prices so startlingly high I almost slam it shut in surprise.

He must catch my expression as he laughs and says, "You can have anything you want."

I exhale, wondering where to start.

"Thank you for coming," he says.

I swallow a lump but don't respond, pretending I'm too engulfed in finding something to eat. I look for something I haven't tried before, which is basically everything.

"Is the lobster good?" I wonder aloud.

His eyes scan his menu. "Probably."

I close my menu as the waitress comes back with an expensive-looking bottle of wine and two glasses.

After pouring each of us a glass, she asks, "You two ready to order?"

I order lobster, and he picks the same.

Once she walks away, he goes into date mode. "Have you lived in Lorimer your whole life?"

"Yeah, but my mom's family was from Mexico." I've always wondered where my father was from, whoever he may be. I look nothing like my mother with her dark eyes and skin, her thick brown hair. I probably took all my father's genes. If I had to guess, I'd assume he had roots in Europe. "Have you lived here your whole life?"

He rolls up the sleeves of his black silk dress shirt. "Not quite. I was born in Rome."

I notice his accent then, faint but not quite Italian, or anything I can place for that matter. Maybe I imagined it, or it's the way he talks. His voice is calming, accented and lilting in all the right places. I could listen to him talk forever. "You don't sound Italian."

He laughs. "I'm not Italian. I've lived all over the world, though. I've only been permanently in Lorimer for a few years."

I wrap my hand around the bowl of the wineglass, bringing it to my lips for a small sip. Bitterness rolls over my tongue, and my throat and chest go cold when I swallow. After taking another tiny sip, I promise myself I won't have more than two glasses, disliking the idea of getting drunk around a guy I don't know. "Your parents are rich, then?" Am I too blunt?

He grins. "Yeah, they were."

I take note of his usage of past tense but decide it's best not to ask him to expand on it. I assume they didn't go bankrupt, considering I'm in a fancy-ass restaurant with him. They're probably dead, unless they really are broke now and he has a good job.

He clears his throat, folding his hands on the table. "I know you already said no, but are you sure we haven't met before? I just can't get over how *familiar* you look."

I take a deep breath and carefully set my wineglass down. Is the only reason he asked me out because he thought I was someone else? *Someone better, even?* "I'm a hundred percent sure I've never met you."

"*A hundred percent*—" His upper lip twitches before he smiles. "Everyone usually calls me Denendrius, if that rings any bells."

I lean back in my chair, squinting at him. He can't let anything go, can he? I already made it clear back at the mall that I don't know him. "No," I articulate.

He pulls his lips into his mouth and gives a little nod. "Okay. I must have seen someone who looks like you in a picture or something."

I don't respond, worried I'll say something to make him leave, so we sit in silence for a moment. He doesn't look as though he feels as awkward as I do. I try to think back to what my friends told me about appropriate date questions to ask him, but I come up blank. Maybe I should have listened.

"What's your job?" My question sounds more like a demand and I wince.

He pulls his water toward him, head bobbing side to side as he carries a tickled grin. Is he trying to think of a way to dumb it down, or does he not have a good answer?

"Jack of all trades?" I offer.

"I suppose that would cover it." He laughs.

I lean closer to him, saying, "Are you like a drug lord or a robber? A criminal?"

He chortles. "Would such a thing make me more intriguing to you?"

I lean backward, shoulders smacking into the metal of the chair. "Maybe."

I'm not really sure what I'd look for in a guy. I haven't really given it any thought. If I had, would it be a drug lord or robber? Or would I be steering clear of anyone with a criminal record and instead looking for someone who had their shit together? Does he have his shit together? Is he loaded because he's the owner of some rich business, or because he's swindled his way into a fortune?

I ask, "If you were some rich criminal, would you tell me?"

His expression falls, turning serious. "We are in public," he says carefully. "I'd tell you later."

Fire licks my veins. I remember how I promised not to sabotage this date, so all I say is, "Right."

He winks at me, folding his hands on the table in front of himself. "Tell me about your family?"

"Imprisoned," I hiss.

My mother, Bonnie, is my only family. But she was arrested when I was nine.

He nods. "Care to elaborate?"

"I wouldn't consider it to be first date material."

He sits back. "Hmm."

I pick my wineglass back up. "Your family?"

He frowns. "I wouldn't consider it to be first date material," he echoes.

That must mean dead. Great first date. I knew I'd fuck it up.

I take a long and bitter swallow of wine and set the near-empty glass on the table while trying to think of a way to resuscitate the conversation.

"Do you enjoy reading?" he asks, veering past the last topic. He refills my glass. "I do."

"Yeah," I admit, though I know it doesn't make me seem very tough.

"What kind of books?"

Such a simple question shouldn't make me shift in my seat and look around like it'd be bad if we were overheard. Maybe I worry my answer half-conflicts with my image. "Horror, crime stuff, a bit of fantasy." I decide to tell him anyway, in case he makes fun of me. Then I can write him off for being a jerk. "I'm a big fan of vampire stories. I think I've read Anne Rice's *Interview with the Vampire* a hundred times."

His smile is kind. *Damn it.* "Vampires are fun, aren't they?"

I offer an indifferent nod, refusing to admit I've always been fascinated by them.

We stare at each other again, me obviously still feeling more awkward than him and his relentlessly amused smile.

"Did you and your friends end up picking out something nice for your birthday, then?" he asks.

I rest my elbow on the table and place my chin in my palm. "Not really, no."

"I'm sure you'll think of something nice to get yourself."

Thinking of how he was old enough to buy me that knife, I ask, "When is your birthday?"

"December fourth."

I lift a brow. "Of . . . which year?"

He chuckles. "I'll answer the question you're really asking. I'm twenty-seven."

I straighten in my chair. "Oh."

His brows lift, his smile relentless. "Is that a problem?"

I chew the inside of my cheek, and he suddenly feels twice as unattainable.

Why would he want me? The thought bumps around my head and makes my stomach twist. My throat tightens and I try to make myself quickly come to terms with the simple fact that I am wasting his time.

"No, that's fine . . . I thought maybe you were in college or something. I don't know."

His lips purse. "I've never gone to college."

"Yeah," I whisper, another awkward silence settling in my seat with me.

"I like your dress, by the way."

I look down at it, noticing the way the chandelier lighting makes it look like a Halloween costume. "Thanks, I got it for eight dollars when I was thirteen," I admit, hoping it will help him understand the kind of person he has asked out.

His chest rolls in a silent chuckle. He pulls at his black dress shirt and mouths, "Stolen."

I guess that answers the job question, and I can't help but wonder if he thinks so low of me that he would say that in hopes of impressing me. Should I be impressed with his stolen shirt? Is a thief the kind of guy he thinks I'm looking for? Should it be?

"I do prefer you without all the makeup, though . . ." he adds. "You were prettier at the mall without it, not that you don't look gorgeous now still."

My teeth slam together, a grenade dropped into my blood-stream. "*I didn't ask you,*" I growl from behind bared teeth, my disappointment making it hard to stop myself from lashing out.

A couple glances sideways from their table and quickly looks away.

He smirks and rests his clean-shaven face in the palm of his hand, elbow propped on the table. There's something about the way his eyes sparkle that makes me wish I'd shut up.

He straightens. "I'm assuming you go to school? Are you a good student?"

"I'd have to actually go to be a good student."

I have been going to school more often lately, probably out of boredom. My attendance has gone up from once a week to an amazing three times lately. I'm definitely not the school's most infamous misbehaved student, though.

I think of telling him this, just to break the silence, but that would mean I'd probably have to tell him which school I go to.

"You should go," he starts. "Your studies are important."

I roll my eyes, but he's speaking again before I can retort.

"Food's coming," he says as the waitress approaches behind him.

She sets our plates in front of us, and I immediately realize there is absolutely no way I'm going to be able to finish the lobster. I'm glad because there's enough food here to keep me from having to talk.

He talks enough for the both of us. I answer his questions when he asks, giving simple answers so I can keep listening to him speak. It doesn't seem to annoy him, as he continues to smile.

I learn he's done more traveling than I could ever imagine, from Argentina to Alaska, to Japan, Africa, Australia, Germany, Indonesia, and Russia. He even lists off a few countries I've never heard of, and some I do know but forget since his list is so long. He says he speaks a handful of languages too, which might explain the way he speaks. Never having even left the state of New York, my life sounds boring in comparison.

When I finish my two glasses of wine and request something else, he snaps his fingers at the waitress.

She fakes a smile as she approaches. "What would you like?"

I'm about to ask for a soda when Denendrius cuts in.

"My date needs something else to drink," he demands.

"Can I have a milkshake?" I interject. "Strawberry?"

"Sure thing," she says, her smile only offered to me.

I stare at him as she walks away.

"You all right over there?" I ask him, hoping he's not getting frustrated with me and taking it out on her.

His flat face quickly turns cheerful and he grins. "Of course, why do you ask?"

I shrug and shake my head, stuffing my mouth full of lobster.

After about two minutes without the waitress's return, he's clearly agitated. His lips are a firm line as he carefully looks around the restaurant.

After ten minutes, he stands up.

I drop my fork on my plate. "What are you doing . . .?"

He straightens his dress shirt. "The service here is horrible."

I pick something from my teeth. "It's packed in here, relax."

At my suggestion for him to relax, his jaw tenses and he quickly looks at me sideways. He opens his mouth, probably ready to retort, but he closes it and sits down.

Normally, I might be upset too. But I'm not letting a late milkshake ruin my first experience at a five-star restaurant.

I continue eating, and thirty seconds later the waitress is bringing me my drink.

"Thanks," I mumble through a mouthful of food.

Denendrius scowls at her. "Don't take so long next time."

She stares at him for a second and then smiles. "I'm sorry, sir." She walks away, probably before she says anything rude or dumps my milkshake on him.

I think of a way to lighten the mood, saying, "So my friend thinks you're some nature freak, that you have a boat."

He tongues his cheek. "Do you like boats?"

"I've never been on one. Why, do you have one?" I ask.

"I used to, but it was taken from me. I could get another, though," he says, brow lifting in suggestion.

I exhale a beat of laughter. "That—that's okay."

Denendrius turns cheery again, rambling on about his favorite movies. I suck back a good fourth of my strawberry milkshake.

Once I'm halfway through my plate, I realize he's not actually drinking or eating at all, just cutting stuff up, moving it around, bringing it to his mouth only to put it back down to speak again. I'm not even sure his wine has moved from where the waitress placed it.

I squint at him, chin scrunched. "You're not eating a damned thing."

His eyes widen slightly in surprise. He clears his throat. "Hmm. I didn't think you'd notice."

I put my fork down, my squint intensifying. "What's the deal? You not like it? You're being—" I bite my tongue.

A grin breaks across his face, his dark eyes bright. "What?"

"You're being weird," I finish for him.

He laughs, pushing his plate away from him. "I'm not supposed to be eating. I have to see the doctor tomorrow."

I roll my eyes, teasing. "Then why would you take me to a restaurant?"

He shrugs. "I was unable to come up with another idea."

I roll my head back. Seriously? I could think of tons of other ideas, and I've never even been on a date before. "You could have taken me to the movies." I stifle a laugh.

His grin widens. "We still can. How about it? We can go when you're done eating—unless you want to stay for cake."

With the date not being bad enough for me to justify cutting it short early, I agree, especially since it has been eons since I stepped into a movie theater.

I use the restroom as an excuse to switch my knife from my purse to my bra since I know I'm leaving alone and going in his car with him. He seems harmless, but at least this way I'm prepared if he turns into a madman once we're alone.

He's watching me intently as I sit back down to finish what I can, too full to even consider cake. I push my lobster away since it's getting cold but decide to suck back as much of the milkshake as I can.

I pull the straw away from my mouth and stare at it in confusion. Somehow it tastes better than before. Sweeter.

"What's wrong?" he inquires, slipping into his leather jacket.

"Nothing." I shove the straw back into my mouth.

I think I'll have to start coming back alone more often, just for the milkshakes.

I'm surprised when he doesn't ask the valet to retrieve his car. Instead, we walk in silence as we travel a few blocks down to where he's parked. Dark hangs above our heads, streetlights and headlights illuminating our path.

When he opens the passenger door of his black Mustang for me, I give the car a long stare, remembering the one that was following me the night I overdosed. But since I can't tell if it's even the same one and know for a fact there are multiple in Lorimer, I disregard my paranoia and I crawl in, propping my feet on the dashboard.

"No seat belt?" he asks, sitting in the driver's seat. He jams the key in the ignition, the car purring. He cranks it into drive, not putting his seat belt on either.

"I don't care if I get thrown out the window," I joke.

He laughs. "Don't fret, I'm a fantastic driver."

We jolt forward, the tires spinning fast enough I'm certain we've already blown past the speed limit.

"Oh yeah, of course," I tease.

He smiles. "So, you were wondering what I do?"

I twist my hands on my lap, picking at sequins. "Yep."

"I count cards, for starters." He turns the wheel, and we barrel around a corner so fast I hang on to the door.

He's piqued my interest. I look at him, brows raised. "Oh? Like in a casino?"

A proud smile flashes across his face. "Yes, like in a casino."

I spin sideways in my seat, back against the window. "How?"

"I have a near-perfect memory." He winks at me. "Also, I have the best poker face."

My lips spread into a wide grin. "Huh, that's really cool. Let me see your poker face."

His poker face is basically an emotionless stare. It could also double as a murder face. It's definitely believable, though, and for a split second makes me think he's not showing his poker face but an I-can't-believe-you-fucking-asked-that look.

I tongue my cheek. "Nice. I assume you're good at reading people too?"

He chuckles. "I suppose you could say that."

"Yeah? Read me."

His brows rise. "Yeah?"

"Yeah."

He adjusts his hands on the wheel. "Hmm." He looks me over. "I think you're flirting."

My heart skips and I swallow. "You think so?"

He responds with a wink.

Denendrius turns a dial on the dashboard and a rock concert comes to life. He brings the volume to a near ear-shattering level, but I don't mind.

Carefully, I study him, hoping he'll reveal something about himself if he doesn't think I'm paying attention. I try to come up with a reason he thinks he knows me.

Instead, staring at him brings about a strange stirring in my gut, like I'm trying to remember the details of an all-too-real dream after starting awake from it. I can feel the shape of the fuzzy edges it holds as I ponder it, the blur of blinding vibrant colors contrasted by a never-ending dark, all mixed in with a flurry of confusion and silence. It's like déjà vu.

But no matter how hard or how long I sift through the feeling, no dream or memory surfaces to offer it clarity. *I don't know Denendrius.* There's nothing about his appearance or demeanor that reminds me of anyone or anything in particular.

Looking out the windshield, I take a steadying breath as we approach the theater.

He finds a place to park in the packed lot, and when we step out of the car, the gentle chill of night makes me wish I'd brought a sweater as I shiver.

"Would you like to borrow my jacket?" he asks.

When I feel his cold hand graze mine, I automatically move my hand away. "I'm fine."

We walk in silence through the white-lit parking lot and into the building, where we are immediately bombarded by the griping of arcade machines. Voices drift over the sound of soda machines and popping popcorn. The place smells of butter and dirt, which also covers the blue-and-yellow abstract carpet.

We easily agree on a horror movie and make our way to the counter for food. He, of course, doesn't order anything, but he insists on buying me cotton candy, specifically blue. I try to tell him we can just grab a purple or pink one, but he forces us to wait as the worker, annoyed, makes a blue one since they're out.

I try to sit in a middle aisle where lots of people can see us, but he gently pulls me back onto the path and directs us to the back corner, seating me between him and the wall. He leans his body toward me and sets my food in my lap.

We chat through the previews, me smiling as he makes suggestions about seeing the advertised movies, as if we are already a couple who visits the theater regularly.

I'm halfway through eating my popcorn when Denendrius's hand moves over the armrest. He slips his fingers through mine. My heart pounds in my ears, my hand turning so sweaty and shaky I avoid looking at him in case he notices.

I learn he likes to talk during movies, mostly comments here and there about how fake the blood and gore is, or how easy it should be for the antagonist to kill the girl. I have to shush him a few times, his remarks making me giggle to the point where I worry we'll be told to leave.

When the movie is over, I begrudgingly acknowledge that our date is too but that I don't want it to be.

We walk back toward the car and he smiles, hand running down my back.

"I had a great time," he tells me.

"Me too," I admit, leaning against the passenger door.

When he wets his lips and leans his head down toward mine, I find myself pulling away. "I live on the west side," I blurt. "But I grew up on the south end of town." My brain tells me to shut up, but the words keep falling out. "I'm a foster kid."

He stares at me, his brow furrowed. "Why—"

"I don't want to disappoint you. I don't live in the north, Den."

He shrugs. "Neither do I."

My brows shoot up. "You don't?"

He shakes his head. "No, I live in the west too."

A strange mix of relief and disappointment fills me. I wanted him to be better than me, wanted someone out of my league to think—for at least a moment—that I might be worth what they are. I realize I don't want to date anyone like me. I don't want to date a drug lord or a bank robber, or someone who might be poor because of a gambling addiction.

"I thought you were rich," I find myself whispering, my words making me sound like a gold digger instead of portraying what I really mean.

I expect him to be angry and accuse me of being after his money. Instead, he leans over and rests his arm on the top of the car behind me, his voice desperate as he says, "No, Marianna, I have money. I promise, okay? I'm not living in the west because I'm broke—"

"I'm not after your money—"

But he keeps going. "I can prove it if you want. I know stability is important to women—"

"Denendrius, stop," I demand.

He stares at me, his dark eyes searching my face.

I pull in a deep breath and release a shaky exhale. "That's not what I meant. It came out wrong."

The corner of his lip lifts in a smile. "That's okay, as long as you like me."

I swallow a lump and try to wipe my sweaty palms on my dress. "You're sweet," I find myself whispering, heat filling my cheeks. "I do like you. I've had a good night."

He grins, his face moving closer to mine. "Yeah?"

"Yeah," I whisper, my breath catching in my tight throat as his soft lips slide between mine, the taste of mint strong on his breath.

My heart drums in my chest, chills running down my spine as he wraps his hand around the back of my neck. Butterflies flutter in my stomach as his hungry lips guide mine, his kiss deepening.

It's the kind of kiss I've seen in sappy romance movies, the kind that's full of passion and love. It's a kiss I would have never expected for my first *true* kiss. It's the first kiss that leaves my knees weak with excitement instead of fear.

I reach my arms around his neck as he pulls my body tight against his, kissing his chilly lips back. Already thinking about our next date, I know I'll be even more disappointed than I first thought if things don't turn out good.

"Come home," he murmurs against my lips before he takes a few more long kisses. "Marianna, come home with me."

I lower my head before he can press his lips back to mine. *I should have known.*

My arms drop from his neck and my hands turn to fists at my sides. I was right to expect disappointment. "I'm not going to your home to fuck you."

His words come out in a panic. "No, that's not what I meant." When he tries to lift my chin, I yank my head out of his grip. "I promise that's not what I meant."

He motions to his Mustang. "I thought you—"

"You thought I'd fuck you because you're rich?" I snarl, crossing my arms and trying to step out from between him and the car.

He leans against the car door with his hand to block me. "No! That's not what I meant."

"Then what did you mean?"

He leans in to try kissing me again.

I turn my face. "What did you mean?"

Den sighs. "I don't know," he says. "I don't know what I meant. Not that. I want to take you on a second date before we even think about that."

My scowl is lethal. "I'm not fucking you on our second date either."

Frustration shapes his face. "I'm not concerned about that, Marianna. That's not my goal here."

I uncross my arms, the fact that he wants to take me on a second date settling in. "Wait, you want a second date?"

His smile is warm. "*Yes*, a second date." He holds my face in his hands, his dark eyes smoldering and unblinking on mine. "Come on a second date with me, okay?"

I can't help my grin when he kisses me again, my stomach bubbling with excitement even though I can't help the thought he could still cancel between now and then. "I'd like a second date."

Den pulls away and laces his fingers in mine. "Perfect, give me your phone number and I'll call you. I'll need a few hours to think through another date plan, though."

I tell him my phone number and ask, "Do you need to write it down?"

He chuckles and shakes his head. "Super memory, remember?" He gives me another kiss. "Let me drive you home."

The idea of giving a guy I hardly know my home address— no matter how sweet he seems—makes my stomach flip. I look pointedly at the bus stop across the street. "It's okay, I'll take the bus."

He holds my hands tighter when I try to slip them out of his, giving me a quick peck on the lips before saying, "It's getting late, Marianna. If I take you home, it'll be twice as fast and safer."

"And my foster mom will be pissed at me for giving out my address." I'm not even sure if she would be, but it's a believable excuse.

He sighs and releases his grip on my hands. "Okay. How long does it take to get home? I'll call you to make sure you got there safely."

I'm torn between thinking his concern is sweet and wanting to tell him that I'm capable of getting home fine without him. Instead, I offer a thankful smile and say, "A couple hours. I'll talk to you soon, then."

He pulls me in for a long kiss before I go on my way.

IV

I'm running on fumes by the time I get home, the excitement of my date and my relapse catching up to me.

I slip my shoes off in the dark before stepping over to the side table to turn on the lamp. Plunking down on the love seat between the side table and TV, I glare across the living room at the uncapped markers on the couch.

Deciding to deal with them later, I pull the phone off the hook and dial Camille since Jenna doesn't have a cell phone and Daina has to give hers to her mom before going to bed.

Her sleepy voice answers with, "Hello? Marianna? Did your date go okay? I tried calling earlier."

"Yeah, it went good. We decided to see a movie after dinner. I just walked in the door." I pull the knife from my bra so I don't forget about it when I lie down, slipping it back in my purse.

She gasps, an excited squeal coming through the phone. "Oh my God! Really? So basically, what you're saying is that we were right about you having a good time?"

I glower into the shadows. "Yep, you were right. Rub it in and I'll hang up."

She giggles. "Okay, okay, spill the beans."

"He held my hand and we kissed," I say with little enthusiasm, though my heart jumps at the memory. "I'm waiting for him to call and ask if I made it home safe."

Her sheets ruffle. "He didn't drop you off?"

"I wouldn't let him."

Camille releases a dramatic sigh. "Of course. Well, what was the kiss like?"

I know her, Daina, and Jenna always gush about those kinds of details with one another, but I find myself wanting to keep them all to myself.

"Like a movie," I admit, twirling the phone cord around my finger when I recall the feel of his toned body against mine. "He's a good kisser."

"Ooh la la. Tongue? What did he taste like?" she inquires.

I scowl in disgust. "Ew, Camille, really?"

I can practically hear her roll her eyes. "It's girl-talk, Marianna. Now that you can relate, you can't zone out. You had your first real kiss tonight, don't you realize?"

I exhale, my tired grin growing. "Yeah, I know," I whisper. "He actually asked me on a second date too."

"Why do you sound surprised?" Camille asks.

"Because it's me," I whisper.

"Well, remember, it's *you* that got a guy to ask you on a second date and got kissed on the first. You can't be *that* awful, right?"

I rub my eyes. "Thanks, Camille." The phone beeps. "Someone's on the other line. I think it's him, so I'll talk to you later."

"Okay, Marianna, talk to you later," she says, a long yawn cut off as she hangs up.

My heart skips, no amount of deep breaths calming enough as I answer the other call. "Denendrius?"

The sound of his voice makes something in my stomach flutter. "Hey there, Marianna. Did you get home safe?" he asks.

I roll my eyes. "Yeah, didn't get murdered." I'm not sure why it bothers me so much to think that someone else might care. Do I think he believes I'm not capable of taking care of myself? Or have I become too used to people not giving a shit?

He doesn't laugh. "That's good. I forgot to ask earlier, but how are you?"

The question throws me off. "Uh—fine, I guess?" I scratch the back of my neck.

"Well, that's good."

"It's midnight now," I tell him, not sure what difference it makes.

"Want me to let you go?"

I sigh when I think of the usual nightmares that await me. "No, it's okay."

"Okay."

Laying sideways on the couch, I put my head up on the armrest. "You forgot?" I tease. "I thought you had a perfect memory?"

His chuckle makes me smile. "Near-perfect."

"Can you tell me how it works?" I pull my knees up since there's not enough space to stretch out.

"I can remember almost everything from the age I started remembering. Specific days, what happened on them, what the weather was like, and what I was feeling or thought. I can recall something I saw or smelled years ago, or what someone looked like in passing."

I mouth my amazement before saying, "That sounds amazing—and also like it could be a curse."

Denendrius's laugh comes out strangely, making me think I'm right. "Tell me what it's like to have a normal memory."

I fidget with the cord. "I don't have a normal memory," I tell him, though considering my past, I'm glad I don't have his.

"Hm. No?"

I'm not sure why I decide to indulge his curiosities with the truth. "No. I have big black spaces in my memory, from my childhood mainly. The things I do remember from back then kind of just . . . smear together. Before I was put in foster care at least."

The sadness in his voice comes clear through the phone. "That's quite unfortunate to hear, Marianna."

I shrug. "It doesn't bother me too much anymore. I don't know." More truths come out before I question if I'm oversharing. "I think it's from all the trauma. I'm glad I can't remember some of the horrible stuff, though sometimes I can't tell the difference between what really happened and the nightmares I used to have as a kid."

"Like what?" he asks, his honey-smooth voice luring me into a strange sense of security.

I decide to tell him something that won't reveal anything my mother did to me. "I had a dream when I was a kid that the police gave me to a better family. I dwelled on it for a long time, considering the situation I was in with my mom, until I accepted that it wasn't true and got over it."

"That's quite peculiar," Denendrius says. "I want to know more about that. Maybe on our third or fourth date we can revisit the subject."

The fact that he still wants to see me past a second date despite my word-vomit makes me giggle.

"What?" he asks, a smile in his voice.

"You're sweet," I find myself telling him again. I yawn and rub my eyes. "Like honey."

"That's a new one. I've never been compared to honey before," he says. "Honey's good."

I giggle again, the deliriousness that comes with exhaustion settling in.

"About dates," he starts, "I was thinking we could go up to the lake and I'll rent a boat."

Hearing someone shuffle around upstairs, I lower my voice. "That sounds fun, but it's too cold to swim."

"Oh. We don't have to swim, then," he says. "We could cruise around on the lake."

"We could do that, plus swimming, in the summer," I say, purposefully throwing out the idea of him being my boyfriend to see how he reacts.

"Yes," he says softly. "We can go to the lake however many times you want."

Warmth fills my chest. Maybe my seventeenth year on earth won't be so bad. Could my life really change for the better? Do I merely need something to look forward to so I start caring about life?

Denendrius starts talking about more ideas for activities he has for us, the lilt of his voice making it hard to stay awake as his words smear together and lose meaning. I fight sleep, wanting to stay awake and hear all his excited plans. But I'm too tired to keep my eyes open, and soon I'm listening to his voice through semiconsciousness.

My eyes only fly open when the soothing sound of Denendrius's voice sounds the same as the last time I was half-unconscious and heard a similar tone tell me why I was puking. Except that voice isn't *like* Denendrius's. I swear it's the same.

"I think I almost overdosed and died last night," I say, desperation for answers and exhaustion taking a toll on my decision making.

There's a long stretch of silence that makes me question if I accidentally fell asleep and he hung up.

"Denendrius?" I whisper. "Did I fall asleep?"

"I saw the bruising on the crook of your elbow and the needle mark earlier," he says carefully. "That's what I was alluding to when I asked how you were feeling."

My stomach flips, embarrassment making me want to retch. I was half expecting him to tell me my drug-induced delirium was reality, but I know Charlie has no reason to lie to me.

I do my best at damage control. "I was clean for a year. It was just a bump on the road to recovery. Last night was really rough."

"I believe you," he says, his words making my breath come easier. "I'll help distract you so it doesn't happen again. Why don't I pick you up after school, and we'll go to the lake? How does that sound?"

"I could skip class and we could go." My eyes fall closed again.

He makes a disapproving grunt. "Your studies are important, Marianna. Go. Tell me where and when you study, and I'll get you."

A headache starts in my forehead from fighting sleep. "Call me in the morning instead. I'll think of a place for us to meet. Maybe we can eat first." That, and I don't have enough brainpower to come up with an excuse to avoid giving him the name of my school. I know the strange sense that I've known him for months—the feeling that makes me keep saying things I shouldn't tell a stranger—doesn't negate the fact I only met him today.

Denendrius chuckles and I hear a kiss come through the phone. "Okay, sweetheart, sleep well."

"Goodnight," I murmur before hanging up the phone.

With my foster mom and siblings fast asleep, I creep up the tight wall-encased staircase and turn left into my room. The dark blue walls greet me when I switch my light on.

With half-lidded eyes, I scowl at my made bed, the cake I wanted from the confectionery sitting securely in its plastic package on my black blanket, my name frosted in baby blue beneath the dolphin.

I snatch it up and cross my aching legs on my futon. Grinning, I open the little gold card taped to the side. In impeccable black handwriting, it reads: *Happy Birthday, Marianna.* A heart is drawn at the bottom.

Although it doesn't say who it's from, I'm fairly certain Charlie is responsible. He'd been talking about how he wished he could get me a gift last week, and he was just out with his social worker. She probably helped him buy the gift and wrote on the card.

Slipping out of my dress, I toss it in the corner with the rest of my dirty clothes and pull on an oversized gray shirt and a pair of ratty boxers, then flop onto my futon. It squeaks, and I can feel the bars in my back, though it doesn't stop me from hitting dreamland with a blissful smile on my face.

Insistent poking jars me awake, Charlie standing at my side in the morning sunlight with a goofy grin.

"Your boyfriend is on the phone. You're supposed to wake up so you don't miss school and your *date*," he says.

My brow furrows and I throw my blanket off. "Boyfriend?" I know he means Denendrius, but isn't it kind of soon to be calling himself my boyfriend? Regardless, the fact he likes me so much to give himself that title fills me with an excitement that has me lunging out of bed and speed-walking to the telephone downstairs.

"Denendrius?" I ask as I pick the phone off the table and hold it to my ear, my fingers fidgeting with the cord.

With a chipper voice, he says, "Good morning, sweetheart. How did you sleep?"

I plop down on the edge of the love seat, my grin wider than it needs to be. "Great, for once," I admit.

"That's good to hear. Are you still up for going to the lake after school?" Denendrius asks. "I can pick you up."

I purse my lips in thought. "How about I call you after school and we can meet up at a burger joint or something beforehand?"

He sighs. "I don't own a phone. If you tell me—"

"You don't own a phone?" I interject. "Then how are you calling me?"

Denendrius's chuckle is strained. "Well, I was waiting for the newest smartphone that is supposed to come out in a couple months, but I might have to make do with the first model for now. I'm using the pay phone from across the street right now."

I give my head a slow shake and roll my eyes. "Okay, well, how about we meet at Buddy's Burgers at three thirty?"

The smile in his voice makes my heart skip. "Sure thing, Marianna. You have a good day at school."

"Thanks. I'll see you later."

I blow a long breath between my lips upon hanging up. After a cigarette and an extra-long shower to shave my legs and scrub my hair, I help Charlie and Samantha get ready for school before setting out on my own with far more enthusiasm for the day than I'm used to.

The fact that it's a guy who has me in a better mood and my mind occupied isn't the most favorable. I'd like to be happy on my own, but I guess any source of excitement and happiness is better than none right now.

Yet, Denendrius is merely one more thing that takes my mind off schoolwork. I carry on through my morning and to lunch in a daze, my thoughts ranging from excitement and disbelief that I went from overdosing to going on a date with a rich man who already wants to be my boyfriend, to panic at the reality that sex will come up if a real relationship ensues.

Daina can hardly contain herself as she weaves through the students in the cafeteria, her red-painted lips in a grin as wide as her brown eyes as she throws herself down in the chair across from me and clasps her hands on the table. "How was it!" she squeals.

I shrug, fighting my smile as I chew a French fry. "It was nice."

"I knew it!" she exclaims, jabbing a gold-painted nail at me. "I fucking knew you'd have a good time! And you told me—"

I playfully roll my eyes. "Yes, I know—"

"Did you tell her he kissed you yet?" Camille interrupts as she sits down with Jenna.

"He kissed you?" Jenna and Daina say at the same time.

My chewing slows and I nod while considering how much detail to give. "He did, yeah . . ." I opt for something jealousy-inducing. "It was super passionate, like in a movie. I felt sparks."

Daina marvels at me, her eyes sparkling. "Oh my God, Marianna! That's so exciting. Look at you, dating and enjoying it!"

Camille and Jenna don proud smiles, like they thought I might've been single for the rest of my life.

The normalcy of everything makes my smile shake. *Normal.* It's all I've ever wanted. To live in a modest house with nice parents, go to school with my normal friends and talk about average things like boys . . . it's a dream. Having one aspect of that—if nothing else—is a nice life change. I can't relive my childhood with good parents or erase my gang days and trauma despite wishing I could, but maybe a normal future isn't completely out of reach.

"How perfect is he?" Jenna practically drools, the hot dog on her plate forgotten.

I exhale a long breath and flop my cheek in the palm of my hand, my elbow propped up on the table. His insistence that I return home with him during the passion of our kiss makes me frown. "He's okay. I like him *a lot*, but he's got a few quirks ..."

Camille straightens. "Uh-oh. What kind of *quirks*?"

I chew the inside of my cheek. "Well, he wasn't the most patient with our waitress. Pretty demanding, honestly, but he was probably nervous. And he asked me to come home with him but swore up and down he didn't mean to hook up."

Daina's eyes narrow. "Then what for?"

"He never said." I shrug and shove another fry in my mouth.

"I can't imagine what else he could've meant," Camille says, shaking her head in disbelief. With a playful wink, she adds, "I can't blame him for trying to score with a pretty girl, though."

Despite his good looks, the thought of sleeping with Denendrius makes me grimace. My past experiences give me a shake that brings my lunch up to my throat and an acidic burn lingers in my chest. It's like the monsters of my childhood don't want me to forget that they're still with me.

"What the hell do I do when he wants to go all the way?" I bemoan.

Camille gives me a gentle smile. "Just take it slow and don't psych yourself out. You don't have to do anything you don't want to, obviously, but wait and see how you feel when the time comes. If you feel comfortable, you could talk about it with him first."

I squeeze my eyes shut and groan, shoving my food away. "I don't even want him to know," I say before opening my eyes again.

Daina reaches across the table and gives my hand a squeeze. "Well, he is older, so maybe he'll be more mature and understanding."

Sighing, I say, "Maybe. He's twenty-seven and *not* a college student, though."

My friends stare at me, Jenna seeming the most put off out of the three of them as she scowls and adjusts in her seat.

With an indifferent shrug, Daina says, "Well, as long as he's not taking advantage of you, right? You're eighteen in a year and you need someone who has his life straight."

Camille, who I thought would have the most adverse reaction out of all of them, says, "Whatever, it's legal. I agree with Daina. My mom and dad were fifteen years apart and they started dating when she was eighteen."

Jenna's scowl intensifies. "Yeah, but your dad's now in prison for fraud—"

With a quick elbow jab, Camille silences Jenna. "We're not going to talk about that. It had nothing to do with their age gap."

I inhale a deep breath to allow a bit of excitement back into me, a grin creeping onto my face. "Anyway, he's taking me to the lake tonight and we're going boating."

Daina's faces scrunches and she flails in frustration in her seat. "Unfair. Does he have a brother? A best friend?"

I can't help but stick my tongue out at her. For once, it's nice that I'm the one they're jealous of.

V

Walking outside when school ends, I spot Denendrius's Mustang parked across the street. Gritting my teeth, I can't believe the nerve he has for tracking me down at school and showing up when we already discussed meeting at Buddy's Burgers.

I tromp down the sidewalk and across the street when there's a break in traffic. The driver's window rolls down as I lift my fist to knock on it.

"You're at my school," I growl. "I didn't tell you where I go to school. How did you find out?"

Denendrius smiles, though his mirrored aviators conceal his full expression. "Is there another high school in the west?"

"Not anymore." I glower and mash my lips together, wishing I could retreat into the school and think my approach through better.

He nods toward the passenger seat. "Hop in."

My knees are weak as I saunter around the car, anticipating —hoping for—a kiss like our first one. He reaches across the passenger seat and opens the door for me. My legs shake as I crawl onto the seat and stare at him expectantly, too full of nerves to make the first move after I shut the door.

A mischievous smirk flashes across his lips before he leans across again and presses his lips against mine. He tastes like mint again, his kisses gentle and long.

I avoid his face when he pulls away and shifts the Mustang into drive. If I look at him, I know my face will heat up and I don't want him to think he already has a firm grip on my heart. As is it, I feel myself starting to sweat, though I'm not sure if it's from nerves when he's got the heat cranked as high as it will go.

When the hot air begins to dry my throat and eyes out, I cough and turn it down. "Jesus Christ. Do you have circulation issues or something?" I ask, thinking of how cold he is.

He glances at the dial and gives me a sheepish smile. "I'll remember to turn it down next time I pick you up."

"Sure. What did you do today?" I prop my feet up on the dashboard as he pulls away from the curb.

Denendrius shrugs and adjusts his leather jacket with his free hand. "I got some things organized."

"For . . . work?" I purse my lips and scrutinize him. He never really answered my question last night when I asked him what his job was. "What do you do? Are you just a professional gambler?"

"I don't go to the casino too often, to be honest," he says.

I wait for him to follow up with more, but when he doesn't, I have a feeling he had no intention of answering me honestly from the beginning.

"What did you study in school today?" he asks, foot too heavy on the gas when he turns a corner.

I cross my arms and glance at the door handle. "Nothing. So, what's your job, Denendrius? Where does all your money come from if you don't win it all?"

He sighs and adjusts in his seat. "Hmm. I was a ship captain for a while," he says, as if that should be a satisfying enough answer.

Clearly, he has *a lot* to learn about me if he thinks that's enough. "Feels like a lie . . . or half-truth. Keep going."

He inhales through his teeth before glancing at me and smiling. "Can't tell you quite yet."

My jaw falls open, brows lifting. "Fucking seriously?"

He reaches over and rubs my arm. "I'll tell you everything when it's the right time. Do you trust me?"

My laugh comes out sharp. "I like you, Denendrius, but I don't trust you. Not yet."

He balks and feigns hurt with a dramatic gasp.

"Tell me or I'm going to think the worst," I demand, my mind returning to the idea of him being a professional criminal.

"Don't. You'll understand when I tell you." He stops at a red light and scoops my hand up in his. "I want us to get to spend more time together first."

"Ah, I see." The only other reason I can think for him not telling me is that he doesn't want his job to be a deciding factor for my feelings. "Are you famous in a foreign country or something?"

He gives my hand a squeeze. "Something like that."

Intrigue rushes through me. "You're mysterious, Denendrius. But in a frustrating way," I tease.

His laugh makes me grin. "I'm glad I'm getting to talk to you, sweetheart. You know a better place to talk? A boat. Excited?"

The fact that he's gone out of his way to rent us a boat makes my heart skip with glee. "Hell yeah. Should we go to Buddy's Burgers now?"

He misses the turn he would have needed to take, saying, "I've got a better idea. Do you like fish?"

"Fish?" My eyes narrow, and I glance in the rearview mirror

on the off chance that there's fishing rods on the backseat. "I guess, but we're not catching supper, are we?"

He laughs. "No. I have dinner waiting for pickup."

"That works." I get comfortable, trying not to overthink how I'll be alone on a boat with him in the middle of the lake. I'm not a great swimmer, so taking to the water wouldn't be the greatest escape plan, but at least I have the knife I got for my birthday if he tries anything.

I watch the beaten houses and unkept yards flash by as we keep west of the city, heading north. The scenery slowly turns to houses twice the size before the buildings subside and make way for busy freeways that separate the west from the richest part of the north.

Denendrius and I sit in comfortable silence, fingers laced together as we listen to low rock music. Eventually he pulls into the parking lot of an expensive-looking seafood restaurant and tells me he'll be right back.

Left alone in his car, I'm unable to control the urge to snoop. I lift the center console and am underwhelmed by what I find. The modest wad of cash doesn't surprise me, and neither does the travel-sized bottle of mint mouthwash. I move them aside and find two packs of gum—mint and bubblegum—and steal a piece of bubblegum after opening it. I scoop the case for his aviators and some gas receipts out and am ready to move on to the glove compartment when a plastic card wedged against the inside grabs my attention.

Sliding it out, I dump everything back in the console and look over the blue and red identification card. The Russian words and his photograph are perplexing, but I might think nothing of it if his name wasn't Markus Kuznetsov instead of what I know him as. I consider the fact that he's foreign, and wonder the odds of him having visited Russia while he was young enough to need a fake identity, especially since it's expired and the registration date would have made him underage for drinking—at least by American standards—though that doesn't explain why he'd still have it now, at twenty-seven.

When Denendrius steps out of the restaurant, I fling the identification card back into the console and try to sit casually as he climbs into the passenger seat. The smell of fish fills the small space and makes me salivate.

"Hey," I greet him before snapping my gum like Daina does to seem cute.

"You can take the whole pack of gum if you'd like," he offers with a friendly smile as he climbs in.

My eyes bug, my chewing slowing. Well, there's no hiding that I was snooping now.

"Thanks," I say carefully as I accept the takeaway bag of food he hands me. "What's with the Russian driver's license in your console?"

He shrugs as he turns the car back on. "My best friend is Russian. He had it made for me some years ago. I didn't realize it fell out of my wallet."

"Oh." I guess my thought process does make sense.

"Does the food smell good?" he asks, cranking the car into drive and pulling out.

"It smells amazing." Patting the boxed fish through the bag, I feel so considerate when I say, "I'll wait until we get on the boat so we can eat together."

"Oh, I didn't get anything for myself."

I give him a you-can't-be-fucking-serious look. "Let me guess, another doctor's appointment?"

He taps his finger on the wheel. "I ate already."

I roll my eyes and cross my arms. "Yeah right, Denendrius."

"You don't believe me?"

I snap my gum again. "*Nope.*"

Denendrius's expression is apologetic. "I'm sorry, Marianna. I was feeling ill and had to stop before I picked you up. It's my health. I'm not as fun to be around when I'm feeling off and starving anyway."

Even though that's logical considering he wasn't allowed to eat yesterday because of his doctor's appointment—some sort of test, I presume—I can't help but scowl. "I'm eating now, then."

He grins. "Have at it."

I'm full of salmon and cheese bread when we park at the empty and secluded docks beside a red truck with a green luxury boat on a trailer. As requested by Denendrius, I stay put as he backs the large boat onto the lake and unloads it.

The late March temperature is far too low to even consider taking a dive, and once we're on the boat, being propelled from shore by the four motors, there's no trees to guard us from the cool wind as we cut through it.

Sitting in the center next to Denendrius as he steers the speeding boat over the calm water, I wish I'd had the fore-thought to bring more than my sweater. I curl up against him on the beige bench seat, but the cold leather of his jacket makes me shiver.

After another minute, he slows the boat to a stop in the middle of the empty lake and the noise of the engine halts.

"You're cold," he notices.

I nod and frown when I see that the weather thermometer is at fifty degrees and the needle on the water temperature gauge is significantly lower. "You're not?"

"No. Besides, I'm used to the cold." He touches a button on the dash and stands, moving around the center console of the boat and to the long double lounge seats directly in front of it and facing the open front deck. Lifting one of the seats, he pulls out a red-and-navy-blue knit blanket and holds his hand out toward me.

"Want to wait for the sunset with me?" he asks, his dark eyes bright and hopeful. Reaching into the inside pocket of his jacket, he pulls out a white chocolate candy bar. "I've got goodies for you."

"Fuck yeah, that's my favorite." I climb off the seat and stretch out on one of the lounging seats as Denendrius lies on the connecting one. He hooks his arm around my waist and pulls me tighter to him.

"What a fun coincidence, then." He hands me the chocolate bar and covers us with the blanket while I rip it open.

My heart hammers in my chest, cocoons cracking open and releasing butterflies in my stomach as I lean my head on his shoulder and take a bite of my chocolate bar. It melts on my tongue as I say, "You should tell me something interesting about you. Like a story, or something."

"Hmm." He purses his lips and looks ahead across the gentle ripples of the water. "I used to train mustangs when I lived down south. I've always been very good with horses. Maybe I'll take you riding one day."

Is there anything he can't do? "That's really cool. I don't think I've even seen a horse in person before, so you'll definitely have to take me."

Denendrius gapes at me like I've said something truly abhorrent. "I can't believe that." Clicking his tongue in disapproval, he shakes his head. "I *definitely* have to take you, then."

I take another bite and try to imagine myself on horseback. Somehow, I can't conjure up a mental image that isn't ludicrous. "Okay, sure."

"Your turn," he whispers, the lilt of his words against my ear making me tremble. "Tell me something interesting about you."

"There's nothing interesting about me," I say simply, looking up at him.

"I think everything about you is interesting." The softness of his eyes, the way he looks at me with such fondness, makes my chest ache.

My hand quivers in his as he takes it, and the heat that fills my chest and limbs distracts me from the quickly dropping external temperature. "I'm pretty good at drawing," I share, unable to think of much else positive about myself.

"You are, hm?" His wide smile exposes his perfect teeth. "You'll have to show me."

I swallow and nod before devouring the remainder of the chocolate bar like I missed supper. "We should have brought drinks."

He flips the blanket off his legs and stands. "I planned ahead."

Denendrius disappears inside a little door on the side of the boat's center wall, his sandaled feet heavy as he goes down steps. "Wine or sparkling apple juice?"

"Sparkling apple juice." There's no way in hell I'm getting drunk with him when we're alone and in the middle of a lake.

"You should come down here and check it out." The sound of a bottle cap hitting something carries out onto the deck. "It's like a tiny apartment down here. There's a little kitchenette, TV, and bed."

The mention of a bed makes me glower at the blanket across my legs. "It's okay, I'm too comfortable here to move."

"Are you sure? It's neat down here. You should see."

Dread makes the cold of the evening return to me. "No, thanks."

I hold my breath as I hear him return to the deck. Even though I have no reason to believe he would, I can't shake the thought of him dragging me from my seat and to the bed as he approaches. My dry tongue is in desperate need of the drink he hands to me while stretching back out at my side. I down half of it and set it on the deck before snuggling back up to him.

We talk until the bare blue sky is smeared with streaks of orange and pink, the little sunlight left reflecting off the water. Our conversation thins as the minutes pass, the words harder to get out with our lips so close together, until our breath is tangled, and the only space left on my lips is occupied by his.

I struggle to keep up with his expert motions, too surprised by the feel of his tongue against mine to think of what I should do. He doesn't seem bothered by my abilities, which makes me think I might be a better kisser than I initially suspected. The gentle rocking of the boat amplifies my dizziness and I peek to avoid losing my balance while sitting.

With the fervor of his kisses, I find myself sliding down the seat onto my back. My hands tighten around his neck until it registers in my mind that he's moving me.

An electric shiver rips through me, my breath shuddering as he lies against my side and drapes his leg over mine. He adjusts the blanket over us before his hand moves to my face.

I'm unable to think of anything other than how we're lying down beneath a blanket, never mind how close his crotch is to mine. My lips falter and my heart hammers, cold sweat wetting the nape of my neck. A wave of nausea smacks into me.

I slide out from under him and stumble to the tall side of the boat. I'm not sure if I'll puke, but I climb up on a raised part of the deck and clutch the silver handrail on the top of the ledge and shiver like I might.

"Sorry, I thought I was going to be seasick for a second," I lie, sheepish as he joins me.

He turns me so my back is pressed against the side, hooking his arms around my waist. "Standing up helps?"

I swallow and nod, his lips back on mine as I lift my head up.

With my arms circling back around his neck, I twist my fingers in the brown waves and curls of his tied-back hair and think of pulling the band out so I can play with it better.

Instead, my hands move to his firm chest and stomach, his breath heavy under my palms.

I can tell he's getting excited by the way he pulls my hips tightly against his and squeezes my waist. The way his eyes dart to the lounging seats when he breaks away to turn his face makes me worry he didn't take me seriously when I said I wouldn't have sex with him even on the second date.

Silver stars litter my sight and prick my skin. "*Stop,*" I mouth soundlessly when Denendrius's lips trail over my chin and down my throat.

When his lips move back to mine, his hand sliding down my back before he squeezes my ass, I don't realize what I've done until my knuckles have already connected with the side of his jaw and he's jerking away from me.

There's no hurt in his eyes like I expect, just instantaneous, all-consuming anger.

My hands cover my wide mouth. "Oh fuck. Holy shit, Denendrius, I'm sorry. I just reacted."

His rapid breath is cold against my face. When his hand comes up, I gasp and lean away from him until he gently places his hand on my cheek instead of hitting me like I anticipated.

I stare at him, waiting for him to settle down, but after a few painful seconds of his wide-eyed and murderous stare, I try to slip away from him. He says something I miss while his other hand moves to my waist, though his reaction to my strike is slow to dwindle.

"Denendrius . . ." I brush my hand down his rigid arm. "Are you okay? Did I hurt you?"

I inhale sharply when he mashes his lips against mine, his shuddery breath filling my mouth as his muscles loosen.

Thankful I haven't ruined everything, I return his kisses and try to focus on the boat rocking and the feel of his tongue searching for mine instead of the demons trying to drag me back into the depths of my mind.

"It's okay," he murmurs against my lips. He kisses the corner of my mouth.

"My only experience with this kind of stuff is . . . bad," I try to explain.

He draws away from me, his hands scooping up mine. He brings one to his lips for a kiss. "It's okay," he repeats. "I understand."

A lump forms in my throat and all I can do is nod.

I squeeze his hands, flinching as I say, "I should go home." I ache for a cigarette—that I know I'll have to snag from Pam—and to be in my own bed, where it's more difficult for me to screw things up with him.

Denendrius sighs and gives my hand another peck. "Have I upset you so much?"

"No, it's just starting to get really cold and I'm tired."

Glancing back toward the center console of the boat, he says, "Why don't we spend the night on the water? We don't have to do anything, I promise, but it's warm down there and I have snacks. I'll drive you to school in the morning."

"I should go home. I really want a cigarette," I admit with a strangled chuckle.

His lips form a tight line, his brows drawn together in clear disapproval. "Hm. Well, there's no better time to quit than now. Besides, I bet you'll get great sleep rocking on the water." A small smile appears on his lips and he holds my hands tight against his chest. "Besides, I love spending time with you."

I sigh, wishing I could let go of my fears and curl up next to him for the rest of the night. But I can't, not yet at least. "Denendrius . . ."

"We should stay," he insists. "Then you can get used to being on a boat. I'm thinking of buying a yacht and taking you out on the ocean this summer."

My brows lift, and I can't help the rush of excitement that

idea gives me. "Then I have all summer to get used to it. Take me home, okay?"

"Okay," he agrees before leaning in for a kiss.

I curl back up next to him as he drives the boat back to shore, no sign of the sun left by the time we climb back in the car and head into Lorimer. The mood picks up again on our car ride, our hands clutched together while we brainstorm ideas for our third date while we listen to classic rock.

"Let me drop you off at home for once," Denendrius says with a wink as we enter the city limits.

I frown and prop my elbow on the console. I suppose going on a boat alone with him in the middle of the lake was dangerous enough that I should be fine to let him drop me off. "Okay, sure. I'll give you directions when we get closer."

Though, the deeper we get into the city, the familiar buildings flashing by, the more I wish I'd accepted his offer of staying on the boat for the night. At least being on the lake was a nice escape from the reality of my life. I can't stop the bounce in my leg or how I bite the inside of my cheek, my hands fidgeting with the hem of my sweater as the car rolls through neighborhoods and past beaten houses I wish I could go without ever seeing again.

When we pull up in front of my foster home, no sign of life beyond the dark windows, I can't help my deep sigh.

He must pick up on how I'm feeling and why, as he turns to me and says, "I want you to know that you can always come to my place if you need to. If your foster mom locks you out or kicks you to the curb, if the government moves you somewhere worse. Even if you just get sick of being there. Okay?" He reaches across the console and holds my hand. "I'll give you my address, just in case."

My hand tenses up in his. "I can take care of myself," I tell him, wanting to make sure that he knows that I like him but don't *need* him.

His nod is quick. "Oh, I know you can. But you don't have to."

"You're sweet. But you don't have to offer that when we've only been on two dates."

"I *really* like you, Marianna, and it feels like I've already known you for so long."

"Okay," I whisper, not wanting to say anything more so I don't insult him. "Thank you."

His hands move to the sides of my face as he kisses me, the passion making me consider his words again. I think that maybe—if we're still together when I age out—his offer isn't such a bad idea at all.

Denendrius quickly writes his address down on the back of a receipt before handing it to me. He tucks my hair behind my ear, his hand resting on my face. "I'll see you later, sweetheart."

I jam the receipt in my pocket and lean closer to him as he rubs his thumb over my cheek and pulls me in for one last kiss.

I'm so warm from his affection that I hardly feel the chill of the night follow me up the sidewalk and to the front door. I'm thankful when the door opens—happy I don't have to resort to going home with him—and turn back to wave goodbye.

It's not until I'm shutting the door behind me that I realize we were so caught up in conversation that I didn't give him directions to my house.

VI

The silence of my dark bedroom weighs on me, my thoughts clanging around my exhausted head. I wrack my brain and try to figure out if I ever told Denendrius my address, but I have no memory of doing so and can't fathom any other reasonable way he would know it.

I cover my face with my hands and groan when I think back to the black Mustang that followed me home before I overdosed, how the sweet voice that was there with me sounds so much like Denendrius's despite Charlie saying there was nobody with me when I came in.

Don't be paranoid. You were in a panic when you saw that Mustang, and half-unconscious when you thought there was a man with you.

I give my head a shake and take a deep breath, but the paranoia only clings to me tighter.

How could I not be paranoid? My paranoid ideas are the only ones that offer my situation any clarity.

But the idea of Denendrius—sweet and gentle Denendrius

—stalking me before I even *met him* seems so absurd. Who would even do something like that? *Why?* He doesn't even seem like that sort of guy—

His reaction to me striking him pops back into my mind, the way he shook with fury and how I was convinced he would hurt me. Sure, I hit him, but he reacted like he was going to snap. Merely thinking about it makes the hair on the back of my neck stand up. Though, with that and the way he treated the server on our first date, I can't help but wonder if there's a short fuse ready to catch fire.

But then I think of the way he kissed me and how much of a gentleman he's been, how much thought he's put into our dates . . .

Maybe I really am paranoid. Am I trying to sabotage things between Denendrius and me?

My thoughts continue, and all the little things come to mind and demand my attention. I think of how he asked me to come home with him the first date but wouldn't tell me what he meant, how he's sort of famous in another country and won't tell me how he makes his money, how he seems to have done far more than what's reasonable for someone his age. The Russian identification makes my stomach tighten, and his insistence about wanting me to stay overnight with him—regardless of if he says sex will happen or not—makes me feel like I have the flu.

The idea of sex alone, that he will likely want it sooner rather than later, almost makes me want to never see him on that basis alone. Sure, he shouldn't expect me to give it up too early, but I know I can't expect him to go without it forever either if we go steady.

The only solution that comes to mind: *break up with him.*

Really, we're hardly even dating, right? Even if he's calling himself my boyfriend, he probably knows we're nothing serious yet . . . *right?*

I groan again and cover my face with the blanket. Despite all the strangeness, I want to see him again. I want to taste the mint on his breath and experience the lust of his desperate lips again.

Maybe I should go on a few more dates and see if things clear themselves up, or at least wait until the morning, when I'm not lying in the dark alone, to consider everything again before ruining a relationship that could be perfectly normal.

Yeah, I'll wait. It'll be a good chance to prove to myself that not everything is horrible, that I don't have to overthink things to death.

Still, as I close my eyes and wait for sleep, I can't shake the unnerving feeling of dread that has settled into me since I came home.

I wake from a dreamless night and drag myself out of bed, across the hallway, and into the bathroom, where I throw myself into the shower. When I come out, there's a hot cup of green tea from Charlie waiting on the windowsill.

When I'm dressed and wide awake thanks to the tea, I join Samantha and Charlie downstairs since they've decided to come home for lunch. Pam is at work, so we're free to enjoy ourselves without consequence. Charlie and Samantha watch cartoons, the sound of the TV muffled by the kitchen's swinging door.

I navigate dirty dishes while I cook boxed macaroni and cheese. There's only enough for the two of them, but I don't have much of an appetite anyway. I pick at my cake as I lean against the yellowed oven, stirring the boiling noodles on occasion.

Charlie comes in as I'm about to throw the empty cake package in the garbage. "Oh, I forgot to thank you for the cake."

"What cake?" He doesn't look at me, just searches through the dirty dishes for two plates to wash.

My hand hovers above the garbage, my eyes locked on him. "What do you mean, 'what cake'?"

He turns around, brow furrowed. "I didn't get you a cake."

I hold the package out for reference in an iron grip. "*You didn't buy this for me?*"

His chin scrunches and he shakes his head, moving the plates to the table.

Fury bubbles up inside me and I slam the plastic container in the garbage before spinning to face Charlie. "You didn't buy me the cake like there was nobody in the house with me, right? Did the cake just materialize in my room like I did through the locked fucking door? Is that what you're telling me?" I screech.

Charlie stares at me with wide eyes, his grip on the plates shaky. "I'm not lying to you, Marianna."

I clench my hands into fists so tight that my muscles ache. "Then tell me how I carried myself inside when I was overdosing, and how I only woke up with a little headache and upset stomach after that? How I *didn't die*. Explain to me where the cake came from too."

Charlie stares at me in bewilderment. "I don't know what to tell you, Mari."

If something's too good to be true, it usually is.

I wipe my eyes, my furious snarl twisting into a deep frown. "You were sleepwalking again, weren't you?" I realize. "When you asked him who he was. That's why you don't remember coming out of your room. You heard me, fell back asleep, then ended up sleepwalking."

"I haven't slept walked in two years," he says. "Not since we lived together at the Andersons."

"I'm not crazy," I say. "You may not be lying, but that doesn't change what *I know*."

Thinking of the little card from the cake upstairs and the

receipt with Denendrius's address in my pants on the floor, I dart upstairs and compare them. Everything from the black ink to the way the impeccable handwriting leans right, to the long *m*'s and curled *s*'s is *exactly the same*.

"I'm not crazy," I whisper to myself, the sorrow of my sudden enlightenment making my eyes sting and my heart ache.

When the phone rings, I scramble downstairs and yank it off the hook. When I hear Denendrius's voice, my body trembles with anger.

"Marianna? I tried calling but I wasn't sure if you were at school. Are you busy? I was wondering if I could take you to a movie tonight," Denendrius says.

My mind spins. "It was you," I accuse. "That was your Mustang following me. That was you there when I was overdosing . . ." I run my hand over my forehead. "Denendrius . . . *what the fuck?*"

"Marianna—"

"Explain!" I holler, wanting him to tell me something rational.

"You were *dying*, Marianna. You were clean for a year and had heroin on you. What was I supposed to do? Let you die? You were so out of it I didn't think you'd remember anything."

I gape and my balance shifts before I plant my hand on the arm of the couch to steady myself. "Den—you—" I'm not even sure where to start.

His voice is gentle as it comes through the phone and makes the ache in my heart worse. "Deep breaths, Marianna. Everything is going to be okay. I know things are messier than they're supposed to be. I didn't want us to meet that way, but you would have died had I not followed you home. I thought it would be better if we met on neutral ground rather than when you were in that state of mind."

I grit my teeth, my shaking hand in a death grip on the

phone. "How things were supposed to be? You've been *stalking* me? How long?"

His groan is tired. "Sweetheart, I wasn't stalking you. I care about you more than you could know." He sighs. "Why don't you go relax and gather yourself. I'll come pick you up and we'll talk about it. I'll explain everything. You'll understand."

"*I'll understand?*" I shriek. "How can I understand that you followed me home, *unlocked my house and disarmed the alarm*, and that you pretended to run into me for the first time the next day to ask me out? Sometime between me leaving for our date and going back home, you broke in and left a fucking cake in my room and made my bed. How can you possibly explain that in a way that makes any goddamn sense!"

"Did you like the cake? I saw it and thought it would be the kind of thing you love—"

My mouth widens in horror, my voice coming out shrill. My heart hammers so hard I see stars. "Holy shit—are you serious? *How the fuck would you even know that's the one I wanted?*"

"You're getting hysterical." The edge in his voice pushes me into a deeper panic. "I will explain, Marianna, I promise . . . just not over the phone. I'm coming to get you. Everything will be okay."

Straightening, I square my shoulders and think of my gun upstairs. "*Do not* come here, Denendrius. Do not! Do you hear me? I don't want to see you again."

"You don't mean that," he murmurs.

"I do. I liked you, Denendrius, I really fucking liked you, but this is *too much*. I'm done."

Stern, he says, "You don't mean that. I know you don't. I'm going to hang up and—"

I talk over him. "Stay away! You're not mysterious, you're just fucking crazy! I—"

Denendrius's voice booms through the phone, my breath

catching at his sudden change in tone. "Shut up! Marianna Shay Cortez, you *shut your mouth* right now and let me speak!"

My stomach drops to my heels.

"*Listen to me*. You need to calm down. I'm going to hang up and come get you in a few hours. Stay put. I don't want to have to come looking for you. We're going to talk it out. You *are not* ending this between us."

I inhale deeply and stand my ground. "You'll regret it if you don't stay away. I've killed people before."

"*Oh, enough*," he snarls. "We're going to be fine. I'm not letting you write me off before I can explain. So *please* go relax and wait for me to come get you."

My lip curls. "I'd rather fucking die."

Darkness looms over his voice. "*Well, then*, Marianna, if that's how you really feel. Just don't say I didn't ask nicely."

The line dies.

VII

Gun in my lap, I sit against the wall at the end of my futon, window to my left and doorway to my right in case Denendrius doesn't heed my warning.

I try to sort through the nonsense in my head, a stale cigarette I found under my bed burning between my fingers. It's barely even worth smoking, but at least it helps keep the tears at bay.

A collection of quiet knocks on my bedroom door brings my finger to hover over my gun's trigger. When the door opens to reveal my friends, I switch the safety on and put the gun away.

"Hello, I guess," I grouse, mentally cursing Pam for forgetting to lock the front door and turn on the security system after coming home from work. Though I suppose it's useless since he's gotten in at least twice now.

Daina hustles Jenna and Camille into my room, kicking random items like books, clothes, and papers aside. She tosses a tacky yellow backpack on the floor.

"Hello to you too," Daina chirps.

"What's up?" I motion to their presence.

"The dance," Jenna reminds me from beside my doorway. Her fingers twist the long ends of her dirty-blond hair.

That's tonight? "I'm not going. I've got enough shit to deal with right now."

"Told you she wouldn't want to come," Camille says as she sorts through a box. She pulls the garbage can from behind my door and drops broken objects and candy wrappers into it after she's removed them.

"Come on, strip. You're coming to the dance, and you're not wearing whatever the hell you are right now." Daina runs her fingers through her hair.

"What I'm wearing is the least of my worries," I grumble, glancing out my window again.

"Why?" Camille asks, wiping something sticky off my floor with one of her makeup wipes.

I shift on my futon. "I've got a stalker."

Camille discards the wipe and quickly straightens. "What? That's why you have your gun out again?"

"Yeah. Apparently, Den isn't as nice as I thought."

Daina gapes at me. "Shit. What did he do?"

"You know that cake I wanted? Yeah, it was sitting on my bed when I came home from our date," I add. "He figured out where I live, somehow."

"You should definitely come to the dance, then," Jenna interjects. "What if he comes looking for you here?"

His words ring loudly in my ears, and as much as I want to pass it off as a bluff, I can't help but wholeheartedly believe that he will show up.

I nod and squish out my cigarette on my windowsill, strategically placing the butt against the window so I'll be able to tell if it has been opened. "That's probably a good idea."

I stand and strip, the other girls following my lead by taking their outfits from the bag and putting them on. I cringe at a pair of short-shorts and tiny-strapped top and fumble while getting into them.

Daina catches my expression and says, "Put them on. Forget about the bullshit for a bit."

I groan. The shorts reveal so much of my butt that anything but the thong I'm wearing wouldn't be an option. The top is low enough that almost half my black bra is visible.

Camille says, "Mom is outside waiting for us still. We should hurry down or else we'll have to take the bus."

I throw on a pair of stolen yellow stilettos and then follow the girls to my door. It wouldn't hurt to get out of the house tonight if Denendrius plans on coming to find me. It's not as if I'll be doing anything other than sitting awake with my gun anyway. I leave it behind, knowing security will be thoroughly checking everyone. At least he can't do anything if I have other students to act as a human shield.

We creep down the tight staircase and slip through the dark living room, shushing each other simultaneously, making more noise doing so than if we were serious about being quiet.

Her mother greets the four of us with smiles while we bicker nonsensically over seating.

Thankfully, the night smears by the moment I walk through the school doors. After trial and error, I finally lose my only friends in the pulsating crowd so I can be alone with my thoughts.

"Hello, Lorimer!" the man on stage shouts into the microphone. Ear-shattering static stings his lips like a bee, and he jerks back before continuing. "How is my favorite city tonight? Y'all ready to listen to some beats?"

I roll my eyes as the suburban thug wannabe paces on stage, belting out cheesy rap lyrics about finding true love.

As the second most violent city in the state of New York, one would think they'd have given up sheltering us from violence by now. Out of the near-million people in this godfor-saken city, all the kids in this shitty school wouldn't be fazed by some mildly offensive lyrics.

I press myself against the cement wall of the high school's gym, avoiding contact with the teens forming grind lines on the scratched wooden floor. Lights spin and twirl hypnotically as if they're having an unsynchronized party of their own.

The school gym is teeming, half my classmates pumping their fists for the sad excuse of a rapper. Most of those kids are clean, no serious records, no hard drugs, no gang affiliation aside from brothers or sisters who run on the streets. Maybe they cheat on tests, fist-fight each other, or party and have drunk sex. Mostly they just happen to be poor enough to live on the west side with their dirty criminal opposites. My three friends are clean kids; there are too many drama-related stab-bings with the dirty ones.

Many of the dirty kids are ignoring the music, the dance just another business opportunity for them. Drugs pass between hands and find their way to clean kids—probably just molly or marijuana—and a lot of dirties. A fight breaks out between two kids in the back corner, almost immediately broken up by security.

Whose idea was this fucking dance? Didn't they think it could turn into a war zone any minute?

It's not long before watching students dance turns into watching Jenna, Daina, and Camille hustling toward me with expressions of oh-thank-gosh-I-found-you on their faces.

"We've been looking everywhere for you!" Camille squeals.

Daina struggles with pulling up the baby-blue dress trying to slide past her breasts. "Yeah, Sarah is looking for you. The details don't sound so pretty."

Sarah. I could never figure out when the drama started with her, but she's hated me since middle school. It doesn't help that I was in a gang and her dad's a cop who was assigned to our area. It doesn't help either that he arrested me once for grand theft auto. Perhaps a few snide comments are responsible too, or maybe it was because the boy she happened to crush on was crushing on me instead. As if that's something I could control or even care about.

I cross my arms. "I'm sick of this stupid shit."

I don't want drama, especially not petty, cliché stuff about boys. I have Denendrius to deal with as it is.

Camille sighs and says to Daina, "See? I told you we shouldn't have bothered her about tonight."

"Incoming." My eyes roll.

CJ weaves through the crowd, biting the crooked hoop in his lip while brushing the long shaggy blond hair from his eyes as he stares at his holey sneakers. Stunned at the timing, they turn and we watch Sarah appear behind him, pulling his arm to turn him. He says something, stumbles in another direction, and rushes away.

Sarah's pale, freckled face that should belong to a twelve-year-old is bright red as she advances with bull-like motions, fists balled at her side. Jenna shrinks behind Camille, grabbing her wrist. Daina recedes into the pulsating crowd, mumbling something about how fights aren't for her. Propped against the wall, I'm expecting her to make a move.

"Hey, what's up?" I block a slap with my arm as if she's nothing more than an annoying fly.

"CJ is mine!" she snarls.

I push myself away from the wall with my heel, invading her space. She flinches against my hot breath. I'm sick of telling her I want nothing to do with him, so all I say is, "*I don't care. Go away.*"

She throws a punch, but I grab her wrist and twist it, forcing a whimper from her. Shuddering at the fringes of my vision, Jenna tries to pull Camille away, telling her how she wants to go home. Camille's mouth is ajar, clearly unsure if she should stay or not. Her shoulders slump, the corners of her lips deepening in wrinkles.

"I'm fine." I laugh and fling Sarah's thrashing body to the ground, capturing her wrists in my fists. I sit on her stomach, ignoring her as she feebly knees me in the back.

"I don't want anyone to get hurt," Camille whines as she allows Jenna to pull her back into the crowd.

"Stop your wailing, bitch," I snap at Sarah.

She screeches, nostrils flaring, face filling brightly with blood. I spit in it and she tries to pull her arms from my grasp.

"I'm going to kill you!" she hisses. "You stupid fucking junkie!"

I spit on her again. "Oh, shut up."

I put both her wrists in my left hand, using my right to knock her head into the gym floor while imagining cracking her skull in two.

Hands grab my limbs and hair, forcing me with severe brutality from where Sarah leaps up and waves the girls on and out the emergency exit door.

I growl profanities like a demon, kicking and clawing, blocking and returning punches as they drag me across a short patch of asphalt and onto the city sidewalk. I strike a girl in the throat with my fist and she topples over to reclaim air.

Managing to twist free, I scramble to my bare feet—my stilettos lost in the scuffle—and take off running. I fly down the street, knowing I've left the girls far behind without even needing to look over my shoulder. All the days of running on the treadmill in the school gym until I puke pay off once again.

Six blocks later, I barrel up the sagging patio steps of an old house, fist pounding on the door until it opens. A vaguely familiar man with a handgun at his waist answers the door with a scowl.

"*Hola*," I quickly greet as I shoulder-shove past him. "Move, please."

My presence ruffles the room of men until my dealer, Manny, waves them back to their video game from where he sits on the couch.

"What's good?" Manny asks from the brown leather couch, his Puerto Rican accent hanging off his words.

Leaping over the back of it, I plunk down beside him. "Just got the shit kicked out of me," I tell him through an exasperated breath. "Having a subpar week."

He looks me over and opens the mini fridge beside him, pulling out a bottle of beer. He pops the cap off and passes it to me. "Well, happy belated birthday."

I groan and sink into the couch, grabbing the beer and taking a quick sip. "I don't even want to think about that anymore."

He rests his elbows on his knees, his own beer bottle hanging in his hand as he laughs. "Why not? You're gon' be all grown up. Freedom! No more shitty foster homes."

Leaning my head against the back of the couch, I groan louder. "Oh yeah, the road after aging out is paved with gold."

He grins and takes a sip of beer before turning to me. "Look at me." He knocks one hand against his chest before lifting them both to reference the room. "I'm doing just fine since aging out."

I lift a brow. "Really, Manny? You've been dealing drugs—in and out of prison—for eight years."

He cackles and rocks back against the couch. "Damn right. Loving every minute of it too."

I blow air between my lips and shake my head. "I don't want that. I don't know what I want, but the street already took my childhood. I don't want it to take my future if I get one. I want out."

Seriousness falls across his face. He plucks a half-smoked cigarette from a dirty ashtray. Cigarette held between his lips as he tries to light it, he mumbles, "Yeah, well, sometimes you don't get a choice, Marianna. This ain't a carnival. You don't just get to leave when the fun stops."

I rub my hand against the old gang tattoo on my neck— now a target—and say, "Yeah, you don't have to tell me."

Unfortunately, Manny is right. Even if I wasn't a year behind in school, I've got a gang tattoo, and a rap sheet to go with it that may as well be a brick wall between me and any job. It wasn't my choice, not at first, but now it'll decide my life in a year. The government will help for a while, but what happens to me when they don't?

I don't even have a family. At least I have a pseudo-mom right now, no matter how shitty she is. I'm not ready to be an adult. Hell, I'm not even ready to be *seventeen*.

"*Oye*," one of Manny's friends says from the front window to my left, the black curtain drawn back a bit for him to peek outside. "This car has drove by at least four times now."

"What kind of car?" Manny asks.

"A black 2006 Mustang. I'd say Yoki's if it wasn't in such good shape."

A chill runs its cold finger down my back, and I stiffen.

Manny's tight eyes meet mine. "Fuck's going on?" he demands.

Sighing, I wave away his worries. "Nothing. Just some dude I was seeing."

His stare only intensifies. "How's he know you're here?"

I chew the inside of my cheek, thumb rubbing the label off my beer. "I don't know," I admit.

Except, I sort of do know how. He probably knows I'm here the same way he figured out where I live, where I sleep, and what kind of cake I'd pick. It's probably the same way we met at the mall.

Manny purses his lips. "What kind of guy are we dealing with?"

I shrug. "I don't know. He's a criminal, but . . ." My lips twist.

"I don't know what he's into. All I got was vague casino-thievery talk. He talks like he's part of some international thing, though, especially with how many countries he's visited. He has a fake Russian driver's license. He speaks a lot of different languages too."

"Why'd you stop seeing him?" he asks.

I swallow. "Aside from the stalking? He was too much too quickly. He called himself my boyfriend after the first date and basically said I could stay with him if I didn't like my foster home on the second."

Manny flicks ash off his cigarette. "I'll admit, that doesn't sound too good. Human trafficking, probably. Targeting you because your life is a mess, trying to get you to rely on him and trust him. I've seen that before."

I shiver and lift the beer bottle to my lips for a long drink.

He inhales sharply and nods a command I don't understand to a man in the recliner. Standing, he sets his video game controller down on the entertainment stand before reaching behind it and pulling out an AR-15.

"He parked," the man says from the window.

"We'll see," Manny's gunman says. He rushes through the living room, swinging the door open. In loud and high-pitched Spanish, he hollers nonsense while running barefoot down the sidewalk.

Manny holds his breath, clearly aware that there's only two ways this could go.

The sound of the Mustang peeling away fills the street and spills in through the open door.

Slinging the gun over his shoulder, he comes in with a toothy grin and hoots.

The room bursts into laughter, and though I join in, I can't shake the feeling that we have nothing to be laughing about.

Manny squeezes my shoulder. "So, a wannabe, huh?"

Laughter fails me, though theirs continues. I hope it's as

simple as they believe, that all he needed was another man to threaten him.

Squeezing my shoulder, Manny says, "Stay a few hours, just in case."

I nod and take a long swig of beer, my stomach bubbling. "Yeah, it's whatever. I've dealt with worse."

He can't be worse than any of the gang members still hoping to wash the streets with my blood.

He passes me a controller, and we take turns racing one another for the next two hours, devouring a delivered pizza halfway through. Despite the fun atmosphere that seems to welcome everyone but me, I can't settle in my skin or shake my disappointment. *I really liked Denendrius.*

I sit and I wait until it feels like a good time to leave. But even when I don't have plans, it feels like I'm always waiting.

Maybe for nothing.

Maybe for anything.

When Manny nudges me in the shoulder, I blink for the first time in who knows how long. My dry eyes burn, my half-smoked cigarette a line of ash.

"You okay?" Manny asks.

"I feel like shit," I grumble, carefully running my fingers over my tender nose.

"Another beer?" He leans toward the fridge, but I shake my head.

"Fuck that. I need something stronger," I say. "Chiva."

He stares at me. "I thought you've been clean for a year. Why would you want to go and ruin a thing like that?"

Manny doesn't need to know that I already ruined my year-long streak. "There's nothing I need to be clean for."

I know I promised myself that last time was the end of my drug use, but will there ever truly be a last time that doesn't end in overdose? After all, opiates have been a part of my life since early childhood. My mother constantly doled out pills, and when she introduced needles, I understood it was her who was sick and not me.

When social services removed me from the home at nine, I got clean with the help of my social worker and programs. But over the years as I understood drugs and where to find them, relapses ended up being inevitable. My gang family did their best to shield needles from finding my arms, and it worked for a while. But nothing, not even life itself, has ever compared to heroin.

His eyes tighten and he mulls me over.

I slap a couple bills on the coffee table. "Manny, give me some fucking black tar heroin," I spell out for him. "And I don't want a lecture from my drug dealer about being clean."

"Marianna—"

I stand. "Fine, I'll go buy it from someone else."

He grabs my wrist and yanks me back onto the couch beside him. "Like hell you will." Standing, he adds, "Why? So, someone else can give you garbage and fucking kill you?"

I smile to myself as he disappears down a hall and into a dark bedroom, returning with my next high. I'm shivering as he sits beside me, my mouth dry as he slaps down a new syringe and a tied-off baggie of black tar heroin on the table.

"Thanks—"

"*Cállate*," he snaps, swooping his video game controller back up. "You're fucking tragic."

As ordered, I shut up. I search the table for the supplies I need, then tear the baggie open.

A string of Spanish curses tumbles off his lips before he inhales sharply and glowers down at me. "You gon' make me watch you dose yourself too?"

"You didn't have a problem selling me drugs a year ago," I tell him before tightening the shoelace around my bicep with my teeth.

"You weren't a year sober a year ago."

"Whatever," I mumble.

He scowls at the television the entire time I prepare my drugs, the lines in his forehead deepening when I search my arm for a vein. I hold my breath as it pierces my vein, and I slam the plunger down.

Quickly, I pull the shoelace off my arm and toss it aside. I lean my head back against the couch. Sunlight rushes through my veins, my worries and aches melting away. Disappointment unblocks itself from my heart and it starts pumping properly again. My breaths are even, and I stop thinking about Denendrius and if he is a human trafficker, if he could do worse to me than my mom did.

After a handful of minutes of warm numbness, I sit upright and sigh. "Okay," I whisper. "Think I'll take the bus home now."

His head sways side to side as he mashes the controller buttons in frustration. "Call me if you need me."

I drift off the couch and out the front door, the crisp air chilling my throat and lungs, my limbs full of warm honey.

When the bus I need to get home zooms by on the road beside me, I pick up my pace and duck down an alley in hopes of making it to the bus stop on the other side of the block before it does.

The air turns thicker, harder to maneuver through, and my eyes droop from the effort. My chin falls toward my chest and my head becomes too heavy to lift back up. The alley stretches, the soles of my feet sticking to the pavement as my steps fumble. The yellow streetlights dim, my vision blurring.

Halfway down the alley, my steps stop, and I waver. The end of the alley is deep with darkness until two enormous yellow eyes open to stare at me.

When the beast attached to them growls, my vision darkens like a bulb breaking.

I don't feel the old asphalt and gravel as I crumple against it. It almost feels like falling asleep.

VIII

I'm twisting in blind disorientation until a touch on my shoulder and warmth beneath me causes my eyes to unstick. Amid the blur, he sits behind the wheel of a car. I try to stop my eyes from wandering so I can look at the man continuing to appear as two.

Fractured memories flit through my mind: the yellow head-lights of a car, collapsing in the alley, skin against my lips while I felt like I was choking on blood. *A man's voice*, and mine—protesting.

Hands shaded with dirt, they're tight on the wheel. As his head turns toward me, his messy medium-brown ponytail slides across the nape of his neck, over his leather jacket. His lips unfold from their tight line to shape words I can't hear.

"*Denendrius?*" I think I say.

A tide rushes in, cleansing away the heavy layer surrounding everything there is to feel. The force quickens my pulse, my chest heaving with thick breaths as I try to catch my balance. His lips move again, and the sound mixes in my ears. I grab around, trying to hang on to something.

"You're disoriented." His voice is another tide. "You hit your head."

I remember his call then, how he told me he was coming to get me and to stay home.

I reach for the wheel to pull us to the side of the road, but he deflects my attempt just as my fingers fold around it. The commotion throws us to the curb. The car stills, headlights rushing past. He stares at the street ahead, jaw tensing and relaxing, paying no attention to me.

I try to speak; try to ask him what he's doing, how he found me.

An edge of danger poisons the air, disturbs my heart and remoistens the blood on my hands with sweat. Cold air sneaks through the crack in the door as I open it to escape, knowing nothing good will come of this.

"Don't you dare!" He pulls me back by my arm and reaches across me to slam the door.

"I'm going to hurt you," I mumble. "Let me go."

My eyes tighten as he says, "You're not in any condition to be making threats. You overdosed *again*. My goodness, it's like you're trying to kill yourself! You don't have a tolerance anymore, Marianna!"

"When I am in the condition—" I grunt and hold my hand against my throbbing head. "You'll be picking your guts up off the floor."

"I don't think you will be anytime soon. You should be in an emergency room."

"Take me there. I think I need—doctor." I press my hand against my forehead as a stab of pain slices inside my head. I say something else, but my words are garbled.

"No hospitals," he says.

Through a mess of thoughts, I manage to slur, "I think I . . . I've got a concussion."

He doesn't respond.

I gag again, my vision smearing from pangs of agony. A wave of nausea clouts me and I gag, my sight reduces to a sliver and the sound coming from his mouth dissolves like mist before reaching me.

I don't realize he's driving again until he slams on the brakes. The door opens and he holds me over the asphalt as I vomit blood. I spit the taste from my mouth, and he pulls me back in.

He shouts at me in a language I don't understand, and I want to yell back, make him shut up with my fists. The gnarled expression drops from his face and he looks back at the still road ahead.

"What happened?" I manage to say.

The leather of the wheel protests under his grip. "You didn't wait so I could explain things to you."

That's not what I meant. What did he do to me when he found me? How did he get me to wake up?

I swallow blood and squint at him, feeling as though I'm swaying, but not being able to tell if I actually am. "I told you to stay away."

His hands tighten on the wheel as he scans the road like he's deciding if he should start driving again. "You can't push me away, Marianna."

I choose my words carefully, saying, "You came on strong and I panicked."

He laughs, clearly not buying it. "You shouldn't have tried to push me away." His words don't sound like a threat, though, more like he's baffled.

My mouth hangs open, not a single word that bumps around in my head finding its way out.

I can't even bring myself to jump in surprise as he leans across the seat in a flash, hand around my throat.

With Denendrius's face only an inch from mine, he snatches my eyes in his hardened gaze. "Tell me you're happy to see me," he articulates.

His hand isn't tight. So why can't I speak? My vision blurs, the blackness of his eyes almost consuming me.

His brow furrows, eyes intensifying. "Tell me you're happy to see me."

"Why would I be happy to see you?" I manage to mumble. My voice doesn't carry the aggressive tone I'd anticipated.

He drops his hand, slitted eyes slowly studying me. He sits straight in his seat, head still turned toward me. I jump when he punches the horn.

"What's wrong with you?" he snarls.

I try to ask him what he means when a sick chill washes through me, my stomach plummeting. My head thumps against the window as I pass out.

The sensation of swaying on ice startles me awake. I open my eyes, coming face-to-face with an upside-down world. The moon peeks through a few clouds, a bystander as I lay limply in his arms.

I stare up at a towering brown building with little balconies. As we approach the apartment, I squeeze my eyes shut, not wanting the light spilling from behind the glass doors to blind me. My foot knocks something metal as I feel us ascend stairs. He turns four times and I hear the jingle of keys as a door creaks open.

"We're home."

My back hits something soft as he sets me down.

I squint at him through the dark, the moonlight making his

skin look paler than the slightly tanned tone it held under the car lights. "Why am I here?"

He pulls a chair away from a metal table, eyes never drifting from me, and sits, expression turning severe. "Because I want you to be my girlfriend."

I blink, face blank. "No, thanks," I mutter.

His fingers curl into a fist. "You've annoyed me, so now I'm deciding for you. Apparently, you thought you were too good for a gentleman. How can you not see we're meant to be together?"

I guess he's moved to the top of the list of people I have to shoot. "So, am I like, a hostage?"

He smiles. "No, I won't keep my girlfriend in a cage."

Blood running down my nose, I try to wipe it away. "All right, well, I'll be going home now, then." I go to move, but nothing happens.

He frowns. "That won't be happening anytime soon. I've barely gotten to spend any time with you."

I try not to think of what that could entail. Instead, I roll my eyes away to study how the moon reaches through the glass windows of the sliding patio door, making the metal shine. I sneak a look at him, wondering if his expression has changed. It hasn't. I can feel him studying me from under his aviators, making my skin crawl.

Hoping to return the feeling, I stare back. He looks cruel in the moonlight, the way the white light plays on the angles of his face, especially his jaw and nose.

"You're asking for trouble bringing me here," I say, throat hoarse. "I know people that could ruin your life."

A line appears on his forehead, fists tightening at his sides, and then shifting to his lap. "That is quite the talk from someone who should be dead. You're welcome for saving you twice now, by the way."

"Sucks," I mumble. "Not really your problem."

"You were a year clean," he lectures, standing. I hear him move to the old fridge in the brown eighties-style kitchen beside the front door. "How could you do this to yourself? You're lucky I was waiting for you or you'd still be lying in that alley, only dead."

"Like I said, it's not your fucking problem."

He slams the old fridge door, a small jug of strawberry milk hooked in his fingers as he returns to the couch. "Here. Strawberry, your favorite."

"Fuck's wrong with you?" I ask as he stops at my side and holds it out.

"Take it."

"I'm not thirsty," I say, my words catching in my dry throat.

He twists the cap, but I don't hear it crack. "You're a liar. Take it."

When I refuse, he caps it and drops it in my lap before walking back toward the front door.

I gaze around the room while I wait for his return, begrudgingly fighting to open the milk as the sight of it only causes me to turn thirstier. While gulping it back, my eyes scan the room. To my left is a black entertainment center, a large analog TV perched inside, a DVD and VHS player on the shelf beneath it.

The wall behind me is covered in black ladder bookshelves filled with videos and books. From where I lie, the rest of the apartment appears virtually empty and spotless. Nothing covers his walls, and not a thing is out of place. It hardly looks lived in.

Denendrius returns with a wet cloth. He takes a place next to my legs and lifts the cloth to my face. When I flinch, he scowls. "You're bleeding."

I hold my breath as he wipes the blood from my forehead.

"This is not how things were supposed to be," he consoles. "You have no idea how much I care for you."

"How were things supposed to be?" I ask, clearing my

throat. I take another swallow of strawberry milk when he pulls away to fold the cloth over, already feeling better with each sip.

"Perfect," he murmurs before sighing.

I wince when his hand reaches for my neck, yet don't stop him from wiping the blood away.

"I wish you didn't have that thing," he says.

My fingers twitch up to touch the tattoo on my neck beneath my ear. I untuck my hair from my ear, and the abstract double Rs inked in red and outlined in black vanish from his sight.

"It's just a tattoo," I mumble.

"Well, there," he says with a small smile, "you're all better."

I don't thank him as he stands and takes the dirty cloth back down the hallway. Instead, I stand to leave. He's back around the corner, blocking the way out of the living room before I've taken my first step.

"Sit down," he says.

"I don't want to."

When he takes a quick step forward, the look in his eyes is enough to make me sit back down—for now.

"Our bedroom is the first room down the hall; the bathroom is after it. Are you tired?" he asks. "Or we could watch a movie. If you're hungry I have some stuff you'll like."

His request for me to come home with him on our first date comes to mind, and I can't help but wonder if I would have found myself in this situation if I had obliged him.

I remain quiet as I study him, study the room around us in hopes I can figure out exactly what kind of situation I'm in. The emptiness of the apartment makes me think he could be transient. An international human trafficker like Manny thought?

Despite any clues that may lie around, all I see is *crazy*, and not the kind Manny and I speculated about. *Worse.*

I consider what kind of weapons he might have lying around. "A movie is fine."

Smiling, he takes the remote from the top of the TV and plunks down beside me. Bringing up the guide, he asks, "What would you like to watch?"

His request to relax and watch a movie is such a contrast compared to what is going on that for a mind-boggling second I question the situation I'm really in.

"It doesn't matter," I tell him, my eyes scrutinizing the sudden calm of his face.

He selects a thriller and slings his arm around me, my aching body now trapped between him and the high arm of the couch. The feel of him at my side sends a pang through my chest and I wish things could have been as real as they seemed.

My heart pounds adrenaline through my limbs, the tired supply quickly drying up to make way for the muscle soreness that comes with stiff stress. Soon, I'm itching for a cigarette while I struggle to keep my eyes open and on the television screen.

I rub my eyes. "Can we go get cigarettes?"

"No," he says, voice gruff. "You shouldn't smoke anymore, you know. It's bad for you."

I scowl at the flames flickering onscreen as they devour a house. *So is being held hostage.*

My hot frustration piles up as the movie continues, and soon I'm ready to risk whatever will happen by shoving him away from me. When I look up at him, ready to snarl something that will definitely result in a fight, he tightens his arms around my shoulders while grabbing my face with his other hand.

"What are you—"

He steals the remaining words from my lips with his mouth, his hand hardening on my face. Fists balled against his chest, I try to push him away, the memory of our first kiss making my eyes burn. He rocks closer to me and I let out a screech. It has the intended effect because he pulls away, eyes searching my face.

"Don't fucking touch me anymore," I snarl, hooked fingers at my side as I prepare to slash my nails across his face.

Denendrius scowls, muscles rigid in his arms and shoulders as he inhales through clenched teeth and sits with his back straight against the leather couch. His dark eyes lock with the television.

Heart pounding, I rein in my breath and wait a few long moments before saying, "I'm sorry, can I use the bathroom?"

He pauses the movie. "Go."

I clamber off the couch and turn around the corner, eyes locked with the front door—unlocked. I take careful and quick steps, only to run the last few feet when I hear him get off the couch.

Somehow, he's at the front door before me. I freeze in my steps.

"Don't be scared," he says, hand reaching out to stop me. "But I don't want you to leave yet. You just got here."

"Get out of my way," I snap. "I want to go home."

"Why would you want to go back there?" he questions, head swaying with disbelief. "Your foster mother treats you poorly and uses you as a maid. There's hardly any food in your house and you don't even have a proper bed. The place reeks of smoke. In a year you'll age out and be homeless. I know that worries you. Pam will kick you out and you'll have no job and no place to live. You won't get a proper job, and even if you did, how can you work and finish high school when you're so far behind?"

I square my shoulders. "It doesn't matter. It's none of your business. That's the home I was put in and that's where I'm supposed to be. The government will help me when I have to leave."

His brow furrows. "Why? I can give you so much better. I

have an apartment, or we can get something else if you'd prefer. But this is close to your school and friends, that's why I picked it. I have a nice car and money."

I glance around for another way to escape, and from the corner of my eye to my right, I spot a sliding bolt at the top of the bedroom door. When he takes a step forward, I know that he's seen me see it.

"I don't want your charity," I spit.

He frowns. "It's not charity, Marianna. I love you."

My eyes widen. "Excuse me?"

"I love you," he articulates.

My heart screeches to a halt, then tumbles like a car down a cliff.

"I love you," he repeats. "You love me, right?"

"I *liked* you, but I don't believe in love," I state icily. I decide that is less dangerous, less personal than *no*.

Lightning strikes in the dark of his eyes.

I guess I was wrong.

"Yet you love *me*, right? You didn't think you could love until *us*, right? With the way you've been kissing me, I know you do."

His persistence is gasoline for my anger. "No, I don't believe in love. And even if I did, I'd never love someone like you. I thought you were nice!"

He takes a deep breath, something more dangerous than anger visibly rolling through his body.

"I can love," he declares as if I said otherwise. "If I can love" —he stabs his index finger against his chest before jabbing it toward me—"then so can you."

I take a deep breath, quickly trying to recalculate despite the flurry in my mind the overdose and this situation have caused.

"Let me out that door or I'm going to scream, Denendrius," I warn.

He leans back against it, simply saying, "Don't."

I curl my hands into fists at my side. "You're in an apartment building. *I will scream*, and then everyone will hear it. Do you want me to do that?"

Lip curled back, he says, "I wouldn't. This place has concrete walls, and people tend to ignore things they shouldn't anyway."

"*Move.*"

The corner of his lip lifts in a smile. "I'll let you scream before I let you go, Marianna."

My eyes challenge his, only tightening when he sighs and stands straight again.

"Go sit down, sweetheart. Things will be fine. You need time to settle."

I snarl, "Fuck you, fuck this apartment, and fuck whatever fantasy you've got going on because I *refuse* to be involved."

A loud growl rips from his throat and he lunges forward and grabs me by the hair at the nape of my neck, holding me in place. "Don't pretend you didn't feel anything. You know we're meant to be together."

I try to twist out of his grip but resort to spitting in his face when that doesn't work.

Denendrius wipes his face with the sleeve of his leather jacket before locking eyes with me and snarling, "You've turned into a nasty brat, haven't you?"

"Fuck you." I whimper when he pulls my hair tighter, his other hand grabbing the front of my shirt to hold me close.

"You have such a foul mouth for someone who looks as innocent as you," he growls, his top lip pulling back in disgust. "What a shame you have to act like this. I loved you."

Before I have a chance to retort, he's dragging me from the apartment. I kick the floor and walls as he drags me—my knees locked—along. I shout curses at the top of my lungs, screaming at him to let me go as I writhe and claw at his arm. Fed up, he throws me over his shoulder, carrying me down the stairs and outside as I use the little energy I have left in an attempt to combat his impossible strength.

He pulls open the passenger door of his black Mustang and dumps me on the seat as if I'm already dead. My head smashes the gear shift, so I pull myself up and try the door handle. As soon as I touch it, it locks. My insides bubbling, I turn to Denendrius, who is already sitting in his seat and slipping his aviators on.

The tires screech as the car pitches us backward. It spins around, my stomach doing the same, and then we're on the road.

"Where are you taking me?" I demand, terrified that Manny was right and that he's bringing me somewhere to sell me off.

His jaw clenches and unclenches. "I'm getting quite sick of those kinds of questions."

My eyes search the clean and bare car for something to use as a weapon. "Tell me where we're going."

"You won't like any answers I have for you," he says simply.

Heart hammering, I twist for the handle, jamming my finger against the button to unlock it. When that fails, I try to flag down the car next to us, but the driver merely stares awkwardly at me before stepping on the gas.

"Sit still!" Denendrius hollers, his voice reverberating through me. I stare at him with wide eyes, my ears ringing.

"I want out," I tell him. "I promise you, you'll want to let me out of this fucking car before my friends come shooting at you."

He ignores me, eyes focused on the road as he speeds through the early-morning traffic.

"Do you fucking hear me?" I bellow.

When he merely glances at me before turning a corner, I decide I'm getting out of this car even if it means crashing it and having paramedics pull me out. Turning to face him, I lean back against the door and kick my legs into him and the wheel.

Voice even, he says, "Stop it."

"Then fucking pull over." I propel more power into my feet, the heels of my bare feet colliding with his hand and bicep. He continues to steer through my efforts.

"I told you to stop it, Marianna."

"And I told you to pull over."

When my heel skips over the top of his shoulder and narrowly misses his face, he slams on the brakes in the middle of the residential road and lunges over the console. His hands lock around my throat like steel vises. I kick harder—this time for breath—as his cold, stony eyes bore into mine while he squeezes.

I feel my pulse in my throat, blood pounding in my ears as pressure builds in my head. A screen of stars pilfers my vision until they explode into blackness and I can no longer feel Denendrius's hands around my throat.

IX

I lurch awake at the sound of the car bottoming out, greenery on every side of the vehicle.

"Where the fuck are we?" I breathe, clutching at my tender throat while I pick through the trees and bushes for something that looks familiar.

Denendrius ignores me as he turns the car off and steps onto a worn path, shutting the door behind him before he circles around to the passenger side.

"Take me home," I demand as he yanks the door open.

He takes my wrist in his iron grip and drags me from the passenger seat. "You're not going home."

When he throws me over his shoulder, I roar and hammer my fists against his back. "Put me down!"

He drops me on the underbrush on my back, towering over me as I gasp for air.

"Then you'll walk," he tells me, placing me on my feet and forcing me forward.

The cold really hits when we slip into the forest. Birds chirp their early songs and a few animals run from our presence. Early morning threatens the navy-blue sky, and the light breeze makes the tops of the trees knock against each other like giraffes fighting.

I think I'm about to faint when the world shifts. A meadow full of short, dead grass straightens around me. Did I pass out? Did he carry me?

His sandals crunch against the dry grass as he drags me along by my arm and out of the trees. I try to wrestle myself away from him, feeling my knee graze something in his pocket that feels a lot like a folded knife.

When I force my hand down his pocket, his confusion gives me the second I need to maneuver the knife out of his jeans.

He merely stares at me, a smile creeping onto his lips as I back up and brandish it in front of myself.

"I'm not fucking scared of you, Denendrius. I'll kill you," I warn, hand still as I hold the blade ready. "Give me your keys. I'm going home."

He grins. "You'll kill me?"

I grit my teeth and nod once, my grip on the knife handle knuckle white. "I've stabbed people before. It'd be easy to kill you."

Darkness drops back over his face. "Come on, then," he hollers. "If you think you're so tough, then show me."

"Give me your keys, or I will." My open hand demands his surrender.

Instead, he decides to gamble on if I'm bluffing by closing the space between us. I focus my strength into thrusting the blade into his abdomen before he can take it from me. He grunts as the sharp metal slices through his flesh and muscle, quickly stepping backward.

His eyes are wide with betrayal, as if he thought I'd never do it.

"Last chance," I tell him. "Give me your keys."

The corner of his lip twitches, any indicator of pain leaving his face. "Or what? You'll stab me again?"

"Yes." I squeeze the knife in my hand, dark blood dripping off the tip and staining the dead grass at my feet.

Slowly, he lifts the bottom of his shirt to expose his unharmed stomach. My heart lurches, sweat starting in my hairline as I look between the bloodied blade and his unwounded flesh. "I think you'll find that useless, Marianna."

When my eyes lift back to his, they're a brooding bright red.

"*What?*" I stumble backward, trip over the heel of my own foot, and collapse in the grass.

He clicks his tongue at me, long fangs descending from where his human canines were. "Of all the things you've forgotten about, *vampires* are one of them?"

"I s-saw you walk in the sun," I fumble, crawling backward as he steps toward me.

It's the drugs, right? I've finally ruined my mind with drugs. That's the only reasonable explanation.

"Yes," he starts. "That took centuries of agony to achieve. So, I wouldn't think anything you may try very worthwhile."

I hold the knife out in front of me as he takes slow steps toward me. "You brought me here to kill me."

I squeal as he appears in front of me, swiping the knife from my hand and wiping it clean on his blue jeans. "It's really the best place for such a thing, isn't it? Kill and dispose in the same place. Nobody will ever know."

The taste of blood stirs on my tongue as his hand clamps around my neck. He lifts me to my feet, and my breath solidifies into a lump in my throat when the tip of his knife appears under my eye.

Only an inch between our noses, he says, "Kiss me. Sway my decision."

I turn my head away. "I'm not playing games," I snarl, trying to hide how my voice quivers. "If you're going to kill me, you're going to kill me. I'm not going to die begging."

Denendrius smiles. "I admire that." The blade moves away from my face.

I exhale sharply when he punches me in the gut, his hand hooking around the back of my neck to stop me from sinking into the grass.

"But that's still not good enough," he whispers. "I'm not impressed."

He pulls away from me, my legs folding beneath me. When I see that the knife in his hand is bright red again, my eyes dart down to where I thought he punched me, and I find my shirt soaked.

I gasp and press my hand against the wound.

He paces in front of me, licking the blade clean. "Don't worry," he says. "You'll live long enough for me to decide how much I truly care about you."

I'm speechless, heart thumping wildly as I stare at him while trying to catch my breath.

"What's wrong?" he says sardonically. "You hurt yourself all the time. What difference does it make if I do it?"

Black dots swarm my sight, a sharp and hot ache radiating through me. "You fucking stabbed me," I cry, eyes stinging.

He licks his lips, eyes locking on me as his chest rises and falls with heavy breaths. "Yeah, I know. Hurts, doesn't it?"

"You stabbed me," I repeat dumbly.

He appears in a crouch before me. "Change your mind and I'll change mine, Marianna."

"Fuck you," I repeat, rolling over to crawl away while kicking at him.

I howl when I feel the knife plunge into my back, twice more after he yanks it out. I bury my face into the grass, sobbing until he flips me over. My curled fist lunges toward his face. His hand locks around my forearm and he twists my arm to reach my wrist, his fangs ripping into my vein. My jaw clenches, teeth aching under the pressure as I squeal. When I tear at his face with my nails—leaving no marks behind, though I try—he stops me by jerking my arm, the sound of my wrist snapping making my stomach turn.

My mouth stretches wide, air trapped in my chest.

Denendrius drops my wrist, face bloody as his hand circles the bottom of my jaw. "Keep squealing," he demands. "I love the sound."

I hold my snapped wrist, blood running down my arm from the twin incisions. "Why? All this because I turned you down?"

He drives the knife into my thigh, and I let out another shriek.

"All you have to do is remember," he snarls. "Remember, and all this ends. You don't want to hear me out? Then you can remember on your own."

"Remember what?" I scream before coughing a lump of spit away.

He grits his bloody teeth, eyes wild as he stares down at me. "Remember," he says, "or you are never leaving this forest."

My eyes challenge his and I huff. "Then you can look me in the eye and kill me because I have no idea who the fuck you are!"

Denendrius makes up his mind, the blade dipping in and out of my torso so many times there's too much to feel. My shirt is shredded, blood painting my skin as I watch his twisted face. Peace shapes itself around me like plastic wrap, my mind empty.

He falls back when he finally finishes, staring at me as he sighs and begrudgingly whispers something to himself.

Denendrius crawls over to me and touches my face with his dirt-stained fingers. "I hope you learned something today."

He straddles me and pins me by the throat. I wouldn't be able to move even if I wanted to.

"You will learn, Marianna. I can't have you like this."

My remaining energy is spent when I feebly swing at him. He pins my wrists against the grass under his knees.

"You are arrogant and cocky. You are not better than me."

He grabs a fistful of my shirt and tears it off, tossing it away.

"You are not God. You are not invincible."

When the blade returns, all I can manage is a loud whimper.

"You're just human."

He holds the knife like a pen in his right hand, the cold tip of the blade touching down on the bruised flesh above my left breast.

My scream swells in my throat, trapped as he starts carving. Crimson bubbles from the wound and he smears it away with the back of his hand to continue his work.

"Do you feel human now? Hmm?"

My mouth opens wide, my hearing blotting as he whispers while cutting me. My own scream doesn't reach my ears. None of this is real, I decide. The world disappears and pulses back. I feel the sweltering pain in my neck as he pulls away from my throat, fangs crimson with my blood.

I black out and wake to a pain I've never felt before. It tears through my insides, igniting me with a feverish heat and chilling cold. My blood-curdling shrieks of pain and terror are foreign, distant to my own ears.

I plead for him to stop the pain. My fingers scratch at the grass, tearing up dirt and everything I can get a hold of. Then I feel my fingernails on my face, trying to claw out my eyes as blood and tears stream from them. I'm unable to understand what he's done to me, and why he's done it.

When his hands pull mine away from my face, I reach out to try striking him. I open my mouth to tell him to let me go, and a stream of blood gags me. I knock my head into the ground, trying to make myself stop screaming, but I can't.

I look up at the sky and watch as the moon turns away from me. The sky flashes different colors as my eyes dart across it.

A woman calling my name makes me turn away from the sky. I search the sparkling meadow for her and see nothing.

"*Marianna*," her whispered voice calls, "*do you want me to sing to you?*"

And as soon as I realize it's my mother, I beg Denendrius to take her away so she can't. I don't want her near, to hear the voice haunting my childhood, the lullaby created from her drug-fueled paranoia that cast nightmares into the depths of my mind. But she sings anyway.

> *Dry your eyes, little girl.*
> *No more weeping, time for sleeping.*
> *The Devil's watching, he knows your fears.*
> *He's been with you all these years.*
> *Mama told him he could have you,*
> *if you dare utter a word.*
> *Close your eyes now or you'll die now.*
> *Go to sleep, little girl.*

"You're hallucinating," he whispers in my ear. "Your mother isn't here."

But the revelation doesn't stop the lullaby from echoing inside my skull as if it's a cave. I think I'm possessed when I start screaming again, and I'm sure my lungs will burst. Tears drip from my eyes, the words clear as bells.

Her voice leaves me, the world jarring still, and my screaming stops. My breath is visible around me as I sit. Snow falls. I look down at myself. Have I merely been sleeping? A brilliant Gothic gown the color of night embraces my frame. I stand, giggling as I twirl, the lace brushing the white flakes layering the ground.

"Hey there," Denendrius's voice says.

With a timid nod, I fix my hair, a smile playing across my painted lips. I look up at him and feel my heart crush in my chest. My breath is taken as I watch the moonlight touch his icy flesh. I stare at his bare chest, the way his lean muscles move through his body. Long black wings spread from his back and brush the air.

"I always imagined death as a man with a cloak and scythe," I say, taken aback by the crystal clearness of my voice. I test it once more. "You are an angel of death, right?"

He smiles and holds an old and battered box out to me, just bigger than a shoe box. "You're forgetting something."

My heart freezes in my chest as my eyes pin the box. I feel the urge to recoil from it, to knock it from his hands like it contains a bomb. But I know one isn't inside, just something much less deadly and twice as terrifying. How I know this, I'm unsure. The box must be what I'm forgetting.

Did I die? Could that be why an angel of death is before me, a forgotten item from my life in his hands? If he killed me, that would explain why the angel looks like Denendrius, but why he stirs no negative emotion within me.

He steps toward me, his wings lifting loose snow into the air. He motions for me to take the box.

I take a deep breath, heat rising around me as I reach my hand out to it.

Something to the right catches my attention, and when I look back to Denendrius, the scene has changed. A sweltering summer burns around us, a little girl standing in the rich green grass between the angel of death and me, the box missing.

She wears the same black dress as I, and even though her back is to me, I know her face is just a younger version of mine.

"Come with me and you will never feel pain again. Nobody

could ever hurt you and you'd never be alone." The angel of death holds his hand out.

To which one of me he's speaking to, I'm unsure.

The little girl—me—says, "We'll be best friends forever?"

"Yes," he promises.

I go to speak, to tell her not to do it, not to go with him, but my lips don't move.

The box appears at my feet, and when my eyes focus on it, the world around me mutes, everything past the cardboard succumbing to a gray fog, their voices scrambled.

"I don't want it!" I scream, kicking it into the fog. A couple black feathers are left fluttering to the ground where it once sat unwelcome at my feet. Whatever it is, I don't want it.

The fog spins in front of me like a tornado—a gray torrent twisting toward me. As I step back, Denendrius rips through, leaving a shriek of surprise to die on my tongue. When he grabs my wrist—wings beating madly—the air turns frosty with snow, iciness crawling up the soles of my feet.

"We're in love," he says.

His words spin around me, echoing in different tones. They're said violently, then sadly, as a promise, then a reminder, genuine, then unsure. Over and over again until my mind trips in confusion and I begin to pull away from him.

"Marianna, why are you doing this to me?" His lips don't move, but his voice rings around me.

I step back into the fog until his face is lost within it, each moment before the last dropping away from me with each step backward. Soon, I forget why I'm stepping, just that I am and that I have to. Scenes appear in the fog around me, most making me step faster. A few times I think to run, but I never do as even those memories drip away and make me question what I was going to run from.

My screams return to my ears and my body is still thrashing

when I come to. I try to hang on to the image of the little girl and death, but it quickly dissolves into a mush of confusion.

I shriek and writhe in agony as pain dances through my body until the sky begins to turn funny shades of orange and pink. Hallucination after hallucination takes hold of my mind, from being raped by Denendrius, to being chased by horror movie killers and living thugs.

X

The music of twittering birds summons me awake. I lurch and spin over, expecting to get a faceful of grass. Instead, I drop a couple feet onto carpet.

Eyes snapping open, I find myself staring back from large closet mirrors.

The events that happened in the forest are muddy, and I can't help but question what I truly experienced.

My overdose could explain the hallucinations and seeing him as a vampire, though he could have drugged the strawberry milk he was so insistent on having me drink.

I yank the oversized T-shirt up and in horror run my fingers over the scarred white letters over my left breast: his name, permanently etched into my skin. Dozens of faint one-inch lines cover my abdomen, proof that the horror in the forest wasn't a complete hallucination. But seeing how I am completely free of bruises and wounds leaves me lacking an explanation. Even the supposed fang marks on my wrist are nothing more than bumpy white scars.

Physically, I feel fine, though my mind is a wreck of confusion and disbelief. How am I even alive? How did I heal so quickly? Why did I experience the things that I did?

Paranoia takes over and I check my gums and eyes in the mirror, trying to figure out if he's turned me. Surely I'd feel different if I was no longer human, so somehow, he must have healed me. Though, how long was I unconscious?

Springing off the carpet, I'm ready to dart from the apartment until I note that I'm not wearing pants. The realization makes my heart stutter. I move to the tall black dresser between the closet and door, carelessly rooting around through his clothes as I search for something I can cover up with. Apartment dead quiet, I listen carefully for him as I open a second drawer.

Cold floods my veins at the sight of a Polaroid peeking from a green photo envelope that sits amongst his folded jeans. My stomach falls like a cinder block through the air when I pull the picture out for a better look, heart stammering as I stare at the little girl's happy face. Her light brown eyes are bright as she holds blue cotton candy in one hand. Her sandy waist-length hair is pushed back by a red headband. She's wearing a navy-blue dress with white polka dots, a red rope belt tied around her waist.

I know the dress. I remember it from my childhood, though I could never remember when or how I came to own it or where it went. It's the same with the bracelet on her right wrist. The envelope slips from my fingers and lands on the carpet. The girl in the picture, who stands in front of a roller coaster at an amusement park I have no recollection of ever visiting, is me.

My fingers tremble, and I remember how Denendrius asked if I knew him in the mall. How at the restaurant he said he must have seen someone who looks like me in a picture.

Why does he have this picture? How does he have it? Why have I never seen it? Did I meet him sometime in my past?

With the threat of Denendrius appearing at any moment, my heart flips. I reach for the envelope. A sharp intake of breath chokes me as the bracelet from the picture falls from it. I snatch it and study the circular white beads. Each has the letter of my first name in black on it.

I shove the Polaroid and bracelet back into the envelope and try to place it exactly as it was in the drawer in hopes he won't notice it has been moved, then I scamper around the room, rushing to find a pair of pants. I shudder at the thought of him undressing me as I adjust the too-big green T-shirt that makes me feel like a child in adult's clothing.

Finally, I find my black shorts inside the dryer in the closet at the end of the hallway. I pull them on, running toward the front door as I do them up.

I pull the door open and turn left so I don't meet him on the stairs we took last time. My feet are light against the red carpet of the empty echo-filled hallway, passing apartment after apartment until I reach a flight of stairs identical to the ones on the other side of the L-shaped building.

When I've escaped from the building, I continue barefooted on the cement, my strong legs putting as much ground as I can between the apartment and me. I feel stronger than I usually do, the crisp afternoon air easily filtering in and out of my lungs.

The sky is spotted with clouds when I sit on a blue bench in a busy park to rest. I twist my feet onto my lap, fingers rubbing the balls of them, massaging out indents of rocks.

On the bench beside me, a woman with frizzy hair in a bun coos to a baby in a stroller, babbling on about family life to her friend beside her.

I'm about to ask her what day it is when the sight of Denendrius's black Mustang skulking along the road at the front of the park plucks me from my seat and drives me in the opposite direction. I rush to the parking lot, waving my arms at a taxi that deposits a teen mom with her son. The driver nods in acknowledgment, and I dive into the back seat, slamming the door so hard the sound seeps into my skull.

I wave him on. "*Drive.*"

My tone makes him jump. The tires squeal as the yellow cab jolts forward.

"Fuck—not that road! Take the other road!"

I've panicked him. He doesn't listen and instead takes the road the black Mustang is rushing down. The front end of the car extrudes toward us as he stops, but we turn to the side and climb onto the main road.

I twist, watching the Mustang from the rear window. He spins a donut in the parking lot and screeches onto the road behind us.

I'm jiggling in my seat, hands tight on the roof handle, feet pounding the plastic mat.

"What's going on?" the man's voice, laced with a thick German accent, demands. "Are you okay?"

"Just drive. Don't let him catch up." I bite down on my lip.

"Okay, I'm driving to the police station," he tells me.

My head snaps back toward him. "You can't."

My eyes move to the bite scar on my wrist, and I think of how he healed so quickly when I stabbed him. Going to the police station is the last thing I need. What would I even tell them when I'm not even sure what's going on? When I have drugs in my system? "My dad's a cop," I lie. "Just drive me home."

He follows my vague directions, and aside from asking what Denendrius wants with me, he doesn't question my demands and is happy with my answer about how the man following me has personal issues with my police officer father.

My heart jostles against my rib cage when Denendrius

comes close enough for me to see through his windshield. He sets a knife on the dashboard, his fangs descending as he bares them in a silent threat.

I gape, the proof that I didn't hallucinate everything in the forest making me reel.

The noise the plastic divider makes when I drum on it with my fists barely drowns out the panic in my chest. "Faster!"

I'm thankful for the driver's quick wit. He turns down a busy street under construction, quickly zooming in behind another car before a man in a neon vest cuts off the line of traffic and moving machinery forces Denendrius to obey the distance.

After I have the taxi driver stop at a safe distance from Sarah's house—where her father's cop car was parked in the driveway—he lets me off without paying and with the request to pass on greetings to my dad. I keep careful track of the cars on the road while I walk home, only to flee at the sight of his Mustang in the driveway. Unsure of what to do in a situation like this, I sneak onto the bus when the driver steps off and ride it to the east side of Lorimer before hopping off in a nice community.

Aimless walking leads to a neighborhood in much better condition than the one where I grew up. The dark skies crawling through clouds above make me feel unwanted as I walk past home after home of families.

I kick a rock ahead of me with my big toe, the thought of running home and seeing Denendrius's car parked in my driveway making me wish I had barged in for my gun and shot him on the way out. I feel exposed when I'm weaponless, like the whole world will try to take advantage of me. And from my experience, that's usually the case.

What had he planned, anyway? Did he think when I saw

his car I would just continue inside regardless? With Samantha and Charlie at school, it's not like he had any real leverage.

Not only did Denendrius being at my place leave me unable to get my gun, it prevents me from having a safe place to sleep tonight. Even with my gun, I'll never be able to sleep without thinking he'll break through my window and snatch me.

My only family member—my mother—is in prison, and I don't want to involve Jenna, Camille, and Daina's families in this vampire hell either. I could go to a shelter, but I'm in too bad of a mood to put up with other street kids. Aside from the street, there's not many options.

I count the streetlamps above, and I wonder what Denendrius is doing. Is he searching for me now? What will happen if he finds me?

My hair ruffles around me like ribbons. I scrutinize every home I pass, fingers crossed for the perfect one. A couple blocks later I see a tall two-story house inhabited by darkness. The pile of newspapers on the front porch and the mail over-flowing from the mailbox gives it a promising look.

Creeping around to the back, I inspect the underside of the welcome mat and find a key. It's old in comparison to the new lock and doorknob and doesn't fit when I slide it in. I sigh and gaze up at the windows.

"Score," I cheer to myself when I spot a way to climb to the window.

The red wooden vine ladder creaks as I climb it, a nail coming loose. When I can reach the roof about five feet away, I hold my breath and throw myself at it, nearly missing. Wiggling the window, I plead with it to open. And it does. It shoots right up into its frame, allowing me to clamber into the room of a teenage girl. I pivot and study the window, wondering why it wasn't locked, and find it was jimmied to stay open—probably by a teenager who enjoys sneaking out. I shut it.

I walk through the house, air soaked with the stench of

potpourri and incense. Finding the kitchen, I leave the lights off so the neighbors won't suspect anything. I spot a calendar on the wall and discover the family's on a trip to Turkey and isn't due back until next week.

Careful with what I touch so they won't think they had a visitor, I explore. I plop myself down at a table in the middle of a green-painted room and bite into an apple from the fruit dish before gulping down a glass of cold water.

I learn they are a family of five, seemingly happy. What are they like? Does the father beat the mother? Is she having an affair? I wonder what there is to know about them.

Awe spills over me the more I search. I'd have to sell my soul and so much more to have a life like this. But it doesn't matter because tonight, the place is mine.

But am I safe?

Thinking through all I know about fictional vampires from books I've read, I decide the answer is likely no. He came into my foster home without being invited in—that I know of, at least—so that means he can likely retrieve me from here without any supernatural force stopping him.

I pace the kitchen, pulling knives in and out of the block and deciding none of them are good enough unless I get enough time to inflict multiple stabs.

Risking a trip to the tree in the backyard, I grab a medium-sized branch from a collection of fallen twigs and leaves, deciding it's the perfect size for a stake.

Bringing it back into the kitchen with me, I find a knife and do my best to whittle the end to a point without cutting myself. After a few close calls, I admire the crude weapon before giving the air a few test jabs, hiding the shavings in the garbage.

I'm not sure if my ideas have any basis in reality or if vampire books are leading me astray, but it's worth a shot.

I move to the fridge for the next part of my plan. With the shelves nearly bare, it only takes me a moment to find garlic on one of them like I was hoping for. It's pre-minced and in a jar, but I take my chances on it working the same. Deciding against putting anything in doors and windows since I don't have cloves to hang, I focus on protecting myself. Unable to come up with a better idea, I find the cutlery drawer and snatch a spoon before unscrewing the jar's lid.

My nose burns when I scoop out a whopping spoonful of minced garlic and hold it up in front of my face. I tuck my stake under my arm and pinch my nose, taking a deep breath before I shove it in my mouth. My eyes tear as it burns down to my stomach and I almost puke it back up. Forcing one more spoonful down, I hope it keeps Denendrius from sinking his fangs into me and that I'm not torturing myself for nothing.

I chug a few glasses of water to help the taste in my mouth, then spread some garlic on the tip of the stake before finding refuge on the couch. Time will tell if my plan is clever or laughable. Sighing, I set my tired eyes on my reflection on the television screen. I look a little crazy sitting in the dim light with a makeshift weapon, though my sudden belief in vampires isn't anything less than that.

I want to blame everything on my overdose or the idea that he drugged me before dragging me out to the woods to murder me, but I was completely sober when he flashed his fangs in the car. Besides, between the fresh scars on my wrist and the memory of his fangs ripping through my vein, there is little room in my mind for another explanation.

Paranoia reenters my mind with my unsettled stomach and burning tongue. Denendrius already bit me. What are the chances that I am yet to undergo some sort of transformation? Would I have already started turning? Or should I expect to begin sweating and aching soon?

The smell of garlic on my rapid breath makes my eyes pop wide. If I'm turning, what will happen to me since I consumed garlic? Will I start puking blood?

My train of thought derails when I remember my head hanging over the crimson water of the toilet bowl.

"*Oh shit*," I breathe when it dawns on me that it wasn't *my* blood I was vomiting. It was his.

Is that how he brought me out of my overdoses? What does it mean for me if I drank his blood? Merely healing? *Turning?*

I leap off the couch and dart through rooms until I find myself in front of a bathroom mirror. I flip the light on and study my eyes and gums, trying to assess how I feel. But aside from an angry stomach and creeping exhaustion, I feel better than I have in a long time—which is also suspicious.

Returning to the couch, I slump down and clutch the stake. I close my eyes and focus on deep breaths, trying to recalibrate from the whiplash the past few days has given me. My heart thuds in my chest, the letdown and fury at myself and Denendrius making my energy dwindle faster.

How could he flip so quickly? And why did I allow myself to like him, to be tricked by him?

I try not to think about the way his lips moved over mine and how sweet he was. The knife he drove through me makes it more painful.

Where do I go from here? Should I be holed up here, or is it more dangerous to leave?

The heaviness of my thoughts weighs on my consciousness, and soon I'm plummeting into dreamland, the horrors of Denendrius stirring up more from my past.

Four hours fly past before the sound of sirens wakes me. I freeze in a cold sweat, wondering if one of the neighbors reported me. But they fade off into the distance, leaving my eyes wide, reminding me of the only time I have ever felt safe in the presence of a cop.

The moon was hidden that night, somewhere safe from the chaos unfolding beneath it. I was nine at the time, tucked in the corner of my room, imprisoned by the locked door and walls mirroring the pain I felt beneath my beaten flesh. The sirens bleated from outside, the sound filling my ears. I sat there quivering, watching the officers through a hole I had made in the newspaper covering the window. They ran from their cars wielding guns, their shouts shaking the house as they disappeared into it.

Gunshots drove me under the bed, the usual drill for when I heard them. And even though they rarely made their way to my room, I watched the door, waiting for someone to enter and kill me.

My mother's furious screams tore through the air, making me crawl back to the window. The officers forced her onto the sidewalk to arrest her, tearing a pistol from her iron grip. Her face was bloodied and beaten, arms red with bruises.

Warm tears streaked my face. Didn't they know only she had the key to my room? Was I going to starve to death?

I shrieked for her to come back, for her to unlock the door so the hunger ravaging my body wouldn't kill me, so it didn't make my body shrivel up to bones like she said it would, saying how only good girls got food and if I didn't start being good, I was going to die.

Eventually, shouts bouncing between people appeared on the landing outside my door, returning me to the underside of my bed. I covered my mouth to choke the sobs and stifle my breathing like my mother had told me to do.

I was screaming and fighting for my life when the police came into my room and pulled me away. Death threats and curses, ones I'd heard from my mother but had never quite understood, flew from my mouth as I tried to make the officers release me. If they made my mother fearful, perhaps there was a reason I should be afraid too.

Their voices were nonsense as they dragged me from the house, my screams and my mother's drowned out by sirens.

They gripped me tightly, stuffing the rag-doll girl I was into the police cruiser. When we arrived at the police station, my mother wasn't in sight, making me wonder what she had done this time. Nobody would tell me; all they did was yell at the officer gripping my hand, asking her why I wasn't in an ambulance and on my way to the hospital.

I had cried about being hungry, the intense pain taking hold of my words. A woman had given me chocolate from a machine, and as I ate it, I couldn't remember ever tasting something so sweet. I could only get a third of the way through the bar before I threw it up, my stomach barely recognizing food.

I haven't seen my mother since and can't even remember the last words she said to me. And to be honest, I couldn't care less if she was rotting right now.

Not long after I was put into foster care, my mother was sentenced to prison on charges of assault, narcotics, illegal gun possession, child abuse, and prostituting herself and me. A few months ago, after being tossed around foster homes like a hot potato, I found a place at Pam's.

I stiffen when I hear the back door open on the other side of the kitchen, sure it's the police or someone else who has come to catch me.

Denendrius's voice sings my name. "*Marianna . . .* where are you, sweetheart?"

XI

I feel like a human maraca as I scramble off the couch and dart behind a bookshelf, the stake clutched tight in my hand. I aim the tip outward at his chest height, ready to attack if he finds me.

"*Marianna,*" he sings again. His voice comes from the kitchen when he says, "I can hear you breathing. And it *reeks* like garlic in here."

I clamp my hand over my mouth, cursing myself for hiding when I should have run to the front door.

The stake is torn from my grip before I see him, and I feel his hand in my hair the moment he snaps into focus.

"Leave me alone!" I screech as he drags me through the living room.

He pulls his hand from my hair as I drop my weight to the floor and try to clamber away.

"Get up," he says, grabbing my arm and pulling me to my feet. "Let's go."

Denendrius's hand clenches the back of my neck as he

forces me to my feet, tightening his fingers and pushing me forward. Anxiety and fear mingle together, becoming one as they seep into my bones.

I lift my chin and set my jaw, knowing those feelings are nothing more than squatters. Eventually, something must come home for them to leave, and it will be relief once I kill Denendrius. Eliminate all threats, the only way to keep power and balance in my screwed-up world. I may not be able to hurt him when he's awake, but he probably sleeps sometime.

He releases me as we reach the car. I take a deep breath and open the door, pulling myself inside. He's there already, eyes tearing me apart. He forces the key into the ignition so hard I'm surprised it doesn't break.

"Miss me?" he asks as the car moves forward.

"Not one bit. How the hell did you find me again?" I demand, glowering at the road as it flies beneath us.

"Your scent. Humans have distinct smells. Things like hormones and blood types play a big part. Drugs have some influence too, especially with taste."

I pull my arms tight around myself, his words making me self-conscious.

He must sense this, as he winks and says, "I love the way you smell when you're sober, by the way. It's like a mix of roses and sea salt."

"Thanks?" My scowl deepens.

Denendrius takes a wistful breath as he turns a corner. His hand reaches deep into his pocket and he pulls out something silver. "Hold your hand out."

I obey, and when he drops a silver heart necklace into my hand, I resist the urge to toss it back at him. "It's nice," I lie.

There's fresh blood dried in the grooves of the heart, and I can't help but wonder how he came to possess the necklace.

He smiles, satisfied, and watches me expectantly for a moment before turning back to the road. I sit rigidly in the seat, counting down from a minute before rolling down the window. He looks at me curiously while I slip my arm out, the icy breeze leaving bumps. Headlights shine around us on the road. A sigh slips past my lips. When a breath returns, I loosen my fingers around the necklace, and it slips onto the street as I'd planned.

His eyes are pits, the fury smothering me. "Why would you throw it away?"

"Because I hate you."

His lip twitches and the window creeps closed beside me. "After everything—"

"What? After everything you've done for me?" I scoff. "Because you took me on a date and spent money on me? Because you think you saved my life? Fuck you! You think I wanted to be tortured? I have no idea what happened when you bit me, but it was the most painful thing I have ever felt in my life. It felt like I was being burned to death in the fucking arctic!" I kneel on the seat, leaning toward him as I think of reaching out to pummel my fists against him.

His fury vibrates the wheel, something rattling in the dash. "I was healing you—"

"I don't care! Who gives a damn if you're a stupid vampire! You think it makes you some sort of god?" I bellow. "You think it makes you extra scary or some shit? I've met humans more fucked in the head than you!"

He jerks the wheel, the car halting.

Before I can blink, I'm sprawled back across the seats. He leans over me, his fingers around my throat. I attempt to punch him away, trying to regain my right to breathe. My legs flail against the steering wheel as his cold grip tightens.

He leans close to my ear. "I taught you a lesson, one you obviously needed. But I'm not convinced it's sunk in. You should never speak to me the way you just did."

Black pilfers bits of light from my vision as I try to break free. It's no use. I'm trapped under stone.

"*Now*, I'm going to let go, and you're going to tell me how sorry you are."

I gasp upon release, greedily sucking air while I try to break my gaze from his amused eyes.

He cocks his head and says, "*I'm sorry, Denendrius. I shouldn't have talked to you so rudely. I deserved it.*"

I spit at him and receive a blow to the cheek.

"Where's spitting going to get you? Say it!"

"I'm sorry," I manage to choke out.

"Wrong!"

Darkness spreads across my vision with the connection of his knuckles to my rib cage. I'm mumbling wordlessly against teasing air. "You still feel tough?" He slaps me gently on the cheek and laughs. "Hm?"

"No," I snarl from behind tight teeth.

"Are you sure?" He lifts me by the throat and slams the back of my head against the passenger window.

Unwanted trembles surge like electricity through my body as his lips reach up my throat and linger. I yelp when his teeth graze my flesh, not enough to leave a mark, but enough to make me say, "I'm s-sorry, Denendrius, I shouldn't h-have talked to you so rudely." I gnash my teeth. "*I deserved it.*"

He slithers back to his seat. "I know."

I turn and sit properly, straightening my back and letting a look of I'm-not-scared-of-anything shape my face as I press my hands together on my lap. I peek at him. The way he feels powerful shows on his curved lips. His head turns to me and as he raises his eyebrow, his smile becomes more severe. I know I'm not fooling him.

He spins a knob on the dash and music pounds from the speakers, heavy metal with screamed lyrics and gut-dropping instrumental. After a few minutes of listening, my head is pounding, and I can't take the sound anymore. I reach toward the dash to turn it to a radio station.

"What are you doing?" he snarls, words serrated. "Did you happen to forget the past few minutes?"

"Chill out, I just want to listen to something else. My head hurts." I turn it to the radio and lower the volume.

His lip twitches at my defensiveness and he grabs my wrist, pulling my hand away from the dashboard. "What are you putting it on?"

"Anything else."

He smiles and licks his lips. "Tell you what—I'll let you listen to what you want if you come kiss me. I've missed it."

As soon as the words leave his mouth, it's no longer about music. I swallow, his challenge making me wish I had put up with the head pain. His tone leaves no room for debate, no choice to change my mind and apologize.

"I ate a shit ton of garlic," I admit, hoping he'll avoid my kisses if they'll hurt him.

He runs his hand up my thigh. "That's fine. I've been exposed to garlic enough now that it hardly bothers me."

"Okay," I whisper, sure he'll react like last time if I say no.

He pulls over on the residential road and parks. Moving his seat back, he tilts it and pats his leg. He removes his mirrored aviators as I climb over to him, flinching when he grabs the back of my knee. I kneel above his lap, my hands gripping the leather headrest. My eyes accidentally meet his, so I quickly close them and press my lips against his.

Maybe I can get away with just a peck.

He exhales and kisses me back gently, immediately moving me to a different position when I try to pull away. My arms end up folded against his chest, and he pulls me onto his lap and tight against his waist, his hands resting on my lower back. I try to focus on breathing through my nose instead of the feel of his soft yet cold lips. I try to move my mind to my happy place, but he's ruined it for me.

Now every time I think of the forest, the smell of vile blood fills my nose, the taste of it stirring in my mouth. It doesn't help much that he tastes of blood too. I try to focus on not throwing up.

He tilts his head in the opposite direction, so I turn mine. I flinch as his mouth turns rougher than I'm used to, his hands sliding up my back with enough pressure to hurt, making me grunt and arch away from them and into his chest. He takes how I've reacted wrong, and I hear a moan vibrate in his throat. I'm grateful his eyes are closed so he can't see me grimace.

I wrap my hands around his shoulders and pull myself to my knees so I no longer have to feel his lap beneath me. He must have taken my repositioning wrong too because he tilts the seat back as far as it will go. I move my hands to his shoulders to avoid crashing into him.

I gasp when his hand jumps to the side of my neck, his lips against my throat in harsh kisses. His lips stop for a moment and I freeze, but I feel him smile and his kisses return harder.

When his other hand disappears from my body, my heart begins to race as I worry about where it went. I peek and discover that he's shoved his hand down his pants. The sight induces a full body grimace and I stress-gag.

Both his hands jump to my face, his eyes staring into mine. "Are you all right?"

"I ate so much garlic that I feel sick now." It's not a complete lie.

"I can make you feel better," he says as he begins to pull my borrowed shirt up.

Yanking it back down, I hear it tear a little. "I don't want to vomit on you," I use as an excuse.

He puckers his lips. "That's fair."

I give a small smile and return to my seat, thankful when he doesn't make anything more of it. I rub my cheek. Why the fuck did I do that? I should have just taken a beating.

He puts his CD back on anyway, and the rest of the drive my

thoughts are on a cycle ranging from how much I need to kill him to whether I would die if I opened the car door and leaped out.

Silence pokes at us with its sharp nails while we climb the stairs to his apartment, overwhelming me with the urge to say something. But I keep my lips tight, my tongue pressing against the roof of my mouth.

I feel his eyes scold my body from behind, the tips of his fingers grazing my arm every so often as they swing at my sides. I swallow, resisting the urge to barrel up the stairs and away.

I wonder if I should be asking him what being a vampire is like, just as girls do on television.

A couple questions might be safe. "You said you were healing me? How does that work?"

"Vampire venom," he says, voice so low I strain to hear. "Once venom enters your bloodstream it begins to work its way through your body, healing as it goes. As it heals, it'll leave you stronger than before, stronger than if you would let your body heal itself. Once all the injuries are healed, it returns to its entry point. It's there that the venom is removed before it has a chance to start the transition to vampirism."

I purse my lips. "Oh. Well, how can *you* heal so fast?"

"It's a vampire thing," he answers with annoyance instead of divulging the info I'd rather have over his attitude.

I wonder if he's still upset about what happened in the car.

He watches me, eyes cloudy with disapproval while opening his door, following too close behind when I enter. I yawn and find a place on the wall and hug myself.

"It's nearly three in the morning. You must be exhausted," he says, his sincere voice opposing the emotion in his eyes. He turns past me and into his room, where it's bright a moment later.

"Sure." I dig at the carpet with my big toe until he comes back.

He nods toward the bedroom and I scurry there, claiming another wall, eyes cautious on his every breath.

A slight grin sits on his lips. "Why are you just standing there?"

"Well, I don't know what the hell you want me to do," I snarl.

His brows pull together, lips parting to say something before he changes his mind. He goes to the other side of the bed and picks up a black duffel bag before tossing it to me.

"This is mine." I gape at him. I pull it open and dig through my clothes from home. "You went in my room again?"

"And told your foster mother you wouldn't be home tonight on my way out."

My head shoots up. "Are you kidding me? What the fuck?"

He sighs and returns to the doorway, leaning his shoulder against it.

"Whatever," I mumble. "Can I have some privacy, please?"

He snorts. "Privacy?"

I grit my teeth and strip anyway, pretending he's not staring at me from the doorway. I throw on a pair of gray sweats and a basketball T-shirt for a team I'd never heard of before owning it.

I toss myself into the queen-sized bed; the blankets are cold as I wrap them around myself. I question whether Denendrius will kick me out and make me sleep on the couch or if he'll take the couch himself.

"How did you get your scar?" I ask after he comes into the room and pulls his leather jacket and black T-shirt off. It travels from just below his rib cage across the lean muscle of his stomach and to his hip. "It looks like someone tried to gut you."

He doesn't turn his back to me as he pulls open a drawer on the black dresser to pull out another shirt. "Precisely." He pulls it over his head.

"Why?" I prop myself up, watching as he pulls his jeans off, leaving him in black silk boxers.

"I hesitated." Denendrius walks around the bed and pulls the blankets back. I want to protest as he slips in beside me. Then I wonder if he's ever been aware of his inappropriateness.

"You don't mind if I sleep beside you tonight, do you? You are my girlfriend, right? This is *our* bed now."

I look at him, study the way his eyes show he won't accept a negative answer and tell him I couldn't give a shit. He pulls the blankets around himself while I push myself to the edge of the bed, forcing my body to balance half on the bed and half in the air as I wish for more space between us.

I wait for him to make his move, to yank me closer so he can rip the clothes from my body and have his way with me. The thoughts are strong enough to keep my eyes open, making me more eager to end his life. I feel fingertips on my face, and I swallow, waiting.

"I won't hurt you like that," he whispers as he moves to the center of the bed and drags me to him.

I cross my legs, keeping them tight and twisting my feet together as I used to when I was young.

He stares, watching my face. "My sister used to do the same with her legs at night when someone would enter her room. My father used to touch young girls and he made no exception for his daughter. Nobody, not even my mother, would say anything about it. I think she was afraid of what he would do. He raped her sometimes too. At night you could hear her crying. Sometimes she would scream. She tried to kill herself when she found out she was pregnant with my youngest sister. I used to think it was because of how it was conceived, but later, my mother said she didn't want to risk any more girls in the house. Not with my father."

I keep my legs where they are, too uncomfortable by his overshared words to move. "Why are you telling me this?"

"I'm not my father."

And if his story isn't enough to convince me, his facial expression is. It's crumpled, and a look of desperation flashes in his eyes. I feel all fear evaporate at the sight of him. He looks weak, easy to kill. I let my legs return to normal and concentrate on the feel of the sheets against my legs.

"What happened to them?" I burrow my cheek into the pillow.

"My youngest sister was six, the second was eleven, and the eldest was fifteen when they and my parents died."

"What happened to them?"

He turns away and without a hint of shame or regret says, "I killed them."

His words leave me staring at the ceiling, the sound of heavy traffic whispering into the chilled air of his bedroom. My eyes are wide and unblinking, staring at the walls that seem to have acquired a blue tinge. I want to sigh and roll over, but I can't help but think of what could happen if I disturb him. So I listen to the creaks of the old building as my limbs turn heavy and begin to cramp from my rigid stillness.

The devil in my subconscious creeps into my dreams as my exhaustion forces me to fall asleep, spinning old memories behind my lids, as vivid as the day they happened.

XII

Trapped in a dream, I scoot my sore body toward the rickety door keeping me confined, my face covered with dried tears and blood. I press my ear to the thin wood and listen. For a few moments, I don't hear anything, but then there's faint whispering and moaning downstairs.

I stand—wobbly-legged—and yank on the door handle. Already loose in the frame, the locked door pops open. I crawl on my hands and bruised knees from my room and onto the landing.

Standing at the top of the stairs, I look down to the living room. My mother sits naked in a broken flower-patterned recliner. Meth smoke rushes from her mouth as she pulls a clear pipe away, the white fog hovering in the air before slowly dissipating. She taps a Latino man with face tattoos on the head, and he looks up from between her legs. She passes it to him and swings her leg over him, pulling herself from the chair.

Spotting me at the top of the stairs, her face contorts and

reddens. My mother screams at me in Spanish, racing up the stairs. Grabbing a fistful of my hair, she drags me down the steps and throws me on the floor.

She calls me disgusting, asking why my face is such a filthy mess. Turning back to the living room, she picks up a gun from the blow-covered glass coffee table. She points it at me and tells me to go into the bathroom. The man in the living room says she shouldn't point a gun at her seven-year-old daughter, but she tells him to shut the fuck up, that he's the reason my face is like this.

She holds the gun to the back of my head and pushes me the rest of the way to the bathroom. Throwing me in the cracked and scum-covered shower, she cranks the water on cold and forces my face into the stream.

Sometime later, I'm in my room. A man sits on the edge of my bed, putting his clothes back on as I lie on the wet covers.

When I wake up, I'm already sitting, eyes wide and mouth gaping with my shrieks trapped in my throat. Trembling, I ball my fists and take a deep breath, holding it until I no longer can, until I'm sure I've sucked the memory so deep inside myself I can't feel the effect of it anymore.

The sky is still thick with night as I sneak off the bed, glancing at Denendrius—who is splayed out on his back—as I tiptoe to the kitchen a few steps away. I open drawers, searching for anything I could use to kill the man.

The last drawer I search is the first containing anything. I let the handle of the large boning knife settle in my hand as I scurry back to his room, my steps soft on the carpet. I can't help but smile while creeping around the bed to where Denendrius sleeps. My insides rush, the slush in my veins from sleep thinning with pulsating adrenaline.

A simple stab may not incapacitate him, but how would he cope with a slit throat?

I set the blade at the side of his throat, my body twitching with anticipation, my hand carefully still. I press down on the knife and rip it across his throat. Instead of red jumping from his throat like it should, his eyes open, falcon eyes snagging mine, surprise lacerating my chest like talons tearing out my heart.

Before I can react, his hands bind my wrists. He pulls me over top of him and leans against me, my back pressing into the bed, the weapon still gripped in my hand. I'm stone as he kisses me, his icy lips rough against mine.

I thrash, trying to turn my head, but he keeps it in place with a cold hand. I kick but he stays unmoving atop me. The feeling of mania builds around him at an alarming speed while the seconds pass, twisting more panic in my gut. I cry out with rage.

He pulls away, hands still imprisoning me. I kick him in the chest, and they tighten, the pain making me gasp.

"Why don't you want me to kiss you? Hmm?" he demands. "I know you liked it."

"Yeah, *liked*. I tried to kill you. How much more obvious do I need to make it?" I fight against his grip and he leans in harder, shaking his head slowly.

"You're confused. Your feelings are stained by fear." His face crumples. "Why are you so afraid of me?"

I'm about to tell him it's because of the Polaroid of me, just feet away, and what he did to me in the forest, but instead, I say, "I'm not afraid of you."

"Then prove it."

I don't react when he glides his lips over mine, stealing my breath in his mouth. I try to guide the knife back toward his face, but it's like arm-wrestling God. He releases my wrists once I drop the knife, the pressure on my wrist from his grip making it hard to hang on. One of his hands moves to cradle my face while the other touches my side. He shudders when I wrap my arms around his neck—mostly hoping I can choke him—and he pushes me back into the bed.

His icy lips aren't enough to numb the emotions, which come in an instant as if they've been poured on me from a hot vat. I keep my eyes tight and my hands in fists. A hot fire swells in my chest, my fingers itching to rip a chunk from his throat. I want to freak out, scream and kick until I can't feel anymore. As soon as I'm about to pull away and punch him, I find myself trying to hold back tears as his breath fills my lungs. Why can't I just fake my way through it? Why can't I just stop feeling like I usually do?

He's fucked my head up, has knocked holes in the emotional walls I worked so hard at building. He must have pushed out some of my sanity when he wedged himself into my life. Something happened when I met him, and the night he took me to the forest. It's like the overwhelming pain rattled my tightly knit barrier, the hallucinations lifting up shit that had taken so long to settle inside me. I feel the unstable girl I spent so long burying—the one I worked so hard to push down until she couldn't breathe, until she died, leaving me a bitter ghost of my past self—creeping up on me. I can feel her settling in now, the girl who'd break down in tears in the middle of class, who'd get so ireful she'd beat other students unconscious for smiling and not even remember it, who walked around like a psycho because she couldn't remember what emotions were, who refused to remember for fear of what they'd bring.

Perhaps being exposed to my past so brutally is why I'm cracking. The picture raising ample questions and the hallucinations from the forest could be to blame.

Denendrius shudders, his fingers finding their way under my shirt, tracing lines against my sides. I want to pull my lips from his, but if I do, he'll think I'm a coward.

I'm not a coward.

The walls close in on me, the emotions spinning tighter around me. Eventually, my mind blanks and my body stops responding. I curl myself into a ball, and he embraces me, pulling my back to his chest and holding me so tight it only encourages the feeling of suffocation.

My eyes are wide as his fingers stroke my face. He whispers how it's going to be okay and how he loves me. His attempts at consolation make me want to kick him away because I know nothing gets better. If no drug is enough to take it away, what can simple words from one of the reasons for my grief do?

My head on his bicep, his arm tucks under my jaw, and for a moment I think I'm being put in a headlock until it moves back. I yelp when his bleeding wrist moves toward my mouth.

"Will it turn me?"

When his sweet whisper comes, I hate how it still soothes me. "Only venom will. I promise it won't make you a vampire. It'll make you feel better. It's how I stopped you from overdosing."

Still, I stare at the wound in terror.

"Hurry, before it closes," he whispers, tucking his bleeding wrist against my lips. I try to move away, but there's nowhere to go.

His blood is already trickling into my mouth, so I'm not left with much of a choice. I panic and swallow, his cold blood spilling over my tongue and down the back of my throat.

The surprisingly pleasant taste is enough to banish my fear. It's not enough to make me drink willingly, but the feeling that washes over me when the flowery sweet taste of his blood enters me is.

I drink steadily when my hand traps his wrist against my mouth.

Heroin—that's the only thing I can compare it to, and even that isn't a good enough comparison. I feel like I've stepped into a replica of reality within myself, one where God himself lives, one without my body, where my muscles are softer than rose petals. It doesn't bring the warmth of opiates, but the cool chill brings a similar calming effect.

"Good girl," he murmurs, his fingers smoothing my hair.

But unlike heroin, my thoughts parade around my head dizzyingly instead of assuming form. It feels like I'm on the edge of falling asleep, a dream waiting for me to tumble into it. Aside from Denendrius and the task of drinking, I'm unable to align my thoughts. They twist together uncontrollably, the varied emotions of them blurring together until I feel absolutely nothing.

It's the purest feeling of insanity. It's the kind where you're screaming and laughing in a padded room, ripping at your own skin and clawing at anyone who comes near you. An eerie calm rides through the feeling with an empty clarity, like I'm thinking everything and nothing all at once. It comes with a strange element of control. Such a feeling would surely put me in a padded room if I was left to experience it in reality.

It's terrifying and wonderful at the same time. *And I like it.*

I feel unplugged when he pulls his wrist away. My thoughts return to normal, my own presence sinking back into me. Some of the calm remains, leaving the feeling of waking up well rested from a nap.

I remain lying on his arm, too comfortable to move. I gasp when the self-inflicted bite on his wrist heals before my eyes.

When I wake, I'm alone. I get up and attempt to call for Denendrius, but my throat itches with thirst. I go to the kitchen and twist so I can get my lips beneath the tap. A long string of cold water expunges the pain.

"Are you home?" I call.

I change quickly into a black halter top and blue jeans—disappointed when there isn't a long-sleeved shirt in the duffel bag—and use the bathroom. Scrubbing my hands until they're pink, I watch myself in the mirror, especially the dark purple bruises in the shape of fingers around my neck, over-lapping onto my collarbone. A small bruise has blossomed on my cheekbone too. Bruises are around my wrists from where he held them last night. A long string of profanity sprays from my mouth as I contemplate how to hide the ones on my neck.

When I exit the bathroom, which reeks of lavender soap, I wander toward the sliding glass door of the balcony. It screeches as if unopened in ages, and once it's slid open over the other pane of glass, enough to wedge myself between, my fingers are throbbing.

Leaving it open behind me, I saunter across the empty wooden balcony, pulling myself up and onto the flat railing, balancing on about half a foot of ledge. I run my fingers over the flaky dark brown paint.

"Jesus," a voice says. "Hey."

A girl in her midtwenties leans against the railing on the balcony next door. Fiddling with her long black hair, she rubs the variegated tattoos on her neck, a lit cigarette poised between two fingers in the opposite hand.

"Hey." I rearrange the hair around my shoulders in hopes of covering at least a small portion of the bruising.

She watches me in disbelief. "What's up with you two?"

"He loves me," I say in disbelief, needing to hear how crazy that is from someone else, even a stranger.

She waves her cigarette at me. "Nuh-uh, don't believe any of that shit. I see girls your age in and out of there occasionally, and trust me, I don't think they're having much fun. I have no idea what the fuck he did to his ex-girlfriends, but there's always a lot of crying and a lot of shouting. Trust me, he's a bad dude."

As if I needed someone else to tell me that. "You can hear everything?"

She flicks ash off the end of her cigarette. "Only the worst. These walls are thick—concrete, I think. Even if I could, someone's rap music or partying would probably drown it out. The guys above me used to party all day until the police raided them."

"Oh."

She finishes the cigarette and squishes it into a full glass ashtray, then opens a battered pack and offers me one as she lights another for herself.

I hop down and stumble a few feet before we both stretch across the gap. When I pull it back between my fingers—careful not to drop it—I place it between my lips and lean back over for her to light it. I take a long drag. I exhale and the smoke rushes past my lips, polluting the air around us.

"You ever talked to him?" I ask. "My . . . boyfriend."

She blows a stream of white through her frown. "Yeah . . . being his neighbor, I've run into him too many times. Nobody in this apartment building has had good run-ins with him. From what everyone says, he's an asshole. We steer clear, ignore him. Occasionally the police get called. I've never seen him in cuffs, though." She flicks the end of the cigarette and gray ash floats onto the mountain previously settled in the tray. Her brows pull together and she shakes her head. "He tried to force himself into my apartment one time. He thought it was the funniest fucking thing when I freaked out and started crying."

"What did he want?"

She shakes her head and swallows. "I don't know, but he beat Tommy black and blue—from 506—but he is annoying, so whatever. It's fucked up because he only cut him off going into the parking lot. Tommy is an asshole anyway." Something buzzes in her pocket before she can answer. She retrieves a cell phone. "Boyfriend," she clarifies as if I cared.

I take another drag. "Does he live with you?"

"Unfortunately. He's a pain in the ass. But I can't afford to pay rent myself, so I'm just waiting for him to get tired of me or until I can afford to move out. Letting him dump me instead of the other way around saves my stuff from getting smashed at least." She chuckles half-heartedly and I notice the scrapes down her arm.

I scowl when Denendrius calls my name.

"Shit," she whispers. "I'm warning you; get away from him. Your boyfriend is scary." She disappears back into her apartment.

When I try to get back into the apartment with my cigarette, Denendrius blocks the way. "Get rid of that thing."

I inhale as much as I can before he yanks it from my hand and flicks it off the balcony.

"Real fucking nice," I grumble, following him into the apartment.

"I'm taking you out for lunch." Denendrius holds the door open.

I slip my sneakers on and follow him out the front door while covering the bruises on my neck with my hands. He rolls his eyes at me, tells me how they should be the least of my worries, and grabs me, inflicting more pain.

The sun beams through the fingerprint-coated doors as we reach the main floor of the building. Denendrius pushes the door open and flinches as he steps back into the sunlight, though he's unscathed as we move quickly to the Mustang and drive away.

I cross my arms tightly over my chest, keeping my eyes on the buildings zooming by. *Get away from him*; it doesn't seem as easy as she makes it sound.

I remember drinking from him last night, hot anger

washing over me. What was I thinking? I feel shame when the thought of wanting more follows.

The date flashes on the dashboard, and I notice it's Monday and realize I'm missing a whole day.

Staring at him, I say, "Is your clock wrong?"

He glances it at it. "No."

"Are you sure? Where did a day go?"

He grumbles. "You didn't notice you were missing time yesterday?"

"Uh, no."

"Well, sweetheart, you slept through it."

What the fuck? His expression says he shouldn't be prodded, but I ask anyway. "How?"

"Healing takes time. I was trying to explain it all to you last night when you were throwing a tantrum," he says.

"*A tantrum*," I mutter under my breath, crossing my arms.

By the time Denendrius stops in the overcrowded parking lot of a diner, I've gone through dozens of scenarios where I try to escape. The only problem is they always end with me being found and either injured or killed.

I grunt and remove myself from the car. Denendrius waits at the hood, watching as if he's expecting me to run. I flinch as he grabs my hand and leads me through the doors of the diner.

Bells sound as we enter. I begin to slip my hand from his, but he tightens his grip. Get away as fast as I can? Not likely.

The place is hoarding people and commotion. Plates clatter and staff shout behind the counter in the kitchen. General chitchat and crying children fill the right side, where everyone is seated. We wait to be noticed by the hostess.

"Table for two?" a waitress with a face plagued with concern asks, grabbing two menus from the metal rack while refusing to remove her eyes from me.

"Yes." I guide Denendrius in her wake, watching her brown ponytail bob against the nape of her olive neck.

She gives us the table closest to the counter and I rip my hand from him like he's contagious. He doesn't hang on again, sitting down as I drag the chair from the table and sit on the bloated teal upholstery.

"My name is Kat and I'll be your server for today." She sets a menu in front of each of us. "What can I get you two to drink?"

"Nothing." Denendrius juts his chin toward me.

I think for a moment and feel her eyes tight on me, her gaze obviously trailing over my bruises.

I drop my hands to my lap. "Just water."

"Okay. Is ten minutes enough time to decide?"

"Yep," Denendrius snaps.

"Okay. I-I'll be back then." She walks away, stumbling over the foot of Denendrius's chair. She apologizes and backs away.

Denendrius pushes his menu away and reaches across to open mine.

"Pick something to eat," he commands. He removes his aviators from his jacket pocket and places them on his face.

"Why do you need to wear those indoors?" I deride.

"Shut your mouth and pick something to eat," he growls. He leans back in his chair, hooking his arm over the back.

The fire returns in my stomach, and I think about reaching across the table to slap him. "If you really loved me, you'd show me some fucking respect." My teeth crunch when I bite down in fury.

"I'd watch your temper. I'll shut you up in front of all these people."

I laugh. "You'll what? Hit me?" I lean back in the chair. "Give me another bruise. If you haven't noticed, one more won't make a difference."

"Keep tempting me, Marianna. You'll see."

We glare at each other in silence—me sometimes breaking away to search the menu—until he gives a warning glance and nods toward Kat. She's walking toward us, a glass of water in her hand. She makes a wide arc in the room so she doesn't pass directly beside Denendrius's chair. Kat sets the water in front of me, condensation dripping down the clear glass, puddling on the table.

Faking a smile, she mouths her concern to me: "Are you okay?"

Denendrius clears his throat. "She's ready to order."

Kat puts her pen to a notepad and smiles.

"I'll have the bacon burger and a cola."

"Make sure it doesn't take too long," Denendrius snaps.

She bites her lip and tells us she'll be back when it's ready, walking away.

I gawk at Denendrius. "Dude, what's your issue with servers? You're going to get my food spat in if you don't chill out."

He ignores me, watching Kat as she strolls back behind the counter. She leans through the gap in the wall, shouting the order to the cooks. She waits until the waitress giving her order is done, and then she turns to speak to her. I must have been spoken of because the other waitress sways to the side so she can look past Kat at me. Our eyes meet and she returns to talking to Kat.

"*I see what you mean,*" Denendrius voices, the words matching the movement of her lips.

The blond waitress tucks her ponytail behind her shoulder.

"*He must have hurt her. You should see how rough he's been with her since they've arrived. Shay, should we call the cops?*" Denendrius voices for Kat.

"*No.*" Denendrius chuckles. "*What would we tell them anyway?*"

"*I don't know, but she looks really hurt. What if she's been kidnapped? I don't want to see her picture on the news tonight, knowing I could have done something.*"

"Just leave it alone. It's none of your business. You always have a reason to complain about customers."

I pull my hands back to my lap and twist my fingers, wanting to jump on Denendrius and throttle him. I turn my face to him, my upper lip twitching slightly, brows pulled together.

"Shay's right. There is nothing Kat can do. There's nothing anybody can do."

I drop my gaze to the flecks of silver in the teal tabletop. "You're an asshole."

"You'll get used to it."

I consider scenarios to get away from him for the rest of the meal, but like before, none of them end in my favor. I could say I need to go to the bathroom, and if there's a window in there, I could break it and run away. But there's no doubt he would hear the glass shatter and meet me on the other side. So, what now? I think about what his neighbor said about waiting for her boyfriend to dump her instead. I digest her words and decide I have two options.

Option one is to keep trying to get away. Maybe if I try hard enough, I'll succeed. I'd finally be as free as I was before. I could go back to feeling nothing. But then there would always be the fear of "what if?" What if he finds me? What if he tires of my blatant attempts to escape and just kills me? How and where would I even hide?

Option two is playing along, waiting for him to grow tired of me until he moves on to another girl or until I find a way to get away for good before he has a chance to stop me. Giving in, letting things slide by, and changing how I react, all to seem like I'm playing along so he doesn't kill me in anger. Maybe if I stop making obvious attempts to flee, he'll calm down and won't expect it when I finally do.

I choose option two.

"I'm sorry," I mumble, ripping off a bite of my burger. There's no better time to start than now.

He's taken aback. "You're sorry? For what?"

I grind the meat between my teeth, my fingers tightening around the bun. I'm not sorry for anything. I never did anything to be sorry. "I'm sorry for everything, Denendrius. I've been such a bitch to you."

"I accept your apology."

I don a false smile and he grabs my hand under the table. I force the detainment of rude comments, the corners of my lips tightening.

I wonder if he knows I'm manipulating him. Does he even have a clue? And if he does, is he pretending like he doesn't?

We eat in silence, and I do my best not to meet his eyes while trying not to be obvious about what I'm doing. I glance around the diner, and on the other side of the black wicker divider, a handful of tables away, my eyes rest on a strange girl.

She's completely clothed in black and lace, a frumpy hat with wide trim covering most of the top half of her face.

I wonder if she's a vampire like Denendrius. She looks like she's from the Victorian era after all. But when her brown eyes shift toward mine for a quick moment, the idea slips away.

I look back to Denendrius but see the strange girl swiftly stand and disappear down the back hall toward the bathrooms.

The thought crosses my mind that I should follow her—that she might know something—and I jump on the urge before I lose my nerve. "Do you mind if I go to the bathroom?" I ask Denendrius.

"Go, then," he mutters.

I speed-walk to the back of the diner, ducking into the women's bathroom but finding it vacant. Opening the bathroom door as slowly as possible, I slip back into the hallway and try the only other door she could have gone through.

Stepping out into the shade of the rear parking lot, I

narrowly miss seeing her turn around the corner of the building.

"Wait," I call while running after her, trying to keep my voice low enough that Denendrius's might not notice, but she will.

But when I turn around the corner of the building, she's darting across the parking lot, her black clothes flitting behind her as she talks on a bright pink cell phone. Her head whips around wildly like she's looking for someone in a panic.

Part of me wants to chase after her, unable to shake the feeling that her leaving had something to do with me and Denendrius.

Instead, I return to the table. I can't tell if Denendrius is aware that I went outside or not when I sit down, his full expression hidden by his mirrored aviators.

I take a long sip of my cola before asking, "You said on our last date that you would tell me about you being sort of famous. Can you now?"

He folds his arms across his chest. "Famous probably isn't the right word."

I consider whether this is a topic I should prod at while I stir the ice in my cup with my straw. "Infamous . . .?"

Denendrius slides his sunglasses off his face, his flat expression unreadable as he stares at me while pulling in a long inhale.

I stop stirring and brace myself. "What?"

"Where do you want to go from here?" he asks, still stolid as he folds his sunglasses over the neck of his deep green T-shirt.

I cock my brow before I realize he's talking about leaving the diner and not of where I expect asking such questions might lead to. "Oh. To Pam's . . . please. She hasn't seen me in a few days, and I don't want her to report me missing. I'll just explain to her that I've been with my boyfriend." My stomach clenches at my usage of *boyfriend*.

Denendrius drives me without a fight, trying to convince me he just wants a normal relationship and that he loves me. Would there have been punches thrown if I hadn't apologized?

He tells me he'll see me tonight and asks what I'll be doing until then. I lean in through the driver's window to give him a quick kiss on the lips, for no other reason than to stop him from firing more questions I won't answer. I turn away and regret coats my stomach with a sickening slime.

XIII

The sun shines brightly across the yard, my feet thumping against the sidewalk. Water from the sprinkler next door looks iridescent as it arches through the sky and wind causes some of the droplets to shift across the green lawn and onto my flesh. The doorknob is dewy when I enter the house and look around for Pam.

I hasten to the stairs. When I ascend, the creaking startles Pam, who is cleaning the bathroom across from my room.

"Where the hell have you been?" she grumbles as she wipes down the mirror, leaving long streaks in the glass.

"I thought he came and told you," I say, hoping she knows I'm talking about Denendrius.

"Your boyfriend? He did, but he failed to mention you'd be gone for three nights. I agreed to you dating him, but I didn't fucking say you could start whoring around at night. And you're lucky your social worker didn't drop in like she's been hinting about. What the hell would I have told her?"

"I don't know." I slowly turn and back into my room. "You

could have told her I was out if you needed to. Make something up, you're good at that."

She grunts. "Jenna's been frantically calling for the past three days. Says she really needs to come over and talk to you."

Jenna? Why would she come to me to talk about her problems? Camille is the go-to girl when it comes to advice. She even insists we do, saying she needs extra practice for when she becomes a therapist one day. And not to mention I'm the person who would give wrong advice and get someone in trouble.

"I'll give her a call." I head back downstairs after throwing a gray hoodie on.

She follows me down the steps. "I'm carpooling to work today, so I have to leave soon. Do you think you can make sure Samantha and Charlie get something to eat when they get home before the babysitter picks them up?"

I huff. She finally got a babysitter? Did Charlie threaten to call his social worker? "I'm pretty sure Charlie can take care of himself and Samantha. They're not babies. Also, why don't *you* try feeding them for once?"

"Because I have to go to work."

"I'm not talking about today. You're never home, or you're locked in your room. God, I don't even know how they still let us live with you." It's not that I have a problem with taking care of them—I love those kids—it's just the principle. I'm not their parent, I shouldn't have to be.

"Hey, watch your mouth. I'm the only one who will put up with your shitty attitude. You can't blame the system when you're the only one stopping yourself. At least I'm not your mother."

"Wow. If it makes you feel any better, you're on the same list."

She shakes her head and walks off.

I plunk down on the love seat and snatch the telephone off

the side table, punching in Jenna's number. She answers on the first ring.

"Marianna?" Her voice cracks.

"Yeah, what's going on?" I pull my legs up and twist the cord in my other hand.

"Oh, thank God you're okay! I thought Sarah had you killed or something! Can I come over, like . . . right now?" she asks.

"Yeah." I know I shouldn't feel like my time is being wasted, her being my friend and all, but I can't take my mind off this situation with Denendrius.

"I'll be right over. Don't go anywhere," Jenna says.

"Meet me in my room."

"Okay."

I return to my room, flopping down on my futon and burying my head in the clean clothes, their scent stale. I try to think of what Jenna's problem could be, but knowing Jenna, it could be anything.

No more than twenty minutes later, she's stumbling into my room. As soon as the door shuts, she bursts into tears and drags herself to sit on the edge of my futon.

"I didn't know who else to talk to. I thought you'd be the only one who understands." Tears drip past her lips and drop from her chin.

I scuttle close to her, awkwardly wrapping my arm around her shoulder. "Well, I'm here. You can say anything you need to." Comforting, right? I'm sure I've heard Camille say it at some point to one of us.

"I don't want to say it." She breathes a ragged breath, wiping tears from her eyes.

"Well, just do it really fast," I suggest.

"I've been shooting up." She sniffs and pulls her arms close to her.

My brows lift, eyes widening. "What? *Why?*"

She rubs her face. "I don't know. Between you and Beth

being hooked, I know I shouldn't . . . but I missed her, so I went and started looking around her room and I found a couple vials and I couldn't help myself."

Beth—her twenty-year-old sister—overdosed on Dilaudid six months ago. I got high with her once when I went over looking for Jenna and she wasn't home, but I haven't been eager to tell her about it since Beth's death. "Jenna . . ."

Her shoulders slump. "I know."

"Do you need a number for rehab or something?" I'm not sure what other help to offer her. I'm not exactly a shining example.

She grimaces as she says, "I was hoping you could give me Manny's number, or one of the other dozen drug dealers you know."

I gape. "Jenna! Come on."

"I'm sorry, Marianna, but it's helping me get through this!"

I roll my eyes. "Yeah, until you overdose."

"Matt from Home Economics taught me how to shoot up. I'm not just jabbing myself silly," she says. "He says legs are a safer place."

My jaw drops. "What, no! And Matt from—dude, I went to juvie with that kid and he could barely string his shoelaces when he got out."

Three years ago, when I was fourteen, was the last time I went to the juvenile detention center. I stole a bait car and tried to outrun the police. It didn't work out well, and Sarah was in the passenger seat of her father's cruiser when he pulled me over. Thankfully, he had another officer take me to the station.

"Are you going to help me or not?" she whines.

"Uh, no."

Her eyes slowly close and she sighs. "Fine, I'll just get it myself."

"Jenna, don't act stupid. What will you do once you're face-down in an alley? Don't you remember my last relapse? Daina had to steal her dad's car so you guys could dump me on the sidewalk in front of the emergency room. Do you want that to be you?"

She wipes a tear.

"You have to get help," I insist, even though it's not even the first thing on my list. "Before you're too far gone."

She shakes her head. "I can't tell anyone else."

"What else can I do to help, then?" I ask. "Because I'm not helping you get drugs."

She stands. "Nothing," she whispers. "I'll just go home. You obviously can't help me, so I may as well leave." She backs toward the door, making a please-stop-me-from-leaving face.

"Wait," I groan. I rummage through a nearby box to pull out a red switchblade, pressing it into the palm of her hand. "I know you're going to look for drugs on your own, so here. Protect yourself at least."

Her eyes fall to the ground and she shoves it into her pocket. "I'll stop soon," she promises.

I shake my head. "Jenna, I've literally said the same thing to you."

"I'm going to go now," she whispers. "My parents don't know I'm skipping school."

"Just be smart," I say.

We say goodbye to one another, and she's out the door. I'm left stunned, unsure of what to do with myself.

Needing escape, I sneak downstairs and grab the keys to Pam's convertible, the nicest thing she owns. With a plan to cruise around the city until the car slurps the gas tank dry, I slip outside and into the garage and crank the keys in the ignition. I back out of the driveway, tires spinning skillfully onto the road.

I learned to drive when I was eleven. My brothers in Red

Revenge would take me with them when they went out to boost cars and showed me the ropes. I was shorter, a smaller target, and since I was so young, I wouldn't be in as much trouble if caught. I was only ever caught once, but it made me better.

After an hour of driving and singing along to the radio, a new nice neighborhood appears in front of me. It's barely connected to Lorimer, attached by a single road, just off the highway that leads into the city.

It sits at the edge of the forest, and a road—where I speed along—divides the neighborhood from the trees. I slow.

The homes are all unique and must have cost a fortune. The yards are a perfect sheet of green grass, little kids out and playing on many of them. Sunshine and happy families, blue skies reaching to the universe, it makes me feel ill. Makes me wish I had been born to one of those families. Maybe then, I would have learned to smile when I was a child.

I stomp the brake, park, and turn the convertible off. I grab a dollar bill from the cupholder and walk toward a lemonade stand managed by two blond children, wanting a slice of their life for just one moment. The boy capers to meet me at the sidewalk.

"Are you going to buy some of our lemonade?" He runs back behind the stand, pushing the blond-haired girl from the center.

"Yeah, as long as you didn't spit in it," I tease dryly.

He picks up a plastic cup and the little girl grabs the pitcher and smiles, pouring the bright yellow lemonade. "I didn't! I promise!"

"One dollar!" the little girl says cheerfully, giving me a toothy grin as the boy hands me the cup.

A bogus smile twitches on my lips as I press the dollar bill into her hand a little too roughly. She doesn't seem to notice, though; she just shows it to the boy and they discuss toys far too expensive for it to cover.

I wonder what it's like to be young and have such high aspirations.

"You're their first customer," a woman's voice calls from behind them.

I look up to see a woman in her early thirties pulling two deck chairs from a yellow shed. The color matches my lemonade and the house.

"It's hot. Come have a seat?" she offers with a smile, unfolding the chair. "I need an excuse to stop gardening."

"Sure," I say, far from eager to get back to Denendrius. "I could use the distraction too." The grass tickles my ankles, the smell filling my nose with a sickening smell of happiness as I plop down in the deck chair. It belches a sound like cracking ice when I sit.

"I'm Carol Greene." She smiles as if I'm her favorite person in the entire world. She unfolds the other chair, placing it across from mine. She sighs and sits, tucking her fluffy fiery-orange hair behind her ears.

"Marianna."

An odd expression crosses her pale freckled face before she plasters a smile back on. "Those two are Julie and James, my foster kids. Cutest twins you will ever see."

I take a sip of the lemonade, let the bittersweet taste roll over my tongue and around my teeth, then swallow. "They're cute."

"So how old are you?" she pries while fidgeting with a pale-colored pant leg.

"Seventeen."

"You're not in school?"

I shake my head and suck another mouthful of lemonade. I wait for a lecture about how education is the key to a good life and other bullshit. But all I get is, "Oh."

I chug the rest of the lemonade.

"Your, um—parents?—don't care?" She readjusts in her chair and gives me an apologetic look, for the question, I think.

"I'm in foster care too," I say bluntly. I crush the cup in my hand, my mind replacing it with a neck.

"Yeah?" She blows air through a little hole she forms with her lips.

I press my lips together as she gets up to answer a ringing phone in the house. She paces in the small living room as she talks, visible through the window. She goes to walk back to the kitchen but stops abruptly, her head snapping toward the photo frames on the fireplace mantel. She says one last thing into the phone before hanging up and looking back toward me.

I freeze, ready to flee. I can tell she's comparing me to something in the photograph. Her mouth hangs open, a look of oh-my-God strikes her, and she runs to the front door.

I bolt across the lawn, the thought of my picture in Denendrius's dresser aggravating fear inside me.

"Marianna! Wait! Please!"

But I don't listen. I cram the key into the ignition and speed away, spinning back onto the road. Whatever is in the picture, I don't want to know. I've got enough bullshit to deal with already. I toss the lemonade cup out the window and pound the gas pedal, turning back into the city.

Police and ambulance sirens wail, the emergency vehicles blocking off the intersection I need to get back to Pam's. Police reroute traffic onto a road I've always specifically avoided.

I catch sight of a kid lying in the road as I'm forced to turn. I'm unsure if he's dead or not as a pool of blood and paramedics surrounds him.

After passing a few cul-de-sacs, a park and a few convenience stores, I finally find a road I can turn onto. It's a dicey street to be on, but at least it's not Red Revenge territory. I'd put the top of the convertible up to hide better if it wasn't broken.

I drive through the parking lot of a gas station and hit the gas when I spot a familiar double-R tattoo on the face of a man sitting alone in a black SUV.

The vehicle takes off after me, and I wonder if I can get far enough ahead of him to get home and grab my gun before he reaches me. I'd keep driving in hopes of losing him, but I know too well how hard that will be, especially when the car is nearing empty.

Fuck.

I remember how all this started, how I used to wander around the streets alone. I was almost eleven, tagging a fence, when a couple of members from Venganza Roja—Red Revenge —asked if I wanted to hang out with them.

They constantly talked about a war that could cause our extinction in Lorimer if we didn't fight back. It was hard not to believe them when they were dying around me. One day, they passed me a black 9mm Beretta and told me to come back with an empty clip and a rival flag if I wanted to be part of the family.

I wanted a family, so a few other recruits and I left eagerly.

When I came back with a bloody bandana, I didn't question whether or not I had done something wrong. My new family said they were proud of me, that I'd proved my ability to protect myself and those around me. It seemed like a good thing to me.

And time after time, they protected me, and I protected them. I tried to make sure they never forgot my value.

But like good things tend to do, it went wrong.

Venganza Roja was founded a few years prior to my joining, a response to the slaughter of members from the main gang founded decades ago. We were just one of many sets to show up across the country with ties to places like Mexico and Colombia. We proved our name true and quickly removed our competition.

Before long, the police were catching on to us. I was distracted. We were getting ready to switch gang houses. I miscounted the product, a horrible mistake to make. Carlos was the boss. He blamed me for stealing blow and selling it on my own. He was high and wouldn't listen to anything I said, wouldn't let me "waste time" by recounting.

He dragged me downstairs, zip-tied me to a chair, and beat me. I was made an example of and left for two days.

Julio was Carlos's second. He counted again and tried to explain things to Carlos, but he wouldn't listen and said he was going to sell me until he got the missing numbers back, then he was going to have me sent overseas.

Julio freaked out and came down to get me. The rest of the gang wanted me dead, said I didn't deserve special treatment. When a fight broke out between Carlos and Julio, I picked up a gun and unloaded on Carlos. Julio said it needed to happen, that Carlos was becoming a liability. He thought Carlos was responsible for the heat on us.

Julio took his place, but the gang thought he was too soft and wanted me dead. They weren't willing to settle for dismissal. Julio tried to argue that I'd done what was best for the family, that Carlos would have made us a prison gang with the way things were going. He was convinced I was still an asset, but most of the gang only saw betrayal.

And as always, they kept true to their name. Last I heard, Julio found himself in Mexico with a missing head, leaving me to be killed on sight.

I spin around a corner and hit the gas, putting as much space between us as I can.

I unhook my seat belt as I race down the road to the house. I'd keep driving, try to lose him, but he'd likely call for backup. Knowing them, I'd end up cornered in an alley with no weapon to protect myself. Or worse, dragged back to the gang house, where they'd do only God knows what to me. I'd have no chance.

Denendrius's car is in the driveway—a godsend—and I pull in beside it, hollering his name at the top of my lungs as I scramble over the car door. I dart across the grass, hoping I can get inside before the gangster gets out of the vehicle or starts shooting.

XIV

I'm thankful for Denendrius's enhanced hearing. The front door swings open, Denendrius's eyes darting around the front lawn and stopping on the black SUV as it jerks to a halt in front of the house. Toting his gun, the man rushes from the SUV and across the law, aiming at me.

Denendrius shoves me behind him, and I'm perfectly fine with using him as a bullet shield.

"Move unless you wanna get shot too," he snarls at Denendrius, finger stiff on the trigger. "Marianna, you're coming back with me or you'll get a bullet next."

"Get back in your vehicle," Denendrius says evenly. "Go on."

I lean out from behind Denendrius. "Yeah, run back home to the rest of your useless brothers before he shoves that gun up your ass."

Denendrius lifts his arm in front of me and I straighten back behind him when I find the gun directed past him and in my face.

"Get back in your car, and leave," Denendrius warns.

When he lifts the gun, there's only a few inches between the barrel and Denendrius's face. "Or what, *pendejo*?"

"Get back in your car, and leave, or you'll find out what I'll do." As Denendrius speaks, the gangster's face adopts a blank and blinkless look.

To my astonishment, he lowers his gun and shoves it in the waist of his jeans, walking back to his SUV while hollering in Spanish at me. "We ain't done with you yet, *puta!*" he yells before climbing back in and speeding away.

Denendrius is smiling when he turns around, steps bringing him back toward the house.

"How the fuck did you make him do that?" I demand in awe while jogging after him up the concrete steps.

"Hypnotism," he says simply.

"*Hypnotism?* You tried that with me," I accuse, shutting the door behind us.

His brown brows twitch upwards and I try to lift my head to challenge his condemning eyes better but can't.

"It doesn't work?" I ask, the answer to my question stalled by Samantha's inquiry about whether her peanut butter and jelly sandwich is done yet as we step into the kitchen.

Denendrius hums for a moment as he returns to a plated half-made sandwich on the dirty counter. "No," he says to me as he picks up the knife and spreads jelly on the bare slice of bread before putting both sides of the sandwich together and cutting it in half.

I wish he would give me more than that, so I don't feel like I'm playing twenty questions. "Why?"

The muscle in his jaw tightens and his shoulders jerk in a shrug. "I don't know. It's always worked on everyone else." A smile breaks his seriousness and he touches my cheek. "It must mean you're special."

When he passes by me to return to the living room, I cross

my arms and scowl while I watch the kitchen door swing back and forth in the doorway.

It takes me a moment to bypass the gang drama to acknowledge that Denendrius has been here *alone* for however long with my little foster sister.

With a furrowed brow and hesitant steps, I wander back into the living room. Denendrius and Samantha sit on the couch on the right wall, her face already covered in a mixture of jelly and peanut butter as she watches a fairy-tale film on the old screen. With a fair distance between us, I plunk down on the couch beside him and cross my legs.

"Why are you here?" I ask him.

He stares at me as if I asked him a question with an obvious answer. "Waiting for you to get back from your *escapade.*" With a forced smile, he adds, "The better question is, *why weren't you* here?"

The look in his eyes makes me swallow.

He's stiff, his motions agitated as he forcefully sits back against the couch. "I came back to get you, and Samantha was here all alone with the door unlocked, hungry and bored, for any sick man to find her. I thought I'd look out for her while I waited."

Does he not realize he's the sick man in his described scenario?

My eyes narrow as I look her over, but it seems like the only thing that has attacked her is her own food.

"Charlie should be home soon," I say.

He smiles. "Good, then you're coming home with me when he does."

An hour later, Charlie is trudging through the front door. He slings his backpack off his shoulder and onto the floor before staring at Denendrius.

"Hi," he greets us, unsure eyes switching between Denendrius and me.

"Hey there, Charlie," Denendrius says as he stands, a sly smile on his lips.

When Denendrius waves me to my feet, I don't dare make a fuss in front of my foster siblings, not wanting to subject them to the violence that would ensue if I refused to go.

I say a quick goodbye to Samantha and Charlie, Denendrius rushing me out and to the car.

The gentle demeanor he used around my foster siblings disappears as soon as we're alone in the car together.

"Where'd you go?" he demands, placing his mirrored aviators on his face before backing out of the driveway. "You never said anything about leaving your foster mother's house."

I kick my feet up on the dashboard and cross my arms. "It's almost like you're not the fucking boss of me, hey?"

The corner of his lip lifts as he glances at me. "*Almost.*"

Gritting my teeth, I stare at the old buildings as we drive by, my head pounding.

"You know, you were very nearly killed," he scolds. "You shouldn't have left the house. Did Jenna convince you to go?"

I shoot a lethal glare at him. "No, she didn't."

He tests his grip on the wheel. "Hm. Well, her scent was in your room. It was only a few hours old, so . . ."

"She didn't!" I growl.

He tsks. "If your friends are going to be a problem—"

I jolt upright in my seat and tighten my fists on my lap. "Don't you dare hurt my friends."

His laugh is one of disbelief. "Well, Marianna, if you're going to allow your friends to come between us—"

"They won't," I insist. I lean my head back against the seat and close my eyes, refusing to say another word until we're at the apartment.

The rest of our night is viciously tense, my muscles sore from sitting rigid through the horror movies he selects for us.

Having to calculate every thought and breath around him is exhausting, and I find myself fighting to stay awake.

When he does decide we should sleep, I'm forced into the same awkward sleeping situation as the previous night. Tucked under the blankets beside him with a stomach full of his blood again, I find myself resisting the urge to close my eyes until I'm sure his won't be opening anytime soon.

The careful closing of the front door on the other side of the closet draws me from my sleep, and I find Denendrius missing from the bed beside me.

"Where did you go?" I ask as I stumble from the bedroom, rubbing my eyes.

He ignores me, placing a knife on the counter before turning to the sink to wash the blood from his face.

I peer at the knife more closely, then at his bloodied appearance. My stomach burns.

"You killed her?" I scream, unable to remove my eyes from the knife I gave Jenna.

He turns around and smiles, which releases another shade of anger into my blood. I shove him, and something in his eyes flares. He shoves back, sending me into the wall.

"Yeah, she's probably dead by now."

"Why? Why her? Out of all the fucking people in the world! You have to pick my friend?"

He sighs. "They're just people, Marianna. It doesn't matter. You have no need for friends now that you have me. They're merely getting in the way."

I spit something angry and unintelligible, jumping at him. He pushes me back against the wall.

"You killed her to hurt me, didn't you?"

He grins, shrugs. I leap at him again, trying to hook him in the throat with my fist. He spins me into a choke hold, laughing.

"You fucking leave my friends out of this. She did nothing to you," I spit.

"She didn't have to do anything," he whispers in my ear, his arm constricting. "I have no current plans to kill the rest of your friends—unless someone was to tempt me . . . hmm?" He throws me back against the wall, pinning me with his forearm against my throat. "Maybe you need to start listening better! I was nice enough to let you go home for a bit. But I didn't say you could leave, did I? No. You had to run off and nearly got yourself shot. What if I hadn't been there waiting for you yet? What if you had died, gotten kidnapped? You need to grow up and start thinking about us!"

Us?

My laugh is flat. "I don't see many threats aside from you."

He shakes his head, eyes heavy with sadness. "Marianna, I just want what is best for you. That's what love is."

I struggle against his grasp, failing. "Take me to her," I demand. "If you love me, you'd let me see her."

He measures my expression. "Why?"

So I'll know for sure if she's dead, so I'll have a chance to save her if she isn't. *So at least I tried.*

"Please, Denendrius. Just . . . *please*?"

He steps back, groans. "Fine, but I don't want to hear any wallowing afterward."

I bite my cheek, trying to push my anger away so I don't do anything to make him change his mind.

I slip into my sneakers and follow Denendrius from the apartment. He keeps a close eye on me as we walk down the stairs, my steps heavy. My skin pricks when we step into the chill of the night, the roads only occupied by the yellow glow of streetlights.

Dark cloaks the sky when we dip into the car. I pull my

knees up to my chest, wrapping my arms around them so I don't kick the shit out his dashboard.

We drive in silence, the only sound between us the hiss of heat from the vents.

After about fifteen minutes, he pulls into a dark alley, headlights illuminating the center of it, the building walls dark.

He opens the car door and exits. I don't move, not sure if I can. I feel weighted, permanently stuck to the seat, and my anger has been replaced by a cold, sweaty fear.

"Coming?" he asks.

I swallow, my arms suddenly sore as I reach for the handle. The car door is heavier than usual, and my legs are fuzzy when I step onto the gravel.

My breath escapes me, my heart hammering so fast I'm afraid it'll cease.

I follow him a handful of steps before he points out a pair of pink shoes a few yards ahead, illuminated by the headlights.

My legs carry me to her before I even think of it. They give out when I reach Jenna, my fingers hesitating over her for a moment as I sit in a heap next to her.

"Jenna?" I manage to say.

When she doesn't respond, I drag her from the shadows and into the light, her flesh still warm.

My chest tightens, shaky fingers searching her bloodied wrist for a pulse. I notice then how I'm sitting in a pool of blood. Her wrists are sliced vertically, an unfamiliar knife in her other hand.

"Suicide." Denendrius tsks from behind me, his voice a million miles away.

I pull her head into my lap, searching her unbitten neck for a pulse instead. *Nothing.*

"I mean, I told her to. You know how convincing I can be . . . it's not like she had a choice."

Her empty eyes bore into mine, my heart feeling as gashed

as her arms. I lay her back down, my hands moving to her chest. I try to pump life back into her, refusing to add her to my list of dead friends.

My hair swings, stray strands catching in my wet eyelashes as silent tears stream down my face.

"There's no blood left in her body to pump," Denendrius says.

My angry huff turns into a strangled sob and I collapse on her chest, my face buried in her purple sweater.

"I'm so sorry, Jenna," I whisper into her chest.

I want to tell her how I never wished for any of this to happen, how if I'd known, I would never have left the house. I would have begged her to stay there with me. We could've talked more and maybe I could've convinced her not to go looking for drugs, to go home and talk to her parents so they wouldn't have to hear how their daughter was found dead in an alley.

"You're going to have to get used to dead people, Marianna. One day, everyone you love will die. Many times, it will be your fault, like now. You must stop caring. It's only you and me now."

If seeing my friends get shot and stabbed in the hood when I was young didn't stop affecting me then, there's no chance of my ever getting used to it now. Each death of a friend is always as surprising and as gut-wrenching as the last.

"I wouldn't be too upset about it, sweetheart. She would have overdosed soon anyway. Don't worry, I got your knife back for you at least."

My muscles tense. My clenched teeth induce a headache. I look over my shoulder to retort, but a flash of black behind the car stops me.

He stiffens, face falling flat. "Time to go."

I shake my head madly as he walks toward me, my fingers tightening on her clothing.

"No," I gasp. "I'm not leaving her here like trash."

He reaches for me and I duck from his grasp.

"She's coming with us!" I shout.

"Not happening. The last thing I need is a corpse stinking up our place."

I slap his outstretched hand away. "Please, we can dump her at the emergency room."

He scoops me up around the waist, ripping my fingers from her clothing.

"No!" I shriek, writhing. "Denendrius, no! We can't leave her—"

His hand clamps over my mouth. I scream angrily into his palm as he carries me away, unfazed by my flailing limbs.

He dumps me in the passenger seat, appearing in the driver's before I have time to move. The car tires squeal as he backs up, rocks kicking up.

He reverses left onto the main road. I duck as the back window shatters, expecting the sound of gunshots. None come. The Mustang rips away, Denendrius mumbling under his breath. I look back, expecting to find whatever came through the window in the back seat, but there's nothing amongst the shards of glass. The doors lock, the speedometer quickly climbing into dangerous numbers.

"What's going on?" I ask carefully.

He doesn't look at me, his eyes shifting from the mirrors to the windows and roads. "Quiet, I need to concentrate."

He quickly swerves around something I can't see, sending me into the door.

"Seat belt," he warns.

I swallow and pull the thing on. A thud sounds on top of us and in the same moment, Denendrius pulls the emergency brake. The air is knocked out of me as the seat belt locks, a screeching sound making me clamp my teeth. The Mustang jolts forward as he hits the gas again. When my eyes adjust, I see five lines across the windshield. They look like they were carved by fingernails.

A figure appears in the headlights for barely a moment before disappearing.

"Was that a—"

"Yes," he says.

Vampire.

Somehow, the likelihood of encountering other vampires in Lorimer never really occurred to me.

I sink into the seat, eyes wide on the road.

"What does he want?" I ask, my voice shrill.

"To kill me."

My eyebrows lift. "Why?"

He tsks. "I may have pissed a few people off over the years."

I gape at him. Apparently infamous was the right word to call him.

A grin breaks across his face. "Okay, a lot of people want to kill me."

He whips around a corner, nearly hitting a woman crossing the street.

"How many people?" I ask in alarm.

He glances at me, face serious. "Well, this isn't the first time this has happened."

"No?" Of fucking course not.

"Only enough that it's starting to get aggravating."

"Oh!" I exclaim. I lean my head back and take a calming breath.

His eyes harden. "That's why I don't want you out of my sight. Who knows what they'd do to you to get back at me?"

I have to pay for his problems? Comforting. I dig my nails into the leather. "And why does this guy want to kill you?"

His loud laughter is abrupt, startling me. "Who knows? My head is worth a lot of money."

I clasp my hands to the sides of my face, heart racing. I don't want to be on the receiving end of whatever vengeance he has waiting for him.

"What did you do?" I demand.

"I don't have nearly enough time to answer that."

I gape. "Denendrius, have you ever thought about not purposely pissing people off?"

He glowers. "Marianna, immortality can get boring. What else am I supposed to do?"

Read? Play Scrabble?

He stops the car in the middle of the road, grabbing my arm.

"What's wrong?" I whisper.

"I don't know where he went . . ." He hits the gas, spins down an alley, and parks. "I'm getting out."

I'm not sure whether or not to protest, unsure of how safe I am alone in the car. He gets out before I can say anything, walking toward something past the hood of the car.

The Mustang jerks, windshield shattering around me. Denendrius lies on the hood of the car, the metal crumpling on impact. When he stands, Denendrius spins a man into where he landed, bones crunching under his grip. The man shrieks, black eyes wide.

I jump sideways when the passenger door opens. It slams shut, the offender pinned to the door by Denendrius. The man from the hood of the car wobbles, his left arm a twisted mess.

There's a gurgling noise, blood drizzling down the passenger window and staining the pink T-shirt of the person pressed against it.

Denendrius disappears, and so does the man from the hood of the car.

I peer through the streaks of blood, barely making out the image of a blond woman lying on the ground, a hole in her chest and fang marks in her throat.

I yelp when the car shifts, the man pressed into the hood as he claws behind him at Denendrius. He sinks his fangs into the man's neck as he holds him down with his bloody hands. I'm doubtful that the man could still be alive, especially when Denendrius forces his hand inside his chest and dislocates his heart from his body.

He looks up at me and frowns, blood smeared across his mouth. "Look what they did to the Mustang!" He throws the heart into the shadows of the alley.

I take a shaky breath as he walks toward the car. He slumps into the driver's seat and sighs.

I'm at a loss for words. Trying to comprehend what I saw, I stare.

He smiles at me as he wipes the blood from his face. "Aside from them wrecking my car, that was fun, right?"

I swallow. "Fun? We could've died."

He laughs. "They were only a few decades old; they didn't stand a chance."

Eyes flitting to the girl on the ground, I say, "Did you—did you drink their *blood*?"

His lids drop over half his eyes, malevolence filling them as they pierce me. I wait for him to say something, but he doesn't.

I run my hands over my bare arms and lean away from him. "What do we do with the bodies?"

His demeanor shifts and he acts as though he wasn't about to crawl out of his skin and into mine. He cranks the car into drive, and it makes a grinding noise. "Their bodies will burn up when the sun touches them at first light."

I wrangle my breath into something that isn't near hyperventilation as he backs up and starts down the road.

He runs his bloodied fingers through my hair, pulling me toward him to kiss my temple. He grins, eyes bright. "I'm sure all that excitement made you forget about Jenna, right?" He snickers.

Storm clouds drift into my mind, my lips curling. I pull away from him and cross my arms.

"Oh, come on," he laments.

He reaches out to touch me and I lean against the door.

Denendrius punches the horn. "Seriously, Marianna? I just saved our lives and ruined my car in the process, and you're still going to act like this?"

I look away from him.

He roars. "Okay, then. What do I have to do to finally please you?"

I look at him in disbelief, my frustration like lightning strikes inside my skull. Do I really have to explain myself?

He spins into the apartment parking lot and parks, turning the battered vehicle off.

I rip the door open and head wordlessly toward the apartment, sunrise spinning at the edges of the sky as I practically stomp over the sidewalk.

He follows in my wake, shouting at me to stop ignoring him, which I continue to do as I race up the steps two at a time. I want nothing more than to hide in the bed with a blanket wrapped around me to block away the world.

I only stop for him to unlock the door, twisting into the apartment as he tries to reach out to me again. He stands in the entryway, waiting for me to shut the door.

He glares. "Do not slam that door."

I kick it into the frame just to make him mad, the force shaking the walls.

His jaw locks, teeth bared.

Racing toward the bedroom, he appears in front of me.

"You need to calm down," he snarls, forearms pressed into the door frame.

I punch him in the throat, but only I receive the pain of the blow.

His lip twitches. "You want to lock yourself in the

bedroom?" He grabs me by the arm and flings me toward the bed. "Fine, then!"

I land on the floor. Before I can get up, the door slams and bolts shut from the other side. The sound of the locks twisting makes me snap, and I leap up, throwing myself into the door as I banshee-scream. Maybe it's the fact I spent most of my childhood locked in a bedroom that makes me scream and fight against the door like a dog on crack.

I try to snap the knob, kick the door down, and uselessly threaten him as he stands on the other side, laughing. The door is solid, though, and even though I end up bruising myself, I keep trying to knock it down. Darkness and crimson struggle to take over my sight as I repeatedly hurl my body into it.

I think of climbing out the window, but he'd have me in a headlock before I fully slide it open.

Nausea wrings my stomach and the world shifts. I'm lying on the floor then, staring up at the ceiling while feeling like I've been hit by a truck. My adrenaline has dissipated into a thick sludge.

The door opens slowly. Denendrius stands above me.

I stare at him with heavy eyes, wondering what happened.

He grins. "You knocked yourself out."

I moan, body throbbing. I wait for fury to pour back into me again, for me to leap up and begin screaming all over again, but I feel used up. I can't make myself move.

At this point, I don't know how to feel anymore. Angry? Upset? I search myself for some sort of sorrow, but I can't find any emotion inside me unless exhaustion counts. It's odd, how fast I go from being angry to not knowing how I feel.

I decide I don't want to think about her anymore. I can't.

"I want to go back to sleep," I whisper, hoping I can pass out again before the tears start. He'd never let me live it down if I cried.

I wince as he brushes my hair from my face.

"Okay," he says.

XV

The photograph of my younger self creeps out from his dresser and into my mind while I sleep. In my dreams, Denendrius is my friend, thoughtful and kind instead of a raging madman.

He sneaks into my room one day while my mom is out turning tricks and whisks me away forever. The photograph of me is from a carnival that stopped in Lorimer. I dream that my life was just one excruciating nightmare, the truth being that I grew up happily in his care.

Still wrapped in my vivid dream, I wake up to the smell of oatmeal on the stove and Denendrius quietly making noise in the living room. I crawl out of the bed and go to find him, the snowflakes on my baby-blue pajamas nowhere as beautiful as the ones that layer the balcony.

He smiles when I enter the living room. He's sitting at a real Christmas tree, rearranging presents and wiping pine needles into a pile.

He kisses me as I sit beside him, and it's not weird because growing up I always had a crush on him, and he was only ever my best friend. He never got older, just me. He stayed beautiful and he was so nice that nothing got in the way of me noticing it, and when I got older, he noticed how beautiful I became too.

Denendrius wakes me up, for real this time. The haze of the dream doesn't fade right away as he asks how I slept.

When I tell him about the dream I had, he looks away to the window, and I must still be half-asleep because his eyes are lost. He excuses himself from the room.

I follow when I hear the balcony door open. His back is to me as he leans his arms against the railing. I place my arms on the rail a few feet from him, the old wood scraping my flesh. He doesn't look at me, eyes hard on the overgrown grass of the abandoned property filled with broken concrete walls across the road.

He looks different this morning, more familiar even. But maybe it's just the novelty of the dream still in place.

The skin on his hands reddens like a sunburn.

"You okay?" I ask, the sun warm on my face.

"I'm worn out," he breathes. "I've been so worried about you that I'm feeding half as much as I usually do, hence why you were able to stab me."

I try to remember the last time I ate and can't.

The dream replays in my head. It's odd how it feels like I've known him for years. It makes me think of the Polaroid of me in his drawer. I take a deep breath. "How long have I known you? There's a picture of me in your dresser." I expect my voice to shake. It doesn't.

Finally, he looks at me. "You really don't remember me, do you?"

I shake my head.

He sighs. "When you were five years old, your adoptive parents brought you to Enchanted Land in California. I happened to be there too. I was approached by a woman who said you were lost. She gave me your photo and told me if I saw you, to notify security. Being the Good Samaritan I am, I decided I would be kind and find you for them."

I gawk at him, mouth agape, no recollection of his story aside from my vague dreams of having a new family as a child. I step back, appalled that he'd twist the information I confided in him. "You're lying! I didn't tell you about my dream as a child so you could spin some bullshit with it!"

He does a double take at my accusation.

"For starters," I begin, teeth clenched, "I lived with my mother until I was nine! It was a consistent nine years of hell! I'm damn sure I would remember something as nice as going to Enchanted Land!"

"I'm not lying." I can hear the fury in his voice, how he's trying to contain it. But I don't care. "You didn't dream it, Marianna. It was real."

I shove him in the shoulder, and he grabs my wrist.

His fingers tighten when I try to pull from his grip.

"You're sick. Why can't you just tell me the truth? Why make up some stupid lie?" I snarl.

He drags me back into the apartment and to the bedroom, shoving me toward the bed before turning to the dresser.

Denendrius rustles around in another drawer before dropping onto the bed beside me with a camcorder. He shoves a tape in it and demands I look at it. Growling, I snatch the bulky camcorder, flip the screen open and press play. The tape makes an unhealthy noise as white and black stripes dance on the screen. After a few seconds, a picture comes to life with a date stamp from 1996.

"*Hi*" is the first thing I hear. It's me. I'm wearing the same blue dress as in the picture. "*Now you say hi, Den.*" I want to look away. I don't want to be reminded of my childhood, of the weak little girl who couldn't stop crying, who couldn't deal with anything.

The shot turns to Denendrius and he waves. I'm surprised to find he looks exactly the way he does now. His aviators are even similar. I listen intently to the rest of the video, further questions drowning my mind at the mention of a woman named Vianna. The video shows him taking me on rides, buying me blue cotton candy and toys, until it abruptly ends. It verifies everything he said.

But by the end of it, I'm fuming. I throw the camcorder on the floor and go to leave Denendrius's bedroom. He appears in the doorway. I scream and kick at his shins as I try to push past him.

"I'm going to kill you if you don't move!" I bellow as I reach for his neck. He blocks my reach a couple more times before shoving me in the shoulders. "Don't touch me!"

"Then calm down!" he commands, shoving me again. "I'd rather not have you black out again."

"Don't—"

He shoves me back again.

"I swear to fucking God—"

And again. But this time he laughs. He pushes me again. "Why are you so angry?" he demands.

"I hate you!" The sound comes from behind bared teeth.

"That's not why." His smile widens. "Why are you so angry?"

Hate, anger, I can't tell the difference. I spring at him again, cursing. All I know is I want him dead, right now, *by my hands*. I start throwing punches and kicking. I think about grabbing my knife and stabbing him repeatedly until somehow, he dies. For killing Jenna, for fucking my life up. He deserves it.

"Want me to tell you what I think is going on right now?" He pokes me in the forehead, which fuels my fury. "You're not angry at me. Yes, you're angry. But you're just taking it out on me. You're furious because there was a life you hardly remember—one you could have had. But then suddenly it's gone! And somehow, you're back in hell with your mother. Did they decide they didn't want kids? Were you too broken to handle? Did they just decide you weren't worth it? Where did they go! They could have saved you from everything. But did they? No!

"And when you think you can put everything behind you, when nearly all your questions are answered . . . there's more! You could have had a good childhood, Marianna. You missed out. And now, when you age out, you'll have *nobody*. You'll be alone for the rest of your life if you don't stay with me, and that truth terrifies you."

I clench my fists at my side. Teeth bared, I scream, "Take it back!"

He just stares at me from the doorway, arms crossed.

I stomp my foot. "I said take it back!"

"Take what back? The truth?"

"Undo it all. Figure out a way to hypnotize me or some shit."

"No."

"Do it." I grind my teeth.

His upper lip twitches. "Stop throwing a tantrum. You're acting like a child."

"Make me forget you, Denendrius."

"*Never.*"

I shriek in his face, a snow-screen of silver dropping over my sight. I take a deep breath, his unimpressed face unchanging.

Unsure what else to do, I flop back on the bed and grumble, "I'm going to hunt them down and kill them. They had no right to abandon me."

He sits back down beside me. "Do you want my help?"

"No," I snarl.

He seems offended for a moment, but a smile shatters any possible evidence. "But I'm your *boyfriend*."

"Fine. Give me some change, I'm going to call my social worker and ask what the fuck is going on."

He pulls a handful of coins from his blue jeans. "There's a pay phone across the street."

I take the coins and jam them in my pocket, Denendrius in my wake as I rip the apartment door open and clomp down the stairs. I don't feel the sun against my skin as I snag the pay phone across the street in my sight, running through a break in traffic to reach it.

I rip the phone off the receiver, the black plastic hot in my palm. I slide in some coins. Jabbing in my social worker's number, I wait for her to pick up and get connected to her voicemail.

I wait until I can leave a message, then shout, "Oh my fuck! Woman, answer your phone!" I hang up. I guess I'll have to wait for my answers.

Denendrius laughs. "That'll get her attention, I'm sure."

I meet his eyes with a death glare. "Shut the fuck up. I'm beyond pissed at you for killing my friend."

He grabs my bicep and pulls me across the street. "Get over it. Everyone dies, it doesn't matter when or how."

Back in the apartment, I flop on the carpet and kick the wall.

He sits beside me. "Sweetheart, if anyone should be upset, it's me. I wait a decade for you, and you don't remember me? You don't see me throwing a tantrum."

I glare at him. I'm pretty sure this whole situation could be classified as him throwing a tantrum.

"Marianna, I haven't even aged a day!"

I remember how I'm supposed to be playing along, acting nice, waiting this shit out. I try to swallow some of my anger surrounding Jenna and change the topic. I'm not going to get anywhere besides a coffin by being angry.

I try to change the subject. "So, immortality is real?"

"Yes. I haven't aged since I was turned." He smiles. "Ask me more questions, like in the movies."

I'm afraid to ask most of the questions I have for him, but he'll be offended if I don't seem curious.

"Where did you grow up?" It's the first question out of my mouth.

He frowns. "Rome, a long time ago."

"How long ago?"

"I was born in 58 A.D."

A vampire from ancient Rome? I try the math in my head.

"I've been around 1950 years," he says as if reading my mind.

I remember him talking about how he murdered his family, so I tell him I want to know what happened. He tells me he doesn't want to talk about it.

"Come on, you know some of my dark shit."

He grits his teeth but agrees. There's a dullness in his eyes when he speaks. "When I was human, there was this beautiful woman, and from the moment I laid eyes on her I wanted to kill her. I followed her home one day and carved her up. I was only halfway done ripping her open when a monster of a man appeared in the room." Denendrius gives an ironic smile, shaking his head.

I try to envision the human version of him with a beating heart and warm flesh, the ability to die . . . How different was he then? He was still a murderer, it seems.

"His black eyes were ravenous in the fire-lit room. I looked up at him from the floor with the intent to kill. Her husband, that's who he was. I'd seen him a couple times in the Forum with her. The next thing I knew was pain. It was excruciating, exactly how you described me biting you. He pinned me to the floor. I could hear his sobbing through the suffocating agony. His tears dripped onto my face as he pulled away from my neck. They burned like acid when they touched my skin. The world was pulsing, and I couldn't stop myself from screaming."

I hold my breath, getting lost in the pictures of his story, feeling the agony. I want to tell him to stop, how I can't bear to remember, that I'd much rather talk about Jenna than this. But I don't. Looking into his eyes, I can tell he remembers the pain too.

"I thought the room had filled with people. Voices started speaking to me. They taunted me; told me I was dying. Told me the man was getting his revenge. A black figure appeared at my feet, a demon. It crawled upon me as I was shouting, demanding it leave me alone. It turned to fog and entered my body, choking me as I thrashed. My sight filled with black voids and I knew I had to run. I pulled myself out of the home and into a nearby collection of trees in a cattle field."

I gawk at Denendrius, awestruck that he managed to move voluntarily. I barely believe it.

"I'm unsure of how long I was in those trees, but it seemed like an eternity. I remember a brief moment when the pain receded. I reached up to my throat and felt the wound entirely healed. Then the pain sprung back, multiplied by millions." Denendrius looks down at his clutched hands and thinks for a moment.

I can't understand how the pain I felt in the forest could be multiplied by anything. Could there be a pain worse? I try to imagine what it would feel like. If I already felt the need to die at the pain healing caused, would I even be capable of pleading with that level of pain?

"I didn't know at the time, but the transformation had begun. This time there were no false images to distract me from the pain; it became the sole thing occupying my mind as it swallowed me with darkness.

"It was night still when I awakened, and I felt extraordinarily strong. My entire body was rippling with energy and strength. I could see every crack and crevice in the trees. I noticed every detail I hadn't before. All the pain had vanished, except for a burning in my throat.

"When I first got up to move, the world bent around me. As soon as I thought of where I wanted to move, my legs took me there. I thought I must have felt how Jupiter did, that I could match him. I thought I had been given a gift—had been avenged, even—by the gods. I could hear animals digging underground, a stream dozens of feet beneath, every tiny heart of every animal surrounding me. I killed animal after animal for blood. I wasn't sure why, but I couldn't help myself and even disregarded how disgusting they tasted. I felt powerful, and I wanted to share the gift with my family."

I purse my lips, turning my hair in my fingers as I stare at the popcorns on the ceiling.

Denendrius smiles and reaches out to take the bit of hair from my fingers. He combs his thumb through it. "The only problem is, not everyone survives the venom. You may as well be playing Russian roulette with only one empty chamber."

"I would survive it," I think aloud, wanting to sound as tough as him.

His eyes brighten. "I know you would."

My chest tightens at the thought of him changing me. It would be an eternal game of cat and mouse. "Of course, I wouldn't want to be a vampire," I add quickly. And I'm not sure if I ever would. Fighting would no longer be a thrill. There would be no danger in life. But on the opposite side of that, I would never have to worry about people hurting me. Maybe if I had a life worth being excited about, I would want to spend forever in it.

His jaw sets. "Continuing with my story," he grumbles. "I was unaware of what I'd become."

"How did you find out?" I sneak in while he takes a breath.

"Do *not* interrupt me again."

I roll my eyes and feel his hand flinch on my stomach like he's holding himself back from smacking me.

"I wanted to share this gift with my sisters and mother, so they could be free of my father. I went to our home during the night, and after explaining where I had been and why my eyes were as they were, I told them what I wanted to do to them. My sister Adelia was first to volunteer. The rest of my family was quick to agree with her. I laid them all on the ground and bit them as I remembered the husband doing to me. Then, I waited."

I find it hard to believe anyone would volunteer for such a thing, but I don't dare voice my thoughts. I wonder how easy it would be for him to get away with lying to me. Would centuries of practice make it impossible to tell?

"I didn't know what to expect. But it wasn't what occurred. My youngest sister was six years old. She died first. While she and the rest of the girls were in hysterics, much as you were when I healed you, the bite wound closed. Blood began pouring from her as she was gagging and screaming. I heard her heart stop, halting everything.

"A few moments later, my middle sister, who was eleven, died the same. Then Mother passed. I remember watching Adelia, who was fifteen, as she thrashed and screamed. I told her it would be okay, that the pain would pass and she would be as strong as the gods. Soon, she silenced as the wound closed, and I knew what she was feeling. I could see the agony in her stiff muscles, so I pulled her into my arms and prayed her heart would keep beating. It was maddened in her chest, on a mission to do as I wished it."

He looks away from me and I wonder how he felt. Was he sad when he killed his family? Did he hate himself? But for some reason, I can't see him feeling like that. I even find it hard to believe someone like him would want his family around forever. He's a lone wolf, the kind who'd kill his own pack just so he could do what he pleases. A family would only inconvenience him. But could he have really cared about them? Could they have been the exception?

I can't help but wonder about his sister Adelia too. And for some reason, I feel close to this girl nearly two thousand years away from me. I find myself wanting to spend time with her, learning about who she is, what she's like. Maybe it's because she was fifteen. We'd get each other, having been hurt the same way. Would she have been like me? Could we have been friends? Exchanging secrets alike while protecting each other? I blink and turn my eyes back to Denendrius, somehow feeling a twinge of loss for a girl I never knew.

He continues. "I was so confused. Why did the other three die and not I? I looked down at Adelia as her heart began to slow. When it stopped, she fell limp in my arms. After, I took them outside and buried them beside each other. I remember looking down at their faces, how they each looked like peaceful replicas of their mother. Long brown hair and soft brown eyes, much like mine. Only they were in the ground and I wasn't." He stares absently for a while, and then his eyes turn to mine.

"Did you feel bad about killing them?" I ask.

He stares at me for a long moment. "No. Why would I care?"

"They were your family."

He shrugs and laughs. "Why would that matter? I tried and they died. So be it. It wasn't the end of the world. I wasn't going to get *torn up* over it."

I swallow. If he could kill his family and feel nothing, then what does that say about what he can do to me?

"I returned after. I couldn't forget about Father. I waited for him to come in, and when he did, I snapped his neck like I'd always dreamed of doing. He was quite surprised to see me."

"Did you drink his blood too?"

Denendrius shakes his head. "No. I wouldn't dream of drinking from a man worse than an animal. But after I killed him, I dug a grave so deep that not even I could smell him after burial."

We sit in silence for a few moments, his story settling like dirt into the crevices of my imagination.

XVI

I stride down the hallway, fifteen minutes late for my nine o'clock class. It wasn't easy to get Denendrius to allow a trip to school since our relationship took a turn for the worse, but he agreed, saying he needed to get the car fixed and feed anyway and that he doubted anyone was going to come after me so soon after he killed those two vampires.

I twist the door handle to the history classroom, but it's locked. I smack the door once with my fist, and it rattles in the frame. "Let me in, Mr. Derek."

Heavy footsteps approach and the door opens, exposing a young teacher in his thirties with the beginning of stress lines in his face. "Need I remind you again, Marianna? It's Mr. Henderson."

"Okay, Mr. Derek Henderson. You're making it so easy to tease you." That and it's officially become a habit. I'm sure he regrets telling us his first name by now.

He sighs, ignoring me as he walks back through the quiet

classroom to the front. I throw myself down in my desk against the wall, mere feet from the doorway.

Mr. Derek sits at his desk and types something on his computer keyboard before looking back up at me. "Marianna, where's your binder?"

"Somewhere in my closet with a bunch of other useless shit."

He leans back in his chair and blows air between his lips. "Well, come get a workbook, then. It's to be handed back in at the end of class. You can continue tomorrow."

I raise my eyebrows and look around at the students, who are scribbling away on a pile of papers. I take an unnecessary amount of time to reach the front of the class and grab the workbook.

By the end of the class, I've drawn multiple scenarios of Denendrius dying. When the bell rings, I go to slip it in the garbage in an attempt to hide that I've done zero work.

"Bring it to me," Mr. Derek says. "Sometimes your drawings are amusing enough to get me through the day."

I huff and hand it to him. When I go to turn around, he tells me to stay for a minute. So I stand at his desk, arms crossed, as he looks over the drawings.

When the last student leaves, he sets the workbook down and sighs. "Marianna, have you ever realized how good of an artist you are? How much potential you have?"

"Who gives a shit?"

"I'm serious," he says. "I just wish you'd put in as much effort into your schoolwork as you do your artwork." He sighs. "If not . . . I don't know what to tell you. You're not going to graduate on the path you're on. You're failing."

"Oh, so you're a guidance counselor now?" I glare.

He rubs the bridge of his nose. "I'm being brutally honest, Marianna. At the very least, go to your art classes and pull up the rest of your grades so you can graduate and maybe even get an arts degree. Make art your reason to succeed, okay? Just . . . think about the future a bit, all right?"

"Jesus Christ," I moan, turning away. "I don't even want to think about my future."

"Wait—" He holds his hand out. "Just listen. If you really are done with school, despite everyone's attempt to convince you, at least try to take art classes outside of school to further yourself. I honestly think you could make something out of this."

"Cut the bullshit, Mr. Derek, I've got no money, no way to get there. I'm sick of lectures."

He doesn't say anything as he looks between me and the drawings. "Can I ask who's in these drawings?" he finally says.

"What do you care?" I rip the papers away from him and stuff them in my hoodie pouch so he can't get me in trouble over it.

He stares at me, more shocked than angry. "Because you obviously have a lot of anger toward whoever is in them. I was wondering if it has anything to do with the bruises on your face and neck."

I pinch the sleeves of my sweater so he can't see the ones on my wrist. "Fuck you," I snarl. "I got in a fight."

"Marianna, I know you don't want to hear it but—"

"Damn right."

He frowns. "I want you to know my door is always open. If you ever need help, whether it's school-related or something going on in your life, even if you just want to have a conversation, I'll be here to help."

"Whatever." I turn and speed-walk through the classroom, slamming the door behind me before disappearing into the crowd of students.

Science drags, but I stick it through for gym, my favorite period. After, at lunch, I gather a mountain of fries and ketchup and sit with Camille and Daina.

"Hey," Daina mumbles, poking at her salad with a plastic fork.

Both have red eyes as if they've been crying nonstop.

"You hear what happened to Jenna yet?" Camille sniffs and rubs her red nose on her baggy sweater.

My eyes burn, my stomach twisting around itself. Still, I shake my head so they'll tell me what they know.

"They, um, found her in an alley. She—" Camille nibbles at the air around her, as if she's hoping to suck in the right words to say. "She committed suicide."

"She slit her wrists and bled to death," Daina adds, shoulders falling and air rushing from her mouth.

"Yeah . . . I was going to leave that part out." Camille's hair falls around her face when she looks down to compose herself.

I chew on my fries slowly, discomfort infecting me like a parasite. I tuck my hair behind my ear and jam my hands between my thighs. I want to tell them everything, but I know I can't. "Does anybody know why?"

My eyes meet each of theirs, glistening. I feel like I'm holding the secrets over their head, but how could I even begin to explain the truth?

"No," they say together and then look at me expectantly.

I shove food into my mouth but can't quite seem to chew it right.

"She was so quiet. Ever since I met her," Camille says softly, as if Jenna will hear us talking about her from the afterlife. "Do you think she did it because Beth died?"

Nobody says anything, the heavy atmosphere around the table numbing.

"I can't believe she killed herself," Camille whispers.

I wring my fingers together, twisting them until I have to grit my teeth to deal with the ache. "Can't we talk about something else?" I plead. My arms and legs flash with heavy heat, but I know I'll end up suspended for doing something rash if I allow myself to feel anything right now.

"How about my party Friday night?" Sarah says cheerily as she slumps down in a chair across from me, next to Daina.

"Sarah, fuck off." I squish a fry into a pile of ketchup and pop it into my mouth, grinding it between my molars while I think of wringing her neck with her shitty blond hair.

"It's okay, though, you're invited too, Marianna. It's at my aunt's place. She's cool with the whole thing."

Camille takes a deep breath. "Whatever, fine. I really need to get drunk."

Daina nods along in agreement, sniffling.

I squint at her, wondering why I'm invited. What shit is she planning?

Startled, Daina pulls her chiming cell phone from her pocket. She wipes her eyes as she stares at the screen after flipping it open. "Who the fuck knows?" She ignores it and tosses it on the salad-dressing-smeared table before leaning her forehead down on her arms.

A few seconds later, Camille's cell phone rings. "Hello? Who's this?" She clears her throat.

I hear the voice on the other end faintly, but not enough to understand words. She looks up at me and gives a quizzical look before forcing a smile. "Yeah, here she is."

I take the cell phone, groaning, and put the thick, flat thing to my ear.

"Hey there, sweetheart." Denendrius's voice lilts on the other end.

"What the hell? How did you get this number?" The cell phone creaks under the pressure I apply.

"In a notebook in your bedroom. It's a mess in here, by the way."

Sarah and Daina give Camille a wondering look.

"Boyfriend," Camille mouths, giving me a long stare.

I shake my head at them, and they give me a yeah-right look.

Sarah plays with the zipper on her blue purse, thinking hard. "Invite your boyfriend to my party!"

"Yeah, Marianna," Denendrius mocks, "invite me to the party."

"Fine, it's Friday night," I mumble. I chew a mouthful of fries ravenously. "While you're there, go in my closet and grab the black long-sleeved shirt and my ripped blue jeans."

I hear metal hangers clanging. "Oh no, you're wearing the short blue dress. The one with black lace ruffles."

"No, it's too revealing," I argue. "And ugly."

The line is silent for a moment, and then a laugh crackles in the static. "It's sexy. I'm grabbing it, so you're wearing it."

I tell him a few other things to gather, like my makeup bag and toothbrush, since he's already invaded my privacy.

Sarah scribbles down the address of her aunt's house for each of us and says there will be some booze but we should still bring as much as we can because she isn't sure she has enough to get everyone as much as tipsy. After general chitchat, she wanders away, and I hope she doesn't begin to suppose we're friends now.

As soon as Sarah walks away, Camille pounces. "Where have you been? You look awful."

I sit back in my chair, grasping for an answer that won't let them in on the trouble I'm in. My head lolls back and I decide to twist the truth. "Well, I'm sure Jenna relayed the message that I was fine, right?"

Daina's eyes dip and they both nod.

"Well, after Sarah's friends beat me up, I called Den, and he came and picked me up. We've kind of just been hanging around his place, eating takeout and watching movies." It's not a *complete* lie.

"I thought he was a stalker . . ." Camille scrutinizes me.

"It was a big misunderstanding." The last thing I need is for them to know the truth about everything. "It turns out Charlie got me that cake. I'm not sure why I jumped straight to Den just because we met him at the mall. I think I was looking for a way to sabotage things with him."

Camille stares at my face. "At least that's cleared up, then. But, Christ, they beat you up bad. Are you sure you want to go to Sarah's party? What if she has you jumped again?"

"He'll be there," I say. "It'll be fine."

While I scrape up the remaining fries on my plastic plate, Daina and Camille beg to stay with me for the night since they can't return home drunk, and Pam doesn't care if we do, but I tell them no since I'm staying with Den. I don't want them too close to him after what he did to Jenna.

My afternoon classes fly by, and then I'm hopping into Denendrius's car.

"Buy me dinner?" I suggest as I slump down into the purring machine, putting my feet up on the dashboard.

I admire the new windshield and hood, sure he *convinced* someone to fix it so quickly. I'd never know anything happened if I hadn't been there.

"Yeah, what do you want?" he says.

I suggest a burger, so we go to a drive-thru and return to his apartment.

"What does that taste like?" he asks me as we sit on the couch, halfway through a horror movie.

I swallow the last bite of my burger. "I don't know. Like a burger? What does blood taste like to you?"

He beams. "Amazing. I'm not sure how I could explain it to you. Perhaps you can think of it as similar to when you drank from me."

My skin itches at the memory of drinking from his wrist, my eyes pinning the thick skin above his veins. It's like someone holding a ready needle just out of grasp. A nauseating need sprouts inside me.

I try to convince myself that I should be disgusted at craving a part of him when every fiber in my body would love to watch that blood stain the carpet. That the blood I drank technically wasn't even his, how he killed someone for it. It doesn't work. I knew what was in heroin and what it would do to me, but I still eagerly forced it into myself.

I try to cut my eyes away from his wrist, but I can't help but let them dart back a second later. He must know what I want, because I watch his wrist move to the devilish curl of his lips.

He reaches out with his other arm and takes a fistful of my hoodie, pulling my head into his lap and hooking his arm around me so I can pull his bleeding wrist to my mouth. "*Drink up*," he whispers.

I drink, mind launching into the same crazed bliss as before. My fingers lock around his forearm so harshly I'd likely tear his skin if I wasn't human. I feel him sink into the couch, surprised at the tension thick in his muscles before it releases. He sighs, his fingers slipping through my hair and down the side of my face. It tickles.

When he eventually pulls his wrist away, reality dribbles into focus. I'm still settling back into myself when he lifts me gently by the throat and sweater, his lips finding mine. He kisses me for a hard second before pushing me back into my seat, his lips twisted in a lofty smirk. His hand moves from my sweater to gently grip my jaw, his thumb pulling at my bottom lip.

Lust stirs in his eyes. "You have more beauty than Venus," he says, gold spun in his voice. "We're Venus and Mars, you and I."

XVII

Thursday passes and smears into Friday night—now—without incident, my perfect-girlfriend act resulting in a day reminiscent of the ones we shared before everything went wrong, though only one of us genuine.

When the horror movie we're curled up in front of is over, it's close to eight forty-five. I use the next fifteen minutes to slip my party dress on after a hot shower and do my makeup, which is basically just trying to cover my bruises.

He picks up a couple bottles of vodka for my friends and me before we head off to a gray house rumbling with music. Yellow light spills from the windows and onto the green grass. The cold night makes the hairs on my arms prick. I fight the urge to shrug away as Denendrius wraps his arm around my waist and kisses my temple.

Gazing up at the starless black void above, I let Denendrius guide me toward the front door. Inside, kids are shouting and dancing while they grip plastic cups full of alcohol. To the right of the front door are stairs leading up, and the entire left side is the living room. Straight ahead, past the living room wall, I can see the kitchen.

Camille and Daina spot me from the couch. They hurry over to swarm us with drunken statements on how epic the party is. I can barely hear them over the music.

"Hi, Den," Daina croons before giggling along with Camille. "I'm so super glad you and Marianna figured things out."

I can tell his grin is driven by amusement.

"Can you get me a drink?" I ask Denendrius. "Please?"

He returns a smile and agrees, walking off. I'm going to need all the alcohol I can get if I'm going to be spending this much time with him.

Sarah jumps off the fireplace mantel and stays squatted for a moment, rubbing her ankles. She strolls over. "So that's your boyfriend?"

I shrug. "I suppose so."

She nods. "Nice. A little old, though—not that I mind."

"Ask him out if you want." I say it like she's asked me if she could have the leftovers from my plate once I've decided I can't eat anymore. Although, if it came to food and she asked, I'd force-feed myself to avoid sharing.

She leans back, raising her eyebrows and scrutinizing me. "What?"

"So, you honestly wouldn't care if I went after him?"

I can see the rusty gears turning in her mind, and I bet she's wondering if I'm plotting to accuse her of being a boyfriend stealer if she does. But I wouldn't care.

"I wouldn't give a damn. Fuck him if you want."

I look over to Camille and Daina, whose mouths are wide.

She grins at me. "Well, I guess maybe you aren't so bad. I'd be a better girlfriend anyway. I can perform."

"Good luck with that, Sarah. And we're not friends," I retort. I know this is just payback for her paranoid ideas about CJ and me, and I doubt she'll find reciprocation from Denendrius anyway.

"Good!" she snarls, looking so smug that I want to test a potato peeler on her face. She sticks her tongue out and dances away.

Camille takes a delicate sip of her drink. "You shouldn't be playing with his emotions," she scolds. "It's not fair to him. Are you *trying* to push him away?"

I glare at her and am about to tell her she doesn't know the first thing about it, but Denendrius exits the kitchen with my drink. He's laughing and joking with a few other people. Did he hear us? If he did, he gives no indication.

I hold out my hand for the cup, and he tells me he'll give it to me if I kiss him. Wanting my drink in my hand instead of on me, I don't protest.

I lean my head back and chug the drink. The taste of vodka is intense as it seeps through the small amount of cola. I watch the teeming house of partygoers as Denendrius retrieves a few more cups. He holds one in each hand as I take my time drinking them.

For the next hour, we chat with random people. Somewhere along the line—after introducing herself—Sarah teases him about not drinking until he tells her to bring him a bottle of vodka.

"How much are you going to drink?" She giggles as she hangs on his arm, trying to hold herself up.

"All of it." Denendrius unscrews the cap. The bottle is at least three-quarters full, and he leans his head back, bottle to his lips as he chugs. His face twists. "*Wow*, vodka's awful," he gripes once the bottle is empty.

Sarah laughs gleefully, practically wrapped around him despite how many times he's shoved her away. I anticipate alcohol poisoning when he stumbles to the bathroom to rinse his mouth, Sarah following him like a shadow.

A shaky hand touches my elbow, and I spin to see CJ holding a bottle of liquid courage in the other. I cross my arms and scrutinize him—from his poorly chosen band T-shirt to his holey blue jeans to the freckles across his cheeks and messy dirty-blond hair—before saying, "What, CJ?"

"I know you won't give me the time of day, but I want you to know I really like you anyway," he says confidently.

"You're the only boy who has ever been stupid enough to genuinely like me, and if you could stop, that would be *great*."

"Marianna, I think if more people could see that deep down you're a good person, more guys would think you're relationship material."

I laugh, the liquid in my cup swaying to the side like a big wave, escaping over the edge and dripping down my fingers. "I think I'm a good person."

"I-I know, but nobody else sees it." He looks at his drink as if it might tell him what to say next.

"How do I know you're not trying to have sex with me?" I slur. I take a sip of my drink, mentally trying to cancel out the taste of vodka from the faint cola while wishing Denendrius knew how to mix drinks.

"If you just give me a chance, I can prove I'm good for you. I'll be there when you need me." He points to my neck. "I would never hurt you."

"What if I already have a boyfriend?"

His lips turn down. "The asshole who's been obsessively talking about you all night? He's a douchebag! I'll be surprised if he doesn't get the shit beat out of him by the end of the night. You can do so much better than him."

"Like you?"

He rubs the back of his neck and sighs. "Yeah, like me."

"Fine."

His smile stretches across his face as I lean in and press my lips to his, realizing too late in my drunken state that Denendrius might do something horrible instead of deciding to treat me better before someone else does. He wraps his arms around my waist, fingers greedily gripping my dress.

I wait for hands to yank me away from behind, but none come. Is he busy with Sarah? But then I open my eyes while our lips stay locked, and I see Sarah about ten feet back, mouth agape, eyes wide, staring at us as if she's witnessed a horrific murder. Tears stream down her face and I realize I just confirmed every false worry she's ever had about CJ and me. In reality, he and I hardly speak at all, but I'll never get her to believe that now.

She rushes past us, hand on the side of her face as she disappears into the crowd. I unlock my lips from CJ's and follow her, leaving him protesting behind us. She finds Denendrius and tries shaking him from his conversation, probably wanting to tell him what she's witnessed.

But he shoves her aside when he sees me, leaving her shaking her head at me as a way of saying I'll pay.

He wraps his arms around my waist, inhales deeply, and grips me so tight I hold my breath. "Hmm . . ."

I grimace. There's no way he doesn't smell CJ on me.

"I want to talk to you," he whispers in my ear.

"Why—"

He grabs my wrist and pulls me through the kitchen and to the basement stairs. He plows through people as he pulls me downstairs. I can hear stomping on the stairs above, going up to the second floor, the distraction making me stumble on the steep steps. The basement is dark, and only a handful of people are down here, mostly doing drugs and making out.

Pushing me into the nearest room, Denendrius locks the door.

"What—"

He pulls me to him by the throat, his lips heavy on mine. I remember my plan, so I entertain his mouth, the taste of the vodka on his lips. Groaning, he walks me backward and I feel a mattress press into my thighs. He dumps me onto it.

"Are you drunk?" I break away.

"I can't get drunk," he mumbles against my lips before returning to kissing me.

He crawls half on me, one of his legs draped over one of mine. His breath is ice and I wrangle with the urge to push him away. Concentrating on the music streaming through the vent above, I wrap my arms around his neck. The ceiling shakes. His tongue traces my lips, and after a few minutes of making out, I can barely feel them.

He yanks the front of my strapless dress down, my bra coming down with it to expose me. I shudder and I feel him smile as he touches me. His thumb runs over the scar of his name and I feel him grin triumphantly against my lips.

I squeeze my eyes together hard and forget to kiss him back. Wintry kisses make their way down my throat and onto my chest, and I watch with paralyzing discomfort as his mouth moves over me.

His lips are restored to mine, his hands gently brushing down my body, over my stomach, until his hand is massaging the inside of my thigh. He kisses me harder until he moves his lips to my neck again while he shrugs off his jacket, breaking away for a moment to pull his shirt off. He sneaks between my bent legs and pulls my dress and bra down to my waist.

I struggle with the decision whether to cover myself like I wish to or give in to stop him from continuing anyway if I say no. Maybe it's the liquor or the fear that traps my words and stops me from moving.

He pushes my dress up to where the rest is at my waist. I swallow a lump of terror and look away to break his attempted eye contact.

When I hear his belt jingle, my eyes shift back to him. Propping myself up, I open my mouth to say something as he unbuckles. My mind can't think of which words to use.

"Just lay there," he says, breath staggered as he shoves me back against the mattress. He unbuttons and unzips his jeans. "I just want you to feel me."

When he begins to slide off his pants, I decide I've had enough. I roll away from him and try to leave, only to have my back slammed against the door and a wrathful face shoved in mine.

"Am I not good enough for you?" he barks. "Hmm?"

"I didn't say—"

"Then why are you willing to give that *boy* a chance and not me?"

I stutter some nonsense while putting my dress and bra back into their proper place.

"You're worthless without me!" he spits.

"No, I'm not." I shove him, but his fingers move to hold me around the throat. "I don't have to take your shit."

"Too bad, you're my girlfriend. I'm not going to lie to you."

"Fine! I don't even want to be with you. I'll go be CJ's girlfriend or something. At least he hasn't stabbed me." I show the smuggest face I can.

An amused smile spreads across his face, eyes twinkling dangerously. "Really? Because he doesn't want you."

"Yes, he does."

He shakes his head sardonically, adding a pouty face. "No . . . nobody else will *ever* want you. Everyone sees you as a low-life druggie who's bound to die on the street. The only person who knows your worth is *me*."

I try to shove him away, but he leans forward, face coming within a few inches of mine.

My lip curls in disgust. "It's not me nobody will want," I spit. "It's you. Nobody has ever really wanted *you*. Not for long, at least."

I wonder if I'm right when his eyes twitch and he takes a step back, his face quickly flashing from dull to dark fury. His knuckles slam me in the ribs, forcing air from my body. I topple to my knees, arms hugging myself.

He sits on the bed and begins to dress. "Get out."

Air catches in my throat as I rise, stumbling from the room while struggling to close the door behind me.

XVIII

I clamber up the stairs, shoving Sarah into the banister as she comes down them. "*Bitch*," I slur.

Drifting through the crowd while trying to keep my balance, I spot CJ on the couch, talking to a group of boys. I tap him on the shoulder.

Turning around, he smiles. "Hey."

I sniff and rub the back of my neck. "Do you have drugs?"

He stands and nods. "I mean, I have weed."

I lick my lips. "Want to get high?"

He agrees, so we make our way upstairs together. I'm nearly too drunk to keep upright, so he holds my arm and helps me up.

After finding an empty room, we shut the door and pile on the bed. I cross my legs and sigh, impatient for something to keep the thought of Denendrius's hands on me away.

He pulls out a rainbow pipe from his pocket and stuffs weed from his grinder in it. He gives it and a lighter to me. My hand wavers when I try to light the pipe, which makes me burn myself, so CJ does it for me.

I inhale until the length of the pipe is empty and then pass it to him. I wait until I can't hold my breath any longer, white billowing around me as I exhale.

"How bad does he hurt you?" CJ asks after taking his turn.

"I don't want to talk about him," I manage to mumble, taking the pipe again.

He nods and sighs. "All right."

We pass the pipe silently between one another until my anxiety has slipped away, my mind twisting over the fuzzy feeling of calm. I lie down on the bright pink kitty cat bedspread and focus on the thrumming of music, the way it turns to magic in my ears. Seconds feel like hours as I stare at the ceiling.

He lies down on his back beside me. "Can I kiss you again?" he asks, eyes scrutinizing his pipe.

"No," I mumble, a lightning strike of anxiety ripping through me.

"Okay," he says.

I wait for him to ask again, to barter, demand, or force his lips to mine, but he doesn't. He doesn't even try to hold my hand, or claim I owe him for the weed.

I turn my head and stare at the boy who's never said a mean thing about me, who's never laid a hand on me, and wonder what drove me to hate him so much. Did he just end up being convenient to hate?

"You're right," I say.

He looks at me quizzically.

"When you said you're a good guy . . . you're right. I don't know why I've hated you."

"I do," he mumbles. "You hate everyone because you can't predict what their intentions are. I get it, you've been hurt. You can't afford to trust anyone. It's an unhealthy attitude, your relentless anger, but I get it."

"Hm, maybe." Maybe I'm just questioning everything since I'm drunk and high.

"Hey, do you remember the year we were in elementary school together?" he asks.

I shake my head. "I don't remember going to elementary school with you."

"I do. We never talked, but we went to the same elementary school, and I was in your middle school for a year."

"Oh."

"I remember you were the saddest kid I'd ever seen. You'd never play with anyone; you'd just sit in the sandbox and sulk. Then you started getting angrier and started pushing kids off the swings and shit and trying to start fights. I tried to figure out why, but when you came to middle school after the summer with a gang tattoo on your neck, I figured it out. Joining a gang at eleven . . . that'll fuck you up."

I remember sitting around the gang house eating mac and cheese while watching the older boys take turns inking each other with the homemade tattoo gun. Having already completed my initiation, it was my turn. I fought not to cry when it came and a red bandana was shoved between my teeth.

My laugh is emotionless. "Yeah, I guess it did. It's weird you remember that."

He shrugs. "It made an impression on me, scared me out of joining one myself. I didn't want to be like you."

"Humph. Thanks."

He chuckles. "Anytime."

We sit in silence for a long moment. My thoughts take no particular direction, just a swirl of colors and broken ideas.

"Are you still in a gang?" he asks.

"I left like a year ago."

He nods. "That's good. Maybe you'll start finding happiness."

I swallow hard. "Happiness and I don't get along."

He thinks for a moment. "I'm sorry you feel that way."

"Me too," I mumble.

He's silent for a long moment. "Did you only kiss me to make your boyfriend jealous?"

"Sort of."

He chews his cheek. "That was my first kiss."

I frown. "Well, sorry for ruining it for you."

"I'm not."

I wonder if Denendrius wasn't involved in my life if this would be the point where CJ and I started being friends. What would he be like to have as a friend? Would we start hanging out at school? Would I hang out with him and his friends? Would we go to the skate park? Maybe he could teach me how to skateboard. Maybe I'd have an identity crisis and pierce my nose and clamp feathers in my hair, or put some crazy colored streaks in. I can't help but giggle at the ridiculous thought.

CJ grins like he's waiting to hear the joke. "What?"

I shake my head, laughter bubbling past my lips. "Nothing, I'm high as fuck."

His smile turns toothy, his bottom teeth crooked. "You're pretty when you laugh."

I stop, chewing the inside of my cheek. "Yeah?"

His eyes trail over my face. "Don't you think so?"

I rub my hands over the blanket and offer a small smile. "I'm content with how I look."

"Well, that's good to hear. The only thing I would change is your smile. I wish I saw it more," he says.

Biting my lip, I study his face. The silver on his lip ring is starting to wear off, his shaggy blond hair nearly covering one eye and needing a trim. His scrawniness shows in his neck and shoulders, and I know if I needed to, I could win a fight against him. He's boyish and cute.

"You can kiss me," I decide on a whim.

His eyes grow wider, and I can tell he isn't sure what to make of my words as he rolls onto his stomach, looking down at me.

"Are . . . are you sure?" he stumbles. "I wasn't saying any of that so I could—"

Resting my fingertip on his lip to shut him up, I scoot closer so my face is under his and nod. CJ places his clammy palm on my cheek, his fingers gripping a section of my hair. He's holding his breath as he closes his eyes and places his wet lips against mine. His kisses are sloppy and taste like weed and cheese puffs, his teeth too close to mine. I guide his lips with mine, curling the back of my hand around his neck. Kissing him . . . it's not nearly as passionate as when Denendrius and I kissed, and there's no fireworks, but it's nice.

For once, I truly feel like a teenage girl. I feel my age in the way we kiss, in his hand as it weighs on my face, how his other is limp by my head while his body hovers above mine like he's scared to touch me. I feel it in the pop music that shakes the walls, the alcohol in my veins, the sound of laughter passing through the door, the childhood memories and drunk tales being made around me.

"I want to date you," CJ says while he pulls away.

"I know, but I'm already taken."

He sighs and flops onto his back. "You should break up with him."

My smile quivers and fails. "I'm trying."

He turns his head, hand coming up to touch the bruise on my neck. "I know, I get it."

When someone knocks on the door, I sigh. CJ gets up to answer it, Sarah on the other side. I groan.

"CJ, can we talk for a few minutes?" Her voice is unusually calm.

He turns to me for a long moment before answering. "Sure, I guess. I'll be right back, Marianna."

"Okay," I mumble.

He leaves and shuts the door behind him. Rolling over, I find fascination in the colorful lines making up pictures on the bedspread. I study them, tracing my fingers over the soft fabric. I wonder if CJ is my friend now. What makes someone a friend?

As the minutes turn over, feeling like hours, I wait patiently. When I hear the door handle turn, I can't help my excitement. But instead of CJ opening the door, it's Denendrius who does.

My stomach tightens when I see him.

"Hey there," he says, holding a cup.

I squeeze my eyes shut for a second as he approaches the bed, hoping he isn't here for the same thing as in the basement. He hands me the cup and I stare into it with stinging eyes, wishing CJ would come back.

"It's getting late. Are you ready to go home?" The bed creaks as he sits beside me.

I exhale sharply. "I'm hanging out with CJ. I'm just waiting for him to come back."

His lips tighten. "I saw Sarah and him getting close on the back porch. It looks like they'll be there for a while."

I huff and grit my teeth. Why did I think he was my friend? I chug my drink, the heavy taste of vodka slamming into the back of my throat, making me wonder if he's purposely doing a bad job at mixing them. "All right," I slur. "Let's go, then."

"We have to go collect Daina and Camille first."

I squint at him. "Why?"

The corner of his mouth twitches in a smile. "They asked to spend the night with us, and I welcomed them with open arms."

"No." My heart hammers in my chest, the dizziness of my drunkenness amplifying. "You leave them alone, Den."

He runs his fingers through my hair and down my back. "Oh, relax, sweetheart." He winks at me. "I need someone to keep a close eye on you at school."

I glower at him and try to climb off the bed, legs giving out under me. Denendrius lifts me up off the floor, and I'm so above any possible anxieties his comments could create, I hardly mind. Techno music fills my ears as he carries me down the stairs and outside since I'm too intoxicated to stand.

He cracks open the car door and sets me on the seat, telling me he's going to go find my friends. His words echo in my ears, making me question if he said them or if I made it up.

It feels like it takes half an hour for two minutes to pass, but finally, the driver's door peels open and Denendrius pushes his seat forward, two drunken bodies clambering into the back and laughing.

Denendrius climbs into the driver's seat and starts the car in motion, speeding through the streets, making me feel like I'm on a roller coaster. The girls sway in the back seat, giggling, but my eyes watch the road, the way it flies beneath us silently.

I turn to face Denendrius, whose eyes flicker to me every so often, a small smile on his lips. I ask him to stop for fast food, and when the sound leaves my mouth, it sounds like I'm listening through a wall. I mellow and he turns the heated seats on.

I must have zoned out, because a few moments later he's setting a steaming burger and fries on my lap, pointing to a soft drink in the cupholder. He passes the same thing back to the girls and they dig in.

Licking my lips, I salivate as I open the cardboard box where a burger sits. I chew slowly, letting the taste spin in my mouth. Taking another bite, I moan into the burger and he laughs.

With a click of a button on the dash, classic rock blares from the speakers, shaking us. I hum and nod along, the sound of girly voices pushing through the music while Daina and Camille laugh about the party and things nonsensical to those sober.

He cruises for a bit and whispers something to me, but only the hypnotic sound of his voice registers, not his words. Reaching over the low console to wrap his arm around me, he kisses the top of my head. I run my fingers over the zipper of his leather jacket, the feeling of metal more interesting than usual.

His hand goes to my lap, fingers wiggling in a way that asks for mine. It draws attention to the tendon in his wrist, to the veins bulging under his skin. I take his hand, my fingernails scraping at his wrist in a failed attempt to draw blood.

His lips fall open and he looks down at me pensively, his breath becoming shorter and quicker. Leaning down, he kisses me, and I let him, unable to fight. For one high moment, I almost forget why I hate him and am brought back to our first few dates.

Daina and Camille giggle in the back seat as if they've never seen anyone kiss before while adding sounds of fake awe.

He pulls away a few seconds later, settling back in his seat and sighing, lips curled in satisfaction.

We appear in the parking lot of his apartment building a few long minutes later. While my friends trip over one another and complain, Denendrius has me tucked at his side. He keeps me upright while I stagger up the stairs, barely able to put one foot in front of the other.

Hanging his leather jacket in the closet behind the front door, he fetches a blanket for Camille and Daina from the closet at the end of the hall and throws it on the couch, telling them to go to sleep. I stare into space like I've gone brain-dead, but he drags me into the room and slams the door, locking it behind us.

He kisses me roughly, pulling my dress off and throwing me on the bed, crawling on top of me. The sound of my heart thumping fills my ears, the taste of vodka and fast food in my mouth. The world spins, his kisses trailing over my body as my mind enjoys the sensation of dreaming. He runs his fingers over my matching plain black bra and underwear while kissing down my stomach.

The world switches from lagging to lightning speed, and I moan as pain bursts around me. I lift my head and see he's bitten my side, drinking. A few drops of blood escape from the corners of his mouth and drip onto the bedding. I want to push him away, but I doubt I could make my arms move.

He kisses me again, the rusty taste of my own blood filling my mouth as his tongue slips inside, his hands carefully moving over my body. My thought process surrenders to my instincts, and since my instincts are numb to the high, I simply do whatever.

Denendrius tears into his wrist, dripping blood over my bare stomach and my chest while my hands slowly chase his wrist. The incisions close before my eyes. I slap at him in slurred frustration, my words garbled. His lips curl mischievously when he laughs.

He lies on his side against mine and rips into his wrist again, giving it to me.

"*Drink up, you little addict,*" he whispers, voice fervent against my ear.

Gold spins in my chest. I close my eyes and lose myself.

Drunk, exhausted, and doubly calm from the mixture of his blood and the weed, I drift into unconsciousness with my lips locked on his skin.

XIX

I stretch and groan, pain pulsing in my side. A pair of cold arms squeeze me, a chilled breath pulsating against the side of my face.

"Morning, beautiful," he whispers in my ear. "How are you feeling?"

I grunt in response and sit up, my mouth thick. His eyes are intent on mine, crinkling in the corners a bit as he smiles broadly. I wipe my hand over my face and brush my fingers through my hair.

Sun shines through the window, a golden streak across us. It's warm where it contacts my flesh, raising goose bumps on areas untouched. The pounding inside my skull wraps my thoughts in a layer of thick fog.

I release myself from the fluffy blankets and land on the floor. The precipitous movement surprises my sleepy mind, and a jolt of pain erupts in my temples. I blink rapidly when silver stars cascade over my sight.

Stepping too close to my bag of clothes, I catch my foot on

the strap and it twists around my ankle. I drag it away by my leg, not having the energy to reach down and untangle it. It clangs and crashes into the walls as my feet fumble toward the bathroom.

I pull the door shut and flick on the dim yellow light. It casts shadows across the brown-flecked countertop and age-stained white walls.

After taking the time to maneuver my foot out of the straps, I peel my bra off and throw it behind the door, followed by my underwear. I run a brush through my sticky hair, grimacing as it rips through knots.

The shower groans as I step into it, the metal rings from the curtain too loud as they squeal against the bar. The lukewarm water spurts me with shocks of cold at random, but I take my time, and eventually, the water cleanses my mind and returns it to a sharp state.

The same floral shampoo, conditioner, and body wash I use at home sit on the shelf. A few old but rarely used bottles with earthy scents sit below mine on the shelf. Probably only for when he's completely covered in blood, since I've never even seen him sweat.

When I step out of the shower, I toss on a fresh set of clothes and comb my hair, leaving it to dry straight on its own.

Denendrius is sitting at the table, staring at Daina and Camille as they sleep. They're sprawled out on the living room floor on a blanket, one of Daina's legs up on the seat of the couch. Camille snores, makeup smeared down her cheeks.

"Wake them up," Denendrius demands.

I nudge Daina in the side with my foot and she groans, rolling over. Her leg slides off the couch and onto Camille's stomach. She jolts awake and slaps Daina.

"Guys, wake up," I demand.

They complain in unison, their deep groans and talk of hangovers loud.

"It's so early," Daina whines.

"It's nearly three in the afternoon," Denendrius says.

I step over Daina and slump down on the couch, pulling my feet up beside me while poking at a droplet of water on my blue jeans.

"Then go home and sleep." His voice cracks like a whip.

"I'm hungry," I interrupt before his verbal lashing turns physical.

"Same." Daina peeks out from under her arm.

Camille wipes hair from her face as she sits. "Me too."

"Well, so am I and you don't see me eating." Denendrius laughs.

I purse my lips at the joke.

Daina stands, knees bent as she sways. She grips the arm of the couch for support. "Man, I thought you were cool. We were going to go to the lake and camp." She wavers to the table and plunks down on a chair across from him. "We still should. We can all get drunk on the beach and shoot fireworks across the lake."

Denendrius's brows lift, his eyes shifting to me for context I'm too exhausted to provide.

"We're not going to the lake, Daina," I say.

She lays her head on the table and moans. "Shitty. It's Saturday, we should keep partying."

Camille stands and wanders toward the table, Denendrius standing as soon as she finds a seat. He sits on the couch beside me, coming into my space.

"You should get us food." I wince at my tone, my words sounding more like a command.

He grabs my bicep and squeezes, fingernails creating ridges in my skin. "Excuse me?"

"Please?" I snap, his action pressing me since I'm sure he's just trying to show off in front of my friends.

"Without the attitude," he hisses, his fingers so tight I'm sure there will be a bruise.

I grind my teeth and fight against the thought of driving my knuckles into his face. "Can you get us food? Please?" I say sweetly.

His face untwists and he smiles crookedly. "Of course." He kisses me on the mouth and gets up, leaving my friends baffled in their seats and me praying a car takes his legs out from under him while he's out.

"What the hell was that?" Camille's voice shoots up an octave.

"Why wouldn't you smack him? It's what you would normally do." Daina stands up.

"Because," I snarl.

"Because why?" Camille pushes. "I've never seen you *not* stand up for yourself."

I choose not to answer, crossing my arms over my chest and turning away. It's not as if I don't want to stand up to him, but what other choice do I have besides taking it? I can't run, which is why I'm remaining fixed on my plan to play along until he leaves me, unless I find a sure way to get away that won't fucking kill me.

"Hello?" Daina calls.

My voice is venomous as it slips from my lips. "You know what? Why don't you mind your own business for once? I know what I'm doing. You think I'm stupid? I know I should smack him. But I don't because I'm not stupid."

Daina rolls her eyes and wanders over to the shelves of movies.

Camille is out of her seat now. "Break up with him."

"I can't."

Daina scowls. "Why? Because he said so? Since when do you take no for an answer? Just tell him it's over and walk away."

My teeth ache. "It's not that easy." I kick the couch.

"Because he'll hurt you?" Camille's question is more of a statement. Her voice is light, gentle like I'll burst into tears if her words are any harder. "Is that why you've been pretending everything is fine?"

I let air fill my lungs. "Yeah, but he'll leave first. He'll get tired of my crap and find someone else."

"You're kidding right?" Daina laughs. "I don't think he's leaving anytime soon. He's completely head over heels in love with you."

I raise my hands in protest. "No, he's not."

Why can no one else see this is just another game to him? Just some stupid control thing?

Daina shakes her head, her eyebrows raised. "No? Well, you should see the way he looks at you. It's all over his face."

"He's not in love with me!" He can say he is over and over again, but I know it's all manipulation.

Daina tosses her arms up in defeat, breath leaving her mouth in a rush. "Whatever you say . . ." She returns to flicking through movies.

Camille's disapproving eyes tighten at Daina before she sighs and takes a few more steps toward me. "I want you to think of the worst thing he's ever done to you."

I pull my lips into my mouth, my chest clenching. It feels like someone is slowly tightening a metal belt around my chest. My breath becomes nonexistent as I think of the night in the forest, the pain as it tore me apart. The vivid hallucinations pulling me back into my past. My skin pricks with heat. I can feel the cold around my body, the taste of my own blood. I fall back onto the couch.

"The abuse will only get worse. Abusers don't stop," Camille says.

"How would you know?"

"We learned about abusive relationships in health class last month. You should have been there."

Maybe this game is ending with my death. Maybe it's his plan. Drive me insane and kill me in the end. I shudder.

"But that's only if you don't get help. I believe in you, Marianna," she says. "You just have to ask for help."

My sight shifts into focus at the suggestion. "Get help? Camille, I can handle this on my own." He's my problem, I'll deal with it. It's hardly a relationship even—what could anyone do?

"Marianna, he's going to take you through hell and back."

I jump up again and step into her space, hands curled at my sides. "I've already fucking been through hell and back. This is nothing. It's insulting you think I can't handle this on my own."

"It's not an insult. You shouldn't *have* to do this on your own. I'll go to the cops with you."

"Did you forget the only reason I'm in this situation is because you and Daina had to be such pushy bitches and convince me to go on that date?" I snarl.

She frowns. "That's not fair. How could we ever have known he'd be this way? This whole time we've been thinking you're bruised from fighting. You're always bruised from fighting."

I almost laugh. "Well, maybe you should have figured it out, Miss Psychology."

Her eyes plead. "Marianna, I'm sorry . . ."

Daina rolls her eyes, pushing Camille toward the door, "C'mon, let's go, let them figure it out alone."

"Wait." Camille looks me dead in the eye and, pleading, says, "I know you may not think an arm grab is a big deal, but it is. Please, please, please, get help from someone, before it's too late. He did that in front of us. If he's so abusive in front of other people, I can only imagine what he's like alone."

I frown and cross my arms. "I can't believe you guys don't get it. I can handle it on my own."

But not even *I* believe my own words.

"She's not going to get it through her thick skull," Daina jeers. "Let's get out of here."

"Mari—" Camille starts.

"Get the fuck out!" I holler.

They whisper to each other as they head out the front door. Just before it closes, Daina turns to me and says, "You've got some serious fucking issues, Marianna. You're lucky you have friends who understand why you're this way. But even if we do, that doesn't mean we have to put up with your shit. You're a time bomb. Figure yourself out before you fucking explode. Don't expect people to stand around and get hit by your shrapnel."

The door slams behind her before I can reply.

I roar and boot the couch, plunking down. I don't need their help. I've always had to be my own hero, and I've done just fine. Besides, the police wouldn't be able to arrest him; they would only make him angrier. I curl up on the couch and cover my face, digging my toes into the cool leather as I groan loudly. I try to guess what Denendrius will bring me to eat in an attempt to distract myself.

By the time he's arrived, I've gotten so sick of thinking about different kinds of burgers, I can barely eat the one he hands me.

The crunch of lettuce is the only noise between Denendrius and me, his eyes unblinking and rough.

"Does it taste good?" Hostility lingers in his voice.

I stop chewing and meet his eyes. They're dark, making my skin twitch with unease. I look away and continue to finish the bite in my mouth before answering, "Yes . . . so, can you not eat food, or what?"

His eyes don't leave my face as he says, "Technically, I can. Aside from there being no point, the taste is atrocious, though."

"What happens to it after you eat it?"

"The venom in my body dissolves it."

"No need for the bathroom?" I tease.

He rebukes my humor with a heavy "No."

I tilt my head from side to side. "Cool," I say into the burger as I take another bite. I get a sly idea, so I ask hopefully, "What about poisons? If someone put some in something, and you ate it, would you die?"

He blows out annoyance and rubs the back of his neck. "Marianna, you can't kill me, no matter what. Give up on the idea."

A hunk of burger lodges itself in my throat and I cough while he stares. Eventually, it goes down, and I ask in a high voice, "Nothing can kill you? Impossible."

He leans back against the couch. "Unless you also happen to be a vampire or can stop me from drinking blood long enough that I grow weak, nothing you can do will faze me. You should know by now."

I swallow hard and shove the last bite—which is falling apart—into my mouth. "Why?"

"I'm strong, a lot . . . older than most vampires. If I'm well fed, I can heal faster than you can cut me. A vampire may be able to, but anything can be a weapon if you have the speed and force behind it that a vampire would."

My eyes tighten. "Oh. What about a bullet?"

He laughs this time. "Sweetheart, I can move faster than a bullet. Besides, I've shot myself before and it was *very uneventful.*"

I swallow. "What are the ways you could die, then?"

He studies me for a long moment before answering. "If I didn't feed for a long time, the sun would destroy me, burn me alive. Decapitation would be another way, or ripping my heart out. A stake would render me comatose, but that would only work if I was a newborn or too weak to move."

"Crosses?"

He rolls his eyes.

"Well, if you've been around for almost two thousand years, what have you done in all that time? How have no other vampires killed you?" I mean, he's an ass, and apparently, that extends to other vampires as well.

He smiles. "Hm, that could be a very long answer."

Then, I remember his comment about the scar on his stomach and ask him about it.

Denendrius smiles. "Yes, I was a gladiator. Do you want the long version or the short version?"

I sigh. Whatever distracts him the most. "Give me something in between."

He thinks hard. "Well, since I wasn't a slave, I chose to sell myself into the life when I was twenty-three. Many free people sold themselves to pay off debt or because they were poor, but being an upper-class patrician, I wasn't short on money. I wanted the fame it brought, the girls and the fortune. But mostly, I wanted an excuse to fight. When I wanted to join, I was assessed by the *lanista*—the trainer—and when they decided I was physically fit and attractive enough to entertain, I was accepted into the Dacian School to train as a *dimachaerus* after I swore the oath to obey, that I was willing to submit to being beaten, burned or killed by sword."

I squint at him. "What is dima . . . cha . . . ?"

He laughs at my attempted pronunciation. "Dimachaerus. It's a fighter of two swords. Instead of a sword and a shield, I fought with a gladius in each hand."

I swallow. "That's brutal. How many people did you kill?"

He grins. "Not every battle ended in death. I only killed a small handful in the four years I fought. But I was very, very good at what I did. Even though I lost some in the beginning, I won very many."

I try to imagine Denendrius in an arena, thousands watching and cheering for him as he spills blood.

"Is that where you fell in love with killing?" I ask.

He winks at me and smiles. "You could say that."

I swallow, remembering the woman he murdered that resulted in him being turned. "But you killed outside of the arena, right?"

He runs his hand over his mouth, feet moving back and forth on the floor. "Yes, you're right. The arena didn't always satisfy me. Like I said, not every battle ended in death."

"Is that why you stopped fighting? It wasn't enough?"

He shakes his head. "No, I was prepared to be a gladiator until I was unlucky enough to be killed or until I could become a trainer. But when I was turned, I knew I couldn't. Everything became about killing after I changed. I was bloodthirsty, in the most literal sense."

I pick at the hem of my shirt. "Can you tell me more about your family?"

His jaw sets. "No."

A thread comes loose from the fabric. "Why not? If you don't care about what happened, then what's the big deal?"

"My family is off-limits for discussion."

I want to press further, ask why he's being so uptight, but I know better. "Fine."

XX

The usual string of news and rumors floating around the school on Monday are much less grim than the story of how CJ's body was found after the party.

From what I've picked up in the hall, someone beat him to death with their bare hands, and I'm probably the only one with a suspect.

Denendrius.

After I heard the news, it took a lot not to grab the person nearest to me and rip them apart.

What was I expecting? For Denendrius to let that kiss go? He didn't have to go as far as killing him, but after killing Jenna for absolutely no reason, I shouldn't have expected anything less.

But for Sarah to be involved? Now that blows me away. Nobody has said anything about her, but after seeing her come down the stairs when I was going up, I can only assume she was going to talk to Denendrius. The question is, did she easily agree to lure CJ to him in spite, or did he have to threaten her?

By lunchtime, things have done the opposite of died down. I hurry to the cafeteria and beat a group of girls to the line. I wait my turn and buy fries with a few bills Denendrius gave me.

Today, the usual groups of students have been smeared across the cafeteria, and it's funny how it takes something like murder to give them an excuse to talk to each other.

I claim a table somewhere near the back doors, close to where Daina, Camille, and I usually sit since the chairs belonging to our table have been stolen.

"Hey." Camille plops down across from me, a few pieces of lettuce falling from her plate upon setting it down.

"Hey back." I stuff a few fries in my mouth after the icy words have vanished from my tongue.

"Daina's still in line," Camille says quietly.

"Good for her," I snap.

"Are you still mad?" she whispers.

"Yep." I chomp more fries.

Daina gawks at her food as she struts toward us, nearly knocking another girl to the floor in her oblivion. She licks her lips as she settles into a chair beside Camille.

"I'm not sorry for what I said, though. But I am sorry for handling it the way I did." Camille points her fork at me and raises a brow.

"Did you hear what happened to CJ?" I deflect.

"Yeah, I did, it's upsetting. So, what's going on with you guys?" she dodges.

"What do you think Sarah thinks of the whole scenario?"

Her gaze tightens. "What's happening between you and Den?"

Our eyes lock, glaring. Out of the corner of my eye, I see Daina's eyes switching between us as she sits still, her jaw the only thing moving as it chews food.

"Stop—" Camille and I both say at the same time.

"Why don't you want to talk about it?" Camille asks.

I push my food away, knocking a few fries onto the table. "See you guys later." I get up and walk from the cafeteria, leaving Camille with nothing but my name in her mouth.

With the gym teacher's approval, I find peace in the school's little workout room after changing my clothes in the locker room. I jump on the treadmill and run for thirty-five minutes, at which point my heart is crushing against my chest as the world spins.

I've always been a great runner, fast. Living in the hood, I had to be. Most of the time too many people were chasing me to fight back, so running was usually the only option. And even if it were me—a five-foot-five, hundred-and-twenty-pound girl—against another thug, I would be pushing my luck trying to fight.

I tried to stand my ground and fight no matter what, but after a while of waking up in alleys and ditches, I learned to stay away from the bigger thugs. Trying to prove myself stopped being worth it in cases like those. So now, when worse comes to worst, I run.

I try to contain vomit as I turn off the machine. The world swings from side to side as I reenter the locker room for a quick shower.

I skip my last classes and sit in the library at an old computer, bringing up a search page and staring at it.

My mind flutters back to Denendrius. I remember him saying there are people after him and wonder how hard it would be to find them and ask for help. I know I can't go out and hunt a vampire down without Denendrius interfering, so the internet might be my best bet. If not, maybe something historical will come up about him.

I cross my fingers and search his name. There are only a handful of results, and most of them are merely pages based on suggested spelling.

I'm about to try a new search when Denendrius's name catches my eye in the description of a role-playing website based on a supernatural video game. When I click, I'm taken to a white nineties-style forum post on a black-and-red background. The post is locked and almost a decade old, but the user responsible for it—suspiciously named Blood_Brothers—talks about how he's trying to find another user in the game by the name Denendrius and how he'll transfer a reward to the account of whoever can locate him. A strange-looking link is embedded at the end of the short write-up.

My sweaty hand sticks to the computer mouse, the cursor twitching over the words as I speed-read them repeatedly.

Could this be a message from vampires hiding in plain sight? The mention of a reward reminds me of how Denendrius said his head was worth a lot of money. Surely if other users had any idea of what he was talking about, there would have been some sort of reply, right?

I take a deep breath, move the cursor over the link full of weird numbers and letters, and click.

A small screen pops up on the computer, disappearing so fast I hardly glimpse it. Nothing happens afterward aside from the antivirus software starting a scan, and I'm left scowling at my screen while I search for a sign-up option so I can message the user myself to ask if we know the same Denendrius.

I grumble when a pop-up appears at the bottom right of the screen to notify me of possible spyware, and I'm glad this isn't my computer.

As soon as I find the sign-up form and type my name in, another internet window opens up.

"*What the hell?*" I whisper to myself as I lean close to the screen, eyes trailing over the block of tiny white words on black.

`Denendrius Sovetta is personally responsible`
`for the deaths and disappearances of`

approximately three hundred Children of Stars. Other crimes include the murders of mortals granted immunity, the murders of mortal children, and the kidnappings and presumed deaths of several Darkling and Children of Star clan leaders.

He is a Darkling and is described as being approximately six foot four with long brown hair.

Denendrius Sovetta was last seen at a restaurant in Lorimer, New York, with a teenage girl. She was assumed to be human at the time of the sighting. She is described as being of Latina or Caucasian descent, short and slim, with light brown eyes and long, straight light brown hair. We are unsure of the nature of their involvement with each other and are currently unaware of her state. We strongly suggest against approaching Denendrius Sovetta if you are Children of Stars, and we warn against Darklings approaching him alone.

Please contact with any information that could lead to his capture.

I take a deep breath and wipe my sweaty palms on my jeans. My next breath is shaky and my heart races at the idea of other vampires now knowing I'm somehow associated with him. Will I be murdered too if he's found?

I try to think of when we were spotted. Was it our first date, or was it when he dragged me to the diner? I realize how bad it would have looked if we were seen on our first date, laughing and talking together.

Even though I don't understand what most of his crimes mean, never mind what Children of Stars and Darklings are, it sounds bad enough to know he'll probably be executed if he's found. And if they find me still with him, will I be killed too? Is someone currently looking for us? Is there a gang of vampires ripping through the city as I sit helplessly at a computer?

But it could be a good thing, right? If I can help those vampires find him, I could explain what's been going on, and they could kill him. If I can convince them to spare me in exchange for information, I could go on with the rest of my life and not have to worry about whatever his plan was for me.

I begin to shake at the thought of how soon I could have him out of my life, and I quickly start searching the block of text and the web page for any contact information. When I come up empty, red begins to shake at the edge of my sight. I slam my fist on the keyboard.

The information screen closes, and a chat box appears.

The red retreats, leaving confusion to dip into me as I stare at the simple chat box. It's like the computer is reading my mind.

Blood_Brothers: Are you still there, Marianna?

I lift my hands off the keyboard, realizing that I likely downloaded some sort of keylogger with whatever spyware the computer detected and they captured my name when I was signing up.

My eyes dart around the busy library, and I double-check that nobody notices me or anything I'm doing.

Taking a deep breath, I quickly type my response.

```
User: Yes.
Blood_Brothers: Do you have information?
```

I swallow a lump, wondering what I should tell them.

```
User: I might.
```

I wonder if my vague response will annoy them, but I need to bide time to think about how to handle it.

```
Blood_Brothers: What information do you
have?
```

```
User: If I tell you, will you kill the
girl he was spotted with?
```

```
Blood_Brothers: Was she you, Marianna?
```

I take a deep breath.

```
User: Yes. If I tell you how to find
him, you can't kill me.
```

```
Blood_Brothers: What is your involvement
with him?
```

Hesitant, my fingers type out the words as I take another quick glance around the library.

```
User: He's forcing me to be his girl-
friend. I'll help you if you don't
kill me.
```

When I hit send, another message immediately appears beneath mine.

Blood_Brothers: My name is Alaire. We know you are at West James High School. Please stay put and we will retrieve you.

My brows shoot up as the chat box and browser pages disappear.

"Wait, what the fuck?" I say to myself, their demand making me reel.

I'm left staring at a blank screen, brain on red alert. I move cautiously away, but since the tables are all taken up by classes, I find a stray chair and sit in the back of the library against the bookshelves, using the mass of studying students as a shield.

My eyes flicker over each exit, so quickly it makes me dizzy. I'm not sure what I'm waiting for. Maybe I'm expecting them to bust in and grab me, move so fast I don't even see it coming, or break down an emergency exit door to get to me.

My legs shake, and I'm not sure if it's out of fear or anticipation. Could the forum post be a trap? Could Denendrius have been behind the screen, waiting for me to fall for it? Is he going to walk into the room, shaking his head, only to take me back to his apartment to beat me? No, that's silly. He doesn't even own a phone.

I run my hands over my knees, still checking the doors. What will these vampires be like? Will they be mean like him? They say they won't kill me, but are they lying so I'd meet them? Will they use me to get to Denendrius? Hurt me to make him angry? Will they kill him, then turn around and kill me to cover up what they've done? Fuck . . . is it forbidden to tell humans about vampires? Will I die because I know what they are?

I look back at the main entrance and my stomach drops. Two black-haired men, no older than their thirties, are standing in the doorway leading back into the school, dark eyes searching the dozens upon dozens of faces of laughing and whispering students. They wear black combat boots and green army coats. I wonder if they can see me over the couple rows of computers. When the youngest looking of the two spots another girl who matches the description from the website, he walks toward her.

"Alaire," I whisper.

The youngest-looking one stops dead, his head snapping toward me. He smiles gently and, with two fingers, motions for me.

Carefully, I stand and walk across the library, stopping a good distance before them.

He smiles again, his French accent slipping through his words. "It's all right. You'll be safe with my brother and me. My name's Alaire."

I have tons of questions, concerns, but I don't dare voice them. I just nod once, knowing that anything I could possibly say will come out rudely.

"Come on," his brother says evenly.

I cross my arms but follow them out of the library. We walk in silence, a brother on each of my sides. Alaire nods at the security guard who stands by the door, and I wonder if they hypnotized him to get inside.

I notice both brothers slide brown leather gloves on before we step outside.

"Fingerprints?" I ask, wondering what we'll be doing to need the forensic countermeasure.

"The sun," Alaire clarifies. "We can't leave fingerprints behind."

My steps falter. "Seriously? Why not?"

He smiles. "Fingerprints are left because of oils on skin, which people like us don't have."

"Shit," I say, impressed.

When we approach a black van with tinted windows, I plant my feet. They stare at me, eyebrows lifted.

"You guys realize you're asking me to get into a rape van, right?" I cross my arms.

The unnamed brother remains serious. "It's precautionary," he says. "A big van is harder to run off the road, and it's big enough in the back to hold a flailing vampire down without anyone seeing them through the windows."

"And if the school sees me get in on camera?" It's not much of a concern for me, but I think maybe it'll make them think twice if they have any unfavorable plans.

The seriousness of the unnamed brother's face doesn't alter as he speaks. "We caused a camera malfunction so Alaire and I wouldn't be recorded. It'll probably take them a few hours to fix. And don't worry, the security guard agreed to let you leave with your uncles to go to the dentist."

So, they did hypnotize him. Their thoroughness makes me want to groan. "Fine, I'll get into your creepmobile."

Alaire chuckles quietly, but his brother's face remains in business mode.

His brother slides the side door open for me, saying, "I apologize for the lack of seating."

The door closes behind me as I crawl into the back. A blanket covers the itchy dirt-covered carpeting, and even though I can see the dried bits of blood, I sit on it anyway.

"So, what's your name?" I ask Alaire's brother as he climbs into the driver's seat. He closes a fancy laptop on a stand between the front seats, tons of wires sprouting from it.

"Edmond." He turns the van on and then brushes his chin-length wavy black hair from his face.

I cross my legs, the sunlight barely reaching me through the windows. If I couldn't see out the windshield, I might think it was evening.

The van jolts forward, leaving the school's parking lot.

"I have to ask. How did you get involved with someone like Denendrius?" Alaire wipes an invisible smudge off the passenger window.

I catch myself from falling backward as we stop at a cross-walk. "I went on a few dates with him but decided to try and end things when I found out he was stalking me. Then, he went full-throttle psycho and made me be his girlfriend." I place my hands behind me, so I don't topple forward when he starts driving again. I realize I'm wrong, though, that we met when I was five. I ponder whether to tell them but, not seeing a reason why it would be important, I don't.

Edmond's puzzled eyes catch mine in the rearview mirror. "And when was this?"

"Almost two weeks ago. Why?"

The brothers exchange a glance.

"What?" I demand.

"You say you just met him, but you have over a decade-old blood mark on you," Edmond says carefully. "It's strong, which means it hasn't been sitting dormant for all this time."

I don't like the sound of that. "A blood mark?"

"It's basically a permanent sign to say 'this is mine, leave it alone' to every other vampire. It alters the marked human's scent a bit."

I grit my teeth. The idea of being claimed makes me want to kill someone.

"And how is that done?" I growl.

"By consuming the vampire's blood, either in something like food or directly," Edmond says.

Eyes widening, my skin burns, and I realize that means I would have drunk his blood as a child.

"I'm just going to assume it doesn't make you stronger either like he claimed, right?"

"It does, but that's never its sole purpose. It forces a bond over time. The more you indulge in the vampire's blood and spend time with them, the more the bond strengthens. It's the reason human slaves and familiars stick around without trying to escape and will do the vampire's bidding." Alaire gives me an apologetic look, like when a doctor is trying to kindly say *you're fucked*.

"So basically, it's the vampire equivalent to Stockholm Syndrome?"

His nod wavers. "I suppose that's a fair comparison."

Denendrius, *that motherfucker*.

Edmond asks, "What did it feel like when you drank his blood?"

I furrow my brow, not sure how to explain. "Like . . . pure insanity. But it was strangely controlled, like a dam holding back a flood, the calm before a storm. It was addicting. All my emotions smeared into one big nothing. Why?"

"The experience when sharing blood can be vastly different," Edmond starts. "It's a way to bond. It connects you and allows you to experience part of the other person."

My breath catches. "So, you're saying I was basically in his head?"

Alaire nods. "And him in yours."

Cold creeps up my neck. "That's . . . that's horrifying."

"From what I know about him, yeah, I can imagine that would be scary for someone in your position." Alaire runs his fingers through his short black hair.

"And what do you know about him?" I ask.

"Just a story, I'm not sure if it's true or not. After he was turned, Denendrius was causing quite the disturbance in what is now Italy. Maybe it was because he had no creator to guide him, or maybe he was just nuts to begin with and vampirism made him snap, but he was killing irrationally and constantly. He was leaving bodies torn up in broad daylight, letting victims get away, torching entire villages. I'm not sure his reasoning, but it seemed he was doing anything and everything he could think of to get noticed.

"And, well, he did. Long before the modern world, a royal clan of vampires in Sirmium—now Serbia—kept our kind in order. They sent men after Denendrius and captured him. They kept him guarded in the dungeon."

I purse my lips. "Why didn't they just kill him?"

Edmond laughs.

"Death would have been a mercy," Alaire says. "Instead they bled him and tortured him, fed him just to torture and bleed him again. That supposedly carried on for decades. Eventually, thirst becomes so horrible it drives the vampire mad if not satisfied—to the point where escape isn't even a thought, just blood. You can barely move, barely speak or think. Thirst consumes you."

I swallow. "How did he escape, then?"

"I guess the guards didn't expect Denendrius to consider cannibalizing the vampires guarding him. The story goes that he drank the guards and kidnapped the vampire king's human niece. They expected a ransom, for him to demand immunity for her return, but he just disappeared. They never found her, and he never caused a big enough disturbance to rile an entire species until he was blamed for an alarming number of missing vampires." Alaire sighs. "I swear the man only has one foot in reality."

"So, vampires don't share blood?" I ask.

"They do," Alaire says. "But what Denendrius does— draining them—is predatory. Vampires share with one another out of love or for a familiar connection, but Denendrius got a taste in the context of a meal."

I allow his words to set in before asking, "Is the royal clan still after him?"

Edmond shakes his head. "No. They were murdered centuries ago by other vampires. Denendrius is far from the only unhinged immortal out there. The entire vampire community can't worry about them all the time unless they start making a scene."

I wrap my arms around my folded legs and clench my teeth. To think a man like that technically owns me by blood . . .

I steady myself when we turn around a corner. "How can I get rid of the blood mark?"

Edmond answers this time. "Either with your death or with his. It can be overwritten by another vampire, but that's not really solving it."

I clench my teeth. "Let's go with his death."

Alaire grins. "That's the plan."

I give a satisfied nod. "Good, so where are we going?"

Alaire turns on the heat, even though it's already hot outside. "We'll find a warehouse at the edge of the city."

We hit a bump. "Why?"

"It's best to be out of the city," Edmond says. "Fewer civilians for him to kill."

"Then what?"

Alaire points the vents at himself as they hiss. "We wait for him."

I scrunch my lips. "What makes you think he'll show up?"

The window rolls down beside me, sunlight blinding me for a moment.

"You're with us. He will," Alaire says.

I roll onto my stomach, propping my head on my hands. "So? Do you really think he'll risk his life coming after me?"

Edmond nods but doesn't say anything, face still blank. I wonder if he ever smiles, ever has anything other than a hardened seriousness to his face.

Alaire turns to face me. "Oh, he will." He smiles. "You're a game to him. He lives for his games. You found us, so you're obviously smart. You're still alive, so he must find something interesting about you too. Trust us. We've been after him for years. He will come. He will probably think we are trying to steal you from him and take it as a challenge."

I chew my cheek. "What do you think would have happened if I hadn't found that forum post?"

Edmond answers this time. "We heard a story half a decade ago. He kidnapped a teenage girl and tortured her."

I raise my brows. "And?"

Edmond purses his lips. "She threw herself out a seventeen-story hotel window. He only had her for a day."

My blood runs cold at the thought of what he must have done to her. Things I probably can't even imagine. To think that could be me is terrifying. Would have there been a point where I would have felt the need to kill myself just to get away from him?

"Hmm." Alaire shifts in his seat, looking over his shoulder and back at me.

"What?"

"He hasn't . . . hypnotized you? That's strange."

I'm reminded of his weird looks. How he looked me in the eye and asked me to show up to the date, his confusion and fury when I wouldn't tell him I was happy to see him.

"Yeah, but it didn't work," I say slowly.

His eyes widen. "Are you sure it didn't?"

"So he says," I respond.

He rubs his chin. "Would you mind if I tried?"

I close my eyes. "Why?"

He sighs. "I promise I won't do anything that will result in harm. I'm only curious to see if it really doesn't work."

I peek at him. "Promise?"

He nods. "Of course."

I open both my eyes and look into his. They aren't harsh like Denendrius's, instead warm, safe like what I imagine a father's eyes would be like. "Fine."

He inches closer, our faces a foot apart, eyes on mine. "Touch your finger to your nose."

I'm so surprised by the absurdity of his request, I laugh.

He moves back, still turned. "Hmm."

"It didn't work?" I ask, still chuckling.

Alaire turns to his brother. "You try."

He turns around to face me, hands still on the wheel as his brother places a hand on it. I sit up and shuffle a few inches closer, bringing my eyes up to his. His are dull with traces of worry.

"What is the first thing you can remember?" Edmond asks.

I move back and cross my arms, the thought of my mother locking me in my bedroom leaping into my mind. I shake my head, jaw set. "No."

"I'm sorry," he says evenly, turning back to the road.

I swallow and uncross my arms. "You guys can't hypnotize me either. What does that mean?"

They stare at each other for a long moment.

"It happens sometimes," is all Alaire says.

I'm not convinced. "Great answer. Care to elaborate?"

"Some humans are just immune to it." He shrugs. "Nothing is perfect. I've met humans who couldn't be marked before. For all I know, the mark is too strong for you to be hypnotized by other vampires."

I squint at him. "Okay . . . but Denendrius can't either, and I've seen him hypnotize people."

Alaire shrugs. "It could be a mental block. He clearly feels enough for you to give you his blood. Or perhaps humans are starting to adapt. Evolution is a peculiar thing."

"Maybe." I roll sideways as he turns. Pulling myself upright,

I ask, "There was mention of Darklings and Children of Stars. What are they?"

"They are two different breeds of vampires. The two of us and Denendrius are Darklings," Alaire says. "There's some debate as to exactly how, but the general assumption is that Darklings were achieved through some sort of eugenics through selected supernatural traits in Children of Stars."

"Huh. Well, what's the difference?"

"Children of Stars can only live in darkness. They have no chance of creating an immunity to the sun. They can appear human, as they keep their human eye color. Unlike us, they can be killed by humans more easily. Though age is a factor, of course. And like us, a lot of popular myths are true for them, like stakes and garlic."

Somehow, I'm surprised by this revelation. But it makes sense why they warned Children of Stars against going near Denendrius. If humans could kill them, then they definitely wouldn't stand a chance against Denendrius, never mind that he killed three hundred of them.

"Oh. Well, how did you guys start following him?"

"He and his crew raided and sank a French ship. From our side, it wasn't difficult to figure out a vampire was responsible, and we picked up his trail for a bit once we realized his description sounded a lot like a man who has been hunted for centuries."

My jaw slacks. "He was a pirate?"

Edmond says, "In the sixteen and seventeen hundreds, yes. He didn't use his name back then. He and his crew—mostly enslaved human men—were somewhat feared, mostly due to ominousness surrounding Denendrius. He didn't make a huge show of his obvious talents, but his crew picked up on certain things pertaining to his vampirism and passed stories along when they would make port. I believe his ship was sunk by the Spanish, but don't quote me on that."

"Wow." My mind itches to know more, and I understand now what he meant when he said how his boat was taken from him and he was a captain.

Alaire's head whips to the side. He mouths at me to be careful what I say.

I squint at him and then realize Denendrius must be near. My heart starts hammering when I realize the fight we're all in for.

Alaire looks at me and puts his finger over his lips. "No, we'll kill her before you can get to her."

My jaw falls open. He smiles and shakes his head at me. I'm on board with what they're doing now, realizing we must make it look like I've really been kidnapped.

"He can hear us?" I mouth.

"He's only a block over," Edmond says. His head snaps toward the back window and he hits the gas. "Scratch that."

Someone lays on their horn behind us, an engine revving.

"No, Denendrius, she's ours now," Edmond snarls. "We're going to rip her throat out."

Alaire crawls between the seats and sits beside me. I think maybe it's to prevent Denendrius from flying through the window to grab me. He gently grabs my arm. I don't mind, though; I'd rather not be pulled through the window.

"Don't touch her? I'll do whatever the hell I want now," Alaire says.

Edmond laughs. "We're in a huge van, you idiot. Do you really want to cause an accident and make a scene in the middle of the street?"

The Mustang revs, and the van jerks so violently on impact that I would have flown into the back doors if it weren't for Alaire's grip on me.

"Of course you do, *asshole*," Edmond mutters as he speeds up.

Alaire mouths at me to scream for help as he puts his hand over my mouth.

I pretend to fight him off, my voice muffled as I scream, "Denendrius! Fucking help me, you psycho!" I elbow Alaire, knowing it won't hurt. "Get off me!"

He smiles at me and nods in approval.

I go one step further by clambering to the open window and waving my arm through. "Get me away from them!"

The Mustang collides again, and fire slices through my arm as I fly backward, head smashing into the metal of the back doors. My vision darkens, and then I'm sitting next to Alaire, his cold arms wrapped around my shoulders. I blink away stars, vision returning.

His lips move silently, asking if I'm okay.

I roll the shoulder of my sore arm, seeing if it's out of its socket. It's not, but it sure as hell hurts. I nod.

"What are you trying to do? Kill her so we can't?" Alaire asks. "No? Sure seems like it." He rolls his eyes. "Really? Going to blame us for denting your car? It's not our fault you can't keep better track of your prey."

"He's leaving," Edmond says.

I take a deep breath. "Where's he going?"

Alaire frowns. "Probably to do something awful." He turns to Edmond. "We need to hurry and get to the warehouse."

XXI

We sit under dim lights on rickety metal chairs in a warehouse, half of which looks like it's being used to build furniture. It's been an hour since Denendrius turned his car in the other direction, and there's been no sign of him since.

"What do you think he's doing?" I grumble as I wipe my palms on my pants, leg shaking with impatience.

"Definitely not healing kids with cancer," Alaire gripes.

Edmond, who sits on the other side of me, says, "He probably went hunting. There are two of us, and he'll want to be as strong as he can."

I cross my arms. "So, are you guys the vampire police or something?"

Alaire stares at the door, unblinking. "We're bounty hunters. People report vampires to us, and we deal with them. It's how we make our money. Plus, somebody needs to keep things in order. We're not the only ones, but we spend most of our time looking for this asshole." A breath rushes past his lips. "It's not easy, though. He's erratic and unpredictable. Sometimes we don't hear anything about him for a hundred years; other times people are messaging us once a week. It's impossible to get a handle on his patterns."

From the corner of my eye, I see Edmond's head turn to me. "No, he has one pattern. For the past eleven years, he's been visiting Lorimer. It started as once every couple years, then once a year, then multiple times a year."

My blood chills. He knows so much about me. How often was he watching me? Has it been *years*?

Old memories dust themselves off, ones where I would sit at the window of my locked bedroom and lift the corner of the newspaper from the window to peer outside. Many times, a shadowed figure of a man stood against the fence separating the abandoned house next door from ours. It comes back to me, the uncertainty, the confusion over who he was and why he masked himself in darkness, as clear as the first time I saw him.

He *has* been watching me for years. And for a couple of them, from my drugged and terrified stupor, I was watching him too.

"I know the pattern."

They both look at me in question.

I take a deep breath. "He took me for a while when I was a child, then returned me. I think he's been checking up on me until he decided to take me back."

"It's only logical considering the blood mark," Edmond says carefully. "Only, that means you're the game of a lifetime. I've never known him to mark humans. This could end in a bloodbath."

Knowing I could be the first one he's ever left a blood mark on is terrifying.

Alaire looks at me with hard eyes, gears turning behind them. "I want to really piss him off," he says. "He'll be less careful, distracted, if he's frothing with anger."

I scratch my knee. "How?"

"Take off your hoodie?"

I squint at him, teeth clamping. "I'm not wearing anything under it."

He's taken aback. "Oh. I apologize."

I straighten. "What were you planning?"

His eyebrows twitch. "I was going to rub my scent on it to make it look like I had my hands all over you."

My chin scrunches when I remember what he did to CJ for kissing me. "Oh. Yep, that would really piss him off."

He holds his hands out. "If you pull your hoodie away from your chest I still can."

It's baggy, so when I pull it away, there's tons of air between me and his hands as he rubs them across the entire front of it. He touches my sleeves next, and I hold my breath when he runs his cold fingers through the length of my hair.

"What have you planned for your life after all this is over with?" Edmond asks.

I swallow a lump and shrug. "I haven't thought that far ahead," I say, not wanting to divulge details of my foster home woes. "I never expected *vampires* to have any part of my future. It's sort of thrown me off."

Alaire draws his lips into his mouth as he nods. He flinches as he carefully says, "I did some digging on you on the way to pick you up. You've had a hard life."

I lift my chin, the backs of my eyes burning. I shrug.

"I'm sorry for that, truly," Alaire says, adding, "And I imagine it will be hard to integrate back into normal life knowing all these secrets. There are options for you, Marianna. I know of a place you can go. It's much, *much* better than how you are living now, and it's safe. For *you*, we could pull some strings to have you go."

My eyes narrow. "What kind of place? Like . . . a reform school, or some shit?"

Edmond smiles. "No, nothing like that. You'd like it there.

Once this is all over with, we'll grab you something to eat, then we'll relax and have a talk."

Something flutters in my stomach, but I bury it with a deep swallow before it can turn into anything resembling hope. Still, I want to know of the place they're talking about. "Sure. That sounds nice."

Alaire and Edmond smile at one another and then at me.

"What are other vampire crimes?" I wonder aloud before I allow myself to think of some *better life*.

Edmond answers. "Blasting our secret to the world, child vampires, and killing another vampire without a reason are the biggest ones."

I cock my head. "Child vampires?"

"It's forbidden to make anyone a Darkling who is immature, but nobody really acts on the broken law as long as the child isn't too young. It's not a huge deal, so nobody usually reports it. Nobody will go after someone if they're a vampire at fourteen or sixteen, but anything much younger and bounty hunters will come after you," Alaire says. "Personally, depending on circumstances, we let anyone carry on over the age of eleven."

I swallow. "What happens to them? You kill them?"

Alaire's eyes widen and he shakes his head. "Of course not. They'll be turned back. But if the vampires turned a toddler, we'd kill the creators."

I purse my lips. "Why is it so bad?" I could probably answer my own question, that a young vampire would be extremely dangerous without control.

"Very young children aren't equipped to handle vampirism. Aside from the obvious social complications, our secret has almost been discovered many times because of them," Alaire grumbles.

"Wait, you can turn them back?"

"Yes, but turning back is hardly a miracle. Something

usually goes wrong, and we've had very little luck. It's for a worst-case scenario, a single chance. Usually, when a vampire turns back human, in the case of Darklings at least, their memories might escape them, especially if they have been around for a long time. There is no guarantee they'll come back—which is the best-case scenario—but they can. Psychological issues are more likely than physical ones, though physical ones do often appear in children who have been turned back. Anything from going blind to having a failed immune system to losing the use of their limbs. We had a child die from a common cold only a few weeks after turning back. That sort of thing. The process of returning to human is violent and unpredictable."

I stare at him. "Then why would you do that to children?"

He sighs sadly. "It's better to try than to just kill them. There have been a few cases that have shown great results but, unfortunately, many that ended up with the child being put down anyway."

"Shit," I whisper.

"It's more an illness than a cure," Alaire adds. "Personally, I'd rather die as a vampire than risk it."

I wring my fingers together. "Wait, but if you kill their caregivers, what happens to the child vampire once they're human again?"

"Usually they'll be placed in a public place, like in a park or a mall. We'll watch them until someone good comes along, like security or police."

Being a child vampire sounds awful. Never growing up, never fully understanding what's going on. I can't even begin to wonder. "Have you two turned children back?"

Alaire says, "Yes, and I've never quite decided how to feel about it."

I wring my hands, pondering. "How do you turn a vampire back?"

"You can't," a lilting voice says from the doorway. "It's a fairy tale. There's no truth in it. You're entertaining liars."

When I blink, they're both on their feet, eyes hard on the doorway. Alaire's behind me then, arms wrapped around my shoulders. My breath leaves and is thin when it returns to me. Denendrius takes a step from the doorway. His face is hard, black eyes blazing.

"Denendrius," Alaire says in acknowledgment.

"I just killed an entire family and set their house on fire," Denendrius's smooth voice says, lips a twisted grin.

Alaire's grip tightens on me.

Denendrius appears a few feet in front of me, and Edmond grabs his arm.

"Give me my girlfriend," he hisses.

Alaire wraps his arm around my waist. "She's mine."

Denendrius leans toward me and inhales. "What did you do to her?"

There's a smile in Alaire's voice. "I'll leave it up to your imagination."

Denendrius's eye twitches, his muscles winding tight until he's rigid.

I hold my breath, thinking he's going to try to rip me away from Alaire. But Edmond and Denendrius disappear, the sound of grunts and war cries breaking out around me. By the time I figure out where they are by sound, their shouts are in another part of the warehouse. I know Alaire can see them, though, as his head keeps moving back and forth.

Denendrius and Edmond appear a few yards in front of us. Edmond takes slow steps backward away from Denendrius, who holds a pointed metal file in each hand.

"Hey, man," Edmond starts, "put those down and let us handle this like men—"

Denendrius thrusts a file into his chest, driving the other one under his armpit when Edmond lifts his arms to wrap his hands around the metal in his chest. Edmond's pained cry cuts through the air, and Alaire disappears. I swallow and hold my arms out to steady myself.

I yelp when cold hands wrap around my arm, my vision blurring. When I can see again, I find myself lying on the concrete floor in front of the door, Denendrius pinned down beside me, the files clattering away from him against the concrete.

Blood seeps through Edmond's shirt.

"You're going to die for the crimes you've committed," Alaire spits.

Denendrius's eyelids flutter, face flat. He catches his breath and laughs. "So, that's what this is about? You kidnapped my girl to lure me away?"

He struggles and they tighten their grip.

Denendrius grins. "I can tell I'm stronger than both of you. Hmm? I must have at least a thousand years on you."

He disappears from beneath them, now standing across the room. When they too turn into a blur, I leap up and press myself against the wall. They're back to screaming at one another, holes and cracks appearing around the room. When I feel them rip by me, a huge dent appears in the wall, an inch from my body. I try to figure out who made it and realize I was probably a fraction of a second away from being grabbed again.

Part of me wishes I was fast enough, strong enough to jump in and help them combat him. But instead, I stay shaking against the wall, flashes of worry ripping through me. Black shakes at the edge of my vision and I tighten my fists, waiting for the outcome of his damned battle.

Someone crashes into the wall beside me.

"Stop it!" Alaire screams. His voice dissipates from beside me and continues on the other side of the warehouse. "Stop trying to grab her!"

Edmond's voice appears on my other side, following another crash. "You'll kill her."

I wonder if that's what most of the struggle has been, him trying to grab me and flee, them trying to stop and kill him.

Somewhere on the other side, Denendrius growls, "I want her back."

"She's not yours to have!" Edmond shouts.

Before I can process it, there's a snapping and crashing sound, right on top of me. My sight is ripped away.

I think I scream at Alaire to kill Denendrius, but I find myself lying on the floor, a gaping hole in the metal wall beside me. My breath is halted, and no matter how hard I try, I can't suck air in. I'm choking. My eyes drift down, and I see my chest covered in blood, looking more sunken than usual.

"Look what you've done!" Alaire snarls, somewhere outside.

I can't even scream when someone swoops by, ripping my throat open.

"No!" Alaire screeches, voice a few octaves too high.

I think his exclamation was for me, that Denendrius was the one who bit me. But a splash of cold sprays across my face, and I see how Denendrius has Alaire pinned against the wall. Alaire is staring past me, eyes wide and frozen, blood dripping from his exposed fangs. Wetness wells in his red eyes.

Fire engulfs me, ice following. When I can finally take a breath, I exhale a shriek. I begin convulsing, a flood releasing from my eyes as screams tear up my throat. My fingernails find the concrete, snapping as I claw at it.

When my head snaps to the side, I see what Alaire's outcry was for. Edmond lays a few yards away from me in a pool of blood that's quickly flooding the dirt. His head is missing.

My fingernails find my eyes. This time, there is nobody to stop me from scratching my sight away.

Their banter is miles away, blood filling my ears.

"No! I wasn't going to kill her! I was fixing your mistake!" Alaire shouts.

"And it only took that millisecond to destroy your brother," Denendrius says.

"You almost killed her for a millisecond?" Alaire asks in disbelief.

"I knew you'd run to help her."

The sound of their quarrel evaporates, the crisp sound of traffic and foreign voices filling my ears. I spin, Paris appearing in front of me.

Alaire grabs my hand, tears running down his face. One finds my finger, my flesh sizzling on impact. I pull away.

"Hurry," he says, "or Denendrius will kill us."

We race down the road, the faces we pass by twisted in a sick mess. I think maybe I'm a newborn vampire now, because the sun blinds me and I can feel my insides boiling. Only, how did we get to Paris so fast? Why did they let me change?

Alaire and I knock through people, and from the corner of my eye, I can see a shadow standing across the street, watching us.

We turn left, away from him, and the shadow emerges in front of us like a thick mist.

"No!" Alaire screams.

When I blink, the cars stop, the pedestrians falling in unison. Blood stains the pale sidewalk, dripping off the curb and onto the street.

I exclaim and trip, dirt manifesting in front of me when my hands catch myself. My head snaps up, the moon hanging above the trees.

My voice comes out ragged when I scream for Alaire. I bolt up and continue to run, breath crushing my chest, the air slipping past my icy lips. I search the forest for him, the shadow constantly standing in my peripheral no matter where I sprint, no matter where I turn.

Denendrius is in front of me then, a shallow crimson gash across his throat. He smiles, teeth stained with blood.

"You're mine," he snarls.

I scream, dashing in the opposite direction, pain ripping through me, threatening my pace.

I'm jerked back to the warehouse, where Denendrius is hunched over me.

"It's okay," he whispers, hand stroking my face.

I'm thrashing, screaming, my arms flailing toward him. I watch the gash in his throat heal before my eyes and wonder if that too was a hallucination.

The ice of his hands as they grip me seeps into my bones, the fire of his eyes consuming my soul, pulling me away from reality.

XXII

When I feel consciousness dribble into me, the blanket my face is mashed into gives no indicator to where I am.

I cling to the immediate thought that I'm in the back of Alaire's truck, wrapped in the blanket to keep me warm. I grasp at the hope he defeated Denendrius, how if I roll over, I won't be in his bedroom. But I don't feel wheels moving under me. I don't hear traffic or the gentle hum of an engine.

I take a deep, strong breath and roll over, ready to be faced with the off-white walls or the mirrored closet doors of his bedroom.

Instead, my own bedroom materializes. I'm alone with the sun drifting through the blinds and my clutter. I listen for the TV, for the sound of chatter. But there's only the heavy sound of silence.

My second thought is that Alaire figured out where I live, put me in my own bed and is waiting somewhere in the house for me to get up.

"Alaire?" I call out carefully.

Denendrius leans against my door frame. "Alaire is dead," he says simply.

The sight of him makes my heart drop into the pit of my stomach. "Oh," I whisper, hoping he can't recognize my disappointment. "Why are we at my house?"

He crosses his arms, face serious. "Did you tell them where we live?"

"No."

He holds his head high. "Well, how was I to know?"

I swallow a lump as he walks across the room and joins me on the bed.

"How did they find you?" he asks.

I know it would be a bad idea to tell him I'm the one who found them. He'd probably beat me for endangering him, for wasting his time. "They showed up at school."

He rubs my shoulder. "Well, you're safe now."

Is safe a real word anymore? If it is, it no longer holds any meaning. *Safe* . . . it sounds made up.

I'm obviously damned. Now I have to start tying up loose ends before it's too late.

Our eyes meet, a hard silence between us. For once in my life, I have not a single word to say.

"Strange," Denendrius mumbles. "You were unconscious for two days this time."

My eyes widen. "Why?"

"Who knows? It's never exact. My friend regained consciousness eight hours after I turned him, which was quite a bit more bizarre. Maybe it's because Alaire's venom works slower than mine since he was younger or something." He sighs and stands. "Who knows? It's not important."

The phone rings, so I race downstairs for it as an excuse to get away from him.

"Hey," I mumble into it.

"Marianna? It's Margaret."

Fuck, my social worker.

"Oh . . . *hey*."

"Didn't you get the message I left with the secretary at your school? You were supposed to call me the other day."

"No, what's going on?"

She makes an irritated noise. "All right, well, Pam's been arrested. Apparently, she was in possession of a stolen car."

I'm a little more shocked than I should be, and I feel the heat drain from my face when I think of how Pam always kept the convertible in the garage and preferred to carpool over driving. Why had I never considered the reason? Someone must have noticed it when I left it parked in the driveway. "Oh? That's . . ." My voice trails off. If she's been arrested, what does that mean for me?

"I tried to tell you days ago, but half the time you're not at school when I show up, and apparently they don't care about passing messages along either. But, seeing as you're home, I'll make my way over."

I jump when Denendrius flops down on the loveseat, arms crossed.

"Why?"

"We have to transfer you to a new foster home tomorrow. Luckily things organized themselves quickly, so you'll only have to spend tonight in the youth shelter. We can pack your stuff in my car for the meantime."

Denendrius pipes up. "You're staying the night with me."

I half-ignore him, saying to Margaret, "It's okay, I guess I have a place to sleep tonight."

A horn honks on her end. "Okay, well, I'll just need the address so I can pick you up in the morning. But other than that, I'll see you in a few."

"All right."

The line dies and I hang up.

I turn to Denendrius and press my lips together. "So . . ."

"Mm-hmm." He gives me a whatever look.

Margaret is knocking on the door about an hour later. Her olive-toned face churns into an expression of concern as she looks at me when I open the door. I pull the sleeves down around my scarred wrists, pinch the hem between my index finger and thumb, and pull the sweater up to cover the majority of scars on my neck.

"Hey, Marianna." She pulls a few boxes in the door. "Lucky, someone brought boxes into the office today. Better than garbage bags, right?"

"Much better," I agree.

She turns to Denendrius and grins. "Hi, I'm Margaret."

He gives her a haunting look. "Where are you taking my girlfriend?"

She forces a grin, looking to the floor as she scratches her neck. Black hair falls around her fingers. "Just to a new foster home . . . it's on the edge of the city."

"Hm." Denendrius scowls.

She gives me a disgruntled look. "Marianna, why don't we go upstairs so I can help you pack?"

"Okay."

I expect Denendrius to follow, but he just switches to the couch and clicks the TV on.

"So, what's up with the *much older* man downstairs?" she asks when we're in my room, door closed.

"What do you mean?" I cross my arms.

"Besides the obvious, I'm mostly concerned about his obscene attitude."

"Don't worry about it." My voice holds a warning, knowing he can hear from downstairs.

"I don't like him."

I shrug. "He's not so bad," I lie, only so she doesn't try to involve herself. "I have a lot of fun with him. He's just abrasive with new people."

She frowns at me and shakes her head. "I know the law is fine with it, but I'm not. You should be dating someone more age-appropriate. What's he, thirty?"

I dodge with, "How did you find me a new placement so quickly?"

She exhales. "I didn't. A handful of weeks ago, Pam requested to have you removed from her home as soon as possible, and then you were requested to be in another about a week ago."

My eyebrows arch. "Oh? Why did Pam want me gone?"

"She basically said you were 'too tough to handle.'"

"Where have I heard that before?" I roll my eyes. "Whatever."

"You have to admit, you've never made things easy on your foster parents," she scolds.

I grunt and dodge again. "Well, then, who would want to foster me?"

"Carol Greene."

My stomach clenches. The woman from the lemonade stand? I take a deep breath, not wanting to know what I ran from. "Oh."

Why would she even think to foster me? Doesn't she know anything about me?

She faces me, her middle-aged eyes serious. "Stop worrying, everything will turn out fine."

I gyre my head from her. "Humph." I swallow. "Wait, what's going to happen to Samantha and Charlie?"

She shrugs. "I'm assuming their social workers will find them new homes."

I wish they could come with me so I can keep looking after them. Actually, it's probably a good idea if we're separated. With Denendrius in my life, they could be in danger.

I recall the woman named Vianna, and my chest heats. If

she had adopted me back then, I wouldn't need to worry about Carol.

"When I was five, was there a woman named Vianna planning to adopt me?"

Margaret stills, narrow eyes on me. "You don't remember Vianna and Kenneth Fenwick . . . *really?*"

"Kind of," I lie. "I want to know what happened to her. Why would she back out of adopting me?" I yank a loose sweater thread, and it snaps.

"Oh . . . Marianna, she and her husband didn't back out of adopting you. They were dead set on having you." Her face is doleful, freezing my bitter expression while I press her to know what happened. "You were already living with them, and the adoption was close to becoming official." She takes a cement breath. "One night the house was broken into and they were killed in their sleep."

I blink heavily once in surprise. "Well, where was I?"

"You were terrified of sleeping alone in your room, so you used to sleep in between them in theirs." She shakes, voice careful on her next words. "They were stabbed."

I swallow a stone-sized lump. "I was next to them when they were murdered?"

She exhales the anxiety of delivering the news and nods.

I'm frozen now, mouth open, eyes unable to shut. I try to identify my feelings, but I can't. Should I be upset? I feel like punching the wall. How do I not remember any of this? Was it so traumatic that I just forgot they ever existed? "Who killed them?"

"The case has been cold for years, not even any suspects. You really can't remember?"

I shake my head, my fingers itching to smack something, so I bite my lips until blood bursts into my mouth. The murderers ruined my childhood. They stopped me from having a good life. They're to blame, and I'm scared *they* is actually Denendrius.

Margaret's phone beeps and she puffs her cheeks up and expels air from between her lips as she reads something on the screen. "Oh boy, I've got to go down to the police station."

I arch my eyebrow at her.

"Don't worry, has nothing to do with you. Do you think you could pack your stuff into his car instead? I'm assuming that's his Mustang outside, right?"

I nod. "Yeah, that shouldn't be a problem."

"*All right*, I'll see you tomorrow at four, then. What's the address?"

I tell it to her, leaving out his apartment number, and then she's off, Denendrius appearing in my room a few moments later.

I greet him with a murderous glare. "Did you kill my adoptive parents?" I snarl.

He's taken aback by my accusation. "I did no such thing."

Crossing my arms, I sneer. "I don't believe you."

His fingers circle my jaw, hard eyes peering down at me as he lifts my head. "*I didn't kill them*," he enunciates. "Why would I?"

When I try to pull from his grip, it tightens. "Jealousy. You killed Jenna and CJ. I'm sure you had a reason to kill them too." Their names make my eyes sting.

"I wear Jenna's and CJ's deaths with pride," he proclaims. "I have no qualms about what I did. Why would I need to lie to you about this? I promise you—swear on my life—that they were already dead when I returned to Lorimer to check up on you."

My shoulders slump. He has a point. "Oh."

Denendrius drops his hand, eyes assessing my room. "From what I heard from you," he starts, "they were lovely people. Quite unlike what I've heard about your biological mother."

I run my hands through my hair, trying to shake the confusion from my mind. "Then who killed them?" I ask.

"I haven't a clue."

Sitting on my bed, I stare at my belongings.

"You owe me an apology," Denendrius says.

I swallow my groan and mind my tongue. "I'm sorry," I mumble. "Can you help me pack?"

"Yes, but I don't know how you've lived in here." Denendrius wipes something I can't see from the wall. "I've been dying to clean this for months."

I pitifully defend myself with, "It's not too messy."

He laughs. "Are you kidding? Don't worry, we'll organize this."

I groan and he pushes stuff aside. Denendrius insists on sorting everything, so it takes us an hour before we make a dent in my room.

"What's this?" Denendrius asks, pulling a brown box—no bigger than a large shoe box—from the back of the top shelf in my closet.

I leap over a bag of garbage and blow on it, a storm of dust latching onto the air. "Oh. It's my keepsake box. I haven't opened it in years. Put it there." I point to the lopsided pile of things I've fought with Denendrius to keep.

"Why not open it?" he asks, pulling off the thick layer of packing tape.

"No!" My heart leaps and I slap his hand away from it.

My entire childhood dwells in the box. Who knows what would be unleashed if it were disturbed from its safety in the past? What if the childhood air compressed inside proves lethal when breathed? I want no part of my past reentering me. I take it from him and cradle it against my chest.

"Well, can I look at least?" he asks. "I'm awfully curious."

"No." I'd rather it remains as is. I haven't seen anything in it since I was taken from my mother's house.

"Please, Marianna, just a peek."

I grit my teeth. He'll open it anyway, no matter what I say. There's no stopping him.

"Fine!" I nearly shout, dropping the box like it'll explode and kill me if I hold it any longer.

He removes the tape, lifting some of the brown cardboard in the process. It's full of papers and items, but I shade my eyes so I don't catch a glimpse of anything. He rifles through, making faces and smiling as he tears through my past. His face falls when he holds a white piece of paper with curled corners.

"What is it?" I ask ruefully.

He flips the picture around.

"*Oh*," I whisper when I see it.

It's a crayon picture of my mother and me. A nice family portrait, especially since I'm stabbing her. I shake my head and look away as he continues to snoop, the sound of papers and objects lifting a headache in my mind. When the noise stops, I freeze, waiting for him to say something or for it to start up again. When neither does, I spin, just in time to catch a glimpse of a pencil drawing, the tip of a black wing catching my eye.

"What's that?"

He stands and begins to fold it as he shakes his head slowly, face innocent. "Hmm? Nothing."

I hold out my hand. Voice firm, a little too high as I say, "Give it to me."

"No."

I cross my arms. "Why not?"

He shrugs and slips it in his pocket. "It doesn't really matter."

My eyes narrow. "Then why are you keeping it? Put it back in the box if it's nothing."

He frowns deeply, merely staring.

My chest tightens. "Denendrius, what's it a picture of?"

He sighs and to my amazement, he pulls it out of his pocket

and begins to unfold it. I swallow and step toward him, my hand coming up. And then, it's snowing.

I look to my feet and see a million little shards of paper sprinkled all over the floor. My hand drops and I look up to see his head cocked, his lips shaping into a triumphant smile.

"You fucking asshole."

My breath turns thermal. Fingers locking into a fist, I draw back my arm. He backhands me into the wall before I can swing. I can feel the drywall give when my head cracks against it. I regain my balance and the fuzz in my vision fades. He's bent back over the box, digging through it.

"Time to put the box away," I growl, staggering forward with my hand pressed against my cheek.

He pulls out a black disposable camera. "Cool, there's one picture left," he says, looking at the number dial. "Let's take a picture of us."

He laces his hand through my hair and forces me to the floor beside him, not even providing me with enough time to protest against the pain. He holds the camera in front of us. I plaster the happiest smile I can muster on my grim face while he wraps his arm around me and snuggles close. He clicks the button and the flash blinds me. I blink hard after the picture is taken, my sight having a lava lamp effect. I slide away from him and flip the flaps closed on the box.

"This is quite old," he says as he turns the camera in his hands. "Do you know what the other pictures are?"

I tug on my chapped bottom lip. "No. I've never seen it before."

He tucks in it in the pocket of his leather jacket. "Well, let's get them developed tonight."

I poke at my teeth, pressing my finger against their dull edges. "Fine, whatever." My skin quivers for a moment.

I wince when he reaches to pull me closer. He rests his head against mine and rubs my knee, his cold touch biting through the fabric of my jeans. I stare at the brown monster, the way it teases me to pull out a portion of my past. Denendrius reaches around my face and pulls my head to face him.

"You know you can talk to me, right? I'm always here to listen," he whispers. "I care about your problems."

"I'm okay." I let out a fake, stale laugh. *He's* my problem.

"How do you feel knowing Vianna and Kenneth didn't abandon you?" His hand wraps around my fingers, pulling them away from my mouth.

"Nothing," I say. "I feel absolutely nothing."

I search my chest, my heart, for any kind of feeling. But where a heart should be lies an empty black room filled with fire-breathing, teeth-gnashing beings. I wonder if my heart is in the box too. After all, I did lose it quite some time ago.

We sit on the grimy floor for a moment, and then I break away when I deem it acceptable to keep sorting. He joins and we finish packing, leaving out a backpack for school tomorrow and a set of clothes since all the ones at his place are filthy. Denendrius stacks the boxes—only about five—according to size while I sit in the corner of my bare room, feeling like I've bathed in dirt. I stare at the dark blue walls of yet another room I'll never be able to miss and wonder what my room at Carol's will look like.

Denendrius sits down on the futon, pulling my gun from beneath my pillow.

I inhale sharply. "How'd you know that was there?"

He studies it, barrel aimed purposefully in my direction. He grins madly up at me. "I've always known about this gun." He puts it in my backpack. "Ready to go?"

I use the wall to push myself up. "Yeah."

We deliver the disposable camera to a drugstore and plan to pick the pictures up tomorrow when school's over. I try to figure out what could be on the film as we drive to his place, but my mind is as empty as the endless stretch of darkness above.

Once at the apartment, I change into my pajamas in the bathroom after takeout and some horror flicks. When I return to the bedroom, Denendrius is already changed and lying on the right side of the bed.

I nearly slip off the bed when I crawl into it. "New bedspread?" I rub my hand over the black silk sheets.

"Yes. Do you like them?"

I nod indifferently, crawling in again. Drawing the new white comforter up past my chest, I twist onto my back, but he flips me on my side and presses his chest against my back. I stare at myself in the mirrored closet doors. He wraps his arms around me and takes a deep breath, the air tickling my neck when he exhales.

"This is perfect. Hmm?" His voice is light, right behind my ear.

I look at the bruise on my cheek in the reflection. I cover it with my hair and close my eyes so I don't have to look. Am I even tired?

"Why don't you have to sleep in a coffin?" I ask, changing the subject.

I flinch when he breathes more cold air onto my neck. "I'm at a point where a little sunlight won't kill me while I slumber. Most vampires don't have that luxury. Though the modern day offers other options now."

"Oh. Can you dream?" I wonder.

He's quiet for a moment. "I do, yes." His fingers slip under my shirt and he runs his hand over my side.

"What do you dream about?"

He exhales forcefully through his nose, though his voice is gentle when he speaks. "My life, mostly. The things I've experienced." He runs his finger along my spine, his lips touching my ear. "*The things I'd like to experience.*"

I swallow a lump. "Dreaming is never fun."

He holds me tighter. "I know you have night terrors. But think about how much I care about you and it will make you feel better."

No, it won't. How could his games cast anything other than nightmares?

"Are you excited to move in with Carol tomorrow?"

"I don't know. But I probably won't be spending many nights here."

He stiffens behind me. "Yes, you will. I'll make sure she lets you."

I squash my lips together, my chin scrunching. He rolls over onto his back and pulls me to his side. I squirm to find comfort and eventually do with my head on his chest and my legs curled up beside me. I clasp my hands together and tuck them under my chin, watching the shadow from the bar in the window above, and how it flickers occasionally, probably when something passes in front of the light outside.

His chest falls and rises with deep breaths as he runs his fingers through my hair. If his heart is still inside him, it doesn't make a peep. Dead. Is his soul too?

"Denendrius," I whisper.

"Hmm?"

I bite my lip. "Do you have a soul?" I wait for his hands to strike me, but they continue through my hair.

"No."

"How do you know?"

He doesn't respond.

"And your heart?" I whisper.

"It's beating."

"I can't hear it."

He holds me tighter. "I know. It's much quieter and slower than yours, but you'll have to trust that it's working."

I listen harder, but the silence in his chest drones on.

The shadow flickers. "I love you," he whispers.

I pretend I'm already asleep.

He shakes me. "Marianna?"

I try to sound like he woke me. "Mm?"

I pull back when I feel his wet wrist against my lips, Alaire's words of warning screaming in my mind.

He huffs in annoyance. "Whatever those two said to trick you, I really hope you aren't stupid enough to fall for it."

I hold my breath, muscles tensing. I don't know what to say. The junkie in me craves his blood, wants me to give in despite knowing what it'll do to me. Drug and cigarette cravings have been kind to me since I've indulged in this, and that fact doesn't help me refuse. But the logical part of my brain tells me not to fucking dare. Then a teensy terrifying voice whispers in the back of my mind, saying I should take it because of what I know and that I should surrender and join the winning side.

He grips the back of my neck roughly. I lock my jaw when he smears blood across my lips, refusing to allow any to trickle past.

"Come on," he whispers gently, "there's nothing to be afraid of."

When I don't obey, his fingers pinch my nose, causing a break in my breath. I bite down on my lip to stop myself from opening my mouth. My lungs beg for air. My head swims. Panic crawls up from my stomach and instinct makes me gasp for air. He shoves his bloodied wrist against my open mouth, the taste of his blood drowning my fear.

My hands wrap greedily around his forearm to hold it in place. He runs his fingers across my back, a kiss finding the top of my head.

"See?" he murmurs. "They got you riled up over nothing."

XXIII

I wake from a dreamless sleep, Denendrius staring down at me as he sits beside my head against the wall. I jerk and look around for a clock that doesn't exist.

"Good morning, my beautiful Venus," he says, gently running the back of his fingers over my bruised cheek. "I've missed you."

Their temperature is enough to jar me into a wide wakefulness.

I notice his leather jacket is on, his mirrored aviators folded over the neckline of his dark green T-shirt. Did he come back from somewhere, or has he been waiting for me to wake up so he can go without leaving me alone?

"Morning," I moan.

I stretch and my shirt rides up. I ruefully notice my hip bones. They were always slightly visible but now appear sharper under my flesh. I realize how little I've been eating, how my appetite has been barely existent. I must be missing at least five or ten pounds; hopefully it hasn't affected my muscle mass.

When Denendrius's fingers reach to touch my exposed skin, I roll off the bed and onto my feet.

"Would you like to go to school today?" His voice is light.

Not really, but it'll be a party compared to spending the day with him. "Sure."

The lunch bell is five minutes away from ringing when Denendrius and I pull up in front of the school.

"Where are you off to?" I ask, checking my face in the visor mirror. The bruise on my right cheek is just as prominent as yesterday.

He slaps the visor back against the ceiling, the reflection of my surprised scowl disappearing.

"Don't you worry your pretty face," he says, his smile sardonic.

Ugh. I open the door, saying, "See you later."

I get one foot on the ground before he yanks on my arm. Eyes narrow, I look back in question, trying not to react to the pain. He releases me and pulls out his thick cash-lined wallet from his back pocket. I can tell some of the money is bloody before he even opens it.

He pulls out a fifty and holds it out to me. "Grab lunch."

Slowly, I reach for it. "You're giving me money?"

He chuckles. "I'd give you anything you wanted, Marianna —a horse to ride through the Sahara if you needed—you've just never asked."

"Really?" My eyes turn to slits. I pinch the edge of the bill, expecting him to rip it away from me. He lets go and it dangles in my fingertips.

He nods. "I'm not sure why you're surprised. Clothes, shoes, jewelry, five-star meals every night . . . you can have anything."

Anything, except my freedom.

I swallow and scrunch the bill in the palm of my hand. "Oh" is all I say.

Denendrius's fingers tease the bottom of my hair. "You just have to want it," he adds. His face turns solemn.

"What do you mean?" I ask carefully.

His hand moves from the tips of my hair to my neck. His fingers curl around the back, his thumb running from under my chin, down my throat and to my collarbones before stopping.

"Just be a good girlfriend," he says simply, "and I'll prove what an excellent boyfriend I can be."

I swallow, and a wicked smile appears on his lips. Cold sweat starts down my back when he pulls me toward him for a kiss. I entertain his lips, wanting the money to stay in my hand.

"See you in a few hours," he says against my lips before nudging me toward the open door.

"Okay, thanks," I mumble, stepping out onto the pavement.

He peels away a fraction of a second after I shut the door.

Grumbling to myself, I walk across the street and into the school, past security and through the empty hallway toward the cafeteria. The bell rings for lunch when I open the door, students already buzzing around tables and in line.

I roll up the sleeves of my blue hoodie, only to shove them back down to my wrists at the sight of the bruise already forming on my left forearm. I heave a sigh and forcefully remove a tray from the stack.

I'd planned on gorging myself on cafeteria foods, but my loss of appetite makes me just grab fries, ignoring the tacos, hamburgers, and pizza I wish I could stomach.

I find my table near the back and pick at my fries, Camille and Daina piling into their seats not long after.

"You know, the cafeteria has all sorts of different foods. You could try something else besides fries," Daina says as she cuts off a piece of pizza from her slice with a plastic fork and knife.

I chew a handful of fries exaggeratedly, a few pieces falling from my mouth. "Yeah? Well, you could eat your pizza like a normal person."

Camille—after blabbering on for a good ten minutes—slams the palms of her hands on the table. "I'm not kidding, Marianna! I'm trying to help you! But I can't if you keep pretending I don't exist."

"Has Sarah been to school the past couple days?" I ask Daina.

She saws off another piece. "Hmm, I don't think so."

Camille kicks the table before storming away, making Daina jump. Her utensils snap in her hands. She curses and throws them on the table and picks up the slice between her long and freshly painted nails.

An exhausted sigh slips past my lips, and I rest my head on my hand. "Well, then." I stuff fries into my mouth.

"On a random note, do you have any tampons? I only have one left." Daina frowns.

"No. I still haven't gotten my period," I grumble.

Maybe if I did, my boobs would grow, not that I need another reason for Denendrius to gawk at me.

She purses her lips. "Maybe you should see a doctor?"

"I'm fine. I guess I'm just a late bloomer."

"You're seventeen . . ."

"What's your point? I'm sure there are plenty of seventeen-year-olds who are late."

She frowns at her pizza. "All right."

I say goodbye and leave my fries behind. I have better things to ponder, like what Camille is up to, which I don't figure out until last period, when the school counselor knocks on the classroom door and asks to see me.

I've never talked to Liz before, constantly dodging all attempts at meetings she's scheduled in the past. Walking out the front doors instead of going to her office, skipping school days when she's had the office give me a note with a date and time. But with her standing smugly in the doorway, face smiling with a look of I-got-you-now, how could I escape?

Groaning, I slink out of my desk, trudging toward the middle-aged woman with a rippled face, like water in a pond when you drop a cinder block into it.

"Yo," I greet dryly.

She waves me out of the room with a single swipe as if she's showing a fancy car in a commercial. The door shudders when she pulls it closed, heels clicking as she walks behind me, an arm's length away. Probably so she can snatch me if I make a break for it.

Herding me toward her office, she hums quietly. My brows knit together, and I glare at the scratched floor, running my fingers along the pastel yellow lockers, the metal cold to the touch.

When my fingers reach open air, I look up and walk across the intersecting hallway to the dull green door with a covered window. With a push from four of her ringed fingers, the door sails backward. She enters and shuts it behind us.

"Take a seat." She grunts, lowering herself into a black chair after pulling it from a cluttered desk.

The tacky blue couch across from her is uninviting, covered with lacy throw pillows plump with misshapen innards. I heave myself onto the middle cushion and watch her grim expression as she leafs through my thick file.

"So . . ." I say, mouth to the side, stretching my cheek.

A practiced smile slides upon her face as she opens a yellow notepad, setting a black pen on it crookedly.

"So, a very concerned friend of yours came to me at noon. She says your boyfriend isn't treating you well, and she thinks you are caught in an abusive relationship." She runs her hands through her yellowy spiked hair.

Camille.

I curl my fingers around the hem of my hoodie, not planning to spew any information about my life to this woman who is obviously too annoyed at me to care. "I don't need help," I clarify. "I'm not in an abusive relationship."

If only she knew it was something, much, *much* worse.

She studies me and nods. "Then we're just here to talk. Sometimes getting everything out of your system can make you feel better."

"Or make a person more paranoid about where the information is going," I counter.

She takes an unsatisfied breath. "I promise anything you say in this room will stay in this room."

I cock my brow. "So technically anyone who comes in this room can be told what I've said."

She twists in her chair and pinches the bridge of her nose. "I promise anything you say will be kept strictly between us."

I lean back against the couch and it squeaks. She must think I'm stupid.

"How long has this been going on?" she asks.

I cross my arms and tighten my jaw. "Awhile."

"I know you don't want to talk about it, but I feel like you could benefit from doing exactly that."

"Probably not." I lean over and jam my flat hands between my knees.

"Why don't you tell me how you two met?"

Oh yeah, why not? Why not tell her that I met him when I was a kid and then he asked me on a date years later? Why not tell her that when I turned him down, he made me be his girlfriend after stabbing me, and that he's probably going to kill me soon? Sure, that's something that totally needs to leave my mouth.

"You know, there are lots of resources to help women in abusive relationships. If you feel like you can't go to the cops, you can go to a women's shelter, you can call a distress hotline, and you can connect with people like me."

I stare at my hands, now twisted on my lap. "I don't need help."

If Alaire and Edmond couldn't help me, then who can?

"I know you probably think it's not that bad, that it could be worse. Do you think you deserve what he does? That he only hits you because you set him off?"

The problem is, sometimes it is my fault. Sometimes I say things poorly, sometimes I shove him. I antagonize him even when I know the consequences. Of course, I only do it because he started it. But if I was a better *girlfriend*, would he be nicer? If I hadn't tried to break up with him, would he still be a perfect gentleman? Technically, I was mean first.

"If you do think that, it's not true. He does what he does because he has issues," she says carefully. "It has nothing to do with you."

"Oh, he's got loads of issues," I spit.

She stacks her hands on her lap, green eyes trying to decipher me. "No relationship is perfect, and I know you two might love each other, but you don't deserve to go through that in the name of love. Love isn't always enough."

Obviously, I don't deserve it. "I don't love him," I say.

He may have said he loves me, but it's a lie. It's manipulation is all.

She purses her lips. "Okay, well, still. I was also told there was a significant age gap between the two of you, and while it's legal, I worry given your personal situation that a power imbalance may come into play. I was told he has quite a bit of wealth. Regardless of age, all relationships should be an equal partnership. Do you find that to be the case here?"

"No," I admit.

Her lips form a tight, flat line. "Mm-hmm. Is there anything, aside from fear, that keeps you two together? I'm sure I could make assumptions on my own, but what is it that has drawn him to you, and you to him?"

I'm unsure of what to say to her, so I stare at the thin gray carpet like the question will answer itself.

"Marianna?"

"I don't know," I whisper. I don't understand why he wants *me*.

The bell rings.

"You can stay to keep chatting if you'd like." She smiles.

My eyes flit to the window; Denendrius's car is parked across the street. I swallow. Did he hear what we said?

I stand. "No." I walk lazily toward the door before turning around to say, "If you call the cops, I'll deny everything."

She just sighs.

XXIV

I wait in Denendrius's car for him to come out of the store with the developed photos. When he returns, he tosses the envelope on my lap.

I stare at him carefully before pulling the photos out of the envelope. My fingers shake, my mind whirring. I take a deep breath.

The first is of Denendrius and me taken in my room. With wide smiles, his eyes are bright, mine dull. I put the photograph behind the others.

I frown at the next photo. It's of me as a child, sitting on a slide in a park I don't recognize. The third is a bedroom, blue and filled with action figures, dolls, and stuffed animals. The next two are blurry, somewhere outside in a backyard, and there's an orange tabby cat. Next, a picture of an amusement park ride, and I wonder if it's in Enchanted Land.

A picture of Denendrius slides between my fingers when I flip through. It's shaky, and this time I know it's in Enchanted Land, as he's sitting at the same blue table from his home video.

His aviators are placed on his face, but instead of his leather jacket, he wears a black-and-white windbreaker. More pictures of rides and low-angled pictures of Denendrius from behind on some street.

Most of the pictures are a blurry mess, or completely black.

The last picture makes my heart drop. It's a family photo, taken with a woman dressed up as a mermaid, her purple tail and hair bright. Vianna holds me, my fingers curled in her long, straight fiery-orange hair. Kenneth stands beside her, balding with a pair of thick old glasses on his face.

I swallow and bite my lip, throwing them back into the envelope.

"Hm. I thought we lost that," Denendrius mumbles before adding, "Is that what you were expecting?"

I cross my arms after putting the envelope in my backpack. I set my feet on the dashboard and stare out the window numbly. "I didn't have any expectations."

Denendrius starts driving, making his way to the apartment so I can meet Margaret. He watches me carefully, measuring my silence. I don't speak much for the next while, barely offering conversation as we pull up to the apartment.

Margaret wants me to ride with her to Carol's, and to my surprise, Denendrius doesn't protest much, though he follows us with the car instead. He calculates my expression as I hop out of his car, and as I say goodbye to him, I see gears visibly working in his head. I try not to dwell on why he appears so troubled.

I sit with Margaret in her car. The sky stirs clouds the color of charcoal and they become too weak to carry the fat droplets of water. The rain taps gently on the windshield, the sound intertwined with the rush of our tires on the dampened highway. They slide down glass, long pure streaks. The forest rushes beside us. I crack the window open, a whooshing noise entering, accompanied by the scent of fresh rain and forest heavy in the air.

After an hour of driving, we near her neighborhood. The road traces along bright green lawns. The beautiful homes are separated by thick trees or shrubs. I can imagine all the warm-hearted families inside again, fireplaces lit, tea in their hands as they surround themselves with smiling faces.

Margaret pulls into the driveway of the yellow Victorian-style home.

A sense of achievement washes over me as Margaret and I get out with my backpack strung over my shoulder, a cold breeze welcoming me into its presence. To hope I'd ever live in a place like this was merely wishful thinking until now. I can't help but think I'm getting a chance to start fresh, a second chance to find a perfect place. But the thought is shattered when Denendrius wanders up behind me. There are no fresh starts.

Taking a deep breath through his nose, he says, "You've got to be kidding me."

"What?" I ask, walking around the rain-kissed purple car and toward the front. Rain drips through my hair, cold as it falls around my face.

He doesn't answer.

I knock on the door and it flies open, exposing a familiar freckle-faced woman with long poufy orange hair in waves and curls.

"Come on in," she says warmly.

As soon as we're hidden from the rain, she turns to Denendrius.

"I'm Carol," she says, extending her hand for him to shake. "You are?"

"Den." He nods, pretending he doesn't notice it. "Marianna's boyfriend."

She lowers her hand slowly, her mouth opening to speak.

Closing it, she stares at him, a confused expression crossing her face. "Um . . . right . . ." She blinks hard as if she's trying to clear her mind of a disturbing thought. "Marianna, I'll show you your bedroom."

Denendrius and I turn left behind her and head up a flight of stairs. My hand glides up the smooth white banister as we walk under the dim white light. At the top of the stairs there's a huge window facing the trees between the neighbors and us. We turn down a hallway once we're on the second floor. The doorway to the first room is across from the wall above the stairs. She enters it and flicks the light on.

The walls are the color of snow, the floor a gray-blue wood. To my right is a large closet with accordion doors and white panels. An actual bed is against the wall—a twin—right after the closet. It's covered in gray sheets and a fluffy white comforter. Straight across from the doorway is a window, standing from the floor to the ceiling and as wide as my arms when they're stretched out at my sides. Through the window, across the road, lies the forest.

"This is beautiful," I whisper as I walk to it.

"I'm glad you like it," she says.

"No, I love it." I sit on the bed. It's like sitting on a cloud.

We carry my boxes up to unpack, but then Margaret says she has to leave soon. She talks with Carol downstairs while Denendrius helps me unpack.

"You should be living with me," he says.

I stare at him for a long moment. "I can once I'm a legal adult?"

"Sure, when you're eighteen." He winks. "Don't worry, this is only temporary. It's convenient for me."

"How so?"

He merely smiles.

When Carol returns, she hangs my clothes in the closet and I unpack books and place them on the ceiling-high white built-in bookshelf left of the window. All my books fill half the shelf.

"Where's the bathroom?" I ask, half out the door.

"Last room at the end of the hall," she says, hanging a long-sleeved black shirt on a clear hanger.

I'm almost at the bathroom door when I hear, "I'm staying the night here with Marianna."

I pause beside the door.

"Uh . . . I don't think so," Carol says.

The bed creaks and I assume its Denendrius who sits because I can still hear her placing hangers on the bar.

"I'm surprised you have a problem with it, considering I'm the reason she's alive now. She would have been kidnapped if I hadn't found her when I did."

What's he talking about? Enchanted Land?

"So that's why you look so familiar." She takes a deep breath.

"Yes. I'm surprised you still remember me."

Wait, *what*? What does Carol have to do with what happened at Enchanted Land?

"Well, you still look the same. And I wouldn't forget the man who brought her back to us."

"So, you agree that I can stay?" he says again, hardly asking.

"No, I don't think so," she says carefully. "I'm sure you know why."

I jump, startled into the banister when there's a loud thump on the other side of the wall where Carol was standing. I don't have to go back in the room to know the sound was from her body being slammed against the wall.

"You're more than happy to let me stay here," Denendrius says.

I imagine the expressionless look on her face, his eyes pinning hers while he messes around with her mind. I'm thankful my head is too fucked for him to hypnotize me.

"It's really no issue," she says robotically. "You're more than welcome."

"Thank you." The bed squeaks.

Her voice returns to normal, and I can almost hear the smile. "Oh, no worries! The rain will probably get worse closer to the city. Soon it'll be too dangerous to drive."

"That's true. I'm surprised you've been so close all along. Small world."

"No kidding. God, I regret going on my trip to Africa. I didn't even know my sister had died until I got back. By then I had no idea what had happened to Marianna." She pauses. "Sorry, I guess you wouldn't know what happened to them."

"I'm well aware."

"What does she remember?" Carol asks. I hear the floor creak. "She didn't seem to remember me."

"She knows about your sister and her husband. But she doesn't remember Enchanted Land. But I think she's slowly starting to piece the rest together."

"That's good."

Denendrius shuffles. "Mm-hmm."

My heart pounds, ready to burst through and shatter on the floor. He's aware I'm outside the door, so he must hear its panicked beating. He must know I'm fitting everything together too. Like how Carol and Vianna were sisters, both at Enchanted Land with me. But why didn't Carol look for me when they were murdered? She could have given me a good life. I could have been saved from my mother.

I back toward the bathroom. Why didn't Margaret prepare me? I know she hasn't always been my social worker, but didn't she know? How do I not remember anything? How is it a memory like this could hide in the recesses of my mind? It's too much. My breathing sounds like a wind turbine. After locking the door, I hide in the bottom of the pearly tub, wrapping my arms around my body. Staring at the golden walls, I hope Denendrius can't hear me.

I need to go back, to undo meeting Denendrius, to stop him from opening a part of my past. Why can't I handle this as I've handled everything else about my past? Brush it off and shrug, tell myself to get over it and move the hell on. Why does it have me hiding, head on my knees as I try to straighten everything out? What's happening to me?

I take a deep breath and use the toilet, then wash my hands. I scowl at myself in the mirror. "Stop being so pathetic," I growl quietly. I place a smug smile on my lips, hoping to trick myself into thinking everything is well.

Walking into the room, my smile still stuck, I look at Carol and try to act as if I'm still clueless about her identity.

"Where are your other foster kids?" I ask, thinking about the twins from the lemonade stand.

She's stuffing folded jeans into the white dresser in the closet. "They're having a sleepover at a friend's house. I'm picking them up after we're done shopping tomorrow. I thought it would be good for us to have some one-on-one time."

"Shopping?" I sit beside Denendrius. He gives me a quick kiss on the cheek, making Carol's face scrunch up with displeasure

"I thought you'd like to get stuff for your room," she clarifies, sliding a wooden drawer shut.

We finish unpacking my things and then she shows me the rest of the house. When we get to the kitchen, I run toward the sliding doors to the deck when I spot a hot tub.

"You have a hot tub?" I exclaim, grinning. I've never been in a personal hot tub before, just the shared ones at public pools. "Can I go in it?"

She chuckles. "Sure, if you want to try it out when I'm done showing you around, you can."

I grin. "Okay, cool."

A few minutes later, she's heading toward wide sliding doors leading to the deck. "I'll get it ready if you want to put your swim stuff on."

I rush upstairs and change into my bikini. Then I go outside onto the wooden deck in the rain, where Denendrius is already bare of clothing and in the steaming hot tub. His eyes are bright, wandering over my body as I approach.

He grins. "The things I'd love to do to you."

"You're naked, aren't you?"

His grin grows.

I mash my lips together, quickly turning uncomfortable with the idea of getting in with him. But he'll be offended if I don't, so I crawl into the hot water and find a seat across from him. He licks his lips as he watches me. I smile weakly as I sink up to my shoulders in water. He gives me a playful look and slides through the floating islands of bubbles to sit beside me.

"Hey there," he says seductively.

I jump when I feel his hand on my knee, water splashing. He stares ahead as he skates his hand up my thigh, a small smile on his lips. He massages the inside of my thigh and my leg twitches in response.

"Mmm." He turns toward me and settles his lips on mine, kissing me gently. His fingers run over my collarbone and rest on the side of my neck. "I love you," he says suggestively.

I don't want to answer, but his fingers are so close to my throat. He could choke me or shove my head under the water, and from the look in his eye, I can tell he's thinking it too. I close my eyes hard, shallow breaths escaping my lips. I don't want to say it, but what will happen if I don't?

"I love you too," I breathe.

His lips turn up. "I knew it."

He returns to kissing me, his hands sliding under the water and beneath my blue bikini top. He touches me and pulls my body close to him with the other arm.

Where's Carol? She should really come out here and break us apart.

I push my fists against his chest as he tries to pull me onto his lap, his fingers pulling at the strings of my bikini bottoms.

My heart leaps into my throat and I gasp. "No."

Water splashes around us in my attempt to swim backward. He steals my wrists.

"If it's because you're worried about Carol seeing us, I told her to go listen to music in her room. She can't hear."

"No, I just don't want to." I try to reclaim my arms, but he doesn't let go.

He kisses my throat, his hands moving to my hips. "I don't believe you."

I feel sick, so I look hopefully to the window of her bedroom.

"I know you've been saving yourself for me," he murmurs, fingers sliding across my stomach.

"I-I'm not a virgin," I stumble, not sure what else to say.

"Those men don't count," he consoles. He pulls the string on my bikini.

I swallow, stomach twisting painfully. "N—"

He kisses my "no" away.

I turn my head. "You're making me uncomfortable."

"Prove you love me. Hmm?" His fingers bend painfully around mine and he puts my hand on his crotch.

"Stop!" I jerk my hand back, but his grip is iron. Fear washes over me. Wetness wells in my eyes and I'm thankful he can't see they're tears because of the rain.

I take a deep breath and stifle my tears, refusing to cry in front of him. I know it'll make things worse.

"I'm good, I promise." He releases my hand but pulls my top off.

I cover myself with my arms, but he yanks them away, eyes lingering before his hands do.

His pout is playful. "Don't pretend I've never seen you naked."

My eyes widen. In my underwear, sure, but bare? This is the first I'm hearing about it. But of course, why would he limit his stalking to only when I'm clothed?

"I'm not ready," I plead, even though I know no words can stop him from getting what he wants.

"You only think so. You're probably worried it will be like when you were little. But it won't be. It'll be good."

I shake my head, pushing my fists into his chest.

He slips his hand down the front of my bottoms. I tighten my legs, but he still manages to hook his fingers inside me. "Feels good, right?" he whispers, leaning forward so my arms fold up.

His lips beg mine for movement. My stomach cramps. My chest is laden, and with my eyes closed, it's hard to tell if I'm with Denendrius in the hot tub or sitting on the dirty floor with some man who's old enough to be my grandfather.

I recline my head and look up at the blackened sky, rain slipping down my face. "You promised you wouldn't do anything like this. You said you wouldn't rape me."

He sighs, breathing out disappointment, and shoves me away. "I'm not a rapist, Marianna."

His denial sparks my fury. I float backward across the hot tub and grab my top, tying it back on. "Are you sure? You can't seem to take no for an answer. I told you I didn't want you to touch me and you did anyway."

He drifts through the water—face displaying hurt—to hold my face. "I don't know what to tell you, sweetheart, but you know I love you, right?"

I push my hands against my chest, and he looks back at me, eyes pained, eyelashes batting a little too much. *Manipulating.*

"Say you're sorry. For once, just apologize."

He shakes his head and pretends cluelessness. "Marianna . . ."

"Honestly? You can't even pretend like you're sorry?" My voice is strained.

He shuts me up with a soft kiss and a tight hug.

Realizing how every time he's put the moves on me, he's gotten a step closer to sex, I whisper, "I know what you're doing."

He's probably hoping I'll tire of his efforts and give in, or that this fucking blood mark will convince me I want him.

He pulls away and tilts his head, lines of puzzlement chiseled deep in his features. "Hmm. What am I doing?"

But when I open my mouth to accuse, the devil glares back at me. My body tingles, an unspoken threat of pain if I dare accuse him of such a thing.

"What time is it?" I ask unsteadily to change the topic, eyes breaking from his.

"Ten forty-nine."

"How do you always know the time?" I lower my head and clear my throat.

"I just do. It's a vampire thing. Like an internal clock."

"Oh." I bring my knees to my chest, my chin dipping below the water. I blow air across the surface.

Ripples disrupt the tiny ones I create as his muscular body cuts through the bubbles and water. "Let's shower and go to bed. You need rest and I don't want to lie next to the smell of chlorine."

He shoves me in the knee, splashing water into my eyes. He turns his back to me and begins to climb out, steam rising from him and spiraling into the air where the rain dampens it. I avert my eyes until he's wrapped a towel around his waist, holding one out to me.

I hurry out of the pool after him, leaving the sound of pattering rain on the water behind me. I stand in a pair of his watery footprints on the deck. Denendrius grabs his dry clothes off a deck chair and herds me into the house. I almost slip in my own steps, but he grabs my hip.

Water drips softly against the carpeted steps when we head up. He passes my room, so I assume he's taking the shower first. Going to turn into my room, he grabs my arm.

"There's no reason why you can't shower with me," he says.

I can think of many, even though he wouldn't accept them.

He smiles. "It's just a shower."

I begrudgingly allow him to pull me along into the bathroom. He locks the door and hangs his towel on a hook on the gold wall.

"I have to pee," I say, hoping for an excuse to either leave the room and go use the bathroom downstairs or make him leave.

He steps into the pearly white tub and draws back the white plastic curtain, water turning on.

"Go, I don't care," he says.

I grumble but go, flushing the toilet when I'm done in hopes of burning him.

Stepping into the tub with my bikini on, I take extra care to keep my eyes above his waist. Denendrius leans against the pink tile to fit under the shower head, water running down the side of his grinning face.

I run my hands under the stream of water and yelp, teeth clamping as I suck back the pain of being scolded. I hold my red hands and notice the handle is cranked as hot as it will go.

"It feels nice," he says softly.

I glower and he sighs, taking my hands in his, cold.

Steam quickly collects in the bathroom as he stands unmoving in the heat. He drops my hands and closes his eyes, using the wall to hold himself up.

My skin crawls as I watch him. I'm reminded of a snake

bathing in the sun and wonder if he'd do the same if it didn't harm him.

"Can you feel the cold?" I ask him, crossing my arms.

He doesn't open his eyes. "From external sources like the weather? Yes, but barely, and not enough for it to bother me. I don't even notice the temperature most of the time." He frowns and opens his eyes. "I'm only troubled by the cold that comes with going thirsty."

"Oh."

His frown deepens then curls into a smirk when he looks me over. "C'mon. I'll switch places with you, but you have to take that stupid thing off. It defeats the purpose of a shower." He turns the water dial to half and pushes past me to steal my spot.

I expect him to stand and gawk at me, but he finds a bottle of body wash and I take the time while he's distracted to pull my bikini off. I use my elbows to cover what little of my breasts has grown while I rinse my hair.

Denendrius chortles, covered in minty bubbles. "I didn't think you'd be so shy."

My face reddens, but I'm unsure if it's from anger or embarrassment. "I'm not shy," I snap unconvincingly.

He winks and pushes me out of the way to rinse off, cranking the heat again.

I grab a random body wash, but he yanks it out of my hand, placing a floral one in my questioning fingers.

"I like you smelling like flowers. It works better with your scent," he says.

I huff but can't say I disagree when it's what I've chosen myself for as long as I can remember. When I rinse off, I try not to dwell on how his eyes are locked on me and instead focus on not looking at him, so he doesn't get ideas.

He notices my aversion and smiles wickedly, holding his

arms at his side. "Go ahead," he teases. "I'm sure you'll like what you see."

My mouth opens silently, heat lifting from my stomach to my face. His smile widens and he reaches for his towel and steps out. I'm just thankful he's amused rather than angry.

The curtain rips back a few moments later, and he turns the water off. He's already dry and in his black boxers. He holds out a pink towel and I quickly take it, covering myself and following him back to my room.

Denendrius plunks down on my bed and watches me, growing visibly annoyed at my ability to dry off without exposing my entire self. When I gather a T-shirt and shorts, his face straightens into something serious.

"I'm not going to touch you in your sleep," he says sharply. "I'm not my father."

I swallow. So much for his good mood. "I'm more comfortable in clothes. I've never slept without them."

"Fine," he says with a shake of his head.

I carefully approach the bed and he moves over against the wall.

"Sure there's enough room on here for both of us?"

He pulls me toward him when I climb on.

"If you stay close like this." He sighs into my neck.

I stare at the ceiling, feeling his eyes on me. When he draws his wrist to my lips, my stomach pinches. I know better now than to try and stop him. I tell myself I'll have to work extra hard at keeping my own thoughts. The self-sabotaging voice speaks from the back of my mind again, louder this time, telling me I'm overreacting and that I'm exaggerating the situation. I push it back and drink, enjoying myself a little too much.

When he pulls his wrist away, I enjoy the residual calm and let him kiss me before rolling over to stare at the forest out the window. The glow of streetlights outlines the trees at the edge of the forest, shows a wolf as it bounds through the grass on the outskirts.

"Do werewolves exist?" I whisper.

He groans. "No. Just vampires. No witches, shapeshifters, wizards, werewolves, warlocks, fairies, etcetera."

"Oh—"

"Go to sleep," he murmurs.

A few minutes trickle by, and eventually, the wolf vanishes into the trees, howling. I breathe out an exaggerated sigh, hoping it will shake him awake. He doesn't move. I suck in air as long as I can, then let it rush out. He still doesn't react.

I start sucking in air again when he speaks.

"Really, Marianna?"

I smile devilishly, content with the response. "I have a question."

He grunts.

My voice turns serious. "Do you think anyone else is going to come after you?"

"No, not after I killed those two."

I frown, disappointment making me feel heavy. "Okay," I mumble.

"Go to sleep."

I make a face and see the wolf return with three more. I observe them through the raindrops on the window, listening closely to Denendrius's breathing and the light pitter-patter of rain on the glass. After at least half an hour, my eyelids don't even droop.

"Denendrius." My whisper cuts through the silence. He doesn't answer, so he must be asleep.

I crawl out from under his arm, thinking about getting a glass of water from the kitchen.

The living room light is on as I tiptoe down the stairs. Carol sits on the overstuffed couch, bent over a coffee table with photographs sprawled out on its surface.

"Hey," she says, turning to me, face somber.

I gnaw on my lip. "Why didn't you take me in when Vianna was killed?" I blurt.

She pats a place next to her on the couch and I wrap my arms around myself. I do a half-walk, half-sprint to her and plunk myself down.

"I'm just going to explain everything, right from the beginning," she says.

Arms wrapped tightly around my stomach, I sit down beside her with my heart thumping so hard I'm worried either she or Denendrius will hear.

"Your mom and dad couldn't have biological children," she starts, setting their wedding photos in my twitchy fingers. "So, they started looking into adoption."

Her phrasing makes me wince, and I'm not sure why. Maybe it's because her words feel like a lie. Maybe because they're dead and I can't remember ever having anyone worth calling mom and dad.

I run my finger over the large eighties-style embellished white dress, Vianna's pink smile as wide as her curled and teased orange hair. Kenneth stands by her side, his large glasses the focal point of his soft face.

"After the process of paperwork and sifting through profiles, they picked you, and you were taken from foster care and placed with them. Then we waited for everything to go through."

My stomach is warm at the idea that they *picked me* above other kids, though I can't shake the thought that another kid probably deserved to be adopted over me.

Carol hands me another photograph. In front of the Enchanted Island castle, Vianna and Kenneth stand on either side of a smiling little girl.

"We knew your beginning years were hard," Carol

murmurs. "Enchanted Land seemed like a great way to start off as a family."

My fingers feel numb as I hold the glossy photograph, and my next breath is dry. "I look like I had fun."

She nods and wipes at her eye. "You did. The four of us had a great time."

I place the photos back on the table before I drop them.

"After our vacation, I took a trip with my boyfriend to Africa for four months. It wasn't easy to get in contact with me, and I didn't know anything had happened to them until I came home." She clasps her shaky hands in her lap and stares down at them. "You were put back into foster care. My sister and Kenneth had no other living family left. I badgered them for you, but the government still held the rights to you, and they didn't think an unmarried twenty-year-old who dropped out of college to travel was favorable. Still, I tried, but your biological mom was somehow cleared of charges and you were put back in her care."

A tired smile curves Carol's lips. "I thought I recognized you when you stopped for lemonade, and when I went inside and saw the old picture of you on my mantel, I knew it had to be you." She rubs my shoulder. "I made a call as soon as you had driven away, and lucky for us, Pam wanted you out, so they were already trying to find a new placement for you."

I return a shaky smile, but it only lasts for a few seconds. "I'm exhausted."

She gives me a caring pat on my shoulder and wishes me goodnight.

Racing up the stairs and into my room, I hide under the blankets, my heart thumping in my ears, my breath so ragged I'm surprised when it doesn't wake Denendrius. I compile the entire story in my head, go over it, and make sure I won't forget any of it like I have before.

XXV

Denendrius's and Carol's voices drift up from downstairs when I wake up. I leap out of bed, alarmed at the thought of them alone together. I throw on a pair of ripped jeans and a tight black halter top with a few cigarette burns in the neckline and bottom hem, slipping into a hoodie to hide my bruises.

My black backpack full of photos catches my gaze as I run a brush through my hair.

I gather my expression and shape it into something appearing to be gleeful and bound down the stairs. I grin widely at Denendrius upon entering the room.

"Took you long enough," he teases.

Carol places a plate of eggs and bacon on the table in front of me as I sit down.

"As soon as you're done, we can leave," she says.

Grease douses my fingers and runs down my thumb when I pick up the bacon. "Where are we going?" I pull the plate a bit closer, ruffling the pink tablecloth as I grab a fork and scoop up a steaming pile of fluffy eggs.

"Just the mall," Carol says.

"Okay," I mumble, my mouth full.

"Well, not to be rude, but you don't have much for good clothes, so that's our main priority," she says.

My "okay" is muffled when I shovel the rest of the eggs into my mouth.

"Ready to go?"

I nod.

Once again, Denendrius bitches about whose vehicle we ride in. Since he claims he won't be caught dead in a minivan, Carol surrenders, clearly playing nice for my benefit, and we pile into his car. Rain spills from the sky, the windshield wipers working overtime, swishing so fast I'm surprised they don't fly off the car. Carol chews her nails in the back seat in the moments when her hands aren't gripping tight to my headrest. The mall is a twenty-minute drive through a slow trickle of traffic.

"You drive like a maniac," she says to Denendrius as he cuts off a truck to get into a parking space closest to the mall entrance.

"Well, you should be thanking me, because the second-closest parking space would have us as wet as the Atlantic by the time we got inside."

She gives an indifferent shrug and pulls the green hood of her raincoat over her poufy mane. "Come on, Marianna, I'll race you guys inside."

The car door opens, and she disappears into the downpour.

Denendrius is smiling as he shoves the car keys into the pocket of his leather jacket. "Isn't she fun?"

"I like her." My words surprise both of us. I've never liked a foster parent before.

"It's a shame her sister and brother-in-law never got to raise you." For once, his words are genuine. He adjusts his aviators and cracks the door open. "They were good people. You would have been much better off, I think."

I feel my small smile come as I dip my head, open the door, and rush through the rain. I shiver under the droplets as Denendrius takes my hand and drags me along, water dripping down my back.

Carol is waiting for us on a bench inside the doors where the cafeteria is. He gives her an amused smile and leads us from the fast-food trap to where the stores are.

"Where to first?" I ask, walking backward through the smog of greasy fast-food scents.

We end up in a skateboard shop, and I leave with a couple pairs of jeans and a few long-sleeved shirts, so I have more options to hide bruises with. Browsing turns into a nightmare with Denendrius looming over my shoulder, who disagrees with half the clothing I choose and tries to make a thing out of my preference for long sleeves. I shut Carol down when she tries to stand up for me and let him pick shorts for me to shut him up. At least bruises haven't made a habit of finding my legs.

After browsing a few more stores and ending up with a handful of outfits, she leads me into a lingerie shop, and I do my best to pick items, with Denendrius trying to dictate.

"Are we done shopping now?" I grumble once we're out of the store. I shake the bags of clothes on my arms. They're nearly numb.

"Almost—where did Denendrius go?" She looks around, puzzled.

I'm almost relieved not to know where he is but also concerned he'll come back with something absurd for me to wear.

An hour and a half later, I spot him sitting on a bench, playing with something. Carol disappears into a store, muttering something about a necklace. I trot over to where he is, let the bags fall to the floor, and plop myself beside him.

He runs his finger across the touchscreen of a flat black phone, a persistent look on his face.

"Let me see, none of my friends have a smartphone for me to play with yet." I snatch it from him and begin to press down on little squares with pictures.

He steals it back, slapping my hands away when I try to grab it again. I wrap my fingers around the cold bench seat. I catch the smell of lavender as it leaks from one of the cosmetic stores facing us, inhale deeply and sigh. Denendrius puts his hand on my knee, his touch reaching through my jeans.

"I still prefer the way you smell," he says. "You taste even better, though."

I clear my throat and rub the back of my neck. "So you finally got a phone?"

"I got you one too." He pulls another box from a bag and sets it on my other knee. It rocks back and forth, and I grab it before it clatters on the floor.

I cradle it between my fingers, my throat growing tight. I tap the box. "Why?"

His expression turns severe, making my knees knock. "So I know where you are. I need to be able to get in touch with you at any time."

"You need to check up on me." I chew on my cheek.

He smiles. "It's because I love you. I want to make sure you're safe."

My knuckles pale from their tightness on the smooth cardboard. I taste blood on my tongue. Could I chew right through my cheek if I tried?

His fingers tighten on my knee as if he's trying to squeeze the words out of me.

"I love you too," I say, my heartbeat drumming in my ears.

"Then open the box. You have to add my number." His lips press against my temple.

I shake my head and set it gently on his lap. "I don't want a cell phone."

He turns rigid, eyes clouded, teeth slamming together. "Why not?"

"They have GPS on them, I heard. I don't like the idea of cops being able to track down where I am. It's why I haven't gotten a cell phone yet." Well, it's not like I can afford one either.

"Poor excuse," he growls. "Open it."

I flex my fingers and slowly reclaim the box. I pull the flap open, unwrap it and turn it on. The screen lights up, welcoming me. Denendrius pulls it from my stiff hands and types in his number.

"You better keep it on you."

"Yeah, whatever," I blurt.

His body turns to me, fingers circling my bicep. "I mean it."

I want to take the phone and throw it against the floor. But instead, I do what any intelligent girl would do. I press my lips against his and claim the phone. I shove it in my pocket and say, "I was just seeing how much it mattered to you."

"So, you promise?" He studies me.

"Yes."

He expels a rushed breath, and a smile breaks across his face. "Good, good."

We sit in silence for a few minutes, him glowing like a child who got his way and me stroking the corner of the phone with my thumb.

I scoot down, resting my head back against the bench. Looking up at the sun breaking through the skylight, I wonder if it's stopped raining.

Against the banister up on the third story, I spot a girl all dressed in black and lace, like the girl in the diner. She looks down at us. It's got to be the same girl. Is she following me?

When she sees me see her, she disappears from behind the banister and I glance at Denendrius to see if he saw her too. No indication that he did, so I keep my mouth shut.

XXVI

When we pull up into Carol's driveway, Denendrius kicks her out of the car, saying he wants to take me out for dinner.

"You were wondering about vampires last night?" he says, backing out of the driveway.

I nod. "Alaire talked about Children of Stars."

He laughs. "Of course he did. I assume I was attached to that topic?"

We turn out of the residential community and head toward downtown Lorimer.

"Yeah," I mumble.

Anxiety drips into me when we pull up in front of a packed Greek restaurant, memories of our last public meals stirring sourness in my gut.

We don't talk much through finding a table and ordering, Denendrius seemingly withdrawn into himself as he stares out the window. I ponder what he's thinking about while taking small bites of my lamb and pasta, or giouvetsi as Denendrius calls it.

A painting is on the wall across the restaurant in a gold frame. Elegant and likely a few hundred years old, it shows numerous half-naked men and women lounging on a cloud, and I think maybe they're Greek gods. I wonder about Denendrius's Roman ones, particularly Venus and Mars and why he's compared us to them.

"Who's Venus?" I ask, trying to fill the space between us.

He doesn't even blink, eyes locked on dead air, his hand in a fist on the blue tablecloth.

"Denendrius." When he doesn't answer, I reach out and put my hand over his curled fingers. "Denendrius."

He pulls his hand out from under mine, eyes jumping to me. "What?"

I pose the question again. "Who's Venus?"

"You don't know who Venus is." His question falls flat, more of a dry statement.

"Or Mars," I add.

"Nor Mars?"

I shake my head and he exhales exhaustion, shoulders drooping as he leans his forearms on the table.

I swallow a chunk of lamb. "Can you tell me?"

"Venus was born from sea-foam and was a beautiful goddess. She stood for love, represented sex and fertility, could give success," he says.

I feel too humble for his comparison of me to her, and not entirely sure what to make of it. "And Mars?"

"The god of war and the protector of Rome, of their farms and livelihood."

"So what's their story?"

The corner of his lip hints at a smile, relaxing me as he speaks. "Venus was trapped in a loveless marriage with Vulcan, an old and lame god. She would often lie in the arms of Mars, her true lover, though they kept their romance secret. After some time, Vulcan suspected them, and he captured the two in a net he fashioned. He called the gods to witness their adultery, only they laughed, and Mars and Venus went on—free—and bore children together."

I poke my lip with the prongs of my fork, careful when I ask, "Do you see their story in us?"

"I can see us anywhere I look."

Laying my fork down, I adjust in my seat. "Who would be Vulcan in our story, then?"

His stare is intense while he thinks. "Anything and anyone who would consider keeping us apart. As of now, that's you."

My throat constricts and I swallow a lump when I can manage a breath.

Denendrius winks, saying, "Don't worry, I would never let anything tear us from one another."

The rain is still mist when we exit the restaurant, darkness spread around us. Denendrius and I find shelter in his car. We back out of the parking lot, tires crunching against the wet asphalt as we depart from Lorimer to claim the highway.

The heat from the seat warms my body, makes me feel like I've drunk hot soup. The silence between Denendrius and me raises the hairs on my arms. The window moans as I roll it down, cold air kissing my face. I reach my arm out, fingers gliding along the black paint of the car. The midnight air dampens my flesh and the beauty makes me feel as empty as a corpse.

I stare at the trees flashing by, and for a moment I swear I can smell the sweet pine. I can taste the grass and feel the tickle of it on my skin. But then I hear screaming, at the back of my mind like elevator music. Then the pain comes back, the burning, freezing. I hear the snowfall, the Gothic dress as it brushes the white snowflakes. My melodic voice rings from the depths of the hallucination as it giggles and flirts with Denendrius, the angel of death, my own personal demon who's come back to open up my own cozy piece of hell. I can hear his wings brushing the air. I feel the pain come back stronger.

My jaw falls open, a gentle gasp barely disturbing the air around me.

"What's wrong?" Denendrius asks.

It's too easy to answer with "Nothing."

Denendrius rubs my knee, offering a friendly smile.

"Where are we going?" My arm is numb now, so I pull it back inside and sit on my fingers.

"You'll see. It's another hour, so you can sleep if you want."

With my feet up on the dashboard, I rest my forehead against my knees, wrapping my arms around my thighs. "I don't think I can." My eyelids droop. Something—a part of the vehicle, I think—vibrates.

I imagine myself running free, laughing, through the trees. Denendrius begins to hum, and I rock my knees side to side. It starts to feel real.

It seems like just when my eyes close, Denendrius wakes me.

"We're here."

I straighten, rubbing my eyes with the back of my hand. Here makes me weary, considering it appears that we're stopped on the same path we took the first time he dragged me into the woods—or at least one like it.

My gaze drifts to Denendrius. "What are we doing?" My voice betrays me. I can't get my first encounter with the forest out of my head.

"You'll see." He steps out of the Mustang.

I follow and slam the door shut when I get out, take a deliberate breath, and face the possible threat within the trees.

Denendrius hooks his arm around my waist, lifting me off

my feet. Before I have the chance to question, I'm dizzy, the world lost to my vision.

Crickets chirp in the tall grass when Denendrius stops. I plunge into it when he lets me down, head spinning like a top. I right myself, sweeping dirt and grass off my pants.

"The house?" I ask, trying not to throw up.

Two floors high, it stands gray and crooked in front of us, its left side sagging into the ground.

Denendrius and I tread through the grass and weeds. The door cries out from his touch as he leads me through it and into darkness. My steps groan and something wooden—the floor, probably—gives under my foot. I grab his arm for stability.

We hasten down a flight of decomposing stairs, steps complaining during our descent. I squint into the dark but can only see a few feet in front of me, and poorly. I hear the click of a flashlight turning on. The yellow light is wide, grazing over the walls of the dirt-carved basement. He hands the flashlight to me and I take the cold thing in my hands, rolling it between my palms.

The light catches something metal as I sweep the room. I shine the light and see a metal cage big enough for a Great Dane . . . or a small person.

Denendrius takes my hand and leads me into a large dirt room where a man is strapped down to a metal table. A brush of light shows me his tight black curls surround by his washed-out face. He opens his eyes and blue irises shine.

"Whatever you do, don't touch him."

"Why not?" I ask, stepping closer.

I wonder how long he's been down here, alone and freezing. What has Denendrius been doing to him? Is this where he goes when I'm not around?

The man's fingers reach toward me, as close as he can get. Lips quivering, he watches me. His mouth opens wide as if pain has overcome him.

"This will answer your question about vampires."

Denendrius grabs my arm and his fangs tear into my skin before he steps away, leaving me stunned. Blood dribbles down my arm from the incisions, causing the man on the table to react violently. He yanks against his restraints, screeching, his bright red eyes wide. A pair of fangs shoot from his gums.

I jolt back. "What the hell?"

"He's a Child of Stars. Cool, hm?" He laughs and plunges a knife into the vampire's arm, silencing him.

The vampire shakes against the table, blood drizzling slowly from the wound, whimpering. Thirsty, I assume.

"He really did look human," I marvel. "How long has he been down here?"

Denendrius laughs. "About a month. He thought he'd try to take me on by himself, and, well . . ."

The vampire squeezes his eyes closed and takes a deep breath, and when he opens them again, they return to blue. I wonder if I could have met this kind of vampire before and not even known it. His fangs slip into his gums and shape themselves into regular eyeteeth.

Denendrius laughs. "So, does he answer your question about vampires?"

Mouth agape with my mind whirring like a freshly oiled machine, I answer, "Not nearly."

He leans against the dirt wall, loosening some clumps as I try to organize the flurry in my mind.

"You killed hundreds of them," I say. "Why exactly?"

He seems to be considering his answer before he says, "Why did I kill hundreds of them? Well, I was thirsty."

My eyes narrow, "Do you . . . prefer . . . vampire blood to human blood?"

He shrugs. "Human blood is like wine—good for anytime you are thirsty—but vampire blood is something much stronger."

My lips purse, more questions on my tongue, but the guarded look in his black eyes makes me turn away from him and back to the vampire on the table.

"How much alike are you two?" I ask. "Children of Stars and Darklings?"

"My kind comes from theirs, but we're quite alike, though stronger. Some of the same rules apply. They can be staked, though the harm that garlic does to them is exceedingly worse with no chance of gaining a tolerance as I have. They burn in the sun, heal, etcetera, etcetera."

"Why *garlic*? I know the idea has been around forever, but why does it work?" I ask.

Shrugging, he says, "Mother Nature needed some sort of defense against them to give mortals a chance. It's said to drive evil spirits away because of its purity and healing properties. People used to hang garlic over their door in hopes of keeping vampires out. It works much better if you soak it in water or make it a paste and put it *around* your doors and windows, though, but lucky entrapment doesn't apply to my kind." He smiles, then references the dirt doorway. "It's why nobody has retrieved him from this room. He can't leave, and they cannot enter."

"Hm. Alaire and Edmond said Darklings came from eugenics," I say, hating that I've brought them up.

He nods, a coy smile slipping onto his lips. "Something like that, yes. That's what I've heard."

The light starts to dwindle. I smack the flashlight and unload another question. "Is the transformation the same?"

"Similar, but a diluted version of what I went through. It's quicker, though probably just as painful. But the fever takes them so fast they don't get *the joy* of hallucinating."

The light disappears from the room. I groan and smack the flashlight, but it slips from my hand and rolls away. I drop to my knees, my fingers moving through the dirt. I feel the metal thing touch them and I take it and smack it against the ground. The light returns and I stand.

The vampire's eyes meet mine, distracting me. I don't realize how close I am until I feel his fingers stretch out and touch my stomach. Fear explodes inside me with an intensity I'd thought only the night in the forest could manifest.

I drop the flashlight and run from the room, adrenaline pulsing through my veins. I clamber up the stairs and race through the house, my hip clipping something metal. Throwing myself into the night, I dart through the trees in hopes of making it back to the car.

The fear is irrational. I don't have a reason to be afraid. But despite it all, I keep a steady pace, sinking further into the dark like my life depends on it. I wait for Denendrius to stop me, or a tree in my path, but instead, a pair of arms around my throat forces me to a halt. I gag and the grip loosens some.

A female voice, thick with a French accent, says, "Listen to me. If you go back and tell your mate to release mine, I promise not to tear your throat out."

My leg shoots back, the force striking her shin. She howls and I propel myself onward, body feeling light with endless energy. She's not nearly as fast as Denendrius, but outrunning her is no easy task, and she quickly overcomes me as I'm forced to slow for an old wooden fence. We both tumble to the ground as she leaps on me, and I frantically search the grass for something to use as a weapon.

Her long nails scratch my skin as I struggle to throw her off and search at the same time. My fingers wrap around a large and long wooden shard of fence post. She tries to knock it out of my hand and my opposite fist connects with her cheek.

Confusion ripples through my mind when the ground disappears from beneath me. She's gripping my clothing and snarling, trying to tear into my neck. We spin, me falling onto her floating body, sitting on her stomach with one leg flailing on each side of her. I raise the makeshift stake above my head and plunge it into her heart. Just as I do, we free-fall.

Her back collides with the ground, my legs bending, knees cracking against the hard and grassy earth. Breathing heavily, I jump off the lifeless vampire corpse, heart hammering in my ears. My mind is crippled by the sudden unexpected event.

I drag her heavy body through the trees and across the short distance to the abandoned house. It takes about ten minutes, but soon enough I have her up the concrete steps and into the house. Denendrius is standing there with a flashlight, the remnants of broken furniture and a forgotten life sprawled around the house.

I scrutinize her body, the white summer dress she is wearing, now stained with blood around where the wooden shard of fence protrudes. Her auburn hair is in dirty ringlets around her pale face, a few strands cascading over her bright green eyes. Lips parted and no sign of fangs, she looks human.

"So how was that?" Denendrius asks as he appears beside me, lips pursed in amusement.

"I'm not really sure what happened," I breathe.

His brows twitch and he crosses his arms. "Not too hard to understand. You touched the vampire downstairs when I directed you to do the opposite, and you ran when his touch attacked your flight response."

I roll my eyes. "So, Children of Stars have special abilities? Thanks for the heads-up." I suppose that's what Alaire meant about supernatural traits.

He nods. "Well, the lucky ones. You have a likely chance of receiving the one your maker does, though they can be quite random."

"Yeah, okay." I clear my airway with a deep breath while trying to force some of my dizziness to subside. "What do we do with her?"

He pokes her with his big toe. "Whatever you want," he says

indifferently. "Pull the stake out if you want. You're the one who wants to learn. So, learn."

My fingers twitch and I bend down. "What happens if I do?"

"She comes back to life."

I bite my lip and wrap my fingers around the wooden piece and pull. She explodes backward, hissing and snarling, eyes on Denendrius. Her green eyes fade into a bright red, and fangs shoot from her gums.

Denendrius reaches out to touch her and she lifts into the air, slowly rising a few feet. Her hands are tight by her side, toes pointed as she hovers, unmoving. It reminds me of the demonically possessed from horror movies.

I marvel at her. She's *amazing*.

Her unblinking eyes are locked on Denendrius, who laughs and says, "You don't impress me. I'll jump up and bring you down."

"Can all Children of Stars do that?" I ask Denendrius, remaining in awe.

He nods.

Her lips spread farther apart, her eyes traveling to me. "I've been waiting for you to come back. Now that you have, *give me Pierre*."

"You could always go get him yourself," Denendrius chuckles, then pretends to remember something. "Oh right, garlic. Guess you're out of luck."

She snarls and her fingernails grow longer and pointed. Like a cat preparing her claws for an attack. I feel the scratches on my throat, free of blood but still stinging.

"You tortured our people!" she shrieks. "You will pay. Kill him, kill me, but Vio—"

In a moment, she's on the floor, her throat in Denendrius's hand.

As he studies her face, he asks, "Did you tell him I'm here?"

She bares her fangs, squirming as she snarls, "Why would I

tell him *anything*? He is not offering nearly as much as others are for you."

"Good," Denendrius says, his hand disappearing inside her chest and returning with her heart.

I stand in stunned silence, staring at her while Denendrius mumbles that he'll be back in a moment. He disappears from the room, his voice appearing downstairs, where his French shouts are accompanied by the man's shrieking.

Then, there's silence.

"Let's go," Denendrius says, back at my side.

"Who was she talking about?" I ask Denendrius as we slip into the night.

He hooks his arm around my waist, my feet coming off the ground. "Wouldn't you like to know?" is all he says before zipping through the trees.

XXVII

Denendrius drops me off at Carol's after deciding he's not going to stay the night. I wipe my hand over my face and get out into the spitting rain.

"I have to meet a friend tomorrow, so I can trust you'll be here when I get back? I'll pick you up after school Monday. You can stay the night at my place."

It's clear to me then why my *temporary stay* here is convenient for him. He's using Carol as some sort of babysitter, knowing she'll want to keep tabs on me.

I grip the door frame, wracking my mind for an excuse to eliminate his plans. "I don't think Carol will let me. And besides, I've just started staying with her. I should probably get settled in."

A beat of breath and half laughter comes while he smiles, eyes hard. "Too bad, sweetheart, I'll be seeing you soon. Stay out of trouble."

I gnash my teeth, rocking on my heels. "Yeah, okay."

"I'll miss you," he says. "I love you."

I swallow and nod. "Love you." I slam the door and walk inside, tires squealing as he speeds away.

I take my shoes off and climb the stairs, nearly tripping over them. "I'm going to bed."

Carol wishes me a good night from the couch after asking me to be quiet since the twins are in bed. "Let me know if you need anything."

"Okay."

I sway up the stairs and strip my clothes off after dumping the shopping bags on the floor. I take my cell phone from my deep pockets and set it on the nightstand, crawling under the blanket and burying my face in the scent of laundry detergent.

Since I don't remember closing my eyes, I'm unable to decide if I'm awake or really visiting my mother in prison.

I'm sitting across the table from her, shouting at her to tell me the truth about what happened when I was a child. But she merely stares, a small smile on her lips until she becomes so frustrated with me she opens her mouth to scream, and I see she doesn't have a tongue.

I wake up with my eyes already open, the numb and chilling atmosphere from the dream remaining enclosed beneath the blankets with me. I tuck them beneath my chin, crisp and clean air filling my nose as I grab my cell phone and curl into a ball facing the wall.

When I press the button to ignite the screen, bold numbers tell me I've only been asleep for ten minutes. After figuring out how to use the browser on my phone, I type in the name of the prison. Do I really want to see her after everything she's done to me? Do I really want to go out of my way to ask her questions she will probably refuse to answer? I click search even though both answers are no. I cling to the hope that she will tell me at least something because I'm resistant to rely on Denendrius to tell me the truth.

I find the number to the women's prison just outside

Lorimer and decide to call them in the morning to ask about visitation hours and if I can see my mother on Tuesday.

I text Denendrius a "hello" and fall back asleep while waiting for a reply. When my phone rattles against the mattress half an hour later, I see he's replied with a "hey there." I ask him what he's doing and he tells me he's with a friend but refuses to tell me who and what they're doing, so I give up and tell him about my plans to visit the prison. He agrees to take me and sends a simple "I love you," which I ignore.

Closing my eyes, I drift into a place of semiconsciousness where I'm trapped inside nonsensical thoughts, unable to take my mind off the ache wrapped around my body. As I teeter between wakefulness and sleep, I can feel the heaviness of exhaustion holding me to the bed. How much sleep will it take to rid this kind of tiredness?

Even through the handful of cell phone vibrations demanding my attention and Carol entering my room every so often to ask if I'm hungry, I stay beneath the thin layer of icelike sleep. Even though I can hear the twins playing down the hall and could break through if I wanted to, I don't.

Instead, I dream of running through the forest, and it would be a nice run if it didn't feel like I was being chased. I don't wake up until Denendrius appears in the forest, raping me and choking me to death.

Shaking in a cold sweat, I unstick the phone from my stomach and see the nearly thirty texts Denendrius has sent me, many of them blank or with various amounts of question marks. I swipe my fingers across the letters on the screen, apologizing for falling asleep while adding that I love him.

Unable to fall back asleep, I lie on the floor facing the window, watching the silver moon pinned in the sky and the mass of forest beneath it. I switch between reading a book from my shelf and drawing pictures of the dream in hopes of pulling the feeling and image of being raped in my first hallucination from my mind.

Once a couple drawings are done, I stare at them for a long time before shredding them with my fingers and tossing them in the garbage. Feeling somewhat better, I draw a detailed picture of me stabbing Denendrius before closing the notebook and sliding it beneath my bed.

The tops of the trees begin to turn pink when I reach up and pull the blanket from the bed with my toes, wrapping it around myself while watching as the sun's arms reach into the forest. The sun pulls the pastel colors from the flowers in the ditch, borrowing the colors to paint the sky.

My mind wanders, and I can't help but think about the girl in black who was watching us at the mall and the diner. What could she possibly want? The same thing every other vampire we have come into contact with wants? If only I could figure out a way to find her.

I watch the clock until I can call the prison and then hold my breath and dial. They eventually give me the okay and tell me their visiting hours.

My stomach growls, so I sigh, stand, and put my clothes back on. I drift into the bathroom, rubbing my eyes and somehow still feeling tired. After flushing and washing my hands, I root through the cabinets and bags until I find a bottle of Carol's sleeping pills dated a few years back in an old makeup bag. I deposit half of them into my hand and place it back in its hiding space, stuffing the little pills in my pocket.

I know I shouldn't take them and even feel a teensy bit of guilt at taking them from the first foster parent I've ever liked, but I don't find a good enough reason to care about putting them back, especially not with what dreams are promised when I fall asleep.

I tread through the thick air and grab a bowl of cereal, my chewing seeming loud in the sleeping house.

Just as I'm about to climb the stairs, Carol comes down the hallway wearing a gray housecoat and a sleepy face and spots me on her way to the kitchen.

"Hey, how are you feeling?" She rubs her eyes and yawns.

"Okay," I mumble.

"Are you sick?"

I shake my head. "No, just really, *really* tired."

She ponders. "Hmm. I wonder why? It could be a cold from the weather."

I shrug and continue up the steps.

"I'll drop you off at school around noon tomorrow, okay?"

I climb back down to the bottom steps and cross my arms, but I realize they're bare and she can see the scars and bruises. I hide them behind my back.

"I don't want to go to school." Maybe if I stay home, I can avoid seeing Denendrius. But then I remember how I have to since he's taking me to see my mom too on Tuesday. I sigh.

Her face twists. "Well, Marianna, we're going to have to talk about school. Margaret told me you hardly ever show up, and you're going to have to change that."

I scowl, wanting the Carol from the mall back, the one who was fun and bought me stuff. "No, I won't."

"Marianna, as it is, you're already behind. Don't you want to pass tenth grade and eventually graduate?"

I lean against the wall and swallow. "I'm not going to graduate."

"Then why are you in school?"

"I like messing around."

She touches her forehead like I'm giving her a headache. "There's got to be more to it."

"My friends are there."

"But doesn't making something of yourself matter to you? Don't you want to succeed?"

I sigh. "I'll be impressed if I even make it to graduation." I can't see myself living past this situation with Denendrius. I can't believe I have to sit around, unable to help myself.

Her eyes widen. "What do you mean?"

I turn and continue up the stairs. "Don't worry about it. I didn't mean anything."

Crawling back into bed, I pull the covers over my head after throwing them back on the mattress. I scowl into the dark. The springs twang when I punch the mattress, my hot breath collecting in the small space beneath the comforter. I punch the mattress again, turn over, and kick the wall. I growl and twist my fingers until it hurts.

The door squeals, footsteps trailing to my bed. Through the blankets, I see the light come on.

"Go away," I snarl.

"I need to talk to you about Den." She wavers.

I prepare myself for another talk on how I need help to leave him while conjuring up words to send her away.

She takes a deep breath, so loud I almost roll my eyes. "Okay, here it goes." She takes another breath, big enough to suck up the entire atmosphere. "What is he?"

I freeze and slowly peel the blankets from my face, greeting her with a condemning look.

She rubs her forehead and gives a little laugh. "Oh dear, I sounded really insane, didn't I?"

I wonder if Denendrius would kill me if I confirmed any suspicions she has about him. I sit up, wrapping the blanket under my chin to hide the marks on my throat.

"Not insane. What makes you think he's anything but human?"

Her expression turns serious again; she's obviously jumping at the chance to voice her ideas. "Okay. It may sound crazy, but he looks exactly like he did when I met him. He doesn't look a day older. And by now, he would have to be around forty. It makes no sense."

I stare at her blankly. "I know."

"And I don't like the way he is . . . I don't know how to explain it." She shakes her head. "He's just . . . not right."

"So, what are you thinking? Any theories?" I pick at a loose white thread, lips pursed.

She lowers her head, the orange-red of her blush matching her hair. "I don't want to say it."

"I bet I'll believe you." I stuff some of the blanket in my mouth and bite down hard.

She shakes her head. "You'll tell me I've been watching too much television. Everyone always tells me I'm too superstitious, that I shouldn't be getting life advice from tarot readings and star signs."

"So?" I mumble into the fabric.

"I'm going to sound like a twelve-year-old girl, and you'll think I'm a whack job."

I yank the blanket from my mouth, gut twisting in frustration. "Just tell me."

She winces dramatically as she says, "He's not a vampire, is he?"

I stare at her with lifted brows and pursed lips, impressed.

She scrutinizes me and moans, standing up. "I knew I shouldn't have said it."

I lean against the wall. "Why? You're right."

She freezes. "I am? How?"

I pull the blanket from my neck and point out the scars from bite wounds. She covers her mouth and sits back down, asking to know everything about what he is. I unload the bare minimum of information—yes, he's immortal, yes, he drinks blood—just enough to feed her cravings for knowledge.

Tears spark in her eyes while she listens to me. "He terrifies me," she whispers when I finish. "Ever since I first met him, when he brought you back to us at Enchanted Land, I knew something wasn't right. He was cold, and he acted like we were taking *you* from *him*."

I don't respond, unsure of what to make of that information. A few minutes later, a thought occurs, forcing out a strangled chuckle.

"What is it?" Carol's eyes search the room.

I shake my head. "I keep expecting a director to jump out and yell 'cut!'"

"Why?"

"This is unreal. Like television. I feel like I'm the victim of a prank that's gone on too long."

"It is real, though, isn't it?"

I twist my lips to the side. "I know."

The truth is carved in stone like someone took their gnarly fingernails and scratched it into the world themselves. Nothing can change the fact that Denendrius is a vampire, that he is utterly obsessed and evil. His plan for me is like a quickly sweltering fire, out to burn anyone and anything in its way. There isn't a break from this, no time to catch your breath to check if you're doing or saying the right thing. Like the angel of death, he knows the outcome of this sick manifestation of intertwined fates, and he's here to collect my soul.

"I don't want you near him anymore." She grinds her teeth, shaking. "He's not to come in this house."

"It's not really for either of us to decide." I touch a lock of her fiery hair, blanket still draped over my arm.

A shaky breath escapes her lips and she shudders. "I just— I'm scared for you. I've worried about you for years."

I press my lips together and rub my face. "I'm scared for me too."

We stare at each other for a few moments before she says, "You know what? Why don't you just stay home from school?"

The idea is appealing, but if I don't go, Denendrius will be infuriated. "I have to. He's picking me up after, and I'm staying the night at his place."

Her eyes widen. "No. Absolutely not."

I regret telling her about anything. *Stupid!* "I have to," I say, voice venomous.

"I'm going to worry about you all night."

"I'll be fine."

She bites her thumbnail. "I'm going to talk to him."

Baffled, I think about how horribly the conversation would go. He'll kill her if she tries to stand in the way of us, probably if he even discovers she knows about his vampirism.

I sink deeper into the blankets, my stomach feeling like it's filling with acid. What if I'm not supposed to tell anyone about what he is? He didn't say I couldn't, but I'm sure it was implied.

"I swear to God, Carol, if you say anything about any of this to him, I will kill you if he doesn't first," I say, my high-pitched voice frantic.

She buries her face in her hands. "I'm starting to wish I hadn't asked."

We sit for another few minutes, her muttering to herself, possibly compiling everything she knows and trying to make sense of it, me glowering at the thought of her confronting Denendrius.

She turns to face me. "You can talk to me about anything, you know? You can trust me. I won't say anything to him."

I swallow and shuffle my feet against the sheets, biting my cheek. "We'll see."

"Okay, well, I'll wake you up before noon." She stands and wobbles toward the door.

I crawl half out of bed when she shuts the door behind her, pulling the sleeping pills from my pocket. I set three on the back of my tongue and swallow, dumping the rest in the drawer of the nightstand.

Even with the pills, it takes some time to fall asleep. Jenna and CJ haunt my thoughts, Denendrius looming behind them. Despite my hopes, the pills aren't enough to keep him from wandering through my dreams again.

XXVIII

A rap on the door stirs me in my bed. I thank Carol for waking me and get up to wash off unnerving thoughts of seeing Denendrius.

I take my time getting ready until she yells that we're leaving in fifteen minutes. Then I throw a knife in my pocket, scurry down the stairs, scarf down a bowl of cereal Carol sets in front of me and hop into her spacious white minivan.

"Where's your bag and books?" she questions, sliding the key in the ignition.

"Don't have any," I lie so I don't need to go through the effort of returning upstairs. I put my feet up on the dashboard.

She turns and gives me a look of are-you-serious. "Feet down, and seat belt on."

"Chill. It's fine." I rock my legs.

"I mean it." She spins the wheel and creeps onto the street.

"What if I just put my seat belt on?"

"Fine," she answers, thoughts elsewhere.

I buckle up but tuck the chest strap behind me and wonder why I bothered listening. I guess it wouldn't be too awful if I had some sort of relationship with her.

"What kind of music do you like?" she asks.

I watch the trees rush by, the stone-gray sky hovering just above them. I wonder when it will rain. "Hip-hop is cool. What about you?"

"Metal and rock, sometimes pop."

Silence fills the small space between us, and I question if it merely makes its appearance due to our history. Eventually, it turns out to be too much for her to handle, because she turns the music on low and peeks at me from the corner of her eye.

"I'm sorry this is so weird," she says.

"It's fine." I wave my hand in an attempt to dismiss her concern.

She swallows and breathes a thick stream of air out of her nostrils. "I think it's because I was used to Vianna and Kenneth being your parents, while I was the cool aunt who gave you everything you wanted. I don't really like the idea of being your parent. It still feels like you belong to them, like I'm trying to replace them."

"Then be my aunt," I say. "Technically your only job is to be a guardian."

She gives a small smile and flinches as a semi passes us in the other lane. "I think that could work."

I nod and swallow hard, but the glob of unease is stuck.

"What were they like?" I wonder aloud.

"They were amazing. I couldn't see how anyone else could be as fit to be parents as they were. They brought a smile to your small face when it seemed impossible. You were their world, Marianna. They told me how one time you said your favorite part of the day was when they tucked you in at night and told you they loved you."

To think I can't even remember the happiest year of my life. I try to imagine all the things we did together. Did we play at parks, at the pool? Did we go skating, rollerblading, and take long walks around the neighborhood? How different was I from other kids? I couldn't see myself throwing tantrums when I was told no; I wouldn't have even dared to ask for anything. I try to envision it all, a bright world full to the brim with happiness, a perfect set of parents wanting nothing more than to make my pain go away. I lost it all.

My jaw tenses, and a fire brews in my stomach. I clench my fists. "Sounds like I was lucky to have them." But my voice comes out dark and sour.

She wets her lips and sniffs, eyes glassy.

"So, what were the twins' names again?" I say, changing the subject so I don't have to see her cry.

"Julie and James. I dropped them off at preschool this morning."

The rest of the ride consists of foot-tapping and humming to the radio. When we reach my school, she drops me off a block away at my request, and I walk to the school, rubbing my hand against the outside of my jean pocket, which holds a few dollar bills from Carol for lunch.

I make sure my hoodie is covering my neck and arms when I enter the school, winding through the halls and to the cafeteria. I order fries and plop myself down at the table where Camille and Daina are sitting. Camille flinches as I sit down beside her, and she gives me a weak smile while chewing the side of a hamburger.

"So, how are you?" Camille says carefully from beside me.

I roll my eyes. "Don't bring up anything to do with what you did, and we won't fight about it." I point a fry at her and then shove it in my mouth.

"Okay, got it."

"Different topic," I say, shoving a few more fries in my mouth.

Daina takes a bite of her cinnamon bun and twists her lips. "Are you going to Jenna's funeral?"

My chewing slows. "When?"

She pushes the half-eaten cinnamon bun away from her and twists her fingers together on the tabletop. Her eyes flutter downward. "Next week."

"Yeah . . . I'll come." I clear a glob of emotion from my throat.

"I still can't believe she committed suicide," Camille mumbles from beside me.

My heart hammers with the knowledge that I'm holding a giant chunk of truth back from them. How would they feel if they knew Denendrius staged her suicide? How they slept in the same apartment as her killer, even talked and laughed with him? I straighten my back and continue eating my fries, knowing I'll snap if I keep thinking about it.

Daina bursts into tears, hunching over. Camille pulls her away from the faces turning to us, muttering a sorry to me as they disappear from the cafeteria.

I have no tears left for Jenna. I want to cry, but I can't. I don't know if I could stop them once they started.

Instead, I toss the rest of my fries in the garbage, heading to the gym to change, then to the fitness room, where I work out into the fifth period until I'm dripping with sweat and ready to vomit.

Slipping into the locker room shower, I turn my face into the stream of water. When I open my eyes and rub the water from them, I stare at the bruises, scars, and cuts on my body. I trace over them with my fingers, scratching at Denendrius's name above my breast while wishing I could cut it off.

I press my fingers against the old burn marks from my

mother and all the little scars dotting and crossing my flesh, too many to recall how they were caused.

My head jerks from side to side and I close my eyes so I don't have to see myself. Water runs over my lids and face in place of the tears I cannot cry. I try to convince myself of something—anything—with a little smile. But it feels fake and disturbing, so I punch the shower wall and hum a little louder.

I thrust my fist into the shower wall again, the anger targeted at myself. I force my eyes open and glower at the wall. How am I just letting all of this happen?

Why can't I stop it?

I take a deep breath, steam swirling in my nostrils and spilling over the tops of the white plastic curtain, making the rusted silver hooks shine. I shake my head and press my fists tight against my temples, biting my tongue. I beat the shower wall until blood is running down it and I'm out of breath, my knuckles ripped open.

I wash and turn the water off, hearing what the sound of the shower had been canceling out: heavy sobbing echoing in a bathroom stall.

Drying off, I pull my clothes back on, double-checking that my injuries are hidden.

The squelch of my wet feet in my sneakers resonates across the oversized locker room. I grumble on my way to the line of teal-painted stalls and knock on the door of the girl who is crying.

"Why are you bawling?" I ask, not sure why I care.

The lock spins and the door swings open, showing a disheveled Sarah. "Oh," she blubbers when she sees me.

I grit my teeth and cross my arms. "So, did you lure CJ to his death?"

"He made me." She wipes her nose with the sleeve of her light gray hoodie with pink polka dots.

"Who did? Den?"

She nods and begins to sob again. "He said he'd kill me if I didn't."

I grit my teeth. "So? You think you deserved to live over him?"

She shakes her head, blond hair whipping across her blotchy face. "I didn't know what else to do."

"You tell the police?"

"No, he said if I did, I was dead." Her eyes widen, lips pulling into her mouth. "And my dad's a police officer, but that just makes it so much harder."

"Maybe you should talk to him, then. CJ didn't deserve that." I spit at her and she covers her face.

She wails. "You didn't even like him!"

I grab the side of the stall, fingers white and knuckles still bleeding. "I don't like a lot of people. But I don't kill them unless they actually need to be killed."

What I want to tell her is that I started to know him, wanted to know him, and that she helped Denendrius take *one more thing* away from me. Now I'll never know if CJ would have ever taught me how to ride his skateboard, never know what it's like to have a boy be so nice to me again.

She hops up. "I did what I had to do to protect myself."

I step into the stall. "Bitch, did you ever think maybe you didn't deserve to be protected? You traded your life for someone else's."

"As if you're any better, Marianna! I can only imagine the shit you've done, especially when you were in a gang," she snarls, jabbing a finger at my neck tattoo. "You have murderer written all over you!"

I step closer, just a few inches from her face. "You're not better than me," I snarl.

She scoffs. "Whatever, Marianna. You're a fucking thug and a junkie and you walk around thinking you're the toughest shit.

'Oh, look at me! I beat bitches and carry heat!' You're a fucking joke."

I sneer. "You're, like, the queen of acting like tough shit, but when it comes down to it, you fucking pussy out half the time. You fucking sent your girl gang after me instead of taking care of me yourself!"

"That's just because I know how crazy you are!" She shoves me in the shoulder. "Want me to deal with you myself? Don't fucking push it, bitch! *I will!*"

My body turns hot, blood boiling as I grit my teeth. I shove her back harder. "Better get your fucking hands up, then," I growl.

When her hands fly toward my face, I grab a fistful of her hair and slam her head against the stall, the sound echoing through the change room. She's shouting nonsense as she tries to peg me with her fist. Hand still tangled in her hair, I grunt and swing her out of the stall. Her fist catches me hard in the jaw, the other one getting me in the stomach. I throw her against the concrete wall, my right fist swinging into her cheekbone. Her head bounces off the wall on impact. I grab her leg when she tries to kick me away from her and send my knuckles into her ribs repeatedly as she tries to get me in the face.

I barely feel anything through the adrenaline, my anger fueled by more than just her and CJ. I continue to beat her, hitting her more than she hits me.

"You ruined my fucking life!" I screech, bloody knuckles splitting her lip.

She receives all the blows meant for Denendrius.

"Fucking cunt!" she screams. "You crazy bitch!"

Sarah cries out in pain when my fist snaps her nose, and instead of throwing more punches, she shoves me away and locks herself in the stall.

I smack the door. "Open up, you coward," I snarl.

"No! You're trying to kill me!"

"You're weak!" I spit. "Open it and fight me."

I can barely understand her through her sobs. *"You broke my nose!"*

"Boohoo!"

The phone in my pocket vibrates and I pull it out to see Denendrius calling. "I'm in the middle of something!" I growl into the phone.

He grumbles. "Yeah, I know. I can hear it from my car."

My surprise shakes some of my anger away. "Really? Where are you?"

"I'm sitting across the street from the school. If you aren't going to kill her, I'd like you to come out."

"School's not over yet."

"Not for another hour, I know. I want you to come home with me right now. I miss you."

I bite my bloody knuckles. "Ugh, give me a minute." I turn my attention back to the door. "Open the fucking door."

"No!"

I kick it. "Open it or I'll fucking kill you!"

"Fuck off!"

I get into the next stall, using the toilet to hoist myself over the divider. I grab her when I'm down, knocking her head into the graffiti-covered green door.

"Someone—"

I ram my fist into her mouth to shut her up, and she starts shoving me away again.

"You want to be beaten to death?" I snarl. "Want to die the same way you killed CJ?"

Her hair swings as I throw her against the toilet. "I loved him, Marianna. I fucking loved him. *But I had to choose.*"

I grab her by the throat and pin her against the wall. For a brief moment, I feel what Denendrius must feel when he does the same to me. "You ruined my life," I hiss. "You've *fucking damned me.* You chose wrong."

I know my anger is misplaced, that she didn't mean for any of this to happen to me, that she doesn't even know what is happening. But she got her friends to drag me off the school grounds, giving me no choice but to run right where Denendrius was waiting for me. Things might have been different had it not been for her.

Sure, he probably would have found me anyway. But she shaved at least a few days off my existence, and someone needs to pay for everything that's happened, and she's the only one involved who can. CJ already paid; Jenna already paid. Alaire and Edmond paid. It's her turn.

I pull the rainbow chrome knife from my pocket and hold in front of her face, her eyes bulging, starting to water.

"Why, Marianna?" she wails.

I twitch and set it against her throat. "Because I'm going to die too." My voice cracks. "And it will be partly your fault."

She stands taller. "Do it, then! Fucking do it! I don't want to live anyway!"

I nick her flesh with the blade, just enough to scare her into changing her mind.

She doesn't flinch. Her blue eyes level with mine.

"Do it," she dares me. Her voice doesn't waver.

When I realize she means it, that I'll be doing her a favor, I slide the knife back into my pocket.

"You deserve to live with what you've done," I spit.

My bloodied hands circle her throat, my thumbs pressing into the bottom of her jaw. She claws at my hands with her sharp fingernails, mouth wide and airless. Maybe it's the adrenaline or a mixture of Denendrius's blood and the healing that makes me strong enough that no amount of her struggling comes near prying my fingers away.

We stare unblinkingly at one another. Her pulse thrums against my palms, the desperation in her irises louder than any pleading words.

"It doesn't matter," I growl to her. "It doesn't matter if you can't breathe."

Her lips move silently, her face bruised, tears streaking through her blood.

"It doesn't matter," I mumble to myself, grip tightening as my eyes sting with tears.

It doesn't matter, though, nothing matters. It doesn't matter if I accidentally kill her, it doesn't matter if I die. Nothing matters. I don't care. I can't care because it doesn't matter. If I run, it doesn't matter. If I don't and sit around waiting instead, it doesn't matter. I'm going to die. And to Denendrius, it won't matter.

Nothing matters.

When her eyelids flutter, I debate whether or not to let go, but eventually, I do.

I check for a pulse, relief finding me when I find one.

Turning, I unlock the stall and am faced with my own bruised face, my own bruised neck. I don't even matter. I'm just a game, a way to pass time. I'm a speck in his life, just another face in a crowd of thousands upon thousands of people he's killed and will kill.

I don't matter.

"You look hot when your face is all bruised," Denendrius says when I sit down in his car across the street.

I wipe the blood from my knuckles on my jeans. "Fuck off."

His eyes turn to slits. "Don't make me add another."

"Whatever."

He starts driving.

"Your moodiness aside, I'm proud of you for handling Sarah the way you did." He smiles. "See? We're not so different, you and I."

Denendrius's approval makes my face and gut burn. It makes me rethink my actions. I don't want to be anything like Denendrius, and the fact that we are similar in some ways is absolutely terrifying. How easy would it be to lose control and follow in his shoes?

I can't find a proper response, so I merely stare at my bloody hands while trying not to cry.

My eyes skim across the bits of city flashing in the open window like a television, until one image snaps my mind into pristine focus.

"Why are you turning down this street?" I demand, wondering how long we've been cruising around the slums.

"Shortcut," he mumbles.

My heart blasts waves of panic through me, my breath short. I need my gun but remember it's at the bottom of my backpack at Carol's. "Turn around! You're going to get me killed!"

Calmly, he says, "What a shame."

"Denendrius! I can't be here! I'm supposed to be dead."

"Fine." He flicks on the turn signal and heads toward safer territory.

When we pull up to a stoplight, the sound of Spanish rap settles into place in the lane beside me. My muscles still and I pray it's just a white guy with good taste. Facing straight, I roll my eyes to the right.

A classic Cadillac convertible, red, sits beside me. They're already staring at me with expressionless faces. With my hair tucked behind my ear, there's no doubt they can see my gang tattoo.

When they notice me notice them, the driver signs.

I don't sign back.

The driver leans closer, eyes tightening on me. He has VR— Venganza Roja—scrawled across the front of his throat, a dark red bandana around his wrist.

The passenger nudges him and shows him something on a flip phone.

They both look back at me, and when their hands disappear from my sight, Denendrius hits the gas, thankfully as aware as I am that we'll be shot at if we don't move.

The car jolts forward and he grumbles about not wanting bullet holes in the Mustang. Behind us, one of them shoots and misses.

I'm grateful Denendrius has had decades to learn to drive. He weaves in and out of alleys and streets, losing them faster than expected.

Our speed only drops when the graffiti thins and we enter a middle-class-looking area.

"Don't stop driving," I snarl. "Drive past a few police stations. If we're being tailed, they won't dare follow us past them."

"Why would that stop them?" He looks bored.

I sit back, propping my feet on the dashboard. "They steal their cars."

"Hm."

I tap my foot loudly, my ankle cracking every few bounces.

"And you might want to get a new license plate." I chew my nail, eyes glued to the side mirror. "They're smart. They could connect it to your place."

"My plates are fakes," he says.

I stare at him. "You've never been pulled over?"

He smiles. "I have. I'm convincing, remember?"

"Right." I wish I could hypnotize myself out of being arrested.

"Do you think they'll come looking for you?" he asks.

I swallow a lump and cross my arms. "Oh yeah."

When I try to explain what happened, he waves his hand at me.

"I'm well aware," he says, smiling. "I know you, remember?"

I wonder how much of my life he's stood around to watch, how much he *really* knows about me. The thought numbs my lips, not that I could think of words to say anyway.

I tuck my swelling hands into the pocket of my hoodie and lean my head against the window, trying to convince myself I'm anywhere but here.

XXIX

The silence has chewed my nerves raw by the time we reach the apartment. When Denendrius opens the door, my stomach lurches into my chest.

All of my belongings from Carol's are packed into boxes and stacked against the wall between the living room and hallway.

I take a step toward them, but my feet feel like they've melted into the carpet. Standing silently, my mind struggles to come to terms with what I'm seeing.

Denendrius locks the door behind us. "What? You weren't under the impression you'd be living with Carol, were you?"

"I—" I lack the proper words.

He kisses me on the top of my head before moving into the living room, draping his leather coat over the arm of the couch. "I would have had you moved in our first night together, but I knew there would be times I couldn't have you around yet." He sighs. "And unfortunately, with the way you've been rebelling, I wasn't about to leave you alone here either."

"I liked Carol's," I whisper.

"You made it simple by telling her what I am, Marianna." He smiles. "She didn't fuss once. She merely took her kids and locked herself in her bedroom so I could pack in peace. I don't even have to worry about her telling anyone. So, thank you." His words are confusingly genuine.

My words come out like a hiccup. "You're w-welcome."

Grinning with excitement, he pulls me into his arms, squeezing the air from me. He steps back, grin still intact as he taps the top of a box. "Go ahead and start unpacking, sweetheart. I'll go get you food."

I bow my head. "I'm not really hungry," I mumble.

He lifts my head back up and kisses me. "I'll help you unpack, and then we'll sleep. How does that sound?"

I nod.

He grabs a box and carries it into the bedroom. "This is a new chapter in our lives, Marianna. You'll see."

By the time I get my box of books to the shelf at the end of the living room, he's already carrying the last two into the bedroom. When I can't get the tape off, I rip into the cardboard with my fingernails, biting back a frustrated shriek. Books fall from my shaky hands on the way to the shelf and I think of chucking them off the balcony. It seems pointless to keep them when I'll probably never have a clear enough head again to crack one open.

When I get up to grab the last box, it's gone and in the room with Denendrius.

I inhale loudly when I spot my memory box on the kitchen counter. I approach it, fingers hovering over the flaps. I think of setting the box on fire. Maybe I'd let the flames catch me too.

He wraps his arms around my waist from behind. "Bed? You seem tired."

Not quite the word I would have chosen, but it's close enough.

"Yeah, okay," I say, shaking him off and heading into the bathroom, where I wash my face and brush my teeth.

Denendrius is already under the covers when I enter the bedroom, rustling around in the sheets and untangling them.

"Where are my pajamas?" I mumble, rubbing my eyes and stumbling into a wall.

He sits up. "Bottom drawer in the dresser."

I yank the drawer open and see my clothes folded neatly. I pull out my bottoms and top from underneath some other articles of clothing, mussing up the order. I strip as Denendrius grumbles about his wasted organization efforts.

I wobble to the bed, the scent of laundry detergent—sunshine and vanilla—filling my nostrils as I climb in.

Denendrius sighs and pulls me close to him, his fingers stroking my arms and sides as he stirs. Eventually, he takes an exasperated breath, flips me onto my back, and crawls on top of me.

His cold breath glides over my throat as he kisses me, lips hovering over my shirt while he slides down. Pulling it up, he runs his lips over my stomach, kissing upwards until he reaches my bra. I shiver from the wintry breath he casts on me, eyes wide while I fight the urge to crawl away from him.

He makes a noise in his throat and his lips jump to mine, kissing hard, his hands pressing against my sides and pulling me off the bed and into his bare chest. His fingers run under my shirt and over my breasts and I kick out. Instead of backing off, he holds me tighter.

I quiver, and he must think it's good because he sighs and presses himself into me. I want to tell him to stop and get off me, but I told him I love him, and if I actually did, I would allow some sort of affection. With his persistence so blatant, I fear what he'll do if I push back like every other time.

My stomach spins, growing uneasy when he tugs my pants

off and throws them on the floor. I feel his cold fingers as they touch me through my thin underwear, applying pressure to places where I might melt if I wanted it.

"Hmm," he hums in my ear, "you're so warm."

I twist my legs together and flinch when he tries to put his hand down my underwear.

"I'm uncomfortable," I mumble.

"Why?" he demands.

I keep quiet.

His lips brush my throat and I lean my head back. He makes a pained sound and wraps his fingers around the back of my neck. Deep breaths are followed by forced ones, and it sounds like he can't catch his breath.

I swallow and try to wiggle away from him. The window emits a blue-yellow light, shadowing his face but exaggerating the hints of bright red in his eyes.

I clutch my hands together, my breath heavy as my throat turns into a sweltering desert.

"Denendrius . . ." I whisper like he'll attack me if I break whatever holds him back from drinking my blood.

His tongue traces my lips, one hand on the side of my face, the other pulling the hem of my underwear.

"I need you," he moans, his hand slipping from my face to between my legs.

I kick out and he growls, hands persistent on my body. I rock back and forth, trying to evade his attempts to pull my underwear down. I twist my legs together and he yanks them apart before using his knees to pin my legs down.

I start thrashing, kicking, clawing, and yelling. He must be enjoying it, craving my reaction because he could just hold me down and have his way. Instead, he smiles.

His hands circle my throat and he throttles me, my pleas trapped. Tears sting. My head swims, too much pressure from the screams building up. Eyes locked with mine, I can tell he's considering whether or not to kill me.

"*Love me, love me, love me,*" he demands madly, hands tightening.

One of his hands moves to his harsh mouth, his milk-white teeth ripping into the pale of his wrist. He presses his bloodied wrist to my mouth, the thick rose-wine scent enticing me to drink, my body craving what my rational mind would refuse.

The cold of his blood trickling over my tongue is almost enough to distract me from the fact I can't breathe, but with his hand so tight I can't swallow. The insanity in his eyes pulsing through his blood and into me is so powerful I can no longer taste the sweet sourness of him.

With his hand crushing my windpipe, blood pools at the back of my throat, my thoughts slowly fading. When darkness robs my sight, my muscles relaxing, he lets go.

I spit a mouthful of blood into his face.

He roars and throws me off the bed. I lie on the carpet sucking at air, heart hammering in my ears. Then I stumble to the bathroom, slam the door and lock it before flicking the light on. I catch a glimpse of myself in the mirror and want to throw up.

A thick red bruise crosses my throat, a cluster of dots and blotches circling my bloody eyes and my cheeks like a mix of freckles and hickeys.

I spin and press my body against the cold of the countertop. Fingernails drag down the door, the sound twisting my gut.

"Go away!" The words shake from my quivering body, my voice raspy.

His voice comes out quiet and innocent. "Marianna, please let me in."

I bare my teeth, a rabid noise behind them. "Go away! You were going to fucking rape me, you pig!"

He rakes his fingernails down the door again. "I was only playing. You know I would never actually do it, right?"

My teeth clang together, knees bent, ready to attack if he enters. "What's wrong with you!" I screech. I rub my hand over my forehead, wiping sweat as I pace in front of the sink.

"Marianna, I just want you to love me," he pouts.

I test a deep breath, but a hiccup-sob type thing comes out.

"Are you crying?" There's something sinister in his voice.

I wipe my nose with the back of my hand, fists clenched so hard it's a wonder my veins haven't popped. I shake my head at the thought of tears.

"You were asking for it," he says.

I kick the wall and hear a crack from the drywall as I leave a heel indent. "Asking for it? I haven't asked for shit! What makes you think you can come into my life and fuck it up!" I take a heavy step back, rubbing my heel raw on the bottom corner of the counter. "I am so sick of you!" I open my mouth wide for a scream? Growl? I don't know, but it shakes me, the energy striking a headache like a match.

"It's going to be okay," he says simply.

I give a bull snort. "Yeah? When? After you kill me?"

"Why would I kill you?"

I throw my hands up. "Well, why not? Goddamn it! What did you do? Search for the most screwed-up teenager in all of fucking Lorimer, just to see how much it would take to make her break?"

"Fate brought us together." Fingernails against the door.

I slam my hands against the door, shooting pricks of pain into my arms. "No. You did. *This is all on you.*"

The door bursts open and I leap back as the lock snaps.

I back into the counter, fingers gripping the countertop.

He holds up my sketchbook, the one I slid under my bed after sketching him dying. My knees wobble.

"Let's get one thing straight." He motions with the book as if to hit me and I flinch. "I *will not* be made a mockery of."

"I didn't mean it," I breathe.

His head tilts in warning.

"I-I'm sorry."

He rips the entire thing in half and tosses it at me, pages scattering. I gulp. When he pulls a plastic bag with the sleeping pills from my nightstand out of his pocket, my blood turns to sludge.

"And these?"

My jaw opens wordlessly.

He crushes the pills in his hand and throws the bag at me too. "I recall telling you to behave."

I try to defend myself by saying, "I didn't leave the house."

He motions to the mess on the floor. "And yet you found a way to defy me."

I try to stand taller, but if it weren't for my grip on the counter, my knees would bring me to the floor.

He takes a deep breath. "Marianna, I am trying. I waited for twelve years, only to be met with this level of attitude and disobedience. It's your turn to put in some effort."

I shake, not in fear but because my blood is churning at a thousand degrees. What was he expecting, for me to just roll over and let him control me, to call him sir and follow him around? Maybe he should have gotten a fucking puppy. I open my mouth to tell him that, only to catch myself. The ache in my throat reminds me of my appearance, and my might fades.

He frowns, eyes filling with pity. He pulls me against his chest and sighs.

"It'll be all right," he says. "You're so young, you can't fully understand. The modern world has digressed and has done no favors for you. Had this been Rome, you would have been just fine."

I'm motionless in his arms with my face pressed against his

cold chest as he runs his fingers through my hair in a failed attempt to comfort me.

His fingers tighten on the back of my neck, cracking it. "But, it's time to grow up." Hand still gripping the back of my neck, he holds me at arm's length. "I gave you a few extra years to prepare. When I was human, our marriage would have been decided by the time you were twelve. You would have been fortunate to be with someone like me."

The idea is appalling and makes tears threaten my eyes. When he pulls me back to him, he burrows his head into the side of my neck.

I push my palm against his hard stomach. "Don't—"

His fangs sink into my neck and I squeak like a mouse. Mouth agape, my eyes flutter. Blood dribbles from the corner of his mouth as he drinks. A few moments later, he stops and whisks me to the bed.

The world is painfully still as I let my pulsing body fall into the sheets. He puts his knees in the crook of mine, fingers sliding over my arm. He pulls the arm I lie on across my chest and rips his teeth into it, giving me his wrist.

I drink more violently than him, so fast I almost choke. The coolness of his blood soothes my raw throat, helps regulate my breath. It's as if he takes my docile exhaustion, me his lunacy. He lets go of my wrist long before taking his away, his fingers stroking my face and neck. Denendrius hums, delivering gentle pecks to the skin behind my ear.

I kick him when he tries to pull his wrist away. He gives in for another minute before yanking his arm from my grasp. I spin around, ready to claw at his face.

"Denendrius!" I snarl, nails stopping inches from his cheek.

At the sound of my voice, I remember myself. His lips curl in delight and I flop back on my side in shame, letting him cradle me against his chest. I pull my bottom lip into my mouth and try not to hate myself.

I imagine myself floating right out the window and up to the moon, where I can cradle the stars in my fingers. I'll be alone, looking over the world. Maybe I'll hear the laughter return through the thick clouds. After all, I rarely hear any when I'm around.

I stroke the bite mark on my wrist, notice how bumpy it is and how red. I'm far too numb to sleep. Perhaps now I'm in a permanent state of exhaustion.

XXX

We watch movies all day while I wait to see my mother. Exhaustion takes its toll and I manage a brief nap before Denendrius is waking me up to leave.

We speed down the sunlit highway and toward the monster at the end of it, my mother. For a path guiding me to something far from a happy past, you'd think something gloomier would be painted around it instead of skies like blue cotton candy.

Maybe if the stretch of road didn't look so inviting and instead was covered in rotting corpses—one for every bad thing she's done to me—we would literally have to stop driving and turn back.

After the drive, we slip into the shade cast by the hulking red-bricked women's prison. I fill my lungs with a heart-stabilizing breath and force myself from the car and to the entrance, my strides long and fast, sucking up every bit of confidence the earth has to offer before I see my mother.

Denendrius waits in the car. After going through the necessary procedures, I'm seated behind a plastic window with holes in it.

My mother's drug-aged face lights up when she sees me sitting down on the other side. Her unkempt mane of dark brown hair is split at the ends and only adds to her wildness.

I set my jaw, trying not to explode and bust the plastic so I can strangle her.

Her deep brown eyes are teary, crinkled from her grin. She holds her hands against her chest, saying through her thick Spanish accent, "I can't believe my baby finally came to see me. I missed you so much. My goodness, you've gotten so big."

I grit my teeth. "After everything you did to me, you're lucky."

Bonnie's smile falls.

I clear my throat, lip twitching. I don't give her the opportunity for chitchat. "How'd you get me back, anyway? How'd you get the judge to clear your charges and deem you worthy to be a mother?" I snarl.

Her chin lifts. "The judge acknowledged that I was a good mother, Marianna. Julio made sure he was thinking in our best interest."

I'm taken aback, my eyes widening. "Julio? As in Venganza Roja's Julio?"

"Julio was my boyfriend." She looks at me like I should already know this. "I asked him to protect you."

I open my mouth, but words don't come out. It makes sense, though, with how Julio treated me. Sometimes it felt like he was trying to be my father. I always assumed it was because he was so much older than the rest of us.

"They used to always be over at the house when you were four." She smiles gently. "Don't you remember?"

I don't remember that, I realize. I don't even know if I remember being four. I don't even remember when I started remembering.

"How is Julio?" she asks. "I haven't heard from him in nearly a year. Does he talk about me?"

"Julio is dead."

She sucks on her upper lip. "Oh."

"What happened to the couple that was going to adopt me?" I wring my fingers.

She glowers. "How should I know?"

I grit my teeth, blood pressure rising. "Did you have something done to them? Because they were *murdered*."

Bonnie sneers. "No," she spits. "God took care of them. Take it up with him."

"Fuck you," I snarl. "You can't convince me their deaths didn't have anything to do with you. *You* found a way to have my parents killed, didn't you?"

Her hands shift in her handcuffs. "I love you. You're *my* daughter, never theirs. But I *did not* have those people murdered."

I cross my arms. "Then why did you do all that shit to me? Why'd you lock me in my room? Why'd you prostitute me? Why'd you treat me like shit?"

She bites her lips, body beginning the quiver. "I had to scare you. I had to protect you." Her voice cracks. "I had to hide you."

I roll my eyes, hands beginning to sweat. "From *what*?"

My mother begins to twitch as she leans toward the plastic. "The devil," she mumbles.

The hair stands on the back of my neck. "What?"

She nods. "He came back after you did and threatened to snatch you from me."

I remember her little song then, scaring me about the devil, telling me he was going to get me.

Her voice rises a few octaves. "I had to lock you away because he would wait outside, watching."

My blood turns icy. The shadow of a man who'd stand outside my window, watching me, sometimes entering my mind. *Denendrius.* My voice comes out detached. "What did he look like?"

Her eyes widen. "You saw him too?"

Slowly, I nod.

She puts her finger up, then nods again. "I saw his face once. He had red eyes," she whispers. "Teeth like a monster!"

She saw Denendrius. I swallow, unable to accept the fact that he added to my mother's drug-fueled paranoid delusions.

"You locked me away . . . because you thought the devil was going to get me." My words are stale.

She nods, brown hair swinging. "*Sí. Sí.* You understand." She gives a broken smile. "*Thank God*, you understand."

I stare at her. "Then why did you sell me?"

She swallows, eyes turning to her lap as she frowns. "They told me he wanted a virgin."

"Who?"

Her eyes dart around like she's looking to see if someone is listening. "*They* did. They said he wouldn't take you if you were impure. I had to make you dirty, or he'd snatch you away."

My heart stumbles, my eyes stinging.

I clench my shaky fingers into a fist. "Is that why you drugged me up too?"

She shakes her head. "No. I did it to help your pain." She takes a deep, trembling breath, tears lining her eyes. "I figured if you were high, you'd forget them."

And forget most of my childhood too, apparently. I may not remember every man, but I remember how it felt, how it made me want to die, how it made me feel sick, dirty, worthless.

I grit my teeth. "Too bad none of it helped," I snarl.

She scratches her neck, lips trembling. "What d'you mean, Marianna?"

"Everything you did was for nothing," I growl.

Her forehead crinkles, her expression carrying a look that

expects someone to hit her. "No, he didn't get you." Her smile trembles. "When I was gone, the gang kept you safe."

I bite my lip, throat thickening. "Yes, he did get me."

Tears well in her eyes. "What?" she cries.

"He got me, Mom," I snarl. "The devil didn't care what you did. He took me anyway."

She leaps up, chair screeching backward, metal clattering around her wrists. "No," she cries. "No, no. I did everything I could to protect you. He couldn't have!"

"You failed as a mother," I snarl. "And I *hate* you."

She slams her fists on the table and receives a loud warning from a guard. Tears stream from her twitching brown eyes. "No! No! You don't say that."

Two guards grab her, pulling her away as she kicks and screams, brown hair flying. "No! I loved you!" she wails. "No! No! Get off me! No! You can't do this! No!"

As they pull her from the room, I know this will be the last time I ever see my mother. The door shuts behind her, her terror-filled face disappearing. Her voice echoes behind the heavy door.

A guard appears angrily beside me, and while he escorts me out, it takes all my strength and will not to grab his gun and fight my way in to shoot her for ruining my life, for taking a perfect set of parents away from me. He tells me not to come back if my only goal is to rile up my already sick mother.

Denendrius is waiting for me in the car. When I get in, I put extra spite into slamming the door.

I turn to him, wiping tears away with a shaky hand. "You drove my mother insane."

He looks at me, his face callous. "She was already insane. If the worst of her abuse didn't start until she got you back, they clearly thought something was wrong with her to have you taken away the first time."

My jaw aches, teeth so tight pain shoots through my face. "As if you had nothing to do with it."

The corner of his mouth twitches in a half-smile and he shifts the car into drive and exits the prison parking lot.

"She claims she didn't have my adoptive parents killed. I don't know why she won't just admit it!"

Denendrius purses his lips in a way that makes my eyes narrow in suspicion.

"*What?*" I demand venomously.

He sighs and adjusts in his seat, tilting his head back and forth like he's considering his words.

Dark fury makes my balance teeter, my sight narrowing as I turn and stare at him with bared teeth. "*You said you didn't kill them!*"

He sucks in air through his teeth. "*I didn't—*"

"You said you didn't *know* who killed them either!" I shriek, hands curling into fists.

"I didn't know their names," he clarifies.

I gape at him, tears burning in my eyes. "What the fuck!" I pummel him in the shoulder with my fist and receive a warning glare. "Denendrius, what the fuck!"

"Marianna..."

I vibrate with fury. "Tell me what happened."

He adjusts his hands on the wheel. "Vampires killed your adoptive parents, Marianna. After I returned you, a couple men threatened you and your family. They told me either I go with them so they could collect their bounty, or they would kill the three of you."

I lean away from him, face twisting in disgust. "And you refused? You chose a child and her parents to die over yourself? *Me?*" It shouldn't come as a surprise.

He waves his hand at me. "Oh, please. I knew they weren't going to kill you. It's against the rules to kill a child, so the likelihood of them doing so when they were coming after *me* didn't make me eager to step in. Your adoptive parents were lovely people, but adult humans are fair game. And look, here you are, with me who's still *alive*, so I was right to call their bluff."

I cross my arms and straighten in the passenger seat. "You are un-fucking-believable. Why would you even take that gamble?"

"Because I didn't want to die, Marianna! That's why!" he exclaims while glowering at the road. "My goodness, sweetheart."

"It should have been you they killed," I growl.

He sighs. "You don't mean that. It's not as if it's *my fault* they were killed. You should be blaming those bounty hunters, not me."

"I do mean that."

I'm stiff as he reaches over and rubs my knee. "Relax, sweetheart. Your visit with your mother has gotten you all upset."

I don't offer a response, my eyes glued to the road as Denendrius speeds along it.

My entire life is a lie, a set of events that happened as a result of him. Who am I but a pawn? What in my life has not led directly back to him? The reason my adoptive parents were killed was because of Denendrius. The shit my mother put me through was because of Denendrius. The reason I was in Red Revenge was because my mother wanted me protected from Denendrius. Everything else that happened in between was just a collection of seconds counting down to the day when Denendrius would finally step in and take direct control of my life.

As always, he has made everything about himself. He has made my life about him.

I exist to amuse him.

I unlatch my jaw to take a calming breath. "Twelve years," I snarl. "You stalked me for twelve years. Why? Why only show up now?"

"There was no more waiting. Your life opened perfectly for me, like the universe knew I was the next step. I saw things weren't going to get better, so I wanted to help before you did something suicidal—like overdosing in a shed."

I chew my cheek. "I've almost died lots of times. I've always gotten by on my own."

"Perhaps so, but there was always something or someone to pull you back from the edge. This time I guarantee you would have died if it wasn't for me. Your heart almost stopped. My blood was the only thing that kept you breathing. If I had been five minutes later, I would have been burying you."

I remember skin against my mouth during a brief second of consciousness, how it felt like I was choking on something. But instead of feeling grateful, I watch the grass smear by in the ditch as we drive, silent anger stewing in my gut.

Barreling down the highway, I slap away every attempt at conversation Denendrius throws at me with a glare. Anger traces a path for my thoughts and locks my jaw so tight I could probably bend steel with my teeth. My mind won't stray from the visit with my mother, frustration piling up inside me.

My thoughts are so blinding I don't even notice when we've parked in the lot of his apartment. After being shaken from my trance, I step heavy-footed from the car, closing the door as hard as I can and receiving a warning from Denendrius.

Clomping up the stairs after him, I slam the door after us. As soon as I turn around, he shoves me against the wall with a few fingers and glares.

"I understand you're angry, but you need to calm down."

I release a frustrated growl from behind bared teeth before stomping and plunking myself on the couch, ramming my fists into my face once as I rest my forehead on them. Unable to find something to project my anger toward, I punch myself in the kneecap and suck in a pained breath.

He sits beside me and rubs my back, only stirring my

boiling blood into something much thicker like molten lava. I ball my fist up and it twitches toward Denendrius when I think of punching him, but he must predict my wish because his fingers turn into a claw on my back.

"I want to see the tape of me again, from Enchanted Land."

"Why?" He stands.

I look up at him, voice strained. "Please?"

I pick at my lips until he returns, placing the camcorder on my lap as he sits beside me. I snatch it up and rewind the tape, obsessively watching it over and over again, each rewind bringing me near hysteria. He stares at the television—off—his hand on my knee, lost in thoughts of his own.

After watching the twenty-minute tape a handful of times, my imagination spinning off the images stained on the film, I begin to hyperventilate.

He pulls the camcorder from my quivering fingers and wraps his arms around me, kissing my cheek. "It'll all be okay, sweetheart."

"I—" My breath catches in my throat and I choke. "Everything is fucked."

He runs his fingers through my hair. "It's getting dark. We'll go lie down. Hm?"

I nod slowly and stand. Denendrius's arms are around me while we walk to the bed. He tucks me in fully clothed and crawls in next to me after dropping his leather jacket on the floor. When I raise my eyes, they meet his, soft and concerned. I roll over and bury my face in the pillow.

His whisper is soft as he crawls in next to me. "You don't need to think about your mother. You don't need her or anyone else. I'll take care of you, okay? I love you, Marianna."

"I love you too," I mumble.

He pulls me onto his chest, our stomachs and chests against one another, my knees on either side of his hips. I notice I've been holding my breath when his chest fills with air and lifts me. I exhale loudly.

Denendrius smooths my hair against my back, his other hand hooked behind my knee.

I try not to cry while thinking about all the things my mother did to me in the name of protection. I try not to remember the sweaty nights, the cold showers, the starvation and beatings. *The heroin.*

My veins burn and my mind twists over the thought of being high.

I think about the one thing more dangerous than heroin, the one thing that feels so much better. I'd much rather feel insanity than the burning ache of sadness.

When Denendrius pulls my fingers from his neck, I wonder how long I've been scratching at him.

I sit up on his stomach, thinking he's going to ask me to get off him. Instead, he rips his jugular open with his fingernails, blood oozing from the wound and staining the white blanket.

When I hesitate, his hand cups the back of my head, pulling me to his throat. He holds me against him while I drink. I'm too absorbed in the high to care about his needy fingers raking down my back beneath my shirt. I don't think I'd be able to pull my lips away even if I put every ounce of strength into the task.

I can barely feel his hand as it trails over me, my body numb to its temperature. I feel like Alice in Wonderland, my mind spinning further and further down the rabbit hole until colors and nonsensical thoughts are smearing across my psyche.

When his hands pull my head away from his throat, I feel like I'm emerging from the deepest depths of the ocean. He kisses me roughly, pulling my body so tightly to his that my bones ache. When he finally lets me go, sighing, it takes me a moment to gather myself, the crispness of reality almost painful. I roll onto my back in the blue moonlight emitting from the window.

My stomach aches, bloated from the blood. The thought almost makes me puke. I think about what a good idea it could be to purge his blood from my system, or is it too late by now? Regardless, I know he'd stop me.

I fall into a sleep so deep I'm surprised and disoriented when I wake and find myself completely alone.

XXXI

When I roll over, Denendrius is nowhere to be found. I know better than to try and leave, instead deciding I want to watch the video again while I wait for him to return, but blown up on the TV so I can search for details. I roll out of bed and stumble to the living room, flicking the light on.

I'm not sure what I'm looking for, why I want to watch it. Maybe I just can't deal with the fact that I can't remember. Maybe I'm trying to lure the memory forward.

When I can't find the camcorder where he left it in the living room, or in any of his drawers, I scowl and stand in the hallway with my arms crossed. Unable to think of any reason why Denendrius would have taken it with him, I dig through the few belongings in the apartment until I uncover not only the camcorder but a large plastic bin in a gap between the dryer and the wall, hidden by the closet door.

The fact it's so purposefully hidden makes my stomach seep through to my knees as I stare at the long, thin green container.

Taking it and the camcorder with me to the living room, I hold my breath when I open it and find dozens of little tapes in their plastic cases, alongside a collection of green photo envelopes. I grab a tape at random and open it to read the title.

Marissa. 2005 – 17

Confused, I put it back and grab one from a different row.

Janice. 1980 – 14

I continue to pull them out at random, hoping one of them will shed light.

Megan. 1990 – 13
Hope. 1989 – 16
Olivia. 1998 – 15
Evelyn. 1979 – 16
Leah. 2007 – 12
2003 – 15

I go back and open them all one by one. Aside from a couple without names and numbers, they're all titled the same way: a girl's name, a year, followed by a number—presumably an age—between twelve and seventeen. I snatch "2003 – 15" and shove it in the camcorder.

Flipping open the screen, I hit play.

The video starts by showing a brown-haired girl sitting on a bed, gagged with cloth. She's white and in her teens.

Denendrius appears in frame and when she protests, he grabs her jaw and hisses, "*Shut up, before you wake the whole house.*"

With my stomach in knots, I take a deep breath, my hand shaking the camera.

Her screams are muffled as he rips her nightgown, followed by a *whap!* as he backhands her.

I slam the screen shut. I don't want to see what I know comes next. Clammy hands shaking, I snatch another tape.

Sandra, 1982 — 12

I press play and am faced with a young girl crying in a sunny forest, a school bag thrown a few feet away from her. This one has brown hair too, and as Denendrius approaches her to unbutton her jean jacket, she begs for her mom.

Tears prick my eyes, blinding me to the image before I control my hands enough to shakily close the screen again.

I start a handful more but can't make myself watch more than a few seconds past the entrance of the girls. Horror creeps into me with each tape. The girls all have long hair, varying from light to dark brown; their bodies are lean and small-breasted. Their eyes, despite being terrified, are all brown or hazel.

From afar, they could all be mistaken for one another . . . *or me for them.*

I toss the tapes in the plastic tub. I don't have to watch the sixty or so other ones to know what they're of. Wrapping my arms around myself, I try to stop the tears from coming. When I realize I've yet to find the tape from Enchanted Land, cold breathes down my back when I realize it has been hidden too.

I hop up and frantically search the apartment, trying to stop myself from sobbing or throwing up. When I find it—and two more—jammed between the piping under the kitchen sink, I almost break the plastic cover when I yank it open.

Marianna — Enchanted Land #2

When I open the second, I feel a slice through my chest

as I gasp for air, sobs strangling me. My wails echo through the empty apartment as it falls from my hand, the tape clanging on the floor. When I remember the rest in my hand, I cough and gag, my hands struggling to take turns opening them.

Marianna, 2008 – 17

"Oh my God," I wail, torn between running to the bathroom to throw up and deciding which of the two newly discovered tapes to watch first.

When I can manage to stand, I grab the tapes and hook the camcorder into the TV, knowing I won't be able to stop myself from turning the machine off if I'm holding it. After crawling onto the couch, I play the most recent.

The video begins with my thrashing body lying on the forest floor. The recording of my screams slice through the silence of the apartment, and I can tell I'm already hallucinating. Denendrius appears in frame and leans over me while I screech and thrash, my fingers clawing at the ground.

Video Marianna whimpers and cries, muscles spasming from the venom-induced fever, her vacant and bloody eyes locked on the camcorder lens.

Denendrius crawls around me, peering at me while checking me over before he removes his belt.

My body tingles and goes numb as I stare unblinking at the television screen. My chest tightens, refusing to allow me any more air. I feel like screaming, punching walls and ripping my skin off, but I can't ground myself in my body. It's as if I'm watching myself watch the video.

Denendrius yanks my shorts off as I convulse and whine. With the hallucinations, I'm hardly fazed by what he does, even as he wraps his hands around my throat. He seems to find enjoyment in my convulsions, barely taking the effort to hold me down as he rapes me like he did in what I thought was merely a hallucination.

It carries on for longer than I can handle. But even when I want to stand and tear the cord from the television, my brain seems to have lost transmission to my body.

When video cuts out and turns to white fuzz, I'm left gawking at the screen, unable to find a way to make myself move. When was the last time I blinked?

My lips twitch as I find a way to drag myself across the ground to switch the tapes. I feel like a zombie. I don't have the energy to make it back to the couch, so I sit on the carpet.

The hidden Enchanted Land tape starts off fairly innocent, with Denendrius and five-year-old me walking down the main avenue of Enchanted Land. The angle of the camera is high above me as he drags me into a shop and lets me select a costume.

"*This one! This one!*" I squeal, pointing to a little black lace gown.

He lifts it off the hook and I smile at the camera. "*Yeah? You want this one?*"

I clap my hands together and hug it. "*Yeah!*"

He hands it to me, and I giggle.

"*Are you getting a costume too?*" my mousy voice asks.

He makes a *tsk* noise. "*They don't sell costumes for grown-ups here, sweetheart.*"

Pointing, I jump at a pair of white angel wings. "*Get those ones, Den!*"

He sighs but submits to my request. "*Do you think they'll fit?*" "*Yeah!*"

His hand extends to a pair of black ones. "*What about these ones? They match your dress!*"

I fake-pout. "*Angels don't have black wings.*"

"*Aw, c'mon. Of course they can! Angels of death do.*"

I stare wide-eyed up at him. "*What's 'angel of death'?*"

He grabs the black wings off the shelf. "*It's just a different kind of angel.*"

We go to the checkout after, and he asks me if I want any of the candy. I eagerly point out a chocolate bar.

"*You're my best friend, Den.*"

"*I am?*"

"*Yeah! The bestest.*"

He laughs. "*Does that mean you love me?*"

I nod madly. "*I do! I do love you!*"

"*You're such a sweetheart.*"

My heart races as Denendrius and my younger version walk toward a hotel when the sky darkens, and when we're inside his hotel room, he sets the camcorder on a table, getting a good view of most of the room.

He lies on the bed and props himself up with his elbow. "Why don't you put the dress on?"

Denendrius trains his eyes on the TV while I change around the corner, eyes flickering back when I appear and say, "*Do I look pretty, Den?*"

"*You look very pretty. You're a princess!*"

I spin and giggle, then bounce toward the bed, wings in hand. "*You have to put these on now!*"

"*Yeah?*"

"*Yeah!*"

He pats the bed and chuckles. "*Come here.*" Pulling his jacket and T-shirt off, he slips the wings on.

I touch the scar on his stomach. "*Did someone hurt you?*"

"*Yes, they did.*"

I show him a cigarette burn on my wrist. "*Me too.*"

We sit in silence for a moment before he says, "*Did you mean it when you said you loved me?*"

I get up and start jumping on the bed, dress twirling around me as I spin. "*Yeah!*"

He sits up. "*I haven't heard that in a very long time. Why do you?*"

"*Because you're fun!*" My feet twist in the blankets and I almost fall off the bed until he grabs my arm.

"*You don't think I'm mean?*" he asks.

I chew on my hair and shake my head.

"*You don't think I'm scary?*"

I smile and shake my head again. "*Nuh-uh.*"

He ponders me for a moment. "*Hmm.*"

I poke him. "*Do you love me?*"

He touches my hair, sadness glimmering in his eyes. "*Do you want me to?*"

I giggle and nod. "*Yeah!*"

"*Okay,*" he says, voice distant.

I stick my tongue out at him and poke his leg. "*Why do you?*" I mimic.

He stares at me for a long time. "*You're familiar.*"

I cock my head. "*Like you think you've seen me before? Sometimes Vianna gets people mixed up in the grocery store.*"

His chin scrunches. "*No, not like that. You make me feel things I haven't felt in a long time.*"

"*Like what?*" I ask, pulling on a loose feather on his wings.

Denendrius's hard swallow looks painful. His black eyes are hollow pits as he stares past young me and turns silent. I don't seem to notice he hasn't answered my question as I move on to playing with my new dress.

Denendrius purses his lips. "*Would you be sad if you never saw your parents again?*"

I frown at him and drop my hands. "*Why would I never see them again?*"

He smooths the tacky floral blanket. "*Well, you want to keep being my friend, right?*"

I grin and nod.

"*If you want to be friends with me, you can't have parents.*"

I furrow my brow. "*I don't get it.*"

He scratches his forehead, thinking. "*What would you say if I asked you if you wanted to live forever? If you come with me, you will never feel pain again. Nobody would ever hurt you and you'd never have to be alone.*"

I giggle. "*We'd be best friends forever?*"

He nods. "*Yes.*"

"*Where would we go?*" I ask.

"*Anywhere you want.*"

I wiggle and laugh. He grabs my hands and tries to stop my eyes from jumping all over the room while trying to make me concentrate on him.

"*Okay, I'll say 'goodbye until next time' to Vianna and then can we go to the toy store?*"

His chin tucks. "*Marianna, if you come with me there will be no next time. You will never ever see Vianna again.*"

I finally still. "*But Mommy says there's always a next time for people that love each other.*"

His smile is pained. He thinks deeply for a while, undisturbed and unfazed by my questions about when we'll be leaving and if I can bring my toys and if I'll need a jacket or snacks.

He only looks up when I say, "*It's not fair that I can't be your friend and have my new mommy and daddy.*"

He swallows. "*I know.*"

My eyes tear. "*I never had a friend before. I don't want to stop having one.*"

He sighs. "*Maybe when you're older we can be friends again.*"

I frown. "*Why not friends now? Why don't you come to my house sometimes?*"

He rubs my cheek with his finger. "*We'll still be friends. You just won't see me again until you're older.*"

"*Do you promise?*" my mousy voice asks.

"*I promise. Do you promise to remember me?*"

I giggle. "*Duh! I won't forget you, Den. You don't forget to come play soon.*"

"*You said there's always a next time for people who love each other, right?*"

I nod.

"*And you love me, and I love you, right?*"

I smile. "*Yes.*"

He touches my hair. "*Then this is only goodbye until next time.*"

I walk with him willingly to the doorway, only to resist when it opens, pulling back on his hand.

He sighs and looks down at me. "*You have to decide, sweetheart.*"

I shake my head and chew my thumbnail. I look down at my dress and back to him, then peer around him outside, making a distressed noise.

He pulls me back into the room and shuts the door, crouching down to my level. He seems to consider something for a moment before making up his mind. "*I'll tell you what. Why don't we have a sleepover and you can decide in the morning?*"

My face lights up and I let out an excited shriek before he covers my mouth. I turn away and race back to the bed, leaping onto it before jumping up and down repeatedly, chanting about a slumber party.

Minutes later he's passing me a room-service menu, ordering everything I point to into a bulky white phone. I giggle gleefully at being spoiled. When he puts a fairy-tale collection on the thick television, I crawl onto his lap.

"*You're freezing,*" I say, rubbing his hands to try and warm them up. When it clearly doesn't work, I wrap our hands together in a blanket. "*There!*"

His smile is small. "*You care. That's sweet.*"

Denendrius is hiding me in the bathroom forty minutes later as a knock sounds at the door. He pulls the black wings off and slips on a black shirt. A cart full of food is wheeled into the room before he takes the cart to the bed and studies it.

He targets a bowl of chili, ripping his wrist open with his teeth. Blood pours from his vein until the wound heals. When he calls me from the bathroom, it's the first thing he serves me.

I happily scarf it down, asking for more. When I don't find a second helping of chili on the cart, I'm near tantrum until he manages to convince me the rest of the food is just as good. When I see the cart is filled with everything else I wanted, I'm happy again, eating with my hands. I make him put his wings back on and I return to watching television from his lap.

When it's over, he tucks me into the bed, propping himself up with pillows beside me against the wall. I'm mumbling in my sleep soon, Denendrius's eyes glowing faintly in the dark like a cat's. He watches me, stroking my hair until I start whimpering in my sleep. When he wakes me up, I'm sobbing and moaning like I've witnessed a murder.

He pulls me onto his lap and holds my head against his chest. "*Did you have a nightmare?*" he asks softly.

"*Mm-hmm.*"

He pets my head. "*What was it about?*"

I'm silent then, my tears dried up. I don't seem able to provide an answer.

I fall back asleep in his arms, sleeping soundly until the video cuts off like it was long forgotten about.

From where I am now and from what Carol said, I clearly made up my mind in the morning.

"You shouldn't snoop," Denendrius says from beside the couch, a sharp and guarded edge to his voice.

My body turns cold, electricity zapping me from my seat. I stand in front of him, in front of the TV.

"How could you?" I shriek at him. "All those girls . . ."

Me.

He gives a disheartened half-smile. "If it's any consolation, you're my favorite."

Wait . . . he thinks I'm *jealous*?

Dumbfounded, I shake my head. "You hurt me. You said you never would."

He shoves his hands in his pockets and scowls. "You don't even remember it."

I motion to the TV. "I don't have to! You immortalized it on video!"

"You didn't have to watch it."

My hands curl into fists at my side. "You didn't have to rape me!"

Denendrius waves his hand dismissively. "I don't know why you're fussing. You can't even remember *anything*, apparently."

"It still affects me! I don't have to remember it! It still happened!"

He just stares, face blank.

"What? So now you have nothing to say? I fucking hate you!" I jam my fists into my eyes, sobs tearing up my raw throat.

"You said you loved me."

"I was five!" I bellow.

Sadness dips into his eyes. "You still said it."

I choke, tears running from my eyes and down the corners of my lips. I want my anger back and my tears gone. I want to have the courage to fight him. Instead, I just lean against the TV, head in my hands, crying.

He sighs.

"Is this what you wanted?" I choke into my hands. "Are you happy now? Are you happy that you finally broke me?" My face scrunches, my voice squeaky.

"No."

My face burns, hands shaking. "Then what do you want from me!" I scream.

"Your love. I love you, Marianna. I want us to be happy."

I feel like my own tears could drown me. "What? So, you waited until I grew up so you could *fuck me*?"

"No," he says, tone desperate. "Nothing like that . . . but I saw how beautiful and strong you were when I came back, and I couldn't help but fall in love with you."

I bare my teeth. "Why me?"

"Because I love you, Marianna. I feel *alive* knowing you. Don't you feel alive knowing me?"

I feel like screaming and ripping my hair out. "You're obsessed with something a kid said twelve years ago!" I scream. "You can't love!"

"I didn't think I could until I met you." He smiles gently. "We're meant to be, Marianna. We are written on the scrolls of time."

The little dam in my head that has stopped me from falling from sanity cracks open. Crimson stains my sight and I banshee-scream so loud that there's no possible way half the building doesn't hear it. I think of my gun in my backpack, how I could shoot him right now.

"You're fucking crazy!" I shriek at him.

"Enough already!" he bellows. "It is not my fault you are terrified of love, that you shut everyone—*me*—out."

I try to bolt past him, but he clasps his hand around my arm and throws me backward onto the carpet.

Leaning down, he grabs a fistful of my shirt and pulls me closer to his face. "I am so sick of you trying to sabotage us," he snarls.

"I will never fucking love you," I say through my tears while batting at him.

His blows come hard as he punches and chokes me. I try to fight back. *God, do I try.* But I'm beneath him on the floor, and my fight is useless against his strength. Even when I feel my ribs crack and my nose break, I keep trying. I only stop when I vomit blood and am covered in it.

He halts, his bloody fist frozen in the air above my head. "Police . . . someone must have heard you."

When his hand loosens on my neck, I take the opportunity to clamber away from him and to the door.

"Go!" he demands. "I'll deal with the cops and find you after."

Teeth gnashing from the pain of my injuries, I clamber down the stairs before he can change his mind.

XXXII

The moon is high in the sky when I make it into the crisp night, the wailing of sirens nearing. A chill breathes down my neck once I'm a handful of blocks away. The night is too empty for how full my head feels. I stop and lean against a fence, hand clutching my broken ribs.

I stand for a moment, twitching, feeling his hands touching me even though I have no memory of him touching those places. I think of my mother again, how I never thought I'd be able to hate someone more than I hate her.

It feels like hours that I'm gripping the fence, watching cars roll by under the haze of golden streetlights. I wipe blood from my nose and spit a mouthful onto the concrete. The sound of Spanish rap pulls my head up, the headlights blinding as two cars race one another down the road.

My heart clutches when I see a flash of red bandanas in both the red and black convertibles, and I start running like they're already chasing me.

They probably would have never noticed me had I not moved.

"*Puta!*" a man hollers through the sound of screeching tires.

I clutch my ribs, feet stumbling as I struggle to decide between darting in a random direction or back to the apartment. I find myself weaving through the posts of a fenced walkway, my name echoing through the street as Denendrius calls me.

I turn, the crack of two gunshots radiating through the night, a member of Venganza Roja leaning half out of his car with his eyes focused on me and his gun clutched in his hand.

It feels like a hot explosion goes off inside my chest as I fall backward. My legs crumple beneath me, the feeling lost in them.

I can't hear the screech of tires as I watch them spin, the man behind the gun yanked to the asphalt by a shadow as the cars peel away. In a blink, the tattoos on his throat are erased by blood.

Denendrius appears beside me, hands pushing and pulling at the clothing covering my chest. "*Marianna.*"

My breath fails me, my throat full. My T-shirt is soaked in blood. A hot blade twists in my lung with each thought to breathe. I try to push myself away from him, but my legs don't even twitch.

Though my mind screams, I offer no sound but gurgling when his eyes turn red, lips pulling back to expose bloodied fangs.

I want to tell him not to heal me, that he should stop forcing fate's hand and let me die already. I should have died when I overdosed, when he tortured me, when he hurt me to distract Alaire. Will he never let go?

Then my eyes find my hands, shaking and gripping his shirt.

I want to accept death. I want to. But even though I know

I'm going to die soon anyway, whether here or later by Denendrius's hand, I don't want to.

He tilts my head, teeth ripping into my throat. Tears blur my sight until all I see is black.

When my sight returns, I'm outside myself. Denendrius crouches over me, wiping blood off my face with the back of his hand. He stares into my blank eyes.

"I've got you," he whispers. "Everything will be okay, sweetheart. I'll never let you die."

I gasp and cower away from my body when black wings spread from his back, feathers disturbed by their descent. He hoists up my limp body, and when he walks away, he's carrying a little girl.

I follow him—me—as fast as I can. He seems to float over the sidewalk, each streetlight dying as he passes by it, leaving behind a trail of feathers.

"Denendrius!" My shout is intertwined with hysteria. And when I reach out to touch him, so he'll notice me, a dark electricity cripples me, my hand clutching at my chest as I fall, my knees cracking against the sidewalk.

He carries on down the road as I stand and run after him screaming, his slow steps somehow no match for my furious gallop.

I follow him into the building and upstairs to his apartment. When he carries younger me into the bedroom, I try to follow, only to have my feet drawn in another direction.

I find myself standing in front of the counter in Denendrius's kitchen, my memory box in front of me. It's wet to the touch and smells of gasoline. I find a matchbox in my hand. Pulling one of the little wooden sticks out, I strike a flame and drop it on the box's top. The gasoline puts out the flame.

I squash my lips together and yank out another match. I strike it and hold the flame to the gasoline-soaked cardboard. The flame dies.

"How?" I shout in frustrated confusion, my voice echoing through the apartment.

How?

How?

The next six matches don't light the gasoline either.

I snarl and throw the box off the counter and toward the dining room. The flaps open, objects and papers flying over the table and floor, black feathers floating through the air. Something thuds against the carpet.

With slow steps, I walk around the counter. In the space between the dining room and living room, a square book lies. I squat to carefully inspect it, and my heart hammers, my palms sweaty. It's a child's diary, a cheap lock holding the glossy ocean-themed covers shut. It's badly beaten and the cartoon fish and dolphins are almost worn into nonexistence.

Black feathers stick out from the top, marking pages.

My fingers shake as I reach out to touch it, only to have my attention snagged by a child's sobbing.

Still crouched, I spin toward Denendrius's bedroom.

Visible through the open door, he sits at the end of the bed, child me on his lap. The blankets are wrong, though, grossly teal and rough like they should belong to a hotel. Tears are streaming from her face and she hiccups while trying to catch her breath.

"*It's okay,*" he consoles, hand running over her back. "*You'll be happy.*"

When he goes to kiss her cheek, I jump to my feet. He looks across the apartment at me.

"Don't you touch her!"

When I step toward them, I'm walking in grass. The moon hangs overhead in the dark blue sky, making the trees glow.

"No," I gasp, spinning in a circle, hoping the scene will change back.

I turn to the sound of movement.

Denendrius leans against a dead tree. "If I take you home, will you think about me from time to time? Remember all the fun we had?"

I bolt away from him, breath loud as I race through the forest, darting through trees and over and under branches.

"I will," child me agrees. Her voice comes from everywhere and nowhere, bouncing between the trees. "You promise to come back?"

His voice appears in my ear, startling me. "*I promise.*"

My black dress snags on a branch and I trip over a fallen trunk and land on my hands and knees in a puddle of blood and matted black feathers.

"You promised to remember me," he says from behind me, voice glum.

I shake. My elbows are weak and threaten to collapse me. My hair hangs around my face, ends submerged in blood.

"All you have to do is remember!" Denendrius bellows, volume rattling my brain.

I slam my hands over my ears and fall onto my side, eyes clamped shut. I shriek until the hard dirt softens under me.

When I open my eyes, I'm lying on Denendrius's bed, the tacky teal blanket still draped over it. He stands in the doorway, eyes cloudy as he watches me.

Cautiously, I sit, the smell of wet grass and dirt flooding my nostrils. Something mechanical hums—invisible—behind him.

"I'll miss you," he mumbles, hands stuffed into the pockets of his black-and-white windbreaker.

Wet beads slip down his face, and I think he's crying for a moment before I hear a gust of wind, and rain begins to patter softly against his windbreaker.

I open my mouth, but blood gags me and floods past my lips. It tastes like his. I try to breathe, but more chokes me. It gurgles when I try to speak.

"I'll miss you too," little me says, her voice escaping from where mine should.

He motions with his head for me to follow. When I blink, he disappears from the doorway like he was never there to begin with, the rain following him. The purring sound fades into the distance, leaving the silence of the apartment.

I fall onto my side, gripping my throat, sputtering and coughing. Heat tingles in my fingers, ice numbing my toes. They meet in my chest and I scream.

The picture around me shudders and slips away, leaving me to float in a black void.

"*Goodbye until next time*," Denendrius whispers softly in my ear.

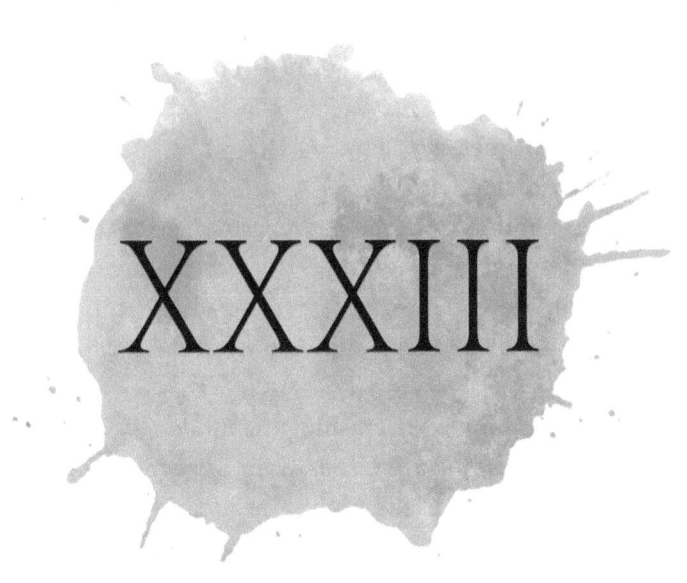

XXXIII

When I wake up, I'm lying in a streak of sunshine on Denendrius's bed. He's dressed me in a clean outfit and brushed my hair, but when I sit, something in my chest is heavy and agitated.

The bed lowers beside me as Denendrius sits, giving me a kiss. It feels like my skin is burning under his lips.

"Did you do it again?" my voice cracks, and I can't help but wonder if he did it the last time he healed me too.

He dances around the rape accusation with another question. "How do you feel?"

My sigh is one of exhaustion. "Fine," I lie.

He analyzes me. "Are you sure?"

Staring at him now, I wish he'd let me die.

I rub my hands over my arm and test my lungs with a deep breath. After seeing the video of him and me when I was a kid, there's no wonder why he appeared as a fallen angel in my hallucinations. Was my subconscious trying to tell me who he was all along?

I leap up, the carpet soft on my feet. I smooth my shirt and look around. "How long was I out? Wednesday is Jenna's funeral," I say, trying to make myself think of something else.

"What time?"

I dust off my memory. "Five."

"Then we're late."

We miss the service at the church, so we go to the cemetery and park behind a long train of cars resting beside the wrought-iron fence. The service has already begun. Mourners wrapped in grief and black attire have formed a circle around the grave.

A few must think we're crashing the funeral—being dressed in street clothes—but a whisper from a weepy-faced mother belonging to my dead friend numbs the idea.

A few people pull apart for us to join the circle as the minister speaks. Daina and Camille give me a small smile, faces moist.

I stare at the chestnut casket, at the big golden metal cross stuck on top, and wonder if there is some sort of God. And if there is, where could he possibly be amongst all this?

Glancing around at the faces, I know she was loved. I curl my fingers, the little monster inside my chest roasting my emotions. *Envy.* But standing here, how could I not feel it? Perhaps it's because if I was lying dead and cold in a wooden box, there would be nobody here but the people paid to lower me into the ground. If nice words could be found to say, there would be nobody to say them. When people find out about my death, will they smile and say I deserved it? Will Camille and Daina be there at least, weeping for me? Or do they secretly hate me, too afraid of me to admit it?

I want to switch places with Jenna. If only there was a way to take her place in that coffin. She could go home, get help and try to get better. Everything inside me could die. All my memories, my feelings, my thoughts, could just *disappear.* I'd be safe inside that little box, nestled deep in the ground where not even the most horrific monsters in the world could disturb me.

I glance up at Denendrius. His head is held high, a hint of a smile on his lips, breath steady as he basks in the sorrow of the souls surrounding.

What do people think is his reason for being here? I bet it's not because he killed her and made it look like a suicide. Biting my tongue, I wish to yell out how he murdered her, just to see how everyone would react, especially Denendrius.

The minister's voice seeps into my racing mind. *"We now commit Jenna's body to the ground, earth to earth, ashes to ashes, dust to dust, in the sure and certain hope of the resurrection to eternal life."*

Eternal life would be nice, depending on how you're spending it. But if there's a hell, I'm not sure the fiery one is as bad as what one would be like as a vampire, forever within reach of a psychopath's grasp. What if you become a ghost, left to wander the earth, invisible to everyone and lonely?

What is Jenna experiencing now? If she's a ghost, is she here standing above her grave? Would she be happy to see how so many people cared about her? How would she react to Denendrius being here?

I glance around, picturing her staring at him as he stands comfortably in his happiness. I shiver as I realize she could be standing right beside me, asking me with words I can't hear why I'm not doing anything to make her death right. Could she want me to tell her family she didn't commit suicide?

They're nearly done throwing handfuls of dirt onto the coffin, so Denendrius takes my hand and pulls me away from my dead friend, deeper into the cemetery, past headstones marking the places of rotting corpses. I watch the names and years engraved on them.

"Can you smell the corpses?" I stroke a smooth marble headstone belonging to a little girl named Emily Parks.

"Some," he says.

We sit on the little patch of green grass provided for the ten-year-old, smelling the red roses leaning against the headstone. I wonder who leaves them for her, why she died.

"I wonder if whoever keeps bringing her flowers knows there was never a body in the casket below us," Denendrius says, hands in his pockets.

I run my fingers through the dehydrated grass. "Then where could she be?"

"The world is a mystery," he mumbles. "Who cares?"

We sit in silence, listening to the crows and sparrows fighting for the oak tree ten feet from us. I watch the leaves flutter on the swaying branches, the shushing noise they make when the warm wind breathes through them. I look at Denendrius's blank face as he watches me, and I swallow. I am the only one alive here, even if I'm not really living.

I follow his gaze down to his lap, where a white velvet box is cracked open, a silver ring with a clear diamond tucked inside. Fear explodes inside me.

"It's a promise ring," he says softly.

"A promise to what?" My voice is an octave too high.

He plucks it out, the sunlight churning rainbows inside it. "A promise of how we will be together for all eternity, forever connected."

My lip quivers as I search his face for any signs of amusement. But there aren't any. I blink hard, a ragged breath pulled between my lips.

"We hardly know each other," I say, desperate.

A gleeful smile breaks across his face. "You know that's not true. Besides, we love each other."

I stare into the diamond as he slides it down to the base of my ring finger. It's like a crystal ball showing my future. And looking into it, I'm terrified by what I see. He breathes dread into me when his lips touch mine in a kiss of death, sealing my fate.

"You know what I was doing when I left you for a few days?"

My breath comes in and out shallow, my jaw so tight I don't think I'll ever be able to speak again. I look to him in question.

"I was getting a passport and identification made for you. You're an Italian citizen now."

His words strangle my breath. "Why?" barely finds a way out.

He smiles. "In two days, my friend is picking us up. He'll fly us back home, and then I'll change you. We can be together forever. Isn't that great?"

The thought of being bound to my rapist forever makes me want to rip the birds from the trees and snap their necks.

This can't be happening.

This can't be real.

I must be in hell, all this a result of the way I lived my life. Yes, that's it. I overdosed. The drugs finally killed me. This isn't real . . . I'm dead.

I have to be.

Denendrius takes my hand. "Marianna?"

"Yeah, great." My voice is a few octaves too high.

Oh God, what am I going to do?

I think of robbing a bank, stealing the fake passport he has for me somehow, and flying to some obscure country. But I know it won't work. I know that wherever I am in the world, he will find me.

His finger rubs the back of my hand. "I know you're scared of how much the transformation will hurt. Hm? But I promise you it will be over, and then we can be happy together forever."

I hope it kills me. I hope to God the transformation *fucking* kills me.

"I assume you'll want to say goodbye to your friends? You can go to school tomorrow and do that if you'd like."

I nod.

I've never wanted caring friends so much as I do now. I've never felt more alone in my life than in this moment. I look back on my life and think of all the awful things I'm leaving behind to my name. When I disappear, people won't be surprised. They'll assume I overdosed, got killed by a gang, left to join some drug ring, or that I got picked up by a pimp. They'll just shrug and say, "Well, I saw that coming."

XXXIV

My goodbyes fall on silent ears the next day, Camille and Daina too grief-stricken to find their way to school. For the first time in my life, I wish I were on good terms with my friends. They were worried about me, but I was too bitter to care. They wouldn't have been able to help me, but still, I could have at least appreciated the sentiment.

I find myself wandering into the counselor's office before school even starts, opening the door and sitting down before she invites me in.

She slowly slides the chair away from her desk, a worried crease in her forehead. "What's going on?"

The lump in my throat is too thick to swallow. My lips don't seem to move either, so I just hold my left hand up, which shakes as I slide my thumb across the silver band of the ring.

Her lips droop, the crease in her forehead deepening. "I'm assuming that isn't good news. You appear sad. Do you want to talk about it?"

I don't feel sad. I don't feel anything. I've used up all my feelings. "I want to leave him," I manage to mumble.

Liz nods. "I'm proud of you. Let's talk about how I can help."

She doesn't understand what I mean, though. What I mean is, is the third floor we're on far enough away from the ground? Or do I need seventeen stories like the other girl?

She opens a drawer in her desk and pulls a few pamphlets out.

"He hurt me," I say, only my voice doesn't sound like mine.

She curls her fingers around the papers, setting them on her lap. "Do you want to talk about it?"

I can't. If I say it aloud, tell it to another person, then that means it has to be true. Even though I know it is, I don't want it to be. I shake my head.

The wheels on her chair are silent as she rolls across the thin carpet, making it seem like she's hovering toward me. "Well, we can use these resources to make sure he can never hurt you again, okay? We can get you in contact with people who will make sure you are safe."

I don't say anything. I let her give me the papers and pretend to listen to everything she says. I focus on the excited undertone to her voice as she rattles off programs, helplines, clinics, and safe shelters. I wonder if she thinks she got through to me, if she thought she'd never be able to help me.

My eyes tear up as I listen to the hope in her voice. What will she think when I disappear? Will she think she didn't help enough? Will she know something utterly horrible has happened to me?

When she finds out—when everyone finds out I'm missing —will she be frantic on the phone, calling the police, telling them she thinks my abusive boyfriend has kidnapped me? What will she think when they never find me? Will she wake up in a cold sweat in twenty years, the fact she couldn't do anything to save me haunting her?

No, she won't. She'll remind herself that she tried, but that I was too stubborn. She'll think I didn't bother to try. She'll know I wasn't really listening to her when she thinks back to this moment. She'll know I didn't bother to call any of the numbers, didn't bother to reach out for help after this meeting.

My file will be lost amongst the rest of the stubborn drugged-up street kids. My life will be reduced to a little percentage added to statistics. She'll sigh and open another file, and she'll focus instead on someone who will be added to a different pile.

Maybe when Camille finally becomes a therapist, she'll end up working here too, years into the future when Liz retires. Do they keep old files? Will Camille find mine one day and remember how I barely scraped by enough to be considered a friend? Will she look through it, reminiscing about me? I can see her now, sitting in Liz's chair, shaking her head as she struggles to remember me. Will she remember how she's the one who convinced me to date him? Will she wish she hadn't? Does she wish she hadn't?

I can practically hear Camille's voice, faint, far into the future, namelessly using me to convince whoever will sit in my spot next to accept her help so they won't end up like me.

The bell rings, so I scoop the pamphlets up in my heavy hands and walk toward the door. I open it but hover in the doorway.

Liz doesn't move from her seat but says, "Thanks for giving me the chance to help you." She smiles. "My door is always open if you need to come in and talk again."

I bite my bottom lip, chapped and sore, blood waiting to break through. I take a good look at the room, my last look, and force myself to remember the crooked gray slats covering the window above her wooden desk, the lines of books, craft supplies, and thank-you drawings that struggle to cling to the cement walls.

I lick my bottom lip and nod once, my eyes turning back to her. "I'm sorry," I think I whisper before closing the door behind me.

I feel like I'm wading through molasses as I walk down the hallway, the rush of students on fast-forward as I make my way to history. By the time I get to the stairs, the students have disappeared.

I look down at the empty steps, the way they seem to go on forever when there's probably less than ten of them. I grip the banister, my feet almost slipping on each smooth step. I think of throwing myself down them, but I'd only give myself a bruise.

Once I make it to history class, I sit in silence, the teacher babbling on about who knows what. I manage to block the sound of his droning voice out.

"Marianna!" he demands.

I jump in my desk, eyes focusing on Mr. Derek as he stands in front of me.

"Why are you just sitting there?" he drones on. "Go on, get in a group."

I look around and notice how all the students have huddled into little groups around the classroom.

"Can I work alone?" I mumble.

He throws a paper on my desk. "No." He points to a group at the back. "Go work with them."

As I stand, my phone rings from my pocket. I freeze midair.

He holds out his hand. "You know the rules, give me your phone."

I bite my lip again, the taste of pennies slipping onto my tongue. "I can't," I say.

I know Denendrius is calling, and if I don't answer, I can only imagine how angry he'll be.

His hand jerks a bit. "Come on."

I sit back down and shake my head.

"Give your phone to me and go to the office," he says evenly. "Marianna, I'm tired of this."

A group of kids laugh and make whooping noises at me.

I want to fight him on it, bounce out of my chair and curse and threaten him, but I can't find it in me. I hold my breath and produce my phone, slipping the ring off my finger, both objects falling into his hand. He doesn't seem to notice the ring between his hand and the phone. I stand and make my way out of the classroom as he demands that everyone else settle down.

I duck into a bathroom on my way to the office and kneel over a toilet when I realize what I've done, how now I don't have the phone or the ring. I should have put the damn thing on vibrate. And what did I think I'd accomplish by getting rid of the ring? I remember what happened last time I pissed him off, and I throw up stomach acid since I haven't had the hunger to eat anything.

Exhausted, I slump onto the floor, head resting against my arm on the toilet seat.

What am I going to do?

I don't realize I've fallen asleep until a knock on the stall door wakes me up.

"Are you okay in there?" a teacher's voice asks. I know her, just can't remember her name.

"Yeah, just sick," I mumble. "I think I ate something bad."

"Oh. Do you need to go home?"

My fingers whiten around the toilet lid and I almost vomit again. "No," I nearly shout.

"Okay," she says. "Head back to class when you're able. You can see the school nurse or ask the secretary to call home for you later if you need to."

"Thanks," I mumble.

"Hope you feel better soon," she says before the bathroom door shuts.

I groan and put my head back down.

When the bell rings for break, I find someone to buy oxy and a cigarette from and leave out the back gym doors, where there's no security. I walk far enough into the football field and off the side where trees separate it from the road; that way the cameras can't see me.

I lie down in the worn grass and dry-swallow one of two pills. I light the cigarette, my next breath slightly easier.

Staring up at the cloud-covered sun, I feel as though I'm spinning. I wonder how many more times I'll see it. A headache forms in the corners of my mind, but I'm not sure if the cigarette or light is to blame. My arm hurts when I lift the death-stick to my lips. I'm glad I never cared enough to quit smoking or drugs.

I try to imagine myself as a vampire. I'd be strong enough— fast enough—to fight off any human but would still have no chance against Denendrius. I wouldn't be able to see the sun for who knows how long. Would it fuck me up like when I was a child, or would being a vampire make me not even care about its existence?

Denendrius will find new ways to mess with me. He'll be able to beat me as long and as hard as he wants, and I'll just heal for him to do it again. If he starves me, I won't die.

How many years or decades will it take for him to drive me crazy? For me to either end up just like him or become so empty that I walk into the sun or find another vampire willing to kill me?

I can't imagine lasting another month of this. The thought of being near him for another decade or . . . *century* makes me want to scream.

Then there's the issue of remembering everything, and vividly. For all I know, that alone could be worse than Denendrius, could break me. Who knows what horrors are trapped in my mind? I'm not even concerned about remembering my time with him as a child. It's everything that happened afterward that shakes my core. I'll remember Vianna and Kenneth's murder. I'll remember every horrible moment my mother and her clients subjected me to, all the unnecessary and gory details.

I pray to every god I can think of that the transformation doesn't work.

I close my eyes, wondering if I can get away with napping. I try to focus my thoughts on the task of breathing, inhaling and exhaling smoke.

"You're either stupid or purposely trying to anger me," a jagged voice snaps from beside me.

My eyes snap open and I jolt upright, Denendrius in the grass beside me.

I gulp as he slaps the cigarette out of my right hand and grabs my left.

"Where's your ring?" he snaps. "And your cell phone?"

"The teacher took my phone when you called," I stammer. "And he took the ring because I was looking at it too much," I lie.

He rolls his eyes. "What am I to do with you?"

I bite my cheek.

He sniffs. "What'd you take?"

"Noth—"

He holds me down and roots through my pockets as I writhe. When he pulls the bagged pill from my pocket, cold sweeps over me.

"I—"

He grabs the back of my neck and gives me a shake. "Throw it up."

"No—"

He tilts me forward, prying my taut jaw open. His grip on the back of my neck tightens when I try to pull my head away.

Cold fingers jam themselves in the back of my throat and I gag until my throat burns. I puke into the grass.

Denendrius rips into his wrist and rests his forearm on his lap, taking a fistful of my hair and bringing my head down. I can't help the greedy gulps I take. The pain in my throat vanishes, and I wish I could take the high his blood gives me and press it into pill form.

To any onlookers, it probably looks like I'm blowing him. He pulls my head up after a minute and wipes the blood from my lips with his thumb before pulling me to my feet by my arm.

"Now, what classroom is this teacher in?" he demands.

"Room 203," I mumble once I get my bearings. "What are you going to do?"

He slaps the car keys into my hand. "Go wait for me in the car."

I walk toward the front of the school, where he always parks. My legs burn like I've been running and I curse myself for not doing exactly that.

Unlocking the Mustang, I dip into the passenger seat and wait. I open the glove compartment to give myself something to do. I find a buck knife, an envelope of money, and a stack of driver's licenses with Denendrius's face but different names on them.

I look at the car keys in my hand and back to the money.

How far could I get before he caught up with me? The end of the block? Mexico?

I lift the keys toward the ignition, my heart thumping, sweaty hands shaking.

He'll be so mad.

The thought drops my hand.

Yet everything makes him mad. Will his level of anger affect how dead I'm going to be despite whether or not I run? Not likely.

I lift my hand again.

He can do worse than kill you.

My mind lists all those things. He could lock me in the bedroom, rape me, blind me, kill everyone I've ever interacted with, cut me up and heal me just to do it again.

I throw the keys in the cupholder and sit on my hands, tears threatening my eyes. I practice deep breaths.

XXXV

Denendrius is back five minutes later. Slamming the door, he slides into the front seat. He throws the phone on my lap and forces the ring back onto my finger.

He glowers at me, jaw taut. "So, do you care to explain why your teacher seemed to know I was your boyfriend and why he was so hostile? Hm?"

I swallow hard, realizing he must have recognized Denendrius from the pictures I'd drawn. "He was just asking about the ring. He thinks you're too old for me," I lie.

He squints at me and sits back in his seat, turning the car on. "Right."

I take a deep breath and jam my hands between my legs, the ring feeling like a million pounds.

My eyes stare past the window as he hums to himself, watching the old houses flash by, paying extra attention to how the sun shines off their windows. I watch the school disappear in the side mirror and wonder if I will really never see it again. He rolls down the windows, picking up speed.

"I might actually miss this city," Denendrius says.

I cross my arms on the door and lay my head down, head half out the window. I watch the front tire spin madly, the sound of the engine in my ears, his voice at the back of my mind as the sun beats down on the side of my face.

"You will like Italy, I promise."

"I can't even speak Italian," I whisper.

He laughs. "That's okay. Your memory will be practically perfect once you're a vampire. You'll be fluent in no time."

My throat turns thick. I cough. "I'm surprised you haven't just changed me already," I mutter.

Denendrius's sharp stare makes my heart thump. "Actually, had things worked out as they were supposed to, we could have stayed in Lorimer for another year or two."

I pull my legs under me. "How was it supposed to work out?"

His teeth graze his bottom lip, jaw shifting. "You were supposed to remember me at the mall, or even before the end of one of our dates would have been fine. You were supposed to tell me how much you missed me and how you didn't want me to go away again. You were going to ask me to take you out of that foster home, and we would pack your stuff and bring it to our apartment. You were supposed to decorate, or I would have found a better place if you weren't happy there. I was going to give you time to say goodbye to being human and to do the things you wanted."

My blink is slow, tears stinging. "I can't have that anymore? What if I try harder to be better?"

He's rough with the wheel as he turns a corner. "No, Marianna. I need you to remember. Once you're a vampire, you'll remember how much you love me, and you'll look back on these past few weeks and see where it all went wrong. Everything will be perfect once you remember."

I snivel, trying to wipe tears before he notices them.

"It's going to be okay," he says. "I will show you all the places I've been." His hand rubs my shoulder before returning to the wheel and I grimace.

His iron grip appears on my thigh. "What's wrong?" he demands.

I project my fear. "What if I don't survive the transformation?"

He chuckles. "Oh, I wouldn't be afraid of that. The chances of it killing you are near nothing."

I try to swallow a lump and fail. "How are you so sure?"

Denendrius smiles. "I've healed you many times now, and you've had plenty of my blood. Your body has already grown much stronger from it. I can almost guarantee you'll survive it."

Well, fuck me, then. A tear drops from my eye and lands on my arm.

He runs his fingers through my hair, and my skin pricks. "Don't be afraid of it. Yes, it's painful, but it's worth it. You'll get to spend the rest of eternity with me. We'll be together forever, as we should."

By now, I've abandoned any hope of getting out of this. I can already see everything playing out. I can already feel the pain of the transformation. I can already feel the cold metal of the cage he's forced me into. I hide my eyes from him so he can't see the fear and pain I know explodes within them.

"Where will we live?" I mumble.

I can practically feel him smiling at my engagement in his plans.

"We will go back to Rome. I put down money on a very beautiful villa for us."

My voice is too high when I say, "What does it look like?"

Fingers through my hair, again. My stomach twists and I feel my fingers turn to fuzz.

"Well, it was built in the fourteen hundreds by a noble family but has since been updated with plumbing and electricity. Imagine lots of white stone, marble and gold, huge windows and vaulted ceilings. It has a massive property with a pool, a garden with a fountain. There's a stable and plenty of trees and privacy. There are tons of bedrooms. Ours has a fireplace with a bathroom and a painted ceiling. There's a library—I know how you love to read. There's a room that would be perfect for an art studio." He smiles. "I hope you'll like it. I've been saving to buy it for you for years."

I nod, the smear of the road beneath making me dizzy. Barely audible, I whisper, "I'm sure it's wonderful. How much did it cost?"

He laughs. "You don't want to know."

Whatever the price, it sounds like a massive target should anyone want to find us.

"You know I'm the only one who will ever love you, right?" he murmurs.

I wonder if it's true. I wonder if I'm so broken, like shattered glass, that nobody would want to come near me in fear of getting hurt in the process. Tolerate me? Sure. Love me? No. Only a sick man like Denendrius could ever find pleasure in sticking his hand in glass.

But then I realize that's what he wants me to think. He wants me to believe nobody else will love me, just so I'll have to resort to him.

"Marianna?"

I choke. "I know."

He nods. "And you know I'm doing this for you, right? Your life isn't very good. I want you to have the best."

I don't respond. I just let the rushing road take me to a dizzying but better place.

He jabs his fingers into my leg, and I wince.

"I love you," he says.

"I love you too," I mumble.

When we arrive at the apartment, I look around, wondering why he hasn't even started packing.

I think of Carol then, how I never got to say goodbye to her. I scratch my head, frown, and wonder if he'd get angry if I asked to see her.

Denendrius sits on the couch and stares at the TV, off.

Leaning against the wall, I shove my hands in my pockets and clear my throat. "Do you think I could say goodbye to Carol?"

He crosses his arms. "No."

My leg buckles. "Why not?"

He takes a long breath and loudly exhales. "If you tell her goodbye, she'll know something is up. Honestly, the last thing I want is SWAT coming to the apartment when I'm trying to pack and move out. That'll be annoying."

I wipe the sweat from my hairline. "What happened to the last pigs that showed up?"

He looks at me blankly. "You mean when you were screaming your head off?"

I give a little nod.

He looks away and smiles. "I dealt with them."

I gnaw at my cheek. "Did you kill them?"

Denendrius looks back to me, his smile turning serious. "No, Marianna, I told them to go away."

Blood trickles onto my tongue and his eyes peer at me harder.

"Do you kill a lot of people when I'm not around?" I ask.

He stares at me for a long moment, eyes hard, threatening. "I have to kill people, Marianna, I'm a vampire."

I swallow and take a step back, causing his eyes to tighten.

"I mean, do you kill a lot of people . . . for fun? Do you kill people and not drink their blood?"

He laughs and looks away. "Let's just say Lorimer's crime rate has ascended drastically since I moved here."

I twist my fingers, unsure of why I care so much. Maybe I'm fishing for evidence to hate him even more. "Yeah, but how many?"

He raises his chin. "Marianna. Stop asking so many questions and stop chewing your cheek. Come sit with me."

My legs threaten to give out as I near him, sinking into the couch. He wraps his arm around me and rakes his fingers through my hair.

"Give me your cell phone," he snarls.

Holding my breath, I pull it out and drop it on his lap instead of in his outstretched hand. He grumbles and proceeds to go through it. He seems satisfied with what he finds and slides it into his pocket.

"Can't have you texting Carol now, can we?" He grins.

"I guess not."

He wraps his arm back around me. "Watch the TV."

I stare at our reflection in the black screen and notice my legs are shaking. I put a stop to it before he notices and say, "There's nothing playing."

He snatches the remote. "Shut up."

I try not to pay attention to Denendrius's arm around me as he flips through channels, barely spending a second on each one before passing to another.

"Why is your heart racing?" he asks, finally deciding on a wildlife documentary.

I swallow and try to focus on not stuttering when I respond with, "I'm just nervous."

He takes my hand, rubbing his thumb on my wrist. "Hmm. You're going to have to be more specific."

"The vampire part," I lie.

"Don't worry, I'll teach you everything you need to know."

He kisses my cheek, breath cold as his lips travel to my neck. He brushes my hair away, and when I see his eyes flash red out of the corner of my eye, I try to brace myself for what I know is coming.

"You know what I'll really miss once you're a vampire?"

I merely quiver in response.

"*The taste of your blood*." His lips run down my neck.

I squeeze my eyes shut as he shoves my head to the side and wraps his other hand around the other side of my neck. I bite my lip as his fangs rip into my throat, hot pain slicing through me. I focus on trying not to make a sound as he drinks from me, the sound of him swallowing my blood filling the room.

The few seconds feel like hours until he finally pulls away. I watch, lightheaded, as his eyes return to black and his teeth return to normal.

"Yeah, I'm definitely going to miss that," he pines.

Fingers shaking, I stick one between my lips and gnaw on the edge of my nail. When I notice the blood dripping down my neck, I exhale heavily and stand, stumbling to the bathroom.

After finding a cloth under the sink, I shut the door and lean against the counter as I wipe the crimson from my neck, fawn legs barely enough to keep me standing. Eventually, I give up on them and climb onto the counter and sit cross-legged while I stare at myself in the mirror.

I look unfamiliar. Darkness sits on the skin under my eyes, a worried crease between my brows I never noticed before. My skin seems paler, but maybe that's just from losing blood, or from constantly feeling like I'm going to collapse.

I feel like an intruder in my own skin. There are no monsters in my chest shouting and screaming anymore, pumping fire into my veins. They've left, probably gone to someone easier to make angry, someone who isn't so exhausted. All that's left is a black hole, quickly sucking up everything inside me until I collapse on myself, nothing but a shell filled with sighs. Where did I leave my determination, my will?

The longer I continue to stare at myself, the more I seem to change. How am I even recognizable to anyone else? I'm not even the same person I was just a few weeks ago. Where did that girl go, and how did I end up here? Maybe I overestimated her.

I close my eyes, and when I reopen them, I feel alone. So alone that I'm not even sure Denendrius exists in the other room.

It feels like I've lost all sense of object permanence. Yesterday doesn't seem to have happened, and the idea of a moment past this seems like the most improbable of things. If I close my eyes, will this bathroom still exist around me?

I feel make-believe, like I could drift through walls. I stare at myself again in the mirror. If I wanted to, could I reach through it and touch my face?

I don't even notice Denendrius has barged into the room and is shaking me until he shouts, "*What are you doing?*"

Then I see the dent my fist has made in the mirror, the shards crumbling around me. When did I do that?

He spins me around. Is he real? He can't be. I broke the mirror and don't even remember it. Have I fallen into a dream?

"*Have you completely lost your mind?*" he hollers.

But his voice sounds faint, and even though I can see his arms moving as he rattles me, I don't feel it.

"Answer me!" he bellows. "What is wrong with you?"

Do I know how to speak?

He growls and backhands me. At first, I don't feel it, but then the tingling, aching pain pounces on me, becomes all that I am in this moment, and becomes the only thing I can feel or think about. I wail hysterically. My breath turns into a stranger, and I'm left staring at the raging monster in his eyes as I sob and gasp for air, tears wetting my face.

"Get it together!"

Denendrius throws me off the counter and onto the floor,

and when my head knocks into the linoleum, everything moves too fast and feels hyperrealistic.

I can feel the square pattern on my face, how cold it is. My hair slips over my face and I can feel every strand. I can hear my heart beating too fast, too heavily, my breath too quick. My clothes are too tight; my skin is too tight. The bathroom light is far too bright. It feels like bugs are crawling over my skin, and I can practically hear their buzzing. My hysterical sobbing seems so far from receding.

"*Pathetic*," he spits. "Have I wasted twelve years on you? Don't make me wish I never met you!"

But he's too loud. I cover my ears. When his hand reaches toward me, I gasp and scramble away into the closet. After closing the door, I pull my knees to my chest, hyperventilating. What's happening to me?

"Fine, whatever," he says. "Stay in there. I'm not going to stand here and entertain whatever you're trying to pull. We're going to Italy."

I'm unsure of how long it takes me to come back to earth, but when I can, I finally force myself to crawl out of the closet and stumble from the bathroom. I notice through the balcony windows that the sun has nearly disappeared, shades of pink and blue smeared across the sky.

The apartment is even emptier than before, boxes stacked in the corner of the living room.

"It's about time you came out," Denendrius says, sitting on the couch. "You were playing 'poor me' for far too long."

I clear my throat, but it still takes a couple tries for my voice to escape. "You packed everything already?"

"Most of the things I plan on bringing."

Everything aside from the furniture and TV seems to be missing.

"Oh."

He leans back into the couch and it squeaks.

"I'm tired," I think aloud.

He huffs. "Yeah, pretending to be a tragedy for two hours can do that."

I twist my fingers together, my bones aching.

Denendrius stares at me, clearly displeased. "You want to go to sleep, then?"

"Yeah," I mumble.

He stands. "Fine."

I open my dresser drawer as he crawls into bed, fully clothed. When I realize the drawer is empty, I sigh.

"Turn the light off," he grumbles.

I listen and crawl into bed. He hums and wraps his arms around me, making me cringe.

"I'm very excited for tomorrow," he whispers.

"Me too," I lie.

I watch him in the mirror intently as he closes his eyes, waiting for an indicator that he has fallen asleep, my heart racing a hundred miles an hour.

He must hear it, because he rolls onto his back and sighs, eyes opening. "I know you're afraid. But you have to trust that I know what's best. I want good things for us, Marianna," he says. "I want the life I was promised as a human but was robbed of."

I chew my cheek. "I'm sorry," I mumble.

He exhales longingly. "I was *so close*. I was near retiring and I was going to train gladiators. I had a hefty inheritance waiting for me, never mind money of my own. Girls were lined up wanting to marry me." He puts his hands on his chest. "There was one woman who wanted me to wait until her newly six-year-old was of age—"

When I give him a horrified look, he shakes his head. "That wasn't unusual, Marianna. Sometimes marriages were arranged long before the girls were twelve. It wasn't about love like it is now."

"I'm sorry." I close my eyes. "I want to hear about the girl."

He exhales slowly. "Anyway, this woman wanted me to wait. I told her she was insane. She was a plebeian and I had girls from wealthy families I could have sooner. I couldn't wait that long to marry. But she wouldn't take no for an answer. She'd approach me every chance she could. She'd tell me I was her daughter's favorite gladiator, that she never saw her happier than when she watched me fight. The woman said I was talked about all the time, and that her daughter wanted to marry me when she grew up. She said her daughter was in love. And I suppose with her age, she had better intentions than the other girls. She had no concept of money, of the loveless arrangements of those days. She saw something that made her happy and wanted it.

"Her mother would bring me trinkets her daughter had made or picked out. She'd hunt me down in the day just to tell me the smallest thing about her daughter. How she smiled, how she laughed, what made her happy, and what made her sad. She'd tell me stories of their day, of her daughter's dreams.

"But I couldn't wait that long. I just couldn't. There were heavier taxes for those who didn't marry, and my father would have thrown a fit. Yet, after a few months of her harassment, I started to wish I could. If she grew up to be anything like her mother, I thought I'd be quite lucky. She had a nice family, one that offered things not even my wealthy parents could. It would have been nice to marry into that despite how poor they were."

He's silent for a long moment. "I had almost made up my mind. I knew if her parents could gather a nice enough dowry, my father wouldn't reject it. I thought I could accept the best of my father's choices while I waited. I could always divorce her later if the woman's daughter turned out to be as good a fit as her mother made her sound."

"Then what happened?" I open my eyes when the light from outside shifts in the room.

"I died before I got to meet her," he says quietly.

I almost feel sorry for him. "What was her name?"

He blinks, jaw tensing. "Mariana. Her name was a letter off from yours."

I lean away from him, the bed creaking. "*What?*" I breathe.

Then it all makes sense why he picked me. I was a year younger than her when he met me. A little girl with the same name, near the same age, who acted like he was the best person in the entire world . . . and it definitely doesn't help that I look the way I do.

"You know I'm not her? Right?" I pray he's sane enough to know. "*Right?*"

"Obviously I know you're not her," he growls. "And if you really are dumb enough to assume I think that, then I was right not to say anything until now. That girl would have married someone else and died thousands of years ago. Besides, your scents aren't even similar." He turns onto his side to look at me. "But now that I have you, I'm going to get what I want. I want you to be my wife and I want children."

My breath hitches. "*Children?*"

He touches my cheek with the back of his hand. "Yes. I want sons and daughters."

I stutter nonsense. "You can have kids?"

I pray he says no, unable to fathom the process and unwilling to be a participant.

Denendrius shakes his head. "But there are tons of babies in the world. You can pick from them any daughters you want, and I'll pick our sons."

He wants us to kidnap children like we're shopping? "But they'll grow up."

"Yes, for a while. But we can change them before they're old enough to stop loving us."

My heart pounds in my ears. Not only does he want to kidnap babies, he wants to create vampire children. To turn them before they're old enough to question us, to question life.

He holds up a finger. "Just one stipulation. They must hold some resemblance to us, all right? We can't have unwanted attention."

I nod, knowing if there's one thing that would be unwise to start a fight over, it would be this. Does he want children bad enough to throw his plans for me out the window and look for someone more willing? This could be the last no I ever say.

He studies my face and frowns. He pulls me to his side and runs his fingers through my hair. "I know it's not ideal. I'd much prefer you to bear my children too. Unfortunately, we don't get such options."

XXXVI

Denendrius sleeps like the dead, my eyes refusing to close. My mind spins off tangents and into horrible places ruled by his dreams for us.

I get out of bed in hopes of clearing my mind, stumbling toward the kitchen to drink from the tap. Blue light wafts into the apartment through the vertical blinds covering the balcony windows. After gulping down rusty-tasting water, I head back toward the bedroom, only for the sight of my memory box on the counter to stop my steps.

I stand in front of it and stare.

Despite its uninviting appearance, it screams at me to open it. I run my fingers over the rough cardboard, my stomach twisting with every dusty ridge.

I've always wondered who packed it up for me. Who went into that bedroom and thought to collect the garbage of my life and box it up like a present for me? Was it an old social worker, a cop?

I carefully take the box by the sides and set it on my lap on the couch. I study its bare exterior for what seems like a century before I muster enough courage to swiftly slap the flaps open.

I exhale a long-held breath and stare at the mangled mess of papers and items. A few poorly taken care of children's books are mixed in with a flurry of crayon-drawn pictures. I push the books aside and pull the drawings out one by one, my eyes lingering on each one for too long.

There's a drawing of an orange cat, princesses, a dolphin with a girl riding it in the ocean. They're innocent compared to others. There's the drawing of me stabbing my mother, of the house on fire. My heart thumps at a drawing of a black stick figure standing outside of a window.

I find a doll. She's naked and scratched up, blond hair chopped jaggedly, with markers used for makeup on her face. I drop it almost as quickly as I lift it up.

At the bottom of the box, I find a blue ocean-themed diary. I nibble my lip as I scoop it up. No key in sight, I wrap my fist around the little plastic lock and twist. It breaks off but scrapes my palm.

Heart pounding in my temples, I open the cover and read the first entry.

April 12, 1996

Hi, Diary. My name is Marianna. I am five. My new mommy gave me this. Her name is Vianna. She said I can write or draw anything in you I want. We went to the park today and it was awesome. I like my new room more than my old one. It is blue and I get to play with boy toys and girl toys! I have so many dolls now. I think I have more toys than anyone else in the world. There's a cat here and I named him Crush because he is orange like the soda, and he likes to crush all the stuff I make out of blocks. I have to go now my new mom is making supper. She has all sorts of yummy food I have never tried before. One day I will try every food there is.

I flip past a few poorly drawn sketches of a bedroom to the next entry.

April 25, 1996

Today I miss my old mom. Kenneth was sad when I said I maybe want to go home. Vianna said my old mommy went to a place to make her better. She is sick. But not a cold like I thought. Vianna said her thinking don't work as good as mine or hers do so she needs her own kind of mommy to tell her what is real and make-believe. She said she takes too much medicine to try and make herself feel not sick anymore and it made her sicker. I hope my old mom is having fun with her special kind of mom like I am with my new one.

May 8, 1996

I saw a teacher person today and she said I am a smarty pants. She thinks I am so cool for being smart at everything without my mommy's help. I get to go to school in fall. I am excited! I can make friends at school. I have always wanted one. They said I am big success. They wanted to know how I have as many smarts as I do but I just always remember having this brain! Maybe I am magic and was born with all this knowing.

I release a long exhale, the memory of being in elementary school and having my teachers accuse my foster parents of doing my work for me and having me copy it in my own writing coming back to me. It didn't help that I could never explain how I learned everything myself when my mother was out of her mind on drugs, but further one-on-one testing concluded that I really was bright for my age, though it seems that intelligence tapered off as I got older. I've always wondered if my father was some genius, though the fact that he slept with my mother doesn't seem like something someone smart would do.

May 21, 1996

I went to the doctor today and it sucked. I made Vianna scared because I asked her what her name is and forgot she is my mommy. I don't understand why she got scared. I only forgot for a few hours. The doctor said not to worry, that I am just stress. I don't want to be stress if it makes Vianna cry. My old mommy never got scared she would just wait until I remembered, and I always did. I heard Kenneth and Vianna talking and they are worried I am sick like my mommy. I know I am not sick, Diary.

I pull my finger from between my lips, the taste of blood in my mouth. I've chewed my thumbnail down so far it hurts. No wonder I can't remember Denendrius or Vianna and Kenneth if I was having memory issues. I wonder if I was a drug baby. Maybe Bonnie dropped me on my head. Maybe it really was trauma and stress. Whatever the reason, I'm glad it resolved itself in my childhood.

I hold my breath and flip the page.

May 27, 1996

I am so happy. Vianna and Kenneth said they are going to take me to the most fun place on earth. I thought my new house was but there is a place even better? I am so excited diary! I will get to meet my favorite princesses and monsters and go on rides and eat candy until I puke. We go in June.

I am just so excited. I will tell you everything when I get back.

I wish I could go back in time and speak to my younger self. I'd tell her to hang on to Vianna's hand and not to dare let go. I'd tell her to scream stranger danger when Denendrius approached. If only that little girl knew what she'd grow up to become, that she will never be happier than she was then.

June 28, 1996

Enchanted Land is the funnest place on earth! I finally made a friend. A best friend too! His name is Den. He is so cool and handsome! He looks like Tarzan but is like a prince. He took me on all the rides and bought me cotton candy and every food I wanted! My new favorite food is chili. I have never eaten such a good food before. We had a slumber party and watched movies. We went on a car ride and I got to see all sorts of dolphins and sea animals! I touched a fish and it was so gross but also kind of cool. He bought me all the toys I ever wanted.

We saw all sorts of cool things and went on so many different water slides and saw the green statue lady. She is so much bigger than I thought! I got to try lots of new foods. Den had loud music but it was okay because he let me shout, shout, shout as loud as I wanted with it. I got sad because I missed Vianna so he took me home. Now I miss Den more. He said I would see him soon again and we will go on a forever adventure just us two! I can't wait! He said he is a secret friend and that's okay because I don't want Vianna to be jealous that I have a better friend than all of her friends.

At the mention of chili, I remember how in the video, he

tainted it with his blood. Would it have been enough to make me miss him, or was I just a naive child under a spell?

On the next page, there are a few crappy drawings of Denendrius and me together on a black car with probably near a billion hearts around it. I resist the urge to tear them out and flush them.

The next few pages are generic banter about playing with toys and my favorite fairy-tale movies. After a few blank pages stuck together by what I assume is peanut butter and jelly, I find more entries. None of them have a date, which doesn't surprise me since I rarely left the confines of my room. Bonnie never knew the date even when I asked anyway.

Hi, diary. They said Vianna and Kenneth went to Heaven. I am with my other mommy now. I do not know if I missed her anymore. There are too many mommies and daddies to miss. If Den was here, I wouldn't have to miss any of them because we would just play and have fun forever like he said. The doctor said mommy is all better now but I think he is lying or stupid.

Sorry diary I still don't know what day it is. Mommy put a sandwich under the door, and it was good, but it made me too full and sleepy to play with my dolls. I moved my blanket to the closet so I can sleep without stupid boys bugging me. I hope if Den comes, he will be smart enough to look in there. I think he will find me easy. He knew all the things, more than any of my mommies and daddies so it will probably take him one second.

Today is Sunday, I think. I saw the man outside the window again. He was dark like a shadow but I think it was Den. Mom keeps all the doors locked like mine so I took the newspaper off the window and opened it so he could come in. He didn't and she got mad and put nails in the wood. I don't remember her being so mean last time. Did I forget because I am stress?

I really think I am stress, diary. I keep forgetting to write in you and it feels like one big day and one big night. So confusing. I am extra sad today because I almost forgot about Vianna and Kenneth until I had a dream.

I miss Den. There are no toys here but my dolls and coloring. I wish I had all the toys Den got me. There were so many it was like one hundred Christmases and birthdays. He was so cool. Did you know he let me sit in the front seat of his horse car like a grown up? How fun does that sound, diary? I don't like the food mommy makes. It tastes bad and makes me sleepy and sometimes she forgets or says no because I am bad. Vianna let me eat anything I want. I miss her.

I asked mommy if she saw Den. I think maybe she did and told him to go away. He is my best friend and he promised to come back and see me. Best friends don't lie to each other so that means something is making him not come. I think he probably went to Heaven like mommy and daddy and the man in the kitchen. Mommy is too worried about the Devil. I tried to tell her if she just got Den to come that he would kick the Devil's butt and that would be that. Mommy is so stupid.

I am sick. Mommy gave me more medicine today, but I hate the needles and wish I didn't have to. She says medicine will help with the boys, but mostly just makes me too sleepy to move. I ask her why the boys? Why can't they go away? She got mad and said I was lucky, that they keep the devil away. She says the devil will take me away if there are no boys. Why can't Den just come and keep the Devil away? Me and Den would go to forever together. He'd say no at the needles! No at the boys! No at Mom! If Den isn't in Heaven I want him to make Mom go dead and go to Hell.

The next page is full of frowning faces and handfuls are ripped out.

Dear diary, I wish I was dead like mommy keeps saying will happen if I'm bad. If I am so bad then she should just send me to Hell with the devil and that would be that!

After that, the topic of Denendrius drops off. Many of the entries are illegible or nonsensical, some only half-written. I read through them all again, paying extra attention to talk about Denendrius.

I slam the diary shut and clomp back into the bedroom, coming around his side of the bed to drop the book straight on his chest.

His eyes open and he looks between me and the book in question, taking no more than fifteen seconds to flip through it, eyes flickering over each page before flipping to the next.

"What's the issue?" he asks.

I snatch the book back and cross my arms. "How long did you have me? Because from the sound of it, it was a lot longer than what your tapes and stories make it seem."

He sits up and exhales, staring me sideways begrudgingly.

"How long?" I demand.

"Twelve days."

Air leaves my dropped jaw like I've been punched. "Twelve days?"

He rubs his face and sighs. "Yes, Marianna, *twelve days*. We were a few hours from Maine when you wouldn't let up about going home."

"Twelve days," I repeat, baffled. I sit beside him on the bed and stare at the white wall, mind whirring. "Why even bother to bring me back?"

He stares blankly at me. "What do you mean?"

I grit my teeth. "Why did you bring me back? If you were just going to watch me for eleven years, why didn't you keep me?"

His eyes tighten in unsure confusion.

"I saw you. At the worst point in my life, *I saw you*. Just waiting, just watching. You knew what was going on and you kept watching." I shake my head in incredulity. "I was waiting for you to come back to save me, but you never did."

His jaw sets, confusion, then wild frustration flashing in his eyes. He looks as if he's about to say something, but he just takes a deep breath and stands.

"*Why?*" I demand.

"You're either mad that I took you or mad that I didn't, because you can't be both," he says.

"Well, I am," I spit.

His hand appears in front of my face, his face twisted, teeth bared, his fingers curled like he wants to strangle the life out of me. He throws his hands up and walks out of the room.

I stand. "You should have done neither! You should never have even met me!" I yell after him.

He appears at my feet and I find myself on the carpet against the wall, face stinging. He storms from the room again.

I get up and follow him into the living room.

"You're trying to blame me, Marianna? You're the problem, not me. If only you could remember how much fun we had, how much you love me. I still gave you an opportunity to get to know me even when you didn't remember instead of throwing everything out the window and you took it for granted. Everything would have worked out if you had just remembered!"

"Then why did you bring me back? All of this could have been avoided."

"Because you would have grown up to despise me!" he screams, his voice reverberating through my core.

I gasp and shrink back against the wall.

He shakes his head, breath heavy. "It wouldn't have mattered if I had taken you, Marianna. If I had, we'd be fighting right now about how I took you away from your parents and stole your opportunity to grow up the same as every other child. You'd be upset that you couldn't have friends or go to school. You would have had to lie about your name, your age, how we knew each other, about *everything*. The FBI was already looking for you. Your face was everywhere. Do you know how many people I had to hypnotize until we got a few states away? You would have hated growing up like that. And you would have blamed me."

He's right, it wouldn't have mattered. It couldn't have worked out, but not for the reasons he thinks. He's still the same person, the same monster. He's still a murderer and a rapist. If I had stayed with him, things couldn't have been so different. If I continued dating him, things would still be the same. It wouldn't have erased all those tapes or stopped him from finding fun in the pain of others. He wouldn't have changed his behavior, his entire life, for a child.

The only difference would be me. He said he gave me a few extra years, which means if I'd stayed with him, he probably would have been fucking me by the time I was twelve. I'd be just as screwed, if not more.

"But the blood mark," I remind him cynically. "I wouldn't have been able to be mad at you."

His eyes flutter and he takes a drawn-out breath. When his eyes level with me, he looks like he's going to lose it. Then I realize he didn't know I was aware of the effects of prolonged blood sharing.

I anticipate his fury, his hands on me, but he just mutters something hateful about Alaire and Edmond and says, "Marianna, you can't really believe my intention was to use it to manipulate you."

I square my shoulders. "Were they lying, then? Were they lying about it forcing an attachment?"

He holds his palms in front of him. "It is what it is. Many things have side effects."

So, I'm right, which means he could be doing exactly what I blame him for doing and is just trying to cover his ass. "Why give me your blood, then?" I challenge.

He looks at me like I've asked him an incredibly intimate but obvious question, and I remember Alaire saying he's never been known to leave a blood mark on his victims.

"Oh," I say.

"I love you, Marianna. Why wouldn't I want to share the utmost of my being with you? I merely wanted to be connected to you."

Fury spills into me. If he sees it as such an intimate thing— even when he was holding me down and forcing his blood down my throat—then that makes it even worse, which verifies he's lying about his use for it too. How could his intention not be forcing a bond when the option is taken away from me?

It takes everything in my power not to scream at him, to stop myself from trying to make him admit how it's not enough for him to control my body, to admit that he wants to have control of my mind too.

He appears in front of me, his eyes searching mine, index finger hooked under my jaw. "Do you understand now?" he asks softly. "Do you understand how all along I've just been trying to do what's best for us?"

My anger turns into a painful slice through my chest at his touch, and I feel my eyes turn glassy. I nod in response to stop my voice from betraying me.

"Good," he says sternly. His fingers move to the base of my neck and he squeezes. "Now stop trying to start fights and let it die."

I nod again and he lets go, moving back toward the bedroom. When I don't follow, he looks over his shoulder and smiles.

"Coming?" he asks. "We have a long flight tomorrow."

My legs are barely strong enough to carry me back to the room.

Denendrius speaks again once we've nestled under the covers. "I didn't know, by the way," he says through a heavy exhale.

My throat tightens when I swallow. "About what?"

His eyes don't stray from the ceiling as he says, "About those men."

It feels like a rock is placed on my chest at the reminder.

Denendrius continues, his face emotionally barren. "I only came to check up on you a handful of times a year. Their scents were all over the property, but I never went close enough to you to know there was any correlation. I knew your mother was a tramp, but I never considered you. I heard you crying one night when I came to check on you, and your mother was being given crack as payment."

My heart thumps so loudly in my ears that I have to focus on his words to truly hear him.

He rests his hands on his chest, eyes snagging mine. His upper lip twitches. "I killed anyone whose scent was in your room." His eyes darken and he smiles. "I killed a lot of evil men. I made them confess and I did wicked things to them so they couldn't hurt you or any other children. I figured I'd leave your mother for you to kill one day."

A strange rush of emotions passes through me. Thankful relief floats in my chest, hot anger pinning my body to the bed. If only he were made up of genuine efforts. Why would he not tell me these things to earn my affection instead of raping and torturing me? Pain starts at the front of my mind. The only reason I can think of is to punish me for not accepting his beginning attempts. Did he think he'd be giving me another reason to be "ungrateful" if he shared this sooner?

"I'm sorry I didn't know to call law enforcement sooner," he whispers.

My heart feels frozen for a moment as I sit up to stare down at him. "What did you say?"

He rolls away from me to face the wall. "I called in an anonymous tip after finding out what she was doing and confronting her. You were out of there before the night was up."

I stare at him wordlessly, unsure what to feel.

I always wondered who ratted on my mom. I always thought the discovery of my abuse was secondary to the discovery of my mother's involvement with crime. My mind stutters to think it was Denendrius. How do I process that information?

"You should thank me," he says into the blanket.

I don't feel my own tongue move when I mumble, "Thank you."

XXXVII

Denendrius shoves me awake in the early morning, walking around the room with his phone tucked between his ear and shoulder. I think I've finally lost my mind as I listen to his garbled speech until I wake up enough to realize he's speaking Russian. He motions for me to get up while walking from the room.

Nothing happens when I try to move, my heart so heavy it has probably pinned me to the bed. It takes effort to blink, to breathe. I don't even think I could get up for a fire. I can't feel the blankets around me, so I doubt I'd even feel the flames.

I want to tell him how I don't want to go to Italy, how I don't want to be a vampire or kidnap kids. How I especially don't want to raise them with him. Instead, I say, "Can I go to school for one more day?"

He appears in the doorway, eyes sharper than knives. He pulls the phone away from his ear. "Marianna..."

I stare at the ceiling and swallow a lump. "Please? You said I could have anything but that I never ask. I just want one more day."

My heart hammers as I wait in the long silence before his response.

"My friend Sergei is already preparing to fly the plane over. Why are you trying to create problems?" he asks in astonishment.

I hold my breath. "None of my friends were there yesterday. I never got to say goodbye."

Able to feel the cold of his stare, I don't dare look. "So?"

"I was too scared to enjoy myself, but now that the day is here, I'm all right," I lie. "I just want one more day of being a teenager so I can put all my focus on being with you and our kids." I hope if I tell him what he wants to hear, it'll help my case, make him feel more giving.

When he doesn't respond, I find the courage to sit. He's staring at me, thinking.

"Please? Can't eternity spare a few more hours?"

We stare at one another in a silent argument before he sighs and rolls his eyes. "Fine, whatever." He points a finger at me. "But after school, we are going straight to meet Sergei and we are not stopping for anything else. You understand?"

"Yes," I say in a hurry, like he'll take the option away.

He shakes his head like I'm the most annoying person he's ever had to deal with and redials his phone. When he continues to speak, he's laughing, and I can't help but wonder if they're talking about me. It feels like they are.

I take a shower, standing in the water and forgetting to wash. I only remember halfway through drying off and have to climb back in. I toss the same clothes on as yesterday since I don't have the energy to spare looking through boxes for clean ones. My makeup is missing from the drawer too, so I go without covering up the shadow of a bruise on my neck and the attention-grabbing one on my cheek from last night.

Denendrius is standing on the other side of the bathroom door when I open it.

"Ready?" he asks.

I nod and follow him to the front door and slip into my skateboard shoes.

The air is empty and cold when we exit the apartment and head for the car. We're silent as he drives me to school. For once I wish he would put music on so I don't have to listen to my own thoughts.

I'm not quite sure what I'm trying to accomplish by postponing Italy. Maybe I think he'll change his mind or tell me he's joking.

Maybe I'd rather he kill me instead and am subconsciously trying to make it happen by pissing him off.

When I think of how few hours I have left, it takes digging my fingers into the sides of the leather seat to stop myself from bursting into tears and hyperventilating. I tell myself that crying will only make things worse. He has no ability for sympathy, and the more I go along with what he wants, the safer I'll be. If I misbehave, it'll only make things harder.

When he pulls up in front of my school, he grabs a fistful of my sweater and pulls me toward him. His lips crush against mine in a kiss. Despite how much I want to break away, I don't want to be the first to do so.

He shoves me away, hand still twisted in the fabric of my hoodie. He smiles. "I love you."

"I love you too," I whisper, the dam behind my eyes almost cracking.

I try to move away and open the door, but he doesn't let go.

"Be good," he says plainly, as if his words aren't loaded with warning.

"Of course," I say. My voice comes out surprisingly strong.

He kisses me again and lets me go.

I grip the door to stop from falling onto the concrete when I open it. My shoes feel heavy when I step out. I shut the door, but his hand stops it. I duck back down to look into the car. He's stretched across the seat, holding two twenty-dollar bills out.

Slowly, I take them.

"Make sure you eat enough," he says. "You won't be able to eat again until we land."

Mr. Derek watches me throughout the entirety of history class. He tries to be subtle about it, but I notice.

I pick at my lips and try to keep my mind off Denendrius. But it doesn't matter how hard I listen to the teacher's lesson on Egypt or how many items in the room I list off in my head, he's there in my mind, demanding to be focused on.

When an assignment lands on my desk, I find myself unable to make sense of the words.

Mr. Derek walks past my desk, saying, "Marianna, can I see you in the hallway for a minute?"

I grouse and follow him, leaning against a creaky pastel yellow locker covered in half-removed stickers.

"I'm sorry I handled things the way I did the other day," he starts. "I've been having issues in my personal life and I shouldn't have taken it out on you."

I wonder if Denendrius convinced him to apologize. "It's whatever."

He jams his hands in his pockets. "I—uh—met your boyfriend afterward . . ." He looks around the empty hallway and lowers his voice. "Do you need me to call someone?"

My breath turns solid. "No . . . why would I need that?"

He motions to his cheek. "Your face."

I roll my eyes. "So? I got punched by some chick in a fight."

His thin lips form a line. I know he doesn't believe me. I also know he can't legally do anything on suspicion alone. I'm glad, though. Mr. Derek isn't so bad of a teacher and doesn't need Denendrius's wrath.

"Are you safe?" he asks.

"Of course," I lie.

I wonder what Mr. Derek will say once I go missing.

An image rises in my mind of police officers trampling into the school and setting up in the office, interviewing teachers and students. I know if Camille, Daina, Carol, and Liz have anything to say about it, the investigation will go from runaway to foul play in a matter of moments.

As if he can read my mind, Mr. Derek says, "Your new foster mother, Carol, has been calling the school looking for you. You haven't been staying at home?"

I shrug. "I've been at Camille and Daina's houses."

His lips form that same flat line of disbelief, but he says, "Okay."

I wonder how many days it will take before I'm considered truly missing, before the police stop telling people to wait, that I'll be home eventually like I always am. Between my gang days and drug binges, it's never been uncommon for nobody to hear from me for a couple days. How long will it take before they assume I'm dead? Will they look for a body?

My stomach pinches. I almost throw up on Mr. Derek's shoes.

"Are you okay?" he asks.

I straighten despite wanting to curl up on the floor. "Yeah, totally. Can I go back to my desk?"

He nods and I wade through curious faces to my seat. I feel colorless, weightless like I'd drift through the window if someone were to open it.

I sit like that through my next class and barely have the energy to stand in line at lunch.

After I've spent a few dollars on fries, I sit at the table where Daina and Camille have already congregated.

Camille frowns when she looks me over.

"How are you?" Camille asks simply.

I chew a few fries. "Fine."

"Really? You look like you're dying or something." Daina takes a bite of her hot dog. "Like, seriously, you look *ill*."

Already? I laugh aloud ironically and chew fries.

Camille stares at me like I've lost my shit.

"*Holy shit*," Daina says, grabbing my hand when I try to bring fries to my mouth. "He gave you a ring?"

I let her stretch my arm across the table, too exhausted to take it back. "Yeah. He wants to marry me."

Daina's eyes look like they're about to fall out of her head. Ketchup is smeared across her chin, but she's too enthralled to notice. She wipes her hands and slides it off my finger, holding it up to the light to get a better look at the large and circular diamond. "Dude, this thing has to be worth thousands. You're not going to marry him, are you?"

The thought threatens my food's place in my stomach. I shrug. She gives the ring back and I slide it on, shoving my food away.

"What are you going to do?" Camille asks. Her finger wags at me. "Because this is not going to be a thing. I'm not going to watch my best friend suffer."

I want to tell her she won't have to worry about seeing me suffer, that she won't ever see me again.

It dawns on me that this is our last conversation.

I remember how upset Daina and Camille were when Jenna died. Will they feel like that once they realize I'm most likely dead?

They stare at me expectantly, like they know just from looking at me what's going to happen, like they know things are ten times worse than I've led them to believe. It feels like *help* is tattooed across my forehead.

I shake my head. "Don't worry. I'm going to get a restraining order," I say for her sake.

She seems to relax a bit. "Good idea. Let me help?"

I nod. "Of course." Faking a laugh, I say, "Do you really think I could get through all that legal bullshit myself? I wouldn't even know where to start."

She smiles a bit. "No kidding."

Daina laughs along and I duck my head for a moment so they don't see my smile crack. When I look up, I catch Sarah staring at me from across the cafeteria. Her healing face is flat, her tray of food untouched. Usually, she's sitting on the other side with all her friends. Today she's alone. Her eyes move to her lap when she realizes she's been caught. I wonder if she's planning something, if she wants revenge.

I shake the thought away and try to focus on the now-relaxed mood at my table, Daina, and Camille laughing about some story in a teen celebrity magazine. They seem pleased with the normality of my snide comments and expressions of hatred for their favorite reality TV stars.

Trying to act normal makes my chest hurt, as all the things I want to shout but can't are piling up behind my ribs.

When the bell demands we head toward class, I wrap each of my arms around their shoulders in a hug as we exit the cafeteria doors. Despite the fact that I rarely participate in any kind of hugging or sisterly behavior, they don't seem to notice. They clearly think I'm teasing them and squeeze back, but all I'm thinking is how I want one last moment of love before I never experience it again.

They wave as they walk toward the stairs. Backing toward the gymnasium, I wave back and don't turn away until their laughter disappears in a flurry of gold and cinnamon hair up the stairs.

I try to hang on to the smell of Daina's vanilla body spray and the pinch of Camille's nails in my side when she hugged me as I enter the gym. I try to hang on to the feeling of their warm bodies against mine since it'll be cold hands on me from now on. The memory fades faster than what should be fair.

My shoes thump loudly against the gymnasium floor as I head toward the gym teacher. He sits on the bench near the back doors with his clipboard, waiting for students to finish in the change room.

Mr. Coulter looks up over his reading glasses when I approach.

"Can I sit out today?" I ask. I know if I try to participate in any kind of physical activity, I'll end up passing out on the floor. I'm already sore from absolutely nothing.

He frowns playfully, old lips crinkled and pale. "You sure? It's dodgeball day. I won't get to penalize and send you to the office for constant headshots."

I want to laugh at his joke, but I can't. "Yeah, I'm sure. I don't feel well."

He slaps me on the shoulder. "All right, go ahead."

I almost question his agreeableness as I sit on the worn wooden bench. Maybe I do look fucked enough that he believes me without a doctor's note. It probably helps my case that he knows gym is my favorite class, that he couldn't even make me sit out after throwing up right in front of him for overexerting myself.

I think about all the times Mr. Coulter tried to get me to join after-school sports, saying if I started showing up to school regularly, he would have no issue putting me on the field hockey or volleyball team. I can't recall all the excuses I gave him. Why didn't I just try? I probably could have done it.

The rest of gym class is spent watching my classmates whip colorful balls at one another, my mind blurring their voices and faces, making me wish I could replace any one of them. I yearn to play, but I can barely find the effort to scratch my nose. I don't want to think about the effort it would take to accurately hit someone with a ball.

When the bell rings for English class, I sneak out before Mr. Coulter can say anything to me. I can't bear to hear the good wishes he always gives to bench sitters at the end of class.

My English teacher gives me flack for not having my binder once again. When she realizes I'm not listening, how I've just sat at my desk against the wall to ignore her and stare at the board, she gives up and starts to collect assignments I wasn't aware of.

I half-manage to pay attention to the teacher as she rambles on about our newest assignment. We have to create a poem based on a news story. Sarah stares at me but tries to hide it. It keeps me grounded in the reality of my desk, her hard eyes making it hard to disappear within myself.

I don't move or say anything to Sarah. I just don't care.

A guy shouts dibs on a news story about a kidnapped girl who was recently found after a decade. I feel the color drain from my face, and I jump up and excuse myself from class. I'm glad there are enough students riled up at his dibs for nobody to notice me leave.

I rush toward the changing room bathroom downstairs so nobody can hear me from the hallway, ripping loudly through doorways. Dropping to my knees on the cold white tile of the accessible stall, I vomit into the toilet. My hysterical sobs make me choke on my own spit. I'm happy nobody is in the locker room to hear me.

Tears fall faster than I can wipe them away, my sobs so violent I have to bite the hem of my sleeve to muffle my squeals. Something rips at the inside of my chest, hot slices chopping my breath as it leaves me. Sight blurred, I shove my sleeve into my mouth and chomp down, my scream tearing my throat. The emotion leaves me like a flood, and no matter how hard I try, I can't stop the tears or hold back my cries.

I turn and hammer my feet against the cement wall when a wave of rage lifts up inside me, the thumping and squealing of my soles echoing. I kick until heat tears at my muscles.

When tingles cascade painfully over my skin like biting insects, I curl into a ball, loud sobs turning into hiccups and whimpers. The tears seem endless. My mind circles around Denendrius repeatedly like a sick record, my heart skipping along.

At the sound of the door, my tears stop like magic, my breath stilling in my throat. I quickly sit up, pushing my back against the white cement wall.

My eyes follow a pair of small blue-and-pink sneakers, gray sweatpants tucked in. They stop on the other side of my stall door.

I'm painfully still, somehow thinking it will stop her from noticing me.

"Marianna?" Sarah's voice, dull, comes from the other side.

I think maybe if I don't say anything, she'll go away. I don't have it in me to fight anymore. She'll have no trouble winning, and it's not like I don't deserve it.

She sighs. "Marianna, I know it's you."

"Fuck off!" I hiccup a sob and slap my hand over my mouth.

She pulls at the door, her fingers—cuticles and nails torn—curling through the gap as she tries to push the lock open from the other side. She gives up. "Marianna, please let me in."

My heart pounds in my ears, eyes sore from crying. "I told you to fuck off!"

When she drops down onto her hands and knees and tries to crawl under the door, I kick at her. She pushes my legs aside easily and stands before me in the stall.

Her eyes widen on me like I'm a ghost. "You're . . . crying," she says.

I clench my teeth together. "Go ahead and rub it in," I snarl.

She swallows visibly, and I notice how awkwardly and

painfully her hips and legs move she when she sits against the wall beside me.

"To be honest, I didn't think you were capable of crying," she says in astonishment.

I smash the palms of my hands into my eyes. "Ugh, Sarah, just fuck off or hurry up and kick my ass." I have so many other things to worry about, I can't even fathom caring about this drama with her anymore.

"I don't want to fight anymore. And to be honest, I don't have the energy to hate you anymore. It doesn't feel fair to hate you when you look so sick." She pulls her hands into her sleeves. "I didn't tell the principal it was you that beat me up, by the way. He even asked and I said no."

I lift my head and glower through damp eyelashes. "I appreciate it, but please fuck off."

Her intense eyes tighten. "Marianna, you seem like a different person. You've lost at least ten pounds. You're all pale and shaky, and I don't think I've ever seen a teenager with bags under their eyes like yours. You're a ghost of yourself. And honestly, if I didn't have a pretty good idea what's going on, I would assume you have a terminal illness."

I curl my fingers around the edge of my hoodie. "Stop trying to be my friend. You're doing a shit job."

"I've never wanted to be your friend," she spits.

I catch it then—that spark of jealousy flickering violently in her eyes—and wonder how I never saw it before.

I swallow. "You don't want to be me."

Her face twists defensively, mouth opening to retort. Then it drops when we both know the truth can't be taken back. She sighs. "No, not anymore."

But I can't understand how she ever looked at me from the outside and thought my life would be better. "No, not ever. You should have never been jealous of me."

Her lip twitches. "Why not, Marianna? You basically get to

do whatever you want, and nobody stops you. Nobody forces you to come to school or do your homework or be home at a certain time. You can get high on whatever you want, party wherever you want, be whoever you want. I bet you've never even been grounded."

I have never been grounded, but I say, "Do you ever think it's because nobody gives enough of a shit about me? At least you have parents that care. Do you really think they ground you because they hate you? You're forced to go to school and do your homework because your parents want you to be success-ful. Your parents make you come home at a certain time so you aren't exhausted the next day, so you don't get shot or kidnapped at four o'clock in the morning. Nobody makes me come home because nobody really cares if I do."

She gulps, eyes misty. "I never thought of it that way," she whispers. Her brow furrows. "Aside from that, my point still stands. People think you're cool. You hang out with cool people."

I laugh. "Really? Like who? I have two normal friends, and everyone else I'm friends with is either addicted to drugs or sells me drugs . . . or both. Half of my friends will be dead or in jail by the time they're thirty." I roll my eyes. "So cool, though, right?"

She stares at her lap. "Everyone . . . guys at least wanted to be with you. I couldn't understand how they could find your hardness and nastiness appealing. How they could want you when you wouldn't even look at them. Meanwhile, I was throwing myself at them and they didn't care."

I groan. "Sarah, how fucking stupid are you? You think any of those guys are worth anything? They see my drug addiction as an easy way to try and get fucked. Like they could get it in if they got me high." I shake my head.

She chews her lip. "Yeah, I guess I knew that." She exhales loudly. "I was so fucking mad when you brought Den to the party. I was ready for some crackhead or gangster and then you waltzed out of a fancy car with an older man who is the equivalent of a Greek god . . . I thought you at least would appreciate that. And when you didn't . . ." She blows air between her dry lips. "I thought if I could take him from you, then I'd win whether you acknowledged it or not."

"And how well did that work out for you?" I ask, thinking of CJ.

Her eyes glaze over, unfocused. "Not well," she whispers to herself.

I shake my head solemnly and lean it against the toilet's water tank. When I inhale, it hurts.

Sarah hums in uncertainty from beside me, eyes watery. She doesn't look at me when she speaks. "Don't say anything to Den, but how long does it take until pregnancy tests work? I don't really know anyone else to ask . . . that won't judge me for something like that, you know?"

My eyes widen in horror. "You slept with him?"

Her eyes flicker to me and away. "Sort of."

I stiffen. "What do you mean 'sort of'?"

She takes an unsteady breath. "At the party, when you went upstairs, I went to see if he wanted to have fun . . . anyway, I tried to get him to use a condom and he wouldn't. Things were good until he started freaking me out, so I tried to get him off me. He wouldn't let me stop, though, and refused to pull out like he promised. My period was supposed to come a few days ago and I keep throwing up. I haven't slept with anyone else."

I'm not sure what to tell her. I know he can't have kids, but I'm not sure how to start explaining her missed period. Maybe the stress Denendrius put her through is enough to make her miss it.

I try to swallow but can't. "What did he do to freak you out?"

Her voice shudders. "Um . . . he started getting rough and hit me. I said I wasn't into that sort of thing and he said he didn't care and wanted me to cry. That's when I realized who was giving you all your bruises and why you were so eager to get rid of him."

A feeling of jealousy rips through my core at the thought of him being with her. I think of slapping her and confronting him. Am I not good enough for him? Her hair is too light, her eyes too blue. She's not even his type! Can she do something I can't? Why would he touch her when he has me?

I tuck my knees against my chest, horrified at my own thoughts. I hope his blood is responsible for them and that I'm not just a bad person. How much of my thinking is a result of this mark? Could I be having other thoughts that aren't mine and not even realize it? I heave, but nothing is left to come up. I think I might start crying again.

I think of the way she moved when sitting down. "Wait, wasn't the party a while ago now? Was it so bad that you still hurt now?"

Tears streak her face, giving me an answer.

I curl my fingers into fists. "He's still fucking with you, isn't he?"

Her breath catches. "I wasn't sure if you knew or not, or even cared. I know he's doing it because he thinks we're enemies and he wants to piss you off. A few nights ago, I went to bed and I found him lying there reading my diary and petting my dead dog. He said you wouldn't sleep with him so he came to me, that he knew you'd come around and would rather wait than cause any setbacks."

I stare, feeling guilty for what's happened to her but knowing I shouldn't. "He killed your dog?" I think of her father's massive German shepherd, the police dog that must have tried to tear Denendrius to shreds when he crept into Sarah's bedroom.

Cries rip up her throat, her eyes closing as she nods. I stare at the wall as I listen to her howl. The stall feels like it's getting smaller each moment.

She looks at me, eyes wild. "What's he going to do, Marianna?"

I don't know what to tell her.

She grabs my arm, pleading. "*I know* you know. You have the same look in your eye that CJ did when he realized he was going to die. What's he going to do?" she wails.

I duck my head, my hair blocking sight of her. I don't want to tell her that she's probably going to be tossed away, that she doesn't even realize how bad things are. There's no way she knows he's a vampire either.

But I know the only way she'll have a chance is if I take one. If I'm going to die anyway, I may as well die trying. Maybe he'll just kill me instead of turning me. Maybe he'll be so busy chasing me he'll completely forget about her. I know it's the right thing to do, and that I owe it to her for jumping to conclusions about her involvement in CJ's death and hurting her, for not considering that maybe she really did think she had no other choice but to lure him to Denendrius.

"I don't know," I say, taking a deep breath. I stand.

She looks at me with uncertainty. "Where are you going?" she asks, her eyes wide.

I stand and almost collapse while walking to open the stall. "To do something really fucking stupid," I say.

XXXVIII

I stand tight against the pastel yellow lockers, eyes locked on the school's main doors. The lump of a security guard paces in front of the foyer, cell phone in hand, the squeak of his shoes and distant trumpets the only sound in the empty space. He looks up momentarily when a locker slams, then his eyes dart back to his phone.

I hold my breath, praying something distracts him soon before a teacher notices me loitering, or someone decides to check in on the cameras. Knowing security guards here are rarely bored, I know I won't have to wait long before somebody fucks around.

A long ten minutes later, another security guard jogs by and collects him to deal with a fight at the other end of the school. Once they're around the corner, I duck and race across the hallway, making sure the doors to the foyer don't slam when I slip through them. Standing between the doors back into the school and the ones leading outside, I quickly check to make sure Denendrius hasn't decided to show up early.

When the coast is clear, I bolt through the front doors, my sneakers heavy on the sidewalk. My feet stop moving halfway down the path and I'm jerked to a halt, breath turning stagnant.

What the fuck am I doing?

Where do I think I can run? Do I really think I can hide from him long enough for it to be worth it? I'm on foot! All he has to do is follow my scent all the way back to me. How stupid! The thought echoes through my mind.

Stupid.

Stupid!

STUPID!

You're so stupid, Marianna!

When I take a step back, it feels safe, like it's the right thing to do. It feels like everything will be okay if I just retrace my steps back to the school. I pause. Surely I should feel the opposite. Should I not find relief in running, in trying to escape?

You'll make him mad . . . he'll be so fucking mad. He'll punish you, and you'll deserve it!

I try to make myself run again, but I only jerk. It's like I'm standing on a stool with a noose around my neck, trying to decide if I really want to kick it out from under me. Do I want to wish I were dead for the rest of my life, or do I want to be dead?

Don't run. Bad idea. Don't do it.

The thoughts continue to swirl around my mind in a flurry. I think about how the smartest thing to do would be to go back to class and wait for him to come get me. Maybe I should tell him I got a little scared, was going to take off but corrected myself before he had to. He'd probably be proud of me for that. He'd be happy I decided to stay with him. Maybe he'd give me his blood. I haven't had any in a few days . . .

The blood.

Is his blood responsible for my dilemma? I can't possibly feel that defeat and subservience is a safer, better option than trying to escape. Why does doing what he wants feel better than what I want? It must be the blood. Right? Or deep down, do I really know it would be stupid to run?

Don't run.

I swallow and shove the thought away. I tell myself running is exactly what I need to do. The worst that can happen is he kills me, which is worst-case scenario despite whatever option I choose.

Don't do it.

But I have to. I'll never forgive myself if I don't try.

I fill my lungs and will my feet to move. After a few steps, terror is choking me, and I stop again.

Run. Fucking run!

I rock back and forth from the balls of my feet to the heels of them, working up the courage. I count my breaths.

One...

Two...

Three...

Run!

I jerk.

I scold myself and take another deep breath, shaking my arms out and cracking my neck like I'm preparing for a race.

Run, Marianna.

Run.

RUN.

I take off down the sidewalk, legs protesting as they carry me away from the school and down the street. Tears blur my sight, breath edging on hysteria. I must look fucking insane racing past houses, checking over my shoulder every five seconds as if he already knows what I've done.

Now you've done it.

I squeal at the thought and almost stumble into a car, righting myself before I continue. The heat beats down on me, and I think I'm already sweating twice as much as I should be. My throat burns.

Half a dozen blocks from the school now, a man crosses the street, cell phone in hand.

"Fuck!" I shout, remembering mine in my pocket.

Could he have a GPS on it? Could he have it set somehow to notify him if my phone leaves the school? The house? Is he already on his way? He might not be technology savvy, but he's smart enough to learn quickly. Not to mention if he has a friend with a plane, he probably knows somebody capable of making my phone traceable to him. He may not need it to find me, but it would make things ten times easier. He could have taken my phone away in the middle of the night and done it too.

I dodge a rusted blue car when I cross the street and the driver honks, obviously not expecting a lunatic to run out from nowhere.

Back on the sidewalk, my fingers fumble at the loose pockets of my jeans for my cell phone. It slips in my shaky fingers, sweat making it harder to grip. I wince when the screen shatters against the pale concrete, but I kick it under a parked Jeep.

I expected to feel better with the phone gone. Instead, heavy guilt begins to erode my gut.

I may have gotten rid of the phone, but now what do I do?

Go back to the school and beg for his forgiveness before it's too late.

"No!" I shout, voice raspy.

I wipe the sweat from my forehead, an intersection surrounded by gas stations and old mom-and-pop shops around me. Cars collect at red lights, the sound of engines polluting the air.

I stop at the crosswalk and slam my hand on the button, leaning over to gasp for air. When I straighten, the colors of the cars smear, bile threatening to climb my throat. Grabbing at the hot rusted metal of the streetlight post, I try to remember the last time I got to work out, the last time I ate a proper meal.

My knees almost meet the road when I try to cross, so I'm surprised when I make it across the street.

Before entering the gas station, I search the road for Denendrius's black Mustang, only taking hold of the hot silver of the door handle when I don't see him.

The bell chimes when I enter, cold air blasting me and tightening the muscles quivering under my skin and lifting my hair. With my sweatiness and the smell of cheap food filling the air and churning the acid in my stomach, it almost feels like I have the flu.

I buy a bottle of water since I have almost forty dollars left and sit outside on the gum-crusted concrete by the blue pay phone on the exterior wall after calling a cab. I try to convince someone to buy me a pack of cigarettes while I wait. It takes some patience—with most people either laughing or flat out ignoring me—but eventually, a middle-aged woman takes pity.

"Better this than hard drugs, right?" she justifies with wrinkled lips when handing me the pack and a lighter.

I shrug. "I guess." I try to give her my ten-dollar bill.

She shakes her head, stringy brown hair swaying at her bruised collarbones. "Don't worry about it, darling, you look like you're having a rough time."

Am I that obvious? I exhale loudly. "Thanks."

She gives me a nod of encouragement before walking away.

I light a cigarette, some of the panic clearing from my mind with that first inhale and exhale.

Kids from my high school collect around the front of the gas station, disappearing and reappearing at random with slushies. School must be out now. I stand against the pay phone, using it to block some of their view of me as I watch the roads for Denendrius. If he didn't know I ran then, he will by now. It could be a matter of minutes before he finds me.

A girl notices me—just a glance—but she doesn't speak or

offer a smile, just continues to talk with her friends like her eyes only landed on me by accident.

A yellow cab pulls into the parking lot and I stomp out my cigarette, relief filling me when I open the door and hop in. The small space smells like meat and cigarettes, foreign music playing quietly.

When he asks me where I want to go, I tell him I don't know the address and that I'll give him directions.

"Roll up the windows, please," I say, hushed.

The glass rolls up on all four doors, trapping my scent inside with me. I direct him onto the street that crosses the one I ran on. He'd just have to drive in a straight line otherwise.

I monitor the windows and mirrors, and we're only a handful of blocks away before the careless driving of a black car catches my attention in the back window. It rips into the parking lot of the gas station and the huddled students from before scatter, making me wonder if the driver almost hit them. It's too far to see any details of the car, but when an imposing man steps out, I know exactly who it is.

I slap my hand over my mouth, heart hammering in my ears. I want to tell the driver to speed up or turn, but I fear Denendrius will hear my voice.

He must say something to the group of teens, because an arm waves him in the complete opposite direction of me. Denendrius gets back in the car and follows their misguided directions.

"Holy fuck," I murmur, wiping my sweaty palms on my jeans. "Turn left," I tell the driver.

I sit in stunned silence, realizing how lucky I am. If they had told him which way I really went, it would have only taken a few seconds for him to catch up and cut the taxi off to pull me out. My muscles loosen a bit, my eyes watering in relief. Why'd they lie for me? Did they think they were playing a prank on him? Or were they able to figure out something was up? Was it the girl whose eyes I met? Did she recognize the fear that must have been plain on my face?

Sitting low in the backseat, I give the cab driver random directions, *far* being the only destination in mind.

I rip through my mind for a plan, but it's hard to concentrate on my thoughts when I'm on constant lookout and every black car makes me duck in my seat. I decide to worry about getting myself lost, thinking it'll be harder to find me if even I don't know where I am.

When the meter climbs near twenty dollars about forty minutes through the ride, I point out a random grocery store and he drops me off. I take the bit of change I have left and find a bus stop a block away, deciding to ride until I can come up with a plan.

Resting on the bench, I look around the neighborhood. The cars are mostly nice and early-century models, the pedestrians decently dressed. The only graffiti covers the bench I'm on, and sparsely. I decide I'm likely somewhere in the north of Lorimer, and probably fairly far from the west side.

The only problem: too many black fucking cars. At least in our part of the city, he's one of few people who own a Mustang. It's an epidemic in this part of town, or maybe they're all I see now that it's what I'm looking for.

I light a cigarette and greedily smoke it. When it burns near the filter, a bus finally arrives.

After practically leaping off the seat and through the doors, I drop change into the slot and collect a ticket. It's just after four thirty when I plop down in a seat adjacent to the back door, in case I need to get off in a hurry.

My lips are a sore, bloody mess after about an hour, and I'm still not any closer to a plan.

I switch buses on a whim in an attempt to make my trail more unpredictable, so he won't be able to follow a specific route if he figures out I got on a bus.

Around seven thirty, darkness is looming in the sky. With a pocket full of used bus tickets, my eyes and brain sore from constant vigilance, the truth starts to settle.

This is my life now.

I'll never be able to stop moving. If I do—especially in Lorimer—he'll find me in a matter of hours like he did the first time. I have to leave, and even then . . .

Getting out of Lorimer would be the easy part. I can steal cars and siphon gas, that's not an issue. Surviving will be the hard part.

I'll have to change my name and dye my hair, but those tricks will only work from afar. I won't be able to risk leaving a trail. I'll still be missing. There will be no ability to find a legal job, a proper place to live. How will I afford to survive? I could sell drugs, but that's a lot of footwork. My scent would be everywhere. It would make me easier to find, especially with my smell being passed on to every buyer.

Since I'll be missing, I can't go to a small town. Not only will there be nowhere to hide, but I risk other people figuring out who I am. I'll have to pick a big city.

There are too many variables.

My life would be dedicated to hiding from him and I couldn't dare consider normality. What kind of life is that?

A dropped gum wrapper could fuck me over.

He, of course, already knows these facts.

I give myself a couple years, and even then . . . that's if I pull it off perfectly. I doubt a two-thousand-year-old vampire is concerned about wasting a handful of years to track down some girl that pissed him off. He's probably killed people for a lot less and would probably have a blast looking for me.

Also, I have a horrible feeling that he's a much better tracker than I know. After all, he's survived for as long as he has with so many enemies. He would have to be smarter than other vampires to avoid being caught by them.

I hold my head in my hands and try not to scream.

When the bus stops, I hop off into the dark, alone on a random street when it pulls away.

I walk. It's all I can think to do. Walk and smoke.

Is there anything else to do?

There's only the sound of my feet and labored smoke-filled breaths as I walk pointlessly. I weave through residential streets and their attached alleys, the harsh yellow of streetlamps and the dropping temperature my only companions.

My steps bring me closer to anger the longer I walk. It feels like it's been hours, and it very well could be. My heart pounds, hands and feet tingling.

I wish I could walk right off the edge of the earth.

I duck into an alley behind a church, using a dumpster to hide me from sight. Leaning against a brick wall, my knees give out and I slide into rocks and broken glass, wincing when the shards poke me through my jeans.

When a black car creeps through the alley, my chest clenches. A shriek builds in my throat, legs pushing my body tighter to the wall.

No, no, no, please no.

I want to close my eyes, but they're so wide, blinking wouldn't even be an option.

The stranger's unfamiliar black car carries on, not noticing me. I pull my knees to my chest and begin to sob. After a few minutes, I can't hold it anymore and I scream, covering my face with my arms.

I'm not sure how long I stay in the alley crying and pleading with nobody. It feels like the rest of my life.

When a woman's voice jerks my head from my arms, I realize I fell asleep.

"Are you okay?" she asks.

I look around me. Oh no, not good. How long have I been

sitting here? Denendrius could be here any moment. I have to get up and keep walking.

I use the wall to guide myself to my feet, eyes passing over her to search for Denendrius on the street.

"I'm fine," I say, voice raspy. I step around her. "I have to go."

I can feel her following behind me as I step from the alley and onto the sidewalk, continuing on.

Then I stop, her image registering in my mind. I turn around, getting an eyeful of her black lace clothing and long, curly black hair.

The girl from the diner and the mall?

She stands there in the mouth of the alley, silently watching me like she's waiting for something.

Knowing what I do now about Children of Stars, I wonder if she could have gone in the sunlight if she was as covered as she was the last two times I've seen her. Could she have been waiting for an opportunity to get me alone, stalking me until a moment like now presented itself? Is she one of the vampires Denendrius scorned, thinking she can use me to get to him?

"Denendrius knows where I am," I lie. "He's on his way to get me."

She doesn't move. "Sure, Marianna," she says evenly.

I swallow at the sound of my name and take a few steps back, my eyes searching the shadows for vampires. The hair stands up on the back of my neck, raised by much more than her gaze. How outnumbered am I? Could these people have abilities like the vampire Denendrius showed me?

"Whatever you want with him, I'll help you," I offer, trying to take advantage of the situation.

She doesn't respond.

"I can help you lure him," I add. "He'd never know you were on to him."

She remains expressionless. "Oh, I know."

My brow furrows, heart thumping. "You know?"

I realize she's a distraction, especially when I catch movement in a white commercial van parked a few feet behind me. I don't react, not wanting her to know I'm on to them.

She folds her hands behind her back. "Yes."

I figure she's positioned in front of me so I'll run away from her and into a trap.

Faking a smile, I say, "Perfect, let's just—" I take off across the street.

"Damn it!" she hollers. "Marianna, come back!"

I push myself as hard as I can, not wanting to find out how fast the others are. When I hear a vehicle door slam and an engine start, I search for a park or alley to cut through.

I hate that Denendrius's warning to stay near him might have been half-justified. I don't regret running away, but being tracked by two different vampires isn't something I anticipated, especially now that there's no knowing who's a greater threat.

XXXIX

I wait in the prickly bushes near the front doors of the closed bank, waiting for the next person to pull up to the ATM and get out of their car.

A blue sedan pulls up and a suited man parks in front of the machine, leaving the car running as he steps out for a moment. When he shoves his bank card into the slot of the machine, I scramble toward the car, ripping the door open and throwing myself into the driver's seat.

He tries to chase after me when I pull away.

My heart pummels the back of my ribs, hands sweaty on the leather wheel. My mind races as I drive, eyes searching the streets for a white plumbing van and Denendrius's Mustang.

I leave the music off, golden streetlights flashing through the sunroof as I try to keep my speed to avoid being pulled over. I try to think of where to go while turning down random streets.

After about two hours, I struggle to keep my eyes open. My hands almost slip off the wheel, body exhausted from stress.

Headlights blind me through the driver's window, my head snapping sideways just in time to be consumed by them. When I see that they're going to try and cut in front of me, I speed up, deciding too late that I should have hit the brakes when they jerk to a stop in front of me and I collide into the front corner of the van.

The car jerks, my vision yanked from me with the deafening sound of crunching metal and shattering glass. My head bounces against something hard, sound dissipating around me, replaced with ringing. I don't hear my own groan, only feeling it roll in my sore chest.

Crippled by confusion, I'm only vaguely aware of the feeling of hands hauling me from the car and the feel of lying on rubber. Something rumbles under me. I feel like I'm trapped under the hush of spinning voices, and I start to wonder if I fell asleep at the wheel and started dreaming.

Unable to completely break through the surface of consciousness, I'm left swimming in nauseated confusion and unable to grasp time.

When I come to, I find myself tied to a metal chair in a dim warehouse, the sound of metal ruffled by the wind. Cold air swirls around me. My feet rest against the gray concrete, roped to the chair legs. My hands are knotted behind my back.

My head throbs and I writhe fruitlessly. "Fuck."

I comb over the warehouse with half-lidded eyes, blinking away stars. Two hallways lead away from the open space I sit in, one on each side of the building. Offices with large windows and closed doors face me, metal tables pressed against the wall under the oil-streaked glass.

Voices move toward me from the left hallway, echoing in the empty space.

"Agatha, please," a girl says. "We're given other ways to protect ourselves from Darklings for a reason. He's too old. This could kill me."

Agatha turns, blond hair wafting around her. "You've had weeks to prepare, Emily."

Emily's small shoulders slump and she nods, brown bangs falling into her eyes. "I know, I know."

"What the fuck is going on?" I demand.

They ignore me and rest against one of the tables, poring over a flip phone in Agatha's hand and mumbling.

I rock back and forth against the ropes, chair legs scraping on the floor. "I know you can hear me."

Emily's eyes dart toward me for a moment before looking away.

"Are you vampires?" I ask.

Agatha looks up this time. "Yes. Now shut up and let us concentrate."

I remember the vampire I staked in the forest and wonder if Agatha would be as easily dealt with. I look around for something wooden, but everything is metal.

I try to loosen the rope around my wrists, sure I'll have rope burn by the end of this. "You didn't have to fucking run me off the road and kidnap me," I say. "I would have told you anything you wanted to know about him. I could have given you his address, license plate, phone number . . . all of that shit."

Agatha laughs. "Sure."

I scowl. "I know one of you has been watching me for weeks. You could have saved yourself some time."

She gives me a pitying look, like I'm some stupid child incapable of grasping the most fundamental of ideas. "You would have ruined everything. The only thing you're useful for is bait."

I'm not sure whether or not to be offended.

"I would have helped. I want him dead as much as you do."

She cackles. "Honey, you're blood marked. You probably don't even know what's going on inside your own head."

I jerk against my restraints, teeth gritting. "He has no

control over me. If he did, I wouldn't have been able to run away."

Her brows rise and she grins. "Really? You had a motor vehicle. You could have been near another state by now. You didn't even try to leave the city."

My jaw hangs. "I—"

When I can't come up with a retort, she *tsks*. "See?"

The black-haired girl comes into the room from the opposite hall, black lace skirt billowing around her. She approaches Agatha. "I did my part. Do I really have to be here when Denendrius comes? He'll kill me in a second if he recognizes me."

Agatha doesn't look up from her phone as she types. "Rayonne, don't be a baby."

I'm glad that Agatha's bitchiness isn't reserved for me.

She folds her arms. "I'm serious. I'll be his first target. How am I supposed to protect myself?"

Agatha rolls her eyes. "He'll be blinded as soon as he's close enough. Don't open your mouth and he won't know who you are."

Rayonne takes a deep breath, shoulders lifting to her ears. "I'm the only other human in the room. You don't think he'll use me as a hostage?"

Agatha turns to Rayonne, hostility twisting her face. Rayonne takes a step back. "Trust us, okay? Like you said, you did your part, so let us do ours and shut up. Go entertain his girlfriend before she starts to piss me off again." She spins back around, continuing to whisper-talk with Emily.

Rayonne's fingers curl into fists and she storms away and down the hall. I catch Agatha's small smile.

I sit like a worm on a fishing line, wondering what the chances are of Denendrius falling for whatever trap they're using me as bait for. The ropes press against my sore ribs when I breathe deeply, probably a result of the crash. My forehead throbs, and I'm glad they haven't turned the main overhead lights on.

Rayonne returns a few minutes later with two bottles of iced tea and a cookie. She sits on the floor in front of me.

"Sorry about all this," she mumbles. She cracks an iced tea open and plops a straw in the top before setting it in the little space between my knees. "The crash especially. Are you okay? I thought you'd stop, not speed into us."

I study her and ignore her questions, my own coming to my lips. "If you're human, how'd you get involved with vampires?"

She nibbles the edge of the chocolate chip cookie. "Recently human. I turned back a year ago, but I was a vampire since Victorian England."

My eyes narrow at that. I remember Alaire and Edmond talking about how Darklings could turn back, but Denendrius called them liars. "You were a Darkling?"

She shakes her head and sighs. "A Child of Stars, like them." She jerks her head toward Emily and Agatha.

My brows lift. For some reason, I'm surprised she seems so normal. After all, Alaire and Edmond did call it a curse. Maybe she got lucky. "How?" I ask.

She bites her lip. "Pretty much the same way you turn a Darkling back . . ."

We both catch Agatha glaring at us, and Rayonne's lips tighten. She scratches the back of her head.

"Why would you turn human just to help vampires?" I question. Wouldn't the point be to get away from the life? I remember her worry of being recognized. "Denendrius?"

"I didn't choose it," she whispers, eyes dropping. "Regardless, he killed my clan. I mean, that's how it ended, five years later. For me, it started when my husband, Alessander, and I came home and Denendrius presented us with our dead son. We ran and joined others, but he found us and burned our church down. I was the only one who got away." She swallows.

"I saw him tear Alessander's heart out as I climbed through the window."

"Shit," I mumble.

She takes a sip of her iced tea, eyes distant. "I've been looking for a way to punish him ever since, and I finally found it." She smiles gently at me. "Don't worry. I've seen some of what has been going on for you. After tonight, we will both be free."

My heart soars, the idea of freedom making my eyes sting. "You're letting me go after?"

She nods. "Our problem is with him. We just needed you to draw him in."

Sweat starts at the back of my neck. "He's coming here? Are you sure your plan will work?"

Do they really stand a chance?

Rayonne takes another bite of her cookie. "Yes. I doubt he has any idea what's going on. We have the element of surprise."

My heart thumps, my mind on red alert as I wait for him to appear.

Agatha's phone buzzes loudly and she looks toward us. "Amy just saw him circling the perimeter," she says to Emily. "Get ready."

Rayonne leaps up and collects my untouched drink, scurrying away from me.

The blood rushes from my face. If it weren't for the ropes, I'd probably fall sideways out of my chair and onto the concrete.

No more than fifteen minutes later, male shouts sound through a door behind me, accompanied by shattering glass and crunching metal.

Denendrius is dropped onto the concrete floor, on his hands and knees between the vampires and me.

He slaps an open hand against the floor. "Whoever is blinding me better stop right now!"

They ignore him.

"We found him circling the perimeter. He killed Amy and Laura before we got him under control," says a teenage boy, no older than seventeen.

Agatha stands and crosses her arms. "I thought I said to stick together."

He blows air through his lips, brushing the shaggy black hair from his eyes. "He split us up, I don't know what happened."

Denendrius doesn't look up, his breath heavy. "Marianna?" he says to the floor.

I don't respond, unsure if I'm glad to see him.

"Marianna?" he asks again, voice sharp.

"Denendrius," I whisper.

He smiles and reaches his arm toward me, still a couple feet away. "Hey there, sweetheart. Why don't you tell me how many vampires are in the room? It seems they're masking themselves too."

Agatha steps in warning toward me and his head snaps toward the click of her heel before he vanishes, appearing directly behind her, grabbing a fistful of her leather coat. Her eyes widen.

"Now, assuming I'm not holding a coatrack, somebody better start listening to me before I shove my fist through whoever is wearing this jacket. You can start by giving me back my sight."

I look around the room, unable to decide who is responsible.

Agatha smiles wickedly. "Go ahead, Denendrius. I'm sure Viorel won't mind punishing you for a few extra deaths."

Denendrius stiffens, an odd expression passing over his face. He hums, unsure. "Viorel? Are you talking about—"

She snickers. "Yes, Denendrius, Viorel. You know exactly

who I'm talking about. What? You didn't think your actions would piss him off the most?"

An expression of God-fucking-damn-it flashes over Denendrius's face and he locks his jaw, inhaling loudly. "He's in Lorimer?"

Agatha tries to wrench free, but he holds her tighter. "You know damn well he hasn't left his castle in a few millennia, never mind Romania. Not with people like you causing mayhem."

Denendrius purses his lips as if he never considered the issue. Then, he smiles. "Well, if he's not in Lorimer, then why should I care?"

"Because you'll be seeing him real soon, Denendrius," Agatha says. "You're going on a vacation."

His eyes widen for a moment, in fear I think, and he swallows. "I don't think so," he snarls.

Emily steps forward and takes a shaky breath, the whites of her eyes visible. She straightens as the black-haired boy and Marcus approach Denendrius. They stand directly behind him and Denendrius bristles, eyes darting around blankly.

Agatha nods at Emily and she closes her eyes, face scrunching in concentration.

When the muscles in Denendrius's body visibly tighten under his skin, he makes a choking sound, his eyes widening. The two vampires quickly shove him to the ground as he twitches and grunts in agony, Agatha stepping away from them. Marcus quickly pulls the lid off a small vial of blood and pours it messily down Denendrius's throat. The two jump away from him just as Emily collapses on the floor.

Denendrius gags, dark blood dripping from the corner of his mouth. "What was that?" he demands.

Agatha snaps her fingers toward Emily, turning to Rayonne. "Make sure she's alive."

Rayonne leaps out of the desk chair and rushes to where she lies on the ground.

I expect Denendrius to leap up and begin tearing off heads, but he just rolls over onto his elbow, head hanging as he groans. He must have his sight back as he looks to me, dazed.

Rayonne shakes Emily and the girl quietly moans. "She'll live."

I flinch when Denendrius appears crouched beside them. He shoves Rayonne away, the sound of Emily's neck snapping as he tears her head from her shoulders filling the room a moment later.

"Not after making me relive my transformation," Denendrius snarls.

He stands and Rayonne stumbles backward toward Agatha.

Denendrius points at finger at Rayonne. "*You.*"

He steps toward her, only to stop short, wavering.

Agatha smiles. "What's wrong, Denendrius?"

He looks between the faces in the room, confused. "What did you do?"

When they don't answer him, he turns to me. "Marianna?" he asks, alarmed.

I'm unsure of what to tell him, afraid of saying the wrong thing.

Agatha laughs. "Go ahead, Marianna. Why don't you fill him in?"

Cautiously, I say, "They fed you blood."

"*Blood?*" His expression falls, eyes bulging. Denendrius quickly wipes his hand over his mouth. "Oh no," he murmurs as he looks at the red transferred onto it.

Agatha grins wickedly, arms crossed. "Marcus."

Denendrius blinks rapidly, and I realize Marcus has been responsible for his loss of sight. When he opens his mouth to speak, he dry-heaves and places his hand on his chest, his face twisting in pain.

I jerk in my chair when he appears on his knees in front of me, shaky hands trailing over me. "I need your help, sweetheart." His twitching fingers run over my thighs, his blank eyes trying to focus on me. "I need you to tell me where the vampires are so I can kill them. I'll untie you if you do it."

Agatha's groan is sardonic. "You've already lost, Denendrius. As soon as you finish turning back, you'll wake up in a cozy little cell in Romania, where you'll either die of old age or succumb to your punishments."

My heart thumps, one big shock wave of sharp surprise radiating through me. *Turning back?*

He shakes his head and heaves again, this time turning his head away from me to vomit blood. I feel his muscle spasms, see the way they clench in his neck and jaw as he gasps for air. "Marianna," he pleads between clenched teeth, "you know I love you."

His desperation leaves me wordless, and all I can think of is how badly I want to push him off me. I want to push him onto the floor and spit on him. I want to move to the back of the room and watch triumphantly as they take him away.

I think how I'll go back to Carol's and try to live my life the way I was supposed to . . . however that is. Maybe I'll join the field hockey team and ask Mr. Derek about those art classes he mentioned. Carol probably would help me pay for them, and if not I'm sure Denendrius won't miss the cash in his Mustang. Hell, I'll probably even be able to get into a better school since Carol lives so far from the hood.

When I feel the smile hint at the corner of my lips, I'm thankful Denendrius can't see.

Agatha hands a revolver to Rayonne, her chin jutting toward me. My heart freezes, blood icy.

Rayonne and I speak at the same time, our tones equally distressed. "*What?*"

Denendrius's fingers curl around the fabric of my jeans like he knows something is wrong, and I wonder what would have happened if Agatha had given her verbal directions.

Rayonne's fist tightens on the gun in her hand. "You said I wouldn't have to kill anyone. You said if I watched her and found a way to get her, that she wouldn't be killed."

Agatha rolls her eyes. "She's useless now. You'll do whatever I say, Rayonne, or you can kiss immortality goodbye."

Denendrius falls sideways, palm slamming into the concrete to prop himself up. His eyes close and he coughs, blood flowing past his lips. His elbow buckles under his weight. "Marianna, please. Where are they?"

Rayonne takes a deep breath. "No."

Agatha shrugs and leans against the wall. "Fine, then. Blaire and Marcus are perfectly able to handle both jobs."

When the two boys walk toward us, I ruefully recognize I'll have to help Denendrius if I want to help myself.

My little bit of hope evaporates when I whisper, "Both sides, three feet behind you."

Tears threaten me when I catch their bodies hit the ground, Agatha's furious shouts filling the air. Blood gurgles in their gaping chests as Denendrius crawls over them to finish the job now that Marcus is too injured to stop him from seeing them. His hand reaches into Marcus's chest first, reappearing with his heart. The bones crunch in Blaire's neck as his head is torn from between his shoulders.

Denendrius tries to stand but fails. He vomits more blood and it sizzles against the floor. He groans, hand gripping his chest.

"Damn it!" Agatha hollers. "Rayonne, she's a witness! She needs to die! Do you really want to chance leaving her alive? She's marked! You should know what lengths people go to for revenge." Agatha steps toward Rayonne, only to have to gun pointed at her. "Stop being so fucking sensitive."

Denendrius pulls himself across the floor toward me, grunting. Blood trickles from the corners of his mouth; he tries to wipe it away with the sleeve of his leather jacket, only to have more spill over his lips when he coughs again.

"Rayonne, put the gun down or I will make damn sure Viorel knows you don't deserve a place in his home. What do you hope to achieve by shooting me anyway?"

Rayonne scowls. "Can you pull a bullet out of your own head fast enough to heal and come after me?"

Agatha frowns. "All this over not wanting to kill her? How could you switch sides so easily?"

Rayonne's eyes water. "That's not it, Agatha. I want Denendrius dead as much as you do. But as it is, I can barely sleep at night since you forced me to turn back. For Chrissakes, you poured the cure down my throat *while I was sleeping.* Do you have any idea what it's like to be human again and remember what it tastes like to kill someone? I still crave blood. You promised me I wouldn't have to kill, and I'm holding you to it. I'm not letting you control me anymore."

I'm shaken from the horror of her words when Denendrius grabs my chair, using it to help him stand. The metal screeches under his weight. He rips the ropes around me and pulls me to my feet.

When he puts his arm around my shoulder for balance, I can feel my ideas for a Denendrius-free future slipping through my fingers.

Agatha groans. "Come on, Rayonne, you're being dramatic. Viorel was clear. He said that if we wanted to be part of the clan, we had to get Denendrius for him. You had to turn back. You were the only one we could find who knew what he looked like, who could find him. We didn't want to waste time by limiting your hunt to nighttime. Now put down the fucking gun or you can kiss going to Romania goodbye, you selfish bitch."

I struggle to hold Denendrius up, our steps toward the door treacherously slow, my body aching under his weight. I pray we can get out before things escalate between the two girls. If Agatha wins, she'll undoubtedly come after us next.

Rayonne runs a shaky hand over her pale face, fingers brushing the edges of her black bangs. "I did what Viorel asked of me. I found Denendrius. That was his only requirement for me. Everyone had their own job, and I did mine. If you won't give me back my immortality, I'll find it myself. Viorel will probably be more than willing to give it back to me after finding out you betrayed another of your kind."

Agatha lifts her chin, brows cocking. "He said to do anything to get the job done."

I wrap my hand around the bar of the door, ready to push it open when Denendrius vomits blood, eyelids fluttering. My arm is almost yanked from its socket as he falls sideways before catching himself on the wall.

Rayonne shakes her head, stepping sideways toward us. "If you really believe he would agree with you, then I guess we'll see which one of us ends up in the dungeon next to Denendrius."

We push through the doors, Rayonne trailing us.

"And how am I supposed to get there if I don't have him!" she hollers after us, eyes wild.

"It's not my job to get him there!" Rayonne shouts back as the door closes. "It's yours! Come fight us for him if you want, but you'll have as much luck as Marcus and Blaire did!"

Denendrius collapses onto the dirt of the warehouse parking lot, pulling me down with him. I yelp, feeling something give in my back. I try to push myself away from him when a deep scream escapes his bared teeth. His head hangs, his hand clutching his chest. He grabs my arm and tries to say something. He chokes on blood before spitting it up as it drips from his nose. When he moans and looks up at me, the black of his eyes flickers to brown for a split second. I gasp and clamber back.

I can hear Agatha shouting at someone—probably over the phone since she's the only one left in the warehouse—as Rayonne drops to her knees beside us.

When she takes Denendrius's arm, his fingers shift from my arm to her neck. I hear the air leave her nose and she quickly mouths that she's helping. He lets go and she sucks in a breath.

He grunts. "Don't try anything."

She swallows and nods. Aside from not wanting my death on her conscience, I question her intentions. Why would she want to help Denendrius after he killed her son and husband?

Between Rayonne and me, we manage to get Denendrius to his feet and hold him steady enough to make it to a purple car that she points out. She takes a single black key from her pocket.

"She's driving. You're in the back seat." Denendrius rips it from her hands and holds it out to me. "I heard her call for backup, so hurry."

We quickly help Denendrius into the passenger seat of the rusted purple car, climbing in after him.

"Why didn't you shoot her?" I ask Rayonne, turning the car on. The check engine light comes on and I scowl.

She braces herself when I crank the car into drive, the tires spinning before they grip the dirt and throw us forward.

"That's not a problem I want," she says.

I don't have to ask what she means, starting to understand that vampires have the same moral code when it comes to hurting another of their species as humans do.

When Rayonne goes to tuck the revolver into her pocket, Denendrius leans into the back and holds his hand out.

"But—"

He snaps his fingers and coughs. "Nope, I don't trust you, and I definitely don't believe your kindness. I still have enough strength to come back there and rip your neck out."

She slaps the gun into the palm of his bloodstained hand

and leans back in her seat, arms crossed and red-painted lips tight.

"Protect me," Denendrius demands, dropping the gun into my lap.

I'm about to retort when he jerks sideways in his seat and retches dark crimson on the beige upholstery. The fabric sizzles on impact like someone tossed acid on it. Rayonne gapes from the back seat, eyes teary at the ruins of her car seat.

I tuck the gun between my thighs as Denendrius moans, his face resting against the headrest. When he closes his eyes, blood runs like tears from the edges of his eyes. He hacks, blood drizzling from his lips. He doesn't wipe it away; instead, he begins to wheeze like someone punched him in the chest.

His hand twitches when he lifts it from where it was limp at his side, his fingers shaking as he slowly moves to his pocket. He pulls his cell phone from his pocket and holds it out to me.

He struggles when he speaks. "I need you to call Sergei when we're home. Tell him what happened, and he'll fix me."

Carefully, I take the phone, disliking the idea of being near another vampire, especially one who considers Denendrius a friend.

"What *is* going on?" I ask, taking a deep breath.

His face twists in agony. "They fed me the cure. It's turning me back human."

"But you said—" I tighten my hands on the wheel and glower at the road.

Of course he'd say Alaire and Edmond were lying about Darklings being able to turn back human. Why would he offer information like that to someone who had already tried to kill him? To someone who would have definitely run to Children of Stars for help the first chance she could?

Rayonne, seeming to sense my confusion, adds, "There's a lineage of vampires with the ability to cure vampirism running through their veins. Viorel has their blood stockpiled, but there hasn't been a known vampire capable of such a thing in centuries."

He reaches toward me. Assuming he's read my thoughts on my face, I flinch and slap his hand back toward him without thinking. He drops his hand and grunts, rubbing the part of his arm where I hit.

Quickly—before he can get mad—I reach across and pull his hand into mine, rubbing his knuckles with my thumb before taking the wheel again. "Sorry, I'm just on edge."

He offers a weak smile.

Then my expression falls. I stare at him.

I moved his arm.

I slapped it away . . . *and he felt it.*

He closes his eyes again and flicks the air conditioning on. I notice the shine on his skin. He wipes his forehead, blood smearing like sweat.

Slowly, my head turns back to look at Rayonne, and from the look in her eyes, I can tell she's already been thinking about what has just sunk in for me.

Denendrius is turning human.

I can hurt him.

He can *die.*

It's no wonder why he's acting like I never ran from him, why he isn't punishing me. Now he has to trust me. Now he has to believe I'll help him. What other option does he have? If he punishes me, there's a chance of me retaliating.

He clears his throat and spits blood onto the floor. His car keys jingle in his shaking hand as he hands them to me. "I need you to take the Mustang back to the apartment for me." He tells me what street it's parked on. "Just in case."

I shove them into my pocket. "Just in case of what?"

He responds with retching, the sound of his teeth slamming together as he screeches in agony.

"Hurry—" He gasps and shakes his head, pressing his

forearm into his ribs. "Drive faster. We have to get to the apartment before they do."

"It's safe?" Rayonne asks from the back seat.

He grunts. "All the entry points have been sprayed with garlic for a long time."

No wonder it was so difficult for them to get near him. Even if they knew where to find him, it would have done them no good.

He turns the air conditioning off when he starts to shiver, his muscles tightening as he struggles to move and relax.

"Are you going to be okay?" I ask, trying not to sound like I'm enjoying his pain.

I am enjoying it, though. It's the best entertainment I've had in who knows how long, and if the situation weren't so dire, I'd probably be smiling too.

"Hurry up," he grumbles again, "or you'll have to figure out how to get me up four flights of stairs if I pass out in the car."

XL

The darkness of the sky fades to navy blue as we near the apartment. If we were followed, there are no signs.

The only sound between the four of us is the constant guttural groans and screeches from Denendrius, the loud chugging of the engine barely able to drown him out. With his head flopped against the seat, he stares blankly at me for the remainder of the ride, only blinking when his face twists in pain or he gags.

"Love you," he whispers before clearing his throat.

The color in his eyes shifts to brown before slowly taking on a crimson tone. His eyes close as he winces, irises bright red when they open.

"Love you too," I mumble, wondering how long it will be before he's human enough for a bullet.

When his eyes droop, I shove his shoulder and he jerks like I startled him.

"We're almost there," I say.

He grunts, lips parted dumbly and covered in slowly drying

blood. He tries to lean toward me, arm outstretched to rest on my lap. If I didn't know any better, I'd think he was looking to be comforted.

"You still love me even though I'm dying?" he asks me, eyes dazed.

I swallow. "Of course," I lie, thinking it's a good idea to add, "Don't worry, we'll fix this." I remove my hand from the wheel after turning a corner to give his leather-covered arm a quick pat.

He nods and takes a deep breath, flinching when his chest falls.

When we pull into the parking lot, I shove the gun into the back of my jeans, slipping the keys from both their vehicles and his cell phone into my pockets.

Denendrius opens his door, the car sinking under his weight when he uses the door to pull him out. Rayonne and I follow as he sways toward the glass door. He struggles to open it, leaning against the glass.

He grumbles when I have to open the door for him. When we draw his arms around our shoulders and guide him through, he leaves behind a streak of blood on the glass.

His feet stumble on the stairs, almost making us fall back down them a handful of times. If it weren't for my iron grip on the railing, we probably would have too.

By the time we reach the apartment door, my shoulders and back ache, and I want nothing more than to duck out from under him so he falls to the floor.

After I unlock the door, he uses the wall to help himself to the bedroom. When he drops onto his side of the bed and pulls a fistful of blanket toward him, I can't help but notice how pathetically weak he looks.

"Call Sergei," he says into the white blanket, now stained with red smears and handprints. "Make sure nobody but you and him come near me," he adds, glaring at Rayonne.

"Okay." I stand in the bedroom doorway, looking him over, trying to decide if he'd die yet if I shot him.

He moves a bunched bit of blanket to peer at me. "Now," he demands. He coughs into the blanket and blood soaks it.

My breath turns heavy, the cold metal of the revolver against my back taking my attention. When he guffaws and tries to stand, I panic and draw it, silver barrel aimed at his face.

His expression remains hard. "I don't find that funny, Marianna."

I draw back the hammer.

Denendrius rolls his eyes and lies back down, pulling the blanket under his face as he stares at me blankly. "Put that away and come comfort me."

I exhale hot air through my nose, knowing he'll wrestle the phone and gun away from me if I go near him.

I keep the gun lifted. "Say you're sorry."

His laugh is soft, causing anger to spill into my blood when I realize he doesn't take me seriously even with a gun capable of killing him in my hand.

Denendrius's fingers outstretch toward me and he smiles, eyes lustrous. "This is why I love you. *You're so cute.*"

Rayonne grumbles quietly from beside me, her head shaking.

"Oh, be quiet. I have no problem with using the last of my strength to kill you." His fist curls around the blanket as he glares at Rayonne. "I have no use for you. If you're still here when I wake up, you'll just be a convenient first meal."

She chortles, leaning against the door frame. "Uh-huh."

I slam my fist against the wall beside me. He doesn't react.

"Say you're sorry," I demand. "Then maybe I'll consider putting the gun down."

He smiles. His hand unclenches from the sheet and he coughs before patting the space beside him. "Come here."

Rayonne straightens. "Shoot him," she urges. "Just don't kill him. Not yet. Viorel will do that . . . in a decade or two, when he's had his fun."

Denendrius's lips stretch. "She won't shoot me. She loves me." He sighs and winces. "She's just a little upset is all."

"I've never loved you," I snarl, trying to force myself to take a fatal shot.

He frowns and coughs, his voice hoarse when he says, "That's a lie. At least make an effort if you're trying to be hurtful."

My hand shakes, something that's never happened before. I was taught never to hesitate or show fear with a gun in my hand, so why am I now? Never once did I waver before pulling the trigger before. I try to stop my hand from quivering but can't. He notices and grins.

I take a deep breath, heart thumping in my temples. "Apologize. Apologize, then beg me not to kill you."

He sits up and grimaces. "Why would I need to do that?"

My palms sweat. I tighten my grip on the gun. "Denendrius, you've ruined me. You raped me and beat me and took everything you could."

He scowls, the corner of his lip twitching. "I never raped you. How *dare you*. We made love."

My breath leaves me like I've been slapped. "What the fuck is wrong inside your head, Denendrius? There's a reason nobody but some love-starved five-year-old has looked your way. That girl is lucky you died before she grew up enough to marry you. I'm sure your mother and sisters prefer death too over having to know someone like you. They're lucky you killed them."

He flinches, a breath forced from his lungs. I can't tell if it's from my words or from pain. Whatever the reason, the look in his eyes is dangerous. He starts to stand, using the side table to help him up.

Rayonne touches my arm and takes a step back. "I'll wound

him if you can't," she says. "I'll take him to Romania myself." She reaches toward my hands in an attempt to take the weapon.

I don't care about Viorel's grand scheme for Denendrius. Having him in a dungeon in Romania does me absolutely no good. He may go through hell, but if his death isn't immediately guaranteed, then what good does it do me? I want him to stop existing, to be unable to think or speak or breathe. I don't want him to die in two years, twenty years, I want him dead *now*. He doesn't deserve for any more time to be wasted on him, even if that time is used to make him suffer.

I want to be the one to kill him. I want to look him in the eye as he takes his last breath. Whether he'll admit it aloud or not, I want him to look me in the eye and know how much I hate him and that his death is a result of the suffering he put me through. Even if he never apologizes, I want to see regret flash through his eyes. I want him to know he fucked up, and that there's no way out of it.

Of course, I might agree with Rayonne if I were in her shoes. If she takes him to the castle, she'll get to listen to him suffer day in and day out without having to lift a finger. She'd get to fall asleep to the music of his screams, wake up and hear them continue. She could probably even pull up a chair and watch his torture like a show, day after day until he finally dies.

Meanwhile, I'd be at home in the ruins of my silent life, wondering and hoping he doesn't break free. I'd never even know when or if he dies. That hardly seems fair.

If someone's going to punish him, it will be me.

In the time it takes me to dodge her grip, Denendrius crosses the room. He throws Rayonne aside, crashing into me. We tumble to the floor, my body trapped beneath him. I writhe as he tries to wrestle the gun from my fingers, trying to pull myself out from under him so I can get the gun at a proper angle to fire.

When Rayonne leaps onto his back and tries to wrap her skinny arms around his throat, he throws an elbow into her face. Something cracks as she yelps, disappearing from my sight behind him on the floor.

I feel like I'm being mauled by a wild animal as we struggle in a tangle of limbs and grunts. He twists the gun in my hands, and I readjust my grip to prevent my wrists from snapping. The blood smeared on it makes it harder to get back under my control, and he ends up ripping it from my fingers. He crawls over me and into the hallway, almost kneeling on my head as he begins to cough and gasp for air.

"*Bastard!*" The word rides between my lips on an exasperated breath.

I roll over and grab a fistful of his jeans before he can get too close to the bathroom, having a pretty good idea of what he plans on doing. He yanks his leg from my grip. When I try to crawl after him, Rayonne pushes me down on her way from the room, blood dripping on the white carpet as she huffs from her bleeding nose. She throws herself onto his back again and he cries out before reaching for a handful of her hair. With a fistful of black locks, he pulls her off and slams her face into the wall.

I catch up to him as he clambers into the bathroom. My fist slams into the side of his head when he tries to open the chamber, and he grabs the edge of the tub to keep himself from falling over. He shoves me backward and flicks the chamber open, his foot kicking me away from him as he sits beside the toilet.

He turns the gun sideways and the bullets fall into the porcelain bowl. When I try to slam the toilet lid on his fingers, he throws his leg over the back of my shoulders. My arms give under me and my chest meets the floor. He flushes the bullets and tosses the gun carelessly behind him. It clangs against the bottom of the tub.

I let out a frustrated cry, and when Rayonne makes it close

enough to the bathroom to see there's no longer a weapon, she vanishes down the hallway. Denendrius laughs and then turns to open the toilet lid and vomit violently. When he looks up, blood is running from his nose and eyes on top of the mess around his mouth.

I think of the knives in the kitchen, no idea where my own gun is. Trying to take advantage of the moment, I stand and step toward the door. Before my foot even touches down, he scuttles forward and pulls the other one out from under me. My face and hands hit the edge of the carpet before he yanks me back in and slams the door.

I bat at him as he tries to flip me on my back and tries to reach the door handle.

"Stop it!" he shouts, pushing me closer to the sink. He stretches across the space, fingers trying to twist the lock as he holds me down with the other arm. Finally, it locks.

He manages to get the phone out of my pocket. I slap it out of his hand before he can unlock it to call Sergei. It skitters across the linoleum and disappears behind the toilet. He freezes and takes a deep breath. I writhe harder.

"Marianna, stop it! Calm down and let's talk about—"

I rake my jagged nails across his face, four gouged lines appearing in his cheek.

"All right!" he barks.

His fingers circle my throat, air trapped in my chest. He may be weaker, practically human now, but it doesn't make much of a difference. I swing hooked fingers at his face, and he tightens his grip, extending his arms so I'm left clawing at his biceps, his face out of reach.

"You're an ungrateful little girl, aren't you? You want love so badly but won't accept any when it's offered," he snarls. "I can give you eternal life, a beautiful home, money, the entire world. Why isn't it enough?"

Pressure building behind my eyes, I punch at his chest.

He winces and tightens his grip. I can feel the muscles spasming in his hands, the uncontrollable shift of pressure as his body fights between human and inhuman strength. My hands move to his as my eyes flutter, a final attempt to pry his hands from me. I sink my nails into his flesh, scraping at his skin until blood trails down his fingers and cakes under my nails.

When he lets go and falls onto his forearms on either side of my head, he gasps in pain, the sound of his guttural breathing against my ear. I choke on air, my throat and chest burning as I focus on remembering to breathe.

"If you could only remember to love me how I love you," he whispers in my ear, tears in his voice. "I just want you to love me again. I've never wanted anything so bad."

If Denendrius wasn't the way he is, I might feel sorry that I was the first person to show him love in almost two thousand years.

I can only grunt in response. My hands move weakly to the edges of his unzipped leather jacket and I take a handful of the material and push in a failed attempt to move him off me. He doesn't move, his breathing shallow against the side of my face. I think perhaps he's nearing unconsciousness.

Where the fuck did Rayonne go?

I try to slide from beneath him, not wanting to be trapped when he passes out.

"*Please don't leave me,*" he whispers, bloody lips touching my skin.

I turn my head away from his and try to push him off me again.

"Are you planning on leaving me when I fall asleep? Don't call Sergei if you do, okay? There's no guarantee I'll wake up anyway, and I'm not sure it's worth it if you aren't there," he whines.

I grit my teeth, hot air blowing from my nose. I want to tell him he won't be waking up anyway, that his sudden expression of sadness won't change my mind or help him in any way.

I tell him what he wants to hear, knowing he could use whatever moments he has left awake to make me regret anything else I could say. "I won't leave, Denendrius. I know you don't want to be alone."

He exhales loudly like he was holding his breath. "I love you."

His bloodied lips mash against mine, leaving no room for any kind of response. He holds himself up, his arms shaking like they're threatening to give out. I try not to gag at the overpowering taste of blood.

When he pushes my shirt up, he closes his eyes, lips slowly trailing toward my waist. His shaky fingers run up and down my thighs.

Something moving under the door catches my eye, and it takes a few moments of confusion to realize it's the end of a knife handle. A set of black-painted fingernails push it through and my heart leaps.

I gently put a hand on Denendrius's head to distract him, in hopes he'll take it as a sign I want him to continue. He does, kissing me harder, his fingers curling around the waist of my jeans. He pauses for short moments randomly, like he's losing bits of time without realizing it.

Reaching carefully with the other hand, I manage to snag the end of the handle between my index and middle finger, pulling it into the palm of my hand.

My breath catches when I realize it's the knife I gave Jenna. My knuckles whiten when I remember her lying bloodless and pale in the alley, when I remember how Denendrius laughed at what he'd done. I think of how he killed CJ, Alaire, and Edmond. My blood heats when I remember the tapes, how he doesn't even consider what he did to me rape.

This time, I don't hesitate. I bring the knife toward him, the blade striking the edge of his shoulder purposefully, just enough to scare him. He cries out in pain, jerking upright and away from me.

Something twitches in his eye when I expect him to react. I think maybe he's lost another moment and that he's close to unconsciousness. I use it to my advantage and jump to my feet. I swing at him again and his reaction is delayed when he tries to grab my wrist. I kick him onto his back, horrible images flashing in my mind, fueling me.

Coughing and sputtering, I manage to straddle him on the floor as he tries to catch his breath while leaning against the counter drawers, blood running from the corners of his mouth. I watch his eyes flicker to brown. This time they don't switch back.

Lifting the knife above my head, I aim for his chest. He grunts and weakly catches my wrist. I pull my hand easily from his grasp.

His face is twisted in bewildered confusion, like he can't comprehend that he's really about to be beaten.

I spit his words back at him. "This is all I've ever wanted."

When the blade rises above my head again, his eyes catch mine. He shouts something in a language I've never heard before, brown eyes wide in confusion.

It's not until I bring the knife toward him that I realize I'm staring into the eyes of a stranger, that his confusion runs far deeper than disbelief in my actions.

Alaire's words ring loudly in my mind, my shock freezing my muscles as the knife stops mere millimeters above his stomach.

"*Turning back is hardly a miracle. Something usually goes wrong. It's for worst-case scenario, a single chance. When a Darkling turns back human, their memories might escape them.*"

In dismay, I realize I don't recognize the man staring back, and that he doesn't recognize me either.

The knife falls from my grip, hands shaking violently as Denendrius turns limp beneath me. His hands thump against the linoleum floor of the bathroom as his breath whooshes from his chest. Brown eyes half-lidded, their unfamiliarity drives me off him, scrambling backward.

My back thuds against the locked door, air ripping up and down my throat. "He doesn't remember me! He didn't know who I was!"

He's just . . . *dead*.

I've seen enough dead bodies to guess that Denendrius won't be waking up. That can't be sleeping.

Fury rolls inside me. I feel cheated. How could he just die? How can everything that has happened end up . . . *erased*. How could he die without knowing who I am? About what he did? There's no truth to my experiences in the brown of his eyes, in the warmth of his blood. He looks like any other dead human.

How dare he.

This isn't fair!

He escaped judgment in the end. He didn't have to die knowing it's because he did wrong. He didn't have a chance to regret, to wish he lived differently. He got to die with a clear conscience, staring incongruously at a girl who didn't even get a chance to make him pay for all he did to her.

I feel outside myself as I stand and pull open the bathroom door. Rayonne is there, her eyes wide as she peers around me.

"There go all our plans. We can carry on with our lives with the comfort of knowing we got fucked once again," I spit. "He's fucking dead."

Her brow furrows, brown eyes contemplative. "Maybe. I wouldn't count on that."

"What else could it mean when someone stops breathing and doesn't have a pulse?" I growl.

"He's turning back, Marianna. Sure, he's technically dead. But I highly doubt he'll remain that way. It's the same as when he would have turned, reversed. He would have died then with no guarantee of waking up as a vampire. If his body doesn't start behaving like a corpse within a couple hours, then we have our answer."

I rub my bloody hand over my tired face, stepping back toward Denendrius. I sit rigidly on the floor next to him and scoop a limp wrist up, fingers pressed against his vein. "Then we wait to see if he wakes up, and hope to hell he remembers everything."

The fight continues in...
BINDING BLOOD

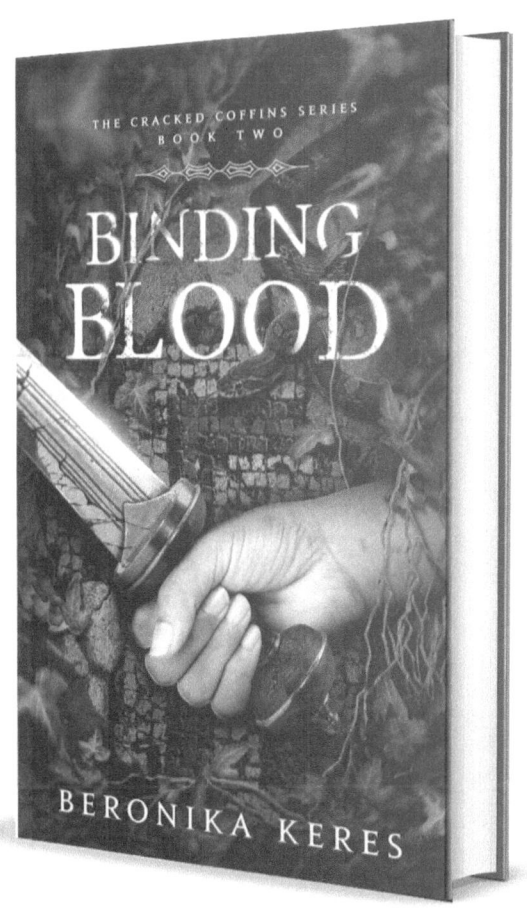

Available Now!

ABOUT THE AUTHOR

Beronika Keres is the Canadian author of the dark fantasy thriller series, Cracked Coffins. In the second grade, she decided she wanted to be an author and has spent her life honing her craft and pursuing her dream. She can often be found chasing plot bunnies and writing books.

When she's not writing, she enjoys spending time with her family or listening to some gothic rock, punk, or metal while working on her newest spike and patch-covered project.

To stay in the loop on future releases and exclusive content, visit www.beronikakeres.com and sign up for the newsletter. You can also connect with her on social media:

facebook.com/AuthorBeronikaKeres

instagram.com/beronikakeres

tiktok.com/@beronikakeres

bookbub.com/authors/beronika-keres

goodreads.com/BeronikaKeres

www.ingramcontent.com/pod-product-compliance
Lightning Source LLC
Chambersburg PA
CBHW020228110726
47898CB00004B/1197